FIRELIGHT

GEOFFREY SAEMANN

Green River Publishing—Deerfield, WI
ISBN: 979-8-9992406-0-6
Library of Congress Control Number: 2025915770
Title: *Firelight*
Author: Geoffrey Saemann
Digital distribution | 2025
Paperback | 2025

This is a work of fiction. The characters, names, incidents, places, and dialogue are products of the author's imagination, and are not to be construed as real.

Published in the United States by New Book Authors Publishing

DEDICATION

To Gabby,

Thank you for believing in me when others did not.

Introduction

This book, like many important events in history, was an accident. And not just a single accident. In fact, this book was the result of several unexpected, and dare I say, at least in hindsight, lucky, events. At the time I began working on it, I had just finished my freshman year of university. I had secured an internship in a molecular biology research lab on campus, having just finished a yearlong project with a different research mentor who worked for the same organization, and actually recommended me for the summer internship. Going into that summer, I assumed I would spend most of my time going back and forth between the lab and my job at the aquatic center on campus. As it turned out, one week into the lab internship, I quit, as I learned that the lab head expected me to put forty hours a week into the lab project without any advance notice. Needless to say, that was the first accident that led to the creation of this book, and the end of my exploration into the world of internships.

I still worked at the aquatic center, but even while working twenty to twenty-five hours every week, I found that I needed something else to fill my days. Towards the end of the spring semester, I had worked on a short manuscript in my spare time. I found the hours I spent working on this project to be very enjoyable and wondered if I should get back into fiction writing. This wasn't my first experience with writing stories. In fact, my first attempt at writing a book took place when I was only twelve years old. However, due to the fact that I did not yet have the patience or the discipline to write an outline and develop my ideas before plunging straight into the writing process, the text was, to put it mildly, a complete mess, a fact I realized even at the age of twelve. Unsure of how I could improve the project, and not having anyone around who could advise me, I ended up abandoning it before it was finished.

I would have another attempt a couple of years later. When I was in the sixth grade, I joined a program called WCATY, a pedagogy of online literature courses based in the Madison area which, as far as I know, still exists today. I thoroughly enjoyed my experience with the program, and I participated in many interesting classes, but three in particular stick out to me. The first involved writing our own alternative version of a classical fairy tale over the course of the nine-week semester. I ended up choosing "The Snow Queen," and I wrote a text impressive enough that the professor in charge of the class recommended that I send it to a publisher. While this didn't end up happening, I still got a lot out of that course. It added two things I hadn't had before when writing: structure and discipline. Assignments every week that forced me to spend the time outlining the story and developing the ideas. Admittedly, I did have a small fight with the professor as I was struggling to keep up with the class at several points, but he was very nice about it and encouraged me to talk to him if I ever had any questions. This was one of the more mature reactions to my grievances I received from an adult, any adult, during those days, and even back then, I appreciated it very much.

I participated in two more WCATY classes which were focused specifically on short story writing. For the first, I wrote a story about a twelve-year-old who is kidnapped and turned into a Jason Bourne-Esque government agent. Once again, I had a bit of a problem with the professor. This time, she complained about the fact that the content in my story was too mature for the class, and she was much less level-headed about it than my previous professor. Still, I was able to make her happy by toning things down a bit, and the class overall was a success. Unfortunately, like many of my early stories, this one does not survive to this day. The last WCATY program I participated in was once again a short story class. Two circumstances combined to make this the best story I'd written thus far. First, I had more experience from the previous two writing courses. I understood how to outline the story effectively and develop ideas into a full narrative text. The second is more personal. I was going through some struggles with mental health at the time due to events that were taking place in school and at home. But once again, it was a lucky accident, as I was able to channel the things I was going through into the story. They served both to inspire and motivate me at a time in my life when I had little of either.

This story went well beyond the original short text that my professor had asked us to write. In fact, it was so large that I only had time to outline it in the nine-week time frame of the class. Fortunately, my professor was so impressed that she allowed me to submit the outline, along with a couple of scenes I had managed to finish, as my final project. One funny story that I still chuckle at to this day occurred on the last day of class, when the professor read a CHAPTER from each of our stories. Now, in the CHAPTER that I had asked her to read, the main character is thinking about a woman he is in love with. The professor read to a certain point, and she suddenly stopped in the middle of a sentence that read something along the lines of "accentuated her breasts," and exclaimed "Geoff!" Everyone started laughing, even the professor, and she sort of just skipped over it and kept reading. I still crack up thinking about it to this day. Once again, this professor encouraged me to finish the story and even send it in for publishing. Sadly, my self-doubts once again got the better of me, and the story was never finished. The outline of this story does survive, buried in the depths of my computer, and maybe in time, given how personal it is for me, when I feel the world is ready to listen, I will feel ready to tell it.

I largely left the writing world for several years after that, focused on school, work, and other things. I wrote several short stories and submitted them to contests over the course of those years. I never won anything, but I did receive positive feedback from several fellow authors who had the chance to read my work. And so, I was sitting around my apartment the summer after freshman year of university, having just told the lab head where I should've been working that I was leaving and not coming back, looking for something to do, and my mind drifted to my old stories. I pulled several of them out of a flash drive where I'd been saving them and read through them one by one. Reading these old works awakened a passion for writing in me that I had nearly forgotten about. "Why hadn't I ever turned this into something more?" I thought after I'd finished. "Why did I ever stop writing?" And now the second happy accident will occur that would lead to the writing of the novel you now hold in your hands. Originally, I discovered the idea for this book hidden away in my treasure trove of notes. It read something along the lines of "A man who seems to have a perfect life falls into a coma unexpectedly and sees the afterlife is nothing like what he expected it to be." I figured with a little preparation I could turn that into a good twenty to thirty thousand word manuscript. Not quite long enough for publishing, but it would be another stepping stone on the road to writing a full-length novel, which remained my ultimate goal, even at the time.

I had nearly finished the work at the time I began to wonder if I could turn it into something more. I was thinking about the project one day while I was walking to work. At around the same time I was reading "The Stand" by Stephen King for the first time. I took inspiration from the post-apocalyptic society King describes in his book, and wondered if I could make a similar thing work in my current project. I began outlining the progression of the book from its current standpoint to its end, which I would come up with later. At the time, Leo Rinolski was my title character, and Jody was nothing more than a side character who served as Leo's good friend. My process during this time was somewhat problematic for several reasons. While I certainly had many interesting ideas, the book didn't have a clear direction or purpose. I had an end goal but wasn't sure exactly how I was going to get there. I had written all my notes at the bottom of the document, separated into three distinct categories: scenes (ordered), scenes (unordered), and general ideas. While I added the ending to this list shortly after I began writing, it still wasn't clear how I would get there. After I'd stumbled around for a while, struggling for a clear direction, I began to plan a bit more by loosely scripting the next few scenes that would occur after the latest one before I began writing. Still, even with this new idea, there was still a lot of blank space in between these scenes and my end goal. I ended up going off on a lot of random tangents that didn't contribute much to the story (a fact that whichever editor read my first draft will corroborate).

I was unable to finish the story that summer. Focused solely on school during the year, it took me until the next summer before I had the free time to come back and finish it. I officially finished the first draft in June of 2024. The problem with these long breaks is that I would sometimes forget the finer details of what I had written previously, which led to inconsistencies. This would lead me to create character and plot outlines for my next project that I am currently in the process of writing, something I had neglected to do for this story. I also wrote this at a time in my life when I harbored a significant amount of frustration due to the events that were happening in the world at the time, and it often exploded out of me when I was writing. As a result, many of my deeply held political and social beliefs became entangled in the book, and these often contributed to the aforementioned tangents about human nature and the mess I believed the world had become. Still, in spite of its top heaviness, I ended up finishing the book and was quite happy with it. I didn't exactly throw a party to celebrate, but I did feel a deep sense of satisfaction as I finished typing out the last few words and saving the final document to my computer. Once again, however, I became busy with schoolwork, and so the draft would sit for several more months before I finally decided to submit it for publishing.

I submitted the first draft of the story to Little Creek Press in March of 2025. A couple weeks later, I received a rejection letter. I was told the plot was confusing as a result of the length of the story. Immediately, the old self-doubts consumed me, and I became visibly angry. All the work I had done was for nothing. The story wasn't good enough for these people. It didn't make any sense. Then, after I had calmed down, I read the email they had sent me again and realized that they hadn't in fact told me the plot was boring, or the story overall wasn't good enough. Because it wasn't. It was simply too long, and the plot was confusing. So, I went back and started re-reading the story and immediately realized what they meant. It hadn't occurred to me until then just how much rambling I had done throughout the course of the story. There were several moments, especially early in the story, where I became confused as to what I was even saying (I can only imagine how the editor must have felt). And so, I did the smart thing. I cut things out, rewrote entire scenes, clarified confusing points, and streamlined the book so that it could be dedicated to the purpose I had finally discovered for it about halfway through writing the first draft. I submitted it to a different publishing company I had discovered during my research of the internet called "New Book Authors Publishing," wondering if my hard work was finally going to pay off. And this time, it finally did.

Trauma. Besides maybe the very rare exception, all of us have experienced it in some form. It was only about halfway through writing my first draft that I decided this should be the focus of the book. The monster, who is known by several names in this book, is a living personification of trauma. He is the voice that whispers in your ear that your classmates don't think you're good enough when you're about to deliver an important presentation. He's the anger and frustration you feel after having a fight with your spouse or being let go from a job. And he's more than that. He takes these experiences and uses them against you so that you will cause destruction, tear yourself down, and destroy the things you love, all of which gives him more power over you. But we can't give in to him. We have to fight back. We are more than just the pain we feel. Trauma can be a very powerful enemy, but, as Jody and the survivors that follow her will learn, so are the forces that exist to fight against it. Let this book serve a reminder to anyone who is in a dark place, that there is something good on the other side. You will fight your way out, and you will defeat whatever pain in haunting you. Sometimes all it takes, as Jody will soon learn, is lighting a match.

CHAPTER 1

Kaden Versantos sat in the back of his American history class, tapping his pencil on the desk out of boredom, but being careful to not let his teacher, Mrs. Vargass, notice. Mrs. Vargass was what most of his fellow students at Calvin Coolidge high school referred to as "Eagle eye," which was a tribute to her wiry frame and skeleton-like hands as much as it was to her uncanny ability to spot troublemakers from a mile away. Kaden's best friend, Marcus Piloty, a boy a year older than Kaden with messy dark hair and a seemingly endless collection of jeans with the knees torn out, often complained about this to Kaden, insisting that "that bitch Vargass," as he called her, must be stalking him, there was no way in hell she could've discovered him committing whatever crime he happened to have been committing that day otherwise, whether it be spray painting a teacher's car, smoking pot behind the school, or tripping some kid in the hallway just for kicks.

Although his parents had never really approved of his friendship with Marcus, Kaden insisted on having him around. Like most inner-city schools, Calvin Coolidge high school could be a rough place for a small, skinny, nerdy boy like Kaden. It probably didn't help that his parents were upper-middle class and had never allowed Kaden to wear what his father described as "dirty street clothes," something that less fortunate kids were apt to take poorly. Kaden had witnessed one of his friends get pinned up against a wall by an older boy for wearing new pristine white sneakers.

While he'd never been targeted specifically, it gave him a sense of comfort to have a friend like Marcus, who, apart from being one of the toughest kids in school, had his back if any of the bigger kids started messing with him. He would always flip open his rather large pocketknife whenever he reminded Kaden of this, and while this might've scared most kids, Kaden felt comforted by it. Kaden also admired how carefree Marcus seemed. While he complained about his parents and teachers coming down on him whenever he smoked pot or keyed a car, he always forgot about it the next day.

Kaden knew he was smart, and he could've been a better student or son, but that was the thing with Marcus. He just didn't care. Kaden wished he could be a little more like Marcus sometimes, just a normal kid who didn't give a shit what anyone thought. He'd express this thought to Marcus sometimes, who would always respond with something along the lines of "Tell them to fuck off then!" to which Kaden would reply by gesturing to his mouth and smiling. It often struck Kaden as funny that Marcus, for all his talk about how Kaden needed to stand up for himself, never realized that this would be difficult, given that Kaden Versantos, in all 16 years of his unusual life, hadn't spoken a single word.

1

A few moments after school had let out, Kaden, standing by the double wide front doors, heard the final bell ring. He texted Marcus "You good?" as the kids began to file out the front doors. No one paid him any attention, for which Kaden was grateful. He waved to his friend Amos, who was with a few of his other friends, all of whom were laughing about something. After waiting for about ten minutes for a reply, Kaden started to walk down the street, figuring he would at least see Marcus tomorrow, when he came bursting out of the school, laughing himself almost hoarse.

"Oh god," Marcus gasped, catching up to Kaden. "Jesus dude, that was so damn funny, I put gum in that bitch Olivia's hair, she was fucking crying! That's worth a suspension any day of the week, don't you think, old buddy?" he said, slapping Kaden good-naturedly on the shoulder.

Kaden nodded and grinned to show he agreed. He had no ill feelings towards Olivia, but it cheered him up to see his friend so happy. Besides, if he was honest with himself, the whole thing was kind of amusing.

"Know the best part? I told that bitch Vargass to suck it when I was in the office. I've never seen her look so shocked, I almost died laughing man," Marcus went on, practically doubled over with the force of his laughter.

Kaden smiled placatingly, wondering in the back of his mind how long it would be before he saw his best friend at school again.

"Hey," Marcus said. "I was wondering..." he paused, seemingly trying to find the words. Kaden cocked his head quizzically to show he was curious.

"Well, not really me, the guys were wondering..." Marcus saw his confused expression. "You know, Amos, and a few of his friends. You know, those guys."

Kaden nodded. Kaden had always enjoyed hanging out with Amos and his crew, who treated him like one of their own in spite of his muteness that kept most of his classmates at a distance.

"Well anyway, we were wondering if..." he hesitated, chewing his lip. "We were wondering if you could do the thing," he said in a rush, as if he thought saying these words quickly would lessen their shocking effect.

Kaden stared at his friend, a mixture of surprise and irritation clouding his expression.

Marcus, looking slightly embarrassed, said, "Look, it ain't my fault man, I let it slip by accident, and they just kept pestering me about it. We were all high, and normally I would never, but..." he trailed off.

Kaden, now thoroughly angry, jerked his phone out of his pants pocket and began typing furiously. A moment later, he turned it around so Marcus could read it.

"I thought I told you never tell anyone about my gift," it read.

Marcus sighed, ruffling a hand through his long greasy hair. "Look I'm sorry man, like I said, I didn't mean to. But since they already know, maybe you could just," he trailed off again, seemingly embarrassed.

Kaden typed another message. "Can't."

"Why not?" Marcus said, a twinge of annoyance in his voice. "Why does it need to be a secret at all? You practically saved my life, imagine how many people you could help!"

Kaden shook his head and held up another message. "That was different. I helped you when you were in trouble. I didn't want to see your life get flushed down the toilet. You'd think that experience would've taught you to lay off the drugs."

Marcus opened his mouth furiously, closed it again, and then looked away, seemingly uncomfortable.

They were both thinking about that night. The first night Kaden had gone into the dark and murky depths of the bathtub. The night he'd confronted Marcus' crew before having ever met him. The night Marcus' dope fiend friend T. J. had almost killed Kaden after he had begged Marcus not to meet the undercover cop posing as their dealer. Marcus looked like he wanted to say something else, but Kaden stopped him.

"I need to leave." Before Marcus could protest, Kaden began walking quickly down the street towards his neighborhood.

"What do I tell Amos then?" Marcus called after him.

Kaden ignored him. As far as he was concerned. Marcus could tell Amos whatever he wanted. Suddenly feeling very stressed, Kaden wanted nothing more than to sit down on the family couch, put on a movie, and write off for the rest of the night. But as he approached the neighborhood where he had lived his entire life, an unpleasant thought occurred to him.

"If Amos knew about the gift...and so did his friends..." Kaden shuddered at the thought. "No one would believe them anyway," he thought. "People would say they're nuts, a bunch of potheads who're too drugged out to recognize a little kid begging for attention when they see one."

While this calmed his anxiety a little, he still found himself thinking about Amos' friends as he opened the screen door to the house. Amos had never tried to hurt him before, nor had any of his friends, but the gift...it changed how people saw him, Marcus was proof of that. Barely a year ago, Marcus had sworn he'd never breathe a word to anyone, now here he was, trying to parade Kaden around to his friends like a zoo animal. Suppose Amos and his friends were pissed off when Kaden refused to show them the gift, suppose they tried to hurt him, suppose they...

"Shoved me up against a wall and put a knife to my throat," Kaden thought, his mind drawn back to Marcus' friend T. J. as he tossed his backpack absentmindedly on his bed and walked into the kitchen, searching for a glass of juice. "What if they decide to take it that far? What if, God forbid, they tell someone else, like your parents. Who might they tell? The police? The FBI? Some government scientists who would haul you off, lock you in a cage, and stick tubes in your arms for the rest of your life? You have to at least be ready." Kaden tried to push the thought from his mind, but it lingered there. Despite his age, the burden of having the gift forced Kaden to be more aware of how the world worked than the typical twelve-year-old.

Ever since he'd first discovered the gift when he was just seven, he'd been well aware of the fact that if the wrong people ever found out, he'd be killed or locked up for the rest of his life, a spectacle for a room full of people in white coats to gawk at. He'd laid awake at night countless times, these worries along with additional ones about what would happen to his mother and father in this scenario consuming him. Kaden sat down at the kitchen table, no longer interested in the orange juice that was sitting invitingly on the counter, squeezing the empty glass so hard he was afraid he might shatter it. He had to go back in to protect himself and his family. He had no choice. He had not moved when his father came home from work ten minutes later. When he asked Kaden how his day at school had been, Kaden absentmindedly signed that it had been fine.

While his mother chatted up a case she had been working with her senior law partner that night over dinner, Kaden picked bleakly at his food. He had no desire to eat. His mind was already focused on the task he would need to accomplish later. He felt like a death row prisoner an hour away from being strapped into the chair; the anticipation was unbearable, but he was helpless to stop it. He stared aimlessly at the untouched hamburger and green beans on his plate, and wondered vaguely if he sat here long enough, might he be able to simply ignore the task at hand until he forgot about it entirely? He shook his head. Wishful thinking, he supposed.

"Everything alright honey?" came his mother's voice from somewhere far away.

It took Kaden a full ten seconds to even notice she'd spoken. He looked at her, confused.

"I asked you if you're alright," his mother repeated, a frown line creasing her forehead.

"I…" Kaden struggled to finish signing out his sentence. "I need to be excused early so I can enter a parallel corridor of existence to try and save both your lives, oh that will go ever well," he thought bemusedly.

His father was frowning now, his own hamburger forgotten.

"I'm not feeling well," he lied. "Can I be excused?"

His mother and father looked at each other. It was difficult to say who looked more worried.

"Okay," his mother said finally.

Kaden waited for another moment, half hoping his father would raise some objection. When he didn't, Kaden got up and walked slowly away from the table, his anxiety worsening with each step he took. He could hear his mother and father saying something about him in hushed tones as he walked slowly towards the bathroom, hoping desperately that one of them would call him back to the table. No such luck.

As Kaden slowly and deliberately undressed himself, he found himself thinking about the night he'd saved his best friend's life. He had not attempted to enter the mist since then, mostly out of fear, but he hadn't forgotten how of course. He wouldn't be allowed to forget the confusing and often terrifying experiences he'd had within the mist until the day he died. He turned on the faucet, the feeling of the hot bath water flowing through his fingers failing to relax him as it had so

4

readily on many a normal night. Kaden stared down at the steaming bath, took a couple of deep breaths, and submerged himself into the scalding hot water, lying flat on his back against the plaster bottom of the basin. Even in just those few seconds, submerging in the blistering hot water should've been sufficient to cause severe whole-body burns that would've landed an ordinary boy Kaden's age in the hospital. But Kaden found the heat not only normal, but extremely soothing. He had done this intentionally, as he always had, to achieve the semi-hypnotized state necessary for submergence into a far deeper and more dangerous pot of water. He closed his eyes, his brain waves gradually lengthening from relaxed theta waves to lower frequency delta waves as his mind gradually separated from his physical body still trapped in the material plane and entered into the dense, tangled jungle that Kaden had long hoped he would be free of forever.

Kaden opened his eyes, greeted by a large living room decorated with ornately curved wooden furniture, a deep purple sofa with matching plush cushions, and a large marble fireplace, logs crackling merrily within the bright orange flames that cast shadows on the opposite wall in the light given off by an oversized reading lamp situated on a wooden side table next to the couch. If he hadn't been terrified of what was to come, the scene might've even been pleasant. Kaden paced in front of the fire, sweating for a reason that had nothing to do with the heat from the fire, his nerves already on edge. After several minutes of dread and anticipation, Kaden forced himself to sit down on the sofa. He stared blankly into the crackling flames, his overstressed mind a thousand miles away. In a dark corner of the room, next to a large statue of "The Thinker," stood a tall figure dressed head to toe in black. A tall black top hat pulled low over his forehead obscured his face. His hands were covered with black gloves. A black magician's cloak was draped over his back. Invisible to the little boy who had just entered his realm, he silently observed his quarry, his anticipation surpassing even the boy's.

He had known of his quarry for many years, but failed to capture him each time he'd come close. Tonight however, there would be no more mistakes. Silently, the figure removed a gleaming stainless steel steak knife from the depths of his robe. He considered it briefly before shaking his head.

"Too easy," he thought. Sheathing the knife in the depths of his robe, he slowly approached the boy, savoring his fear. The magician smiled. The boy knew he was there, he was sure of it, but he could do nothing. He circled around the boy, who sat motionless on the sofa, staring into the flames. It would make it all the more satisfying when he finally performed the deed. He suddenly turned his attention to the wooden door on the other side of the room, smiling coldly as he felt the approach of his newest marionette. Kaden, startled, glanced up from the fire as the door burst open, revealing a trembling little girl who looked no older than eleven or twelve. Panting, her dark eyes, wide with fright, darted around the room before landing on a small closet on the opposite wall. She sprinted for it, her long dark hair flying behind her, and threw herself inside, slamming the slatted wooden door behind her.

Kaden stared at the closed closet door for a full thirty seconds, debating whether to go and comfort the little girl cowering inside before remembering that

5

he was invisible to her. He turned as a second figure stalked into the room, a little boy who was about the girl's age. The boy's dark eyes darted around the room searchingly, his expression calculating. Something about it made Kaden extremely nervous. Getting up from the sofa, Kaden cautiously approached the boy, who was now examining the thin space behind a large mahogany bookshelf. A few seconds later, the boy shook his head and strode past Kaden into the center of the room, his dark eyes gazing around, coming to rest on the slatted wooden closet door. The boy's bottom lip curled in a way that reminded Kaden unpleasantly of a starving wild dog preparing to attack. It was only then that Kaden noticed the gleaming blade clutched in the boy's hand. Kaden let out a high-pitched scream heard by no one as the boy charged, throwing himself on top of the little girl, her terrified screams echoed off the polished oak walls of the room as the boy buried the blade ruthlessly into her over and over, blood spurting onto the walls and floor of the closet from dozens of deep stab wounds.

Finally, the boy, breathing hard from the effort, stood up, covered in the little girl's blood, who was now lying like a dropped puppet on the closet floor, her eyes staring lifelessly off into space. The boy stared down at his victim impassively, casually wiping a speck of blood from the nose. Slowly, he turned to face Kaden, his black eyes glittering like diamonds. Kaden stared, his mouth opening and closing uselessly like a fish.

"He can't see me," Kaden thought. "it's not possible, how can, how can…"

Then the boy smiled. Kaden moaned in terror. He seemed to smile with only his canines, every tooth in his mouth far too sharp to belong to a normal human. Kaden screamed, throwing up his hands to shield himself as the boy charged, the knife brandished over his head.

His vision suddenly went dark just as the boy reached him, as if someone had flipped off a light switch, the grisly scene replaced by a black, empty void. Kaden, suspended in midair as if held up by invisible strings, glanced around at the space, his eyes met with identical inky blackness no matter which way he turned.

"You have failed, my friend." The booming voice pierced Kaden's eardrums as effectively as a hypodermic needle, echoing through the empty space as effectively as if it were a giant auditorium.

Kaden's eyes darted through the darkness for the source of the voice but saw nothing. It seemed to be coming from all around him, as if hundreds of voices were speaking in perfect unison.

"You cannot protect them," it continued.

His parents' faces flashed before his eyes, followed by Marcus', every feature covered with blood and bruises. Kaden moaned in terror.

The little girl's broken and bloodied body suddenly appeared in front of him, floating suspended in midair, her limbs dangling lifelessly in front of her, her eyes closed. The strength suddenly disappeared from Kaden's legs, sending him sprawling to his knees. He felt tears come to his eyes.

"I will take them," the girl whispered. "Just as I will take you."

Kaden stared open-mouthed as the girl began to rise higher into the air. Ten feet…twenty feet…fifty…Kaden had to crane his neck to keep her in view. She was now at least a hundred feet above him, her limbs dancing bizarrely on invisible strings. She tilted her head back and screamed, her eyes rolling into the back of her head, revealing only the whites. Kaden screamed, and then an invisible hand clamped over his mouth, cutting off his airway, lifting him into the air to join the girl, higher, higher...

...His father's strong arms lifting his limp body out of the water, the sudden glow of the bathroom lights nearly blinding him after the suffocating darkness. Kaden sputtered and coughed, expelling inhaled water from his lungs, his entire body trembling. He felt a hand slap him hard several times on the back in between his shoulder blades, and he vomited more water along with the remains of his lunch onto the bathroom tile, struggling to catch his breath.

"Jesus that was close," came his father's voice from somewhere far off.

"Kaden, Kaden, honey?" came a second voice, fraught with worry.

His mother. He looked up to see his mother and father standing over him, their faces anxious.

"Oh honey," his mother cried, tears spilling down her face. "We thought we lost you, you nearly drowned..." The rest of her words died in her throat as she pulled him into a crushing embrace, sobbing uncontrollably.

"Molly, give him some space," his father said, pulling her off him with some difficulty. Kaden barely registered their words. He was breathing hard, struggling to get words out.

"Dad, dad, we have to help her..." he signed frantically.

"Should we bring him to the ER?" his mother interrupted.

"He's fine Molly, just had a little scare," his father replied, embracing his wife.

"Dad, we have to..." he tried again.

"Christ," his mother whispered from somewhere inside her husband's arms. "I almost lost my little boy. He almost..."

The rest of her words were lost in a fit of sobbing. Kaden, now thoroughly angry, winced as a white-hot spark of pain exploded in his chest, its warmth rapidly spreading throughout his entire body. He opened his mouth before he even knew what he was doing.

"Dad!" Kaden shouted, the single spoken word from Kaden, who had been mute his entire life, hitting his father like a bolt of thunder.

His father stared at him, dumbstruck. His mother glanced at him, confused.

"Dad, we have to help her, he's..."

"Who son?" his father said gently, laying a comforting hand on his shoulder. "Are you in trouble?"

"No," Kaden said quickly. "Not me. The girl. She's..."

He paused, unsure of how to communicate what he needed to say effectively. Both his parents looked very worried now.

"Mom, dad, I saw something tonight. Something terrifying. I saw..."

He paused again, struggling to find the words.

"What, son?" his mother asked gently. "What did you see?"

"The magician."

CHAPTER 2

Jody Razitsky snapped awake, bright morning sunlight streaming in through the small empty window frame high above her head. Her entire body was covered in a fine layer of cold sweat. Her dark eyes darted around her unfamiliar surroundings, causing her to momentarily panic before she recalled where she was. She was in the home of the Gonzalez family, who had agreed, along with a few other local families, to host the small team of Peace Corps volunteers she was leading while they were on mission in Ecuador. The small bedroom, it's smooth balsa wood walls decorated with a brightly colored mosaic posters of American bands, colleges, and photos from various family outings, had belonged to Carlos Gonzalez, the eldest son of her host family before he'd left a few weeks ago for Columbia University on scholarship.

He was a kind, hard-working, and highly intelligent young man, and Jody had become very fond of him in the time they'd gotten to know each other. He'd even been the first to volunteer his room when the family had agreed to sponsor them while they were on mission. Jody smiled at the memory. She hoped he was doing well. Jody smoothed her dark hair out of her face and swung her legs out of bed, but before she could stand up, Isabella Gonzalez, Carlos's mother, still wearing her long flannel nightgown, hustled through the open bedroom door.

"¿Estás bien?" she asked. *"Are you okay?"* The worry on her face made Jody feel slightly embarrassed.

"Sí, estoy bien," Jody replied, trying to sound as cheerful as possible in spite of her slightly frazzled nerves. "Tuve un mal sueño." *"Yes, I am okay. Just had a bad dream."*

Mrs. Gonzalez continued to watch her anxiously as she walked over to the small closet to retrieve a navy-blue t-shirt and bright green shorts. Jody felt herself flush a little with embarrassment as she tied her dark hair back into a tight ponytail. This woman had been so kind to her, she did not need to be troubled with Jody's childish night terrors.

"Lamento escuchar eso. ¡Pero tu español está mejorando!" *"I'm sorry to hear that, but your Spanish is really improving!"*

Jody grinned. Since they'd arrived a few months ago, it had been Mrs. Gonzalez's mission to make sure they all spoke Spanish fluently, and in the last couple of weeks, Jody had finally started to get the hang of it.

"Gracias," Jody said as she started toward the kitchen to meet the others. *"Thank you."*

"¡Por supuesto!" Mrs. Gonalez replied cheerfully. *"Of course!"*

"¿Está Leo despierto todavía?" Jody asked. *"Is Leo awake yet?"*

The words had barely left her mouth when Leo Rinolski appeared in the doorway to the living room, his messy black hair disheveled, heavy dark circles visible beneath his eyelids. The way he was slumped over made him look slightly shrunken.

"¿Dormir mal?" Jody asked. *"Sleep badly?"* She flashed a grin that Leo did not return. He sat down heavily at the kitchen table and laid his face in his hands. Jody's grin faded immediately.

"It happened again, didn't it?" she asked, quickly pulling over a chair and sitting down beside him.

Mrs. Gonzalez, who knew about Leo's nightmares, quickly busied herself with the coffee pot, knowing it was best to let Jody handle the situation.

After a moment, Leo nodded. He sighed and ran a hand through his disheveled dark hair.

"I'm good," Leo said, although he felt far from it.

Jody, who didn't believe for a second that Leo was alright, hesitated before saying her next words.

"Did you see your dad again?"

Leo remained silent. It had been the same dream as always. Walking down the street in New York where he'd grown up, his father running to him in a panic, gunshots, and his own screams echoing through the dark night as he stared down at his father's lifeless body. It wasn't really a dream at all, but rather, a reenactment. It always happened just as it had when he was a kid. He slowly nodded before staring down at the floor, pointedly averting his gaze. Jody, feeling useless, clumsily put her arm around Leo's shoulders. Mrs. Gonzalez, watching the scene unfold from across the small kitchen, continued to work on the stubborn coffee pot, knowing better than to interject.

Leo squeezed his eyes shut, struggling not to cry in front of his two best friends.

"Hey," Jody said softly. "Do you know what I used to tell myself whenever I wake up from a nightmare?"

Leo looked at her.

"I'd tell myself that I'm back in the real world, and the nightmares don't have any power over me here. And when I go to sleep, I remind myself that the nightmares only have power if I let them, if I let myself be afraid of them. Don't give them that power."

Leo smiled.

"You're right," he said. "I can't stay sad when I'm here with you two."

Jody pulled him into a tight hug, for which Leo was grateful. Jody could empathize with Leo, having been subjected to the American foster care system from the age of twelve till she'd been thrown out by her foster parents the day she'd turned eighteen. Ever since they met, they'd bonded over the mutual trauma of losing a parent. And while Jody had largely made peace with the trauma of being abandoned by her biological parents, she remembered how hard those first few years had been when she'd been out on her own.

"Monsters only have power over us if we give it to them," she whispered.

"I know," Leo whispered back, releasing her from his embrace. "You'll never let them get me, will you?" he said jokingly.

Jody grinned and socked him playfully on the shoulder.

"Not until you help me get that well dug today," she teased. "After that, I'll have to think about it." Leo laughed.

"Gracias," Leo said gratefully as Mrs. Gonzalez set a plate of eggs down in front of both of them.

Mrs. Gonzalez smiled.

"Un niño en crecimiento siempre tiene hambre," she said, smiling humorously. *"A growing boy is always hungry."*

"What'd she say?" Leo, who was still working on his Spanish, asked Jody.

"Nothing," Jody replied, grinning sheepishly as Mrs. Gonzalez went back to fixing the coffee maker.

"C'mon," Leo said, finishing his eggs and quickly tossing the plate in the sink. "They're waiting for us. Let's go lead the death march," he said, flashing his crooked grin.

"After you, partner," Jody grinned, tossing her own plate in the sink and hurrying after Leo. She turned at the front door to catch Mrs. Gonzalez smiling at her.

"Eres una buena amiga, Jody." *"You're a good friend, Jody."*

"Hey Leo, what held you up this morning?" Leo's friend Jonas asked teasingly as they walked side-by-side up the narrow mountain pass. Overhead, the blazing sun beat relentlessly down on them, and although Leo was dying for a drink of water, he was investing all his remaining energy in putting one foot in front of the other on the path, and worried that if he stopped to remove the water bottle from his pack, he might find it impossible to get moving again. He was so fatigued from the heat that it took him a moment to process what Jonas had said.

"Hey Leo, you alive back there?" Jody called out, eliciting a chuckle from Jonas.

Leo wiped the sweat from his brow, realizing that he might, in fact, need to stop for a water break to prevent himself from passing out from heat exhaustion.

"Yeah, Jody, I'm still alive and kicking back here," he said sarcastically as he caught up with her. "If I die from the heat one of these minutes, I'll be sure to let you know." Jody laughed and socked him playfully on the shoulder.

"No way, man, you're not dying on me yet, not when we still have a well to dig once we get to the top of this mountain," Jonas said, eliciting a laugh from Leo.

Jonas started to say something else, but he was quickly drowned out by the ringing of Jody's cell phone. It took her a moment to recognize the number. She gave the screen a quizzical look before accepting the call. Wondering why her supervisor would be calling her, she held the phone up to her ear. Leo, still joking around with Jonas and a couple of other guys about his non-existent sex life, glanced at Jody and saw that she was on a call. Leo watched their group leader anxiously as she listened intently to her supervisor, her facial features tightening apprehensively as the message came through. Finally, after several minutes, she hung up the call and turned to her friends. Her expression was grim.

"What's up?" Leo asked, struggling to keep his voice steady. Something about Jody's expression made the hairs on the back of his neck stand up.

"We've got a problem." Jody leaned back on her heels and cupped her hands around her mouth in a megaphone gesture. "Storm's coming in! Let's pick it up people, we've got less than an hour to reach the village before it breaks!" Jody spun on her heel suddenly and strode up the path so quickly that Leo practically had to run to catch up with her.

"Storm?" Leo gasped once he'd reached her.

"Yeah," Jody replied, keeping her eyes trained on the path ahead. "Real bad one, we need to get off the mountain fast."

Leo glanced up at the village in the distance, dismayed to see that they still had a lot of ground to cover. At the same time, he saw out of the corner of his eye a gathering mass of black storm clouds approaching them from the west, and he began to pick up the pace.

"So we've got to walk in the rain for a bit, how bad can it be?" he joked. He had meant to lighten the mood but his growing nervousness left him sounding more like a scared little kid asking his parents whether everything would be okay than anything else.

"Not just rain," Jody replied without looking up. "Sounds like a real nasty thunderstorm, chief was saying there's a potential landslide warning on the horizon, too."

It was the news that Leo had been dreading. Jody stopped suddenly and turned on her heel to face the rest of the group, most of whom were lagging significantly behind the two of them and did not seem overly concerned with the prospect of the incoming storm.

"C'mon people, let's move, we've gotta get off the mountain!" Jody called a little more urgently this time.

"Point is," Jody continued, turning back to Leo, "we need to get to shelter now."

Leo glanced up at the village again, and Jody followed his gaze. To both Leo and Jody, it seemed farther away than ever. They were both thinking the same thing: there was very little chance that they would reach the village before the storm hit, and if they were still on the mountain pass, they would be in serious trouble.

"Hey, what's going on?" Jonas asked cheerfully as he caught up to them. "It's a little rain, so what?" he said casually, socking Leo playfully on the shoulder.

"Landslide doesn't sound like a little rain to me," Leo said, suddenly not finding Jonas's antics funny in the slightest.

Jonas's smile immediately faded.

"Jesus, did you say landslide?" he asked, sounding slightly panicked.

A few of the others suddenly looked nervous as well, and they noticeably picked up their pace at Jonas's words.

"Yeah," Jody said, turning back to the group. "Pick up the pace!" she shouted. "Let's move!"

"Point being," Leo muttered to Jonas, whose eyes were suddenly wide with fright, "we need to get to the village now."

But with every passing minute, that scenario seemed less likely to Leo.

11

Overhead, Leo felt the first drops of rain, and before long, it had intensified to a full-on downpour.

"God, I can't see shit," Jonas called out through the driving rain.

"Keep going," Jody called out. "We're not far off now." Privately, Jody knew they were much closer now, but she still had her doubts as to whether they could make it there before the landslide hit.

"You guys alright back there?" Jody shouted over the pouring rain.

"Depends on what you mean by alright," Jonas called back, his shaggy head bowed against the driving rain. "I mean, we're alive," he added. Jody couldn't tell if he was trying to be funny or if he was serious.

"I can see the village, it's right up there!" Leo called through the driving rain. "Let's hurry this up, c'mon!"The group had broken into a full run in the last several minutes and Jody could hear several of them panting right behind her.

"C'mon guys, we're almost there!" she shouted over her shoulder, although she doubted that anyone besides Leo could hear her over the pounding rain.

Leo stopped so suddenly that Jody smacked into him and nearly fell to the ground as she bounced off his back.

"What the hell is that?" Leo exclaimed, pointing at something on top of one of the houses. Jody followed his gaze and immediately felt her blood run cold.

The shadowy figure was sitting on top of the thatched roof of one of the huts, legs crossed, apparently completely unperturbed by the storm.

"No," Jody thought. "He's not sitting, he's floating." Initially, the thought seemed completely absurd, but as she watched him, fascinated, she saw that no part of his body touched the roof, and he was indeed levitating only a few inches above it. Although the downpour had made it difficult for Jody to see anything more than a couple feet in front of her, he appeared perfectly clearly to her. As she stared, dumbfounded, he slowly rose higher into the dark sky. Twenty feet, forty, one hundred...when he finally came to rest, he was so high up that Jody had to crane her neck to see him, at least half a mile up. His arms and legs hung limply in the air, and his head rolled forward on his neck so that Jody couldn't see his face. Then came the voice.

"Jody..."

Whimpering, Jody fell on her knees on the path, her eyes leaving the man but still seeing him in all directions. No matter where she turned her head, he was always right in front of her, as if she unknowingly had entered some twisted hall of mirrors.

"Jody..." it said again.

Jody screamed and squeezed her hands over her ears, but the voice did not need to be heard. It was inside of her. Then it slowly raised its head, revealing its face to Jody. Jody began howling like a wounded animal and fell flat on the ground, shaking uncontrollably as if in the throes of a seizure, squeezing her eyes shut to block him out, but he would not be blocked out. His face remained painted on the inside of her eyelids, causing her to wail ceaselessly in pain and terror, the world around her vanished, nothing existing but the empty inky black void where the thing's face should've been.

But she no longer saw the void. She saw her parents' faces. Her beautiful mother with her tender smile. Her handsome father with his strong chin and thick bushy black beard. And then her father changed. Those warm dark eyes that always lit up at the sight of her darkened, suddenly burning with uncontrollable malice. And then her mother was screaming. Blood was flying everywhere. Her mother's screams mixed with her own terrified wails. And then she was running for her life, screaming for help that would never come as the monster that had become her father bore down on her, her mother's blood streaming from the knife in its hand as it bore down on her with each step, getting closer, closer…Jody screamed as she felt the thing grab her from behind and twist her so that she could see the empty black void where its face should've been. She let out a final pitiful cry as the darkness tilted upward to meet her, swallowing her whole into its soothing embrace.

Leo stared, transfixed, as the shadowy figure rose into the air, higher and higher, until he had to crane his neck to see.

"Jesus, he's a mile off the ground," Leo whispered.

The monster grinned, and he felt himself shudder violently as its face became an amorphous mass, shifting and twisting. Leo gasped. He was staring into the face of his mother.

"Leo," his mother said in a voice roughened by years of smoking. "You aren't going out again tonight, you hear?"

Leo's mouth opened and closed soundlessly at her words.

"I know what you did last night, Leo," his mother went on. "You killed that poor kid driving drunk, didn't you?"

The memory flashed before his eyes. The thud as the child's body hit the windshield. The mother's screams mixed with his own as he slowly realized in his delirious state what he had done.

"I'm sorry, mama," Leo sobbed, tears spilling down his face as he collapsed to his knees. "I just…"

"You just what?" his mother snapped. "Got on a bender? Got good and pissed off about your dad? Someone call you a name? Hell, I've heard all the excuses Leo, and I don't wanna hear 'em no more."

"Mama, please…" Leo wailed, sounding exactly as he had on the day his mother had thrown him out.

"GET OUT," his mother screamed, and Leo crawled into a ball as a hundred feet flew into his body, pounding every available inch of his flesh.

"GET THE FUCK OUT OF MY HOUSE!"

"I'm sorry," Leo whispered through choked sobs as the blows continued to rain down on him. "I'm so sorry, ma…"

The Puppeteer smiled at the lifeless bodies of Jody and Leo. The task was almost complete. He turned and stared pensively out into the dark and pouring rain, knowing he still had another marionette to string up before the night was over.

CHAPTER 3

Russian president Ivan Petrov sat alone at the ornately carved wooden desk with his hands clasped stiffly in front of him, the darkness of the room only serving to further emphasize his total isolation. He stared at his hands folded onto the desk, the events of the last 72 hours playing over and over again in his head like a bad record that had been superglued onto the record player. No matter how many times he told himself he needed to push the thoughts from his mind and focus on what needed to be done, he remained completely still, unable to force himself to use what little strength remained in his exhausted body to get to his feet and walk down the hall to the situation room, where his ministers had spent the last several hours discussing the fate of the country, and perhaps the entire world, in hushed tones, as though talking about it more quietly might delay the terrible events that were almost certainly about to unfold.

He sighed and dragged a hand across his aching forehead, as though it might serve to soothe the terrible pounding of his overwrought nerves against his skull. He had no desire to leave the modicum of comfort his seclusion provided him and face the world again, only to be confronted by the same dull-witted people he'd trusted for so many years, begging for answers on how they should resolve the crisis that they themselves had created. He reached beneath the desk and retrieved a 40-ounce bottle of Smirnoff vodka. He considered it for a brief moment before overturning the bottle into a miniature shot glass, puddling it onto the desk in his haste. He downed the alcohol in one gulp and slammed the shot glass back onto the desk hard enough to send a jagged crack spiderwebbing up the side of it.

Even as a child, Ivan Petrov had harbored a great respect for the United States. Like all other Russian schoolchildren who'd passed through the public education system during the cold war, the gregarious amounts of anti-western propaganda he'd been spoon-fed had more or less forced him to harbor some hatred of America beside the respect he held for it. Still, even as a teenager sitting in his world history classes listening to his professor's lecture about the evils of the western world, he'd still viewed the U.S. as a formidable opponent, an enemy that could be admired for their strength and innovation as much as they were hated for their imperialism and greed. But gradually, as he'd grown older, the respect had been lost as he'd watched the United States weaken and allowed corruption to run steadily more rampant until he no longer recognized it.

He'd watched as NATO had been formed and spearheaded by the United States, began to encroach on the old Soviet satellite states, spreading their sick and twisted ideologies and gradually isolating his country diplomatically and economically. Still, he had to admire them for applying the Marxist strategy of Rudi Dutschke. America no longer used military force to impose their will on the world. Rather, they

14

imposed their agenda by invading the institutions of those countries. The thought might've made him smile under different circumstances. It was something he would've done. Still, he'd watched over the years as the west encroached on Russian soil until finally in 2014, he decided he could stand idly by no longer. It was time to liberate the people of those nations hijacked by the United States. It was time to take back what was rightfully his.

When Russia had liberated Crimea in 2014, he'd visited Simferopol personally and been greeted with crowds who'd cheered his arrival. It only served to strengthen his image of himself as the great liberator. And so, in 2022, with the United States in the midst of an economic and political crisis, he'd sought to liberate Ukraine. He'd been confident. He'd visited Ukraine many times over the years and been greeted warmly each time. The people there loved him. They wanted his leadership. Petrov sighed, rubbing his aching temples. So, what had gone wrong, then? He'd turned the question over and over again in his mind for the last several months, struggling for clarity. It was not until about 72 hours ago, when everything had truly gone to hell, that he had finally come up with a satisfactory answer. He had expected the war to only last a number of weeks. In his mind, the numerically superior and better-equipped Russian forces would sweep aside the smaller Ukrainian force and take Kyiv easily.

A surrender wouldn't be necessary. The people in Kyiv would welcome the Russians. The fighting spirit of the Ukrainian people, combined with the terrible losses, had quickly shattered his brief fantasy. The Ukrainians fought for country, family, freedom, those three words that the Americans used to be fond of bull horning whenever they went off to war. Petrov's army had bombed cities, committed brutal atrocities against Ukrainian civilians, even come within twenty miles of the Kyiv itself. Yet the Ukrainians fought on relentlessly, never even considering the idea of surrender to the overwhelming Russian onslaught. He had never been able to break the will of the Ukrainian people.

"Just like the Americans used to be," he thought. He almost smiled.

Then calamity had struck. A group of around 100 defectors from the Russian Volunteer Corps had launched a sudden invasion of the Belgorod Oblast. They launched attacks in several cities, burning most of them to the ground, but it had all been a smokescreen. Three days ago, his defense minister had come to him in a panic to inform him that the RVC had captured the Belgorod 22 Nuclear Weapons Storage Facility. Petrov, who had always prided himself on his calm and self-control, had barely left the room in time to stop himself from strangling the idiot for allowing this disaster to take place. He himself had desperately appealed to the company commander in control of the facility, but the requests had been outright refused. A few hours ago, he'd been informed that the terrorists had hit St. Petersburg with a nuclear warhead.

The city where he'd grown up, where his parents were buried. The attack had been personal. He stared down at his hands, which were trembling slightly, a terrible anxiety filling him like lead as the weight of his failure finally crashed down on him.

"MAD…" a voice whispered in his head. He'd learned the acronym during his KGB days.

"The bastards took everything from you, Ivan." He sat stock still, his hands beginning to shake with anger.

"They deserve it." He slowly got to his feet, suddenly feeling more energized than he had in weeks.

"You know what to do, Ivan," it whispered. He stormed out of the room, slamming the door behind him.

"They'll see," he thought savagely as he approached the situation room, where his ministers were sitting anxiously around a large round wooden table.

"There will be MAD, the tyrants in the west can be sure of that."

His ministers got to their feet as he entered the room.

"Mr. President…" his foreign affairs minister began.

Petrov ignored him. He turned to his defense minister, Ruslan Parmov, the man who, at that moment, he hated almost as much as he hated the terrorists who had attacked his beloved childhood home.

"Launch a retaliatory strike," Petrov barked.

"Sir…" Parmov began.

He felt his hands slowly ball into fists. There would be no talk of de-escalation, of decency, of lives.

"MAD…" the voice whispered again.

"Do it," he said firmly, before turning to leave.

"Sir, we can't…"

Petrov whirled around, his fist swinging hard and catching Parmov in the jaw. He collapsed to the floor, roaring in pain. Several of his ministers shuddered, but the murderous look in Petrov's eyes kept them from speaking up.

"DO IT!" Petrov roared. "MAKE THOSE SONS OF BITCHES PAY!" Without waiting for a reply, he turned on his heel and stormed out of the room. His ministers stared after him in shock. None of them noticed the shadowy figure standing in a dark corner of the room, a tall black top hat pulled low over his face. He grinned viciously as he watched the Russian president storm down the hallway, thinking bemusedly about how easy it had been to string up the angry little man.

"Just another helpless plaything," he thought, chuckling coldly.

CHAPTER 4

"**W**ake up you little shit!"

Leo recoiled as someone smacked him hard across the cheek. "WAKE THE FUCK UP!"

He shielded his face with his hands as blows began to rain down on him from all sides. "WAKE UP! WAKE UP!" the woman screamed over and over.

"Okay, ma, okay, I'm awake!" Leo begged, still cowering under the hail of blows. He swung his legs out of bed, and came face to face with his mother, who finally lowered her hands, her chest heaving up and down. Leo was able to see now that he was in a hospital room.

"Jesus boy, if I had a dollar for every time I've had to get your lazy ass out of bed, I could get the fuck out of this shit hole neighborhood we live in!" his mother spat.

"Oh c'mon mama," Leo sighed, rubbing his exhausted eyes.

"SHUT UP!" his mother roared, smacking him hard enough to send tumbling into the side of the bed.

Leo groaned in pain.

"Oh, stop your whining," his mother said. "The only person who has any right to complain is the mother of that little boy you hit last night!"

Their eyes met for a brief moment, and beneath the burning anger that really left his mother's gaze, Leo saw something even worse. Apathy. He'd finally broken her. For all the times she'd complained about having to raise him on her own, for all the times she'd been disappointed in him, for all the times she'd said she didn't care about him, she'd never looked at him like this. She was truly done with him this time. For good.

"Mama," Leo whispered, reaching out to embrace her.

She shoved him away, looking at him as though he were a dead rat on her kitchen counter.

"You've been a bad boy Leo," his mother said coldly. "You've been REAL bad this time Leo," she whispered, her voice trembling with rage.

"No mama," Leo whispered. "I'm not a bad boy. I promise I'll be good, I promise, I promise, I'll be good, I'll be good!" he screamed, breaking down into hysterical sobs as he fell to his knees, the room around him blurring through his tears.

His mother stared down at him wordlessly, her face twisted with disgust. "You've been a bad boy, Leo," she murmured.

"No, no, no…" Leo sobbed, clutching onto her leg.

"You've gone too far this time, Leo," she murmured, shaking her head in disappointment."

"I ain't bad, ma," Leo begged. "I ain't bad, ma. I AIN'T FUCKING BAD!"

17

"I've had enough, Leo," his mother said, flatly, kicking at him with the toe of her crimson high heeled boot. "I'm throwing you out this time. You want to live like a homeless man, robbing and stealing from honest people, go be homeless, boy!" She shook him off and started for the door.

"NO MAMA PLEASE DON'T GO!" Leo screamed, dragging himself across the floor.

She paused momentarily, her hand on the doorknob.

"Please, please, please…" Leo gasped.

"Well," his mother said slowly. "Alright." She turned, bending down so she was level with him. "But first, you've gotta show me you can be a good boy, Leo."

"Yes, yes," Leo gasped, reaching from the floor to embrace his mother. "I'll be good, ma, I promise I'll be good."

The Puppeteer wrapped Angelica Rinolski's arms around her crying son.

"Good," the Puppeteer whispered in Angelica's voice, a wicked grin crossing the woman's face. "I love you, son."

"I love you too, ma," Leo sobbed.

CHAPTER 5

arlos Gonzalez charged through the automatic glass double doors into the silent waiting room at New York Presbyterian hospital and into the waiting arms of his mother who embraced him more tightly than she ever had, sobbing her heart out on his shoulder.

"Está bien, mama, está bien," he kept saying over and over again, trying to calm his hysterical mother. *"It's okay, mom, it's okay."* But when he saw the look on Jonas's face, as well as the other members of the mission team that had been flown back from Ecuador on the medical flight along with their two injured teammates, he immediately realized that it would not be alright. He looked up as a door opened to their left and a young woman in a white lab coat strode towards them, her expression grim.

The sight of them didn't help her mood. They sat sentinel in a semi-circle, eyes downcast, hand clasped over their navels in a gesture of silent prayer, although how many of them were actually praying Raeburn never found out. They resembled the mourners at her mother's funeral procession which had taken place barely a year ago.

Everyone from the mission team, most of whom had been sitting in chairs or against the wall, stood as she approached, their expressions anxious. Releasing his mother, who immediately collapsed back into a chair, still crying uncontrollably into her hands, Carlos nervously approached the doctor.

"How bad is it?" he asked before she had a chance to open her mouth.

The doctor slowly shook her head, averting her gaze.

"Are they going to be okay?" Carlos demanded, his voice rising slightly. He grabbed the doctor by the shoulders hard enough to make her flinch. He felt a pair of strong hands grip his shoulders and drag him away from the doctor, who didn't look the slightest bit perturbed by his outburst, as if she dealt with this regularly. Carlos shook Jonas off and collapsed into a chair. He angrily wiped the tears from his eyes. From the moment he'd met Jody, he'd loved her. She was everything he could possibly want in a woman. Beautiful, sweet, kind, sexy, gentle, every positive adjective he could think of came to mind at the mere sight of her. He'd spent every available minute with her, even insisting that he teach her Spanish himself just to give himself an excuse to be alone with her for hours.

"They're stable," the doctor informed them. "They gave us a good scare, but no life-threatening injuries. They'll pull through." She saw a collective feeling of deep relief ripple through the group, and a small smile crossed her face. Raeburn Ingolstadt was only twenty-seven years old, having just finished her residency at Presbyterian. Her only regret in focusing on her career exclusively was that she'd never had the chance to fall in love, get married, and start a family. The lack of a

19

single deep emotional connection often caused her to do something that mentor in her residency had strongly warned her against: forming emotional attachments to her patients. And watching this group right now, even from a distance as they sighed with relief and hugged each other at the news, many of them crying, she felt a connection to them, as if she'd become a symbolic member of their mission group. Even in the few minutes she'd known them, she could tell they were very close. She envied that. It was the one thing in her life, a life that was otherwise very full, seemed to lack. She turned as Isabella Gonzalez, her face still streaked with tears, stood up and approached her. Raeburn willingly pulled her into a tight embrace.

"Thank you," Isabella whispered, her tears staining the collar of Raeburn's lab coat. "Thank you."

Carlos, whose own face was stained with tears, slowly pried his mother off of Raeburn and guided her back to a chair where she sat motionless, her face buried in her hands. Carlos laid a comforting arm around her shoulders.

"Thank you, doctor," he said, refusing to look Raeburn in the eye.

Raeburn nodded.

"I've got to go check on them, but I promise, they'll make it through this." She hurried away before anyone could say anything else, immediately feeling like an idiot for making such a promise. Yet another piece of advice from her old mentor that she hadn't followed. Never make promises that you can't keep. As she strode towards the hospital room where Jody Razitsky was lying, unconscious, she increasingly began to feel the weight of what she had just done. In her effort to soothe the exhausted and scared group, she'd conveniently left out the fact that mere hours ago, she'd been forced to order Leo and Jody to be put into medical comas to keep them both alive, and that the odds that they came out of them were minimal. She sighed heavily as she entered Jody's room, running a hand exhaustedly through her long blonde hair. Even by the standards of an emergency room doctor, it had been a long night, but Raeburn Ingolstadt had the strange feeling it wasn't even close to being over yet.

Raeburn stared silently at the lifeless body of Jody Razitsky, sighing heavily at the thought of what she was going to be forced to tell her loved ones in the morning. She traced her thumb gently down Jody's cool wrist, resting it over the small patch of skin where the steady thrumming of the radial artery could be felt by an outsider. The various monitors and screens by her bedside indicated her condition was stable. She was perfectly healthy, apart from the fact that she was in a coma. The absurdity of it was almost enough to make Raeburn laugh. Instead, she hung her head in defeat.

"I'm sorry kid," she whispered, holding Jody's cool palm in her own. "You've got a lot of people out there who care about you who don't know what to do. I know you can pull through. For them." For an instant, Raeburn saw Jody's lifeless eyelids flicker. She nearly jumped in surprise.

"The strings have been cut," Jody whispered.

Raeburn, suddenly rigid with fright, stared at Jody, unwilling to believe what she was seeing. She nearly screamed as Jody's eyes shot open. Her hand shot out and caught Raeburn's wrist in a vice grip.

"He's here," Jody whispered, her voice shaking with terror. "You have to get out of here before..."

They both jumped with fright at the sound of pounding on the hospital room door.

"Hey Rae, you done in there? I've gotta scrub the room down," came the voice of Violet Sharian, one of her CNAs. Raeburn turned to Jody, who shook her head.

"Don't," she mouthed.

"Jody what..." Raeburn started, but Jody silently held a finger to her lips.

The pounding on the door came again, more incessant this time.

"Open the door, Raeburn."

Only it wasn't Violet's voice this time. It was deeper, rougher, stronger. The sound of it made the hairs on the back of Jody's neck stand up. They were running out of time.

"What's going on?" Raeburn whispered, her voice trembling.

Jody shook her head, her eyes suddenly brimming with tears.

"I'm sorry," she whispered. "I'm so sorry, I..."

The rest of her words were lost in a high-pitched scream as the door to the room exploded inward off its hinges. In the doorway stood Leo Rinolski, still wearing his hospital gown, his face contorted into a mask of rage. Where his eyes should've been, were a pair of soulless black holes.

"RUN!" Jody screamed, a second before she was dragged into the air and launched across the room as if hoisted by an invisible rope.

Raeburn screamed and dived for the open door. She never saw the gleaming steel scalpel clutched in Leo's hand until it swung up to meet her, splitting her jugular in two. She collapsed to the tile floor, the room fading to black around her as blood poured out of her neck in an unstoppable torrent.

"NO!" Jody screamed as Leo bore down on her, his gaze as pitiless as his cold black eyes.

"Leo," Jody begged as he raised the scalpel. "Leo please..."

The blade smashed into her breastbone with the force of a battering ram, plunging into her heart tissue.

Jody gasped as a spurt of blood erupted from her mouth, nearly choking her. Leo squatted down beside her, staring at her coldly as her life flowed from her body.

"I told you," he whispered. "I am the end all be all. The alpha and the omega. All who do not fear me are foolish."

Jody, the room fading to gray around her, turned to look into Leo's lifeless eyes.

"This isn't you," she gasped through a mouthful of blood. "You're a good person, Leo."

"You're wrong," Leo whispered. "I was born sick, just like you. Just like those people out in the waiting room, all of whom will be dead in a few minutes." He stood up to leave.

Jody, her consciousness rapidly fading, whispered, "You can't let it control you. Leo, please, remember who you are. Find...the others. Fight...back..." And then she slumped forward as the room finally faded to black, and everything was gone. Somewhere far off, a woman screamed.

Violet Sharian, the orderly Raeburn had sent to clean Jody's room a few moments before her death, sprinted down the hall in a blind panic. Leo stalked towards her, the blood drenched scalpel brandished. She ran blindly, not caring where she was going, her mind still struggling to comprehend what was happening. A moment later Violet burst into the waiting room, gasping, struggling to catch her breath. No one paid her any mind. She ran to the first person she identified, tears spilling down her face.

"Listen to me, the coma patient, I don't know what happened, he's..." she stopped.

Jonas's expression was completely blank, as though he barely noticed she was there. He was staring at the miniature TV set in the corner of the room. Violet followed his gaze, and then she understood.

"A second nuclear missile is bound for New York city, and will likely impact in the next five minutes," the reporter on the TV blared. "We encourage any citizens of New York city or the surrounding areas to evacuate as quickly as possible."

Violet didn't hear the rest of what the reporter was saying. A strange high-pitched ringing sound had filled her ears. She stood up slowly, sat down next to Isabella, and threw her arms around her, hugging her tightly, the tears now pouring freely from her eyes. Isabella, crying hard herself, hugged the young woman who had been taking care of the two people she had come to love as much as her own children back fiercely. The others in the room, at the sight of the two young women, snapped out of their trance and began hugging each other, many of them crying, several cries of "I love you!" ringing out through the deserted waiting room.

Leo Rinolski strode silently down the hall, his mother's words echoing in his ears.

"You gotta be a good boy Leo, can you do that for me, honey?" He grinned coldly as he approached the doors to the waiting room, the blood-soaked scalpel gleaming in the glow cast by the flickering overhead fluorescent lights.

"Oh don't worry, mama," he thought. "I'm gonna be a real good boy! From now on, I'm gonna be as good a son as you could possibly ask for!"

"Good," his mother's voice whispered in his head. "There's some more bad people in the lobby I want you to get rid of, Leo. Can you be a good boy and do that for me?"

"Of course, ma," Leo whispered enthusiastically. "Anything for you!"

A moment later, Leo Rinolski burst through the double doors into the waiting room, scalpel in hand, murder written on his face. As he turned to face the group assembled in the waiting room that gave him no notice, ready to purge them all from existence, the world disappeared in a blinding explosion of white light, purging both the encroaching darkness of the abyss and the fading firelight from that place.

22

CHAPTER 6

The doomsday report delivered by the newscaster Brian Fallstan, who, despite being impeccably dressed in a three-piece black business suit complete with a stark-white tie, looked like an absolute wreck, was not isolated to the New York Presbyterian hospital or even the whole of New York city. By 11 PM that evening, the broadcast from CBS News and World Report had reached every major city across America, with enormous crowds numbering in the tens of thousands gathering in the streets of Chicago, Los Angeles, Philadelphia, San Francisco, Dallas, Houston, Phoenix, and San Diego to hear the news of what had by now taken place in New York city. In Los Angeles, despite the massive crowds that had gathered in the street and were practically trampling each other to get close enough to see Fallstan's unshaven face and bloodshot eyes on the giant monitor positioned above the CBS News tower, this jostling immediately ceased as Fallstan delivered the message that doomsday had, after many years of anticipation, finally arrived.

For approximately seven minutes and forty-five seconds, the streets of LA were eerily silent as the crowds stared up at the monitor, open-mouthed as the footage of the explosion and the mushroom cloud of gray smoke played over and over again with Fallstan's voice falling into a disinterested monotone as he lacked the strength or the will to continue to put any emotion into his hastily prepared speech. Finally, in the last thirty seconds of his speech, he simply couldn't go on any more and broke down sobbing on camera. The camera team at CBS got him off the air as quickly as possible, but not before he was able to deliver one last sentiment to the American people listening anxiously down below: "God have mercy on your souls." He committed suicide in his dressing room a few minutes later.

Following the doomsday report, it was as quiet as a grave in the streets of downtown LA for about thirty seconds before the anarchy began. The crowd stampeded in all directions, thousands of them going no more than a few steps before they were shoved down under the panicked horde, never to re-emerge from their asphalt graves. A homeless man was thrown through the window of a small jeweler's store by a group of teenagers, who then jumped through the broken window and continued to beat the man until he lost consciousness. A two-year-old girl in a heavy pink winter coat was hit by a stray bullet and passed away in her screaming mother's arms. A group of five middle-aged men wearing shirts that sported the Patriot Front ensign broke into a firearms shop and stole several automatic rifles as well as around five-hundred spare rounds a piece. They quickly re-entered the fray and opened fire on a group of black teens, who returned fire with their own weapons.

Another black boy of around thirteen witnessing the firefight grabbed an AR-15 from the store and gunned down the group firing on the black teens before they even knew what was happening. A store front for a local insurance company went up in flames as a Molotov cocktail was thrown through it. The chaos in the streets continued unabated for about fifty minutes before the missile finally made impact, obliterating both the rioters and those fighting to escape the chaos in a cleansing explosion of heavenly white light.

CHAPTER 7

The following radio communication was recorded at 12:30 AM between a US Army National Guard contingent based on S. Michigan Ave. and local base command at the National Guard station on Calumet Ave:

"Base command to checkpoint 1, come in checkpoint 1, over."

"Checkpoint 1 to base command, I read you loud and clear, over."

"Base command to Checkpoint 1, what's your status, over."

"Checkpoint 1 to Base command, situation all clear, over and out."

About 15 minutes of silence passes before the communication resumes:

"Checkpoint 1 to base command, come in base command, over."

"Base command to Checkpoint 1, I read you, loud and clear. What's your status, over."

"Base command, we've got a bit of a situation here. There's a large group coming down Michigan avenue approaching the checkpoint, over."

"Checkpoint 1, how many are there, over."

"There are about 100, maybe more. They're getting to within one hundred yards, and it doesn't look like they intend on stopping."

"Checkpoint 1, do not engage, I repeat, do not engage. We're here to keep the peace, do not use force unless absolutely necessary, over."

"Base command, I read you. They're within seventy-five yards now, and most of them look like they're armed. Oh shit, I see some automatic rifles."

"Checkpoint 1, I repeat, avoid confrontation unless absolutely necessary, allow them through if necessary, but do not fire unless fired upon, I repeat, do not fire…"

"Base command, one of my men has just been shot! I repeat, they're opening fire, we need immediate backup! We need EMS immediately! I repeat, we need…"

The transmission ends at this point. In the background, automatic rifle fire, shouting, and screams can be heard. Then an explosion, chants of "Fuck the law!" that gradually fade into the distance, and silence.

CHAPTER 8

Jeremy Garson stood in the unusually cool summer night with the other eight men from his unit that command had been able to scramble on such short notice. They had been abruptly awakened about an hour ago and taken a Humvee to the corner of East Camelback Road and North 44th Street adjacent to a small, upscale eatery called "The Henry," with orders to contain the chaotic rioting currently taking place in downtown Phoenix after, in the words of his unit commander, "That idiot Fallstan picked up a bullhorn and announced that the world is ending." The near constant sounds of gunfire, shattering glass, explosions, and screams, as well as the blazing light coming from several raging fires, all of which seemed to be getting closer to their position with every passing minute, was making Garson increasingly nervous and, even in the semi-darkness, he could tell his comrades were thinking the same thing.

A strapping young African American man named Lance nudged Jeremy, shaking him out of his thoughts.

"Hell of a party down there, eh?" he said, grinning. At the same moment, what sounded like a rocket screamed through the air and collided with an enormous glass-paned office building a few blocks away, exploding thunderously and igniting, melting the glass around the impact crater.

"Yeah, hell of a party," Jeremy said sarcastically, tightening his grip on his M4. A crackle of radio static suddenly emitted from Jeremy's breast pocket.

"Base to unit 1, come in unit 1, over."

"Base, this is unit 1, unit commander Jeremy Garson speaking, I copy, over."

"Unit 1, you've got a crowd of about twenty-five people approaching you from the north. They're about a mile north of you, currently heading in your direction, over."

Lance, all hint of humor gone, exchanged a look with Jeremy. Even in the semi-darkness, Jeremy could see he was extremely nervous.

"Base, we've got less than a dozen men out here, requesting immediate backup, over."

"Negative unit 1, we can't spare the manpower, we've got blockades on all streets going into the city center, we're spread thin as it is. You're gonna have to make it work with what you have, over."

Jeremy, cursing under his breath, ordered his men to form a picket line in the road next to the Humvee with weapons at the ready, and positioned himself in the machine gun turret on top of the Humvee.

"Unit 1, crowd is now less than a quarter mile from you, looks like a group of men, women, and children. Most of the men and women are armed, over."

"Don't use force unless absolutely necessary…" Jeremy thought, recalling his CO's orders from earlier in the evening. It seemed like a moot point now.

"Fire on my signal," he called out.

Lance, also recalling the CO's orders, turned to Jeremy.

"Sir, our orders were not to engage…"

"Lance, to be frank, I don't give a damn what our orders were," Jeremy spat furiously. "If the CO loves his orders so much, he can join us out here and get killed along with the rest of us. If he's unwilling to do that, I'll tell him where he can shove his orders."

Lance turned back to the street, tightening his grip on his own M4.

"Incoming!" came a shout from the end of line, and now Jeremy saw the crowd, rapidly approaching them from a few hundred yards down the street, and, to Jeremy's dismay, he saw that several of them were, in fact, armed with automatic rifles.

When they had gotten to within a hundred yards, Jeremy shouted, "Stop right there," aiming the scope of the machine gun directly at them.

The crowd's progress immediately ceased. Some of them exchanged worried glances. Then, two of the men raised twin AK-47s, and Jeremy aimed the mounted machine gun in their direction, prepared to die fighting for the men that he loved.

"Stop! Stop!" came a shout from somewhere in the midst of the group.

The two men immediately lowered their rifles and turned to a young African American man who emerged from the crowd. Lance aimed the scope of his rifle directly at the man's forehead.

"Stop right there!" he shouted, and the man's progress halted.

He raised both hands in a gesture of surrender. Jeremy, without even realizing, had removed his grip from the machine gun.

"Please, sir," said the man, looking directly at Jeremy, who couldn't help but feel a stab of pity at the man's pleading expression.

"You need to leave now," Jeremy said bluntly. "We have orders to prevent anyone from exiting the city center."

"Sir, you don't understand…" he began.

"You heard him," Lance said, who had lowered his rifle but now began to raise it again. "Disperse immediately, or we will open fire."

"Please," he continued. "We have children."

A small African American girl, no older than five or six years-old, emerged from the crowd, led by the hand by a young African American woman who appeared to be her mother. Unnoticed by Jeremy, more people had joined the crowd during this exchange, so that it now numbered around fifty, and more were emerging from the dark street by the second.

"I'm afraid we can't allow you through," Jeremy said firmly. "Disperse immediately, or we will open fire." He returned his grip to the machine gun, aiming the sight at the man standing in front of the crowd.

"Please sir," the man pleaded, slowly approaching the Humvee.

"That's far enough!" Jeremy shouted, a hint of desperation creeping into his voice.

He desperately did not want to shoot this man, but the man just kept coming, step by step, inch by inch. As if in slow motion, he saw the man's hand travel towards his waistband, only to reemerge brandishing a silver Desert Eagle, the chrome reflecting brilliantly in the moonlight. Jeremy's grip on the machine gun tightened, and his finger slid inside the trigger guard, but he could not pull the trigger, even though he knew he must. He heard the shot that would surely end his life, but somehow found he could still open his eyes, only to see the man lying on the ground, a bullet hole clearly visible in the center of his forehead. Jeremy heard a woman scream, a little girl's terrified cry of "Daddy," followed by shouting from his men, automatic weapon fire, and more screams of the wounded and dying. He felt his hands grip the machine gun as it exploded beneath his fingers, lighting up the cool night air with long flashes of gunfire. More screams and bodies fell to the ground all around him. He gasped as a blinding pain erupted in his shoulder. He fell from the machine gun turret to the pavement below, his vision blurring as his head cracked sickeningly against the asphalt. Just before he lost consciousness, he heard a scream of "Grenade," an explosion, and then the cool, blissful darkness mercifully enveloped him.

CHAPTER 9

The chatter in the situation room at the White House died down immediately when President Randolph entered the room, rubbing his eyes in exhaustion. He'd only managed to steal a few hours of sleep in the last seventy-two hours, ever since he had gotten word of the RVC's capturing of the Belgorod 22 Nuclear Weapons Storage Facility in Russia, and at his age, his body did not take kindly to such a long and brutal ordeal. He'd spent much of the last seventy-two hours trying to reach the commanding officer in the RVC unit that had captured the facility, while simultaneously mobilizing the U.S. army into full combat readiness in case of a nuclear strike inside of Russia. Then it happened. The missile strikes on Kyiv and New York had left him no choice but to launch counterstrikes in Yekaterinburg and Rostov-on-Don.

With the attack on Los Angeles, however, the president had a new problem to deal with, which was why they were all sitting in the situation room at 1 o'clock in the morning, looking to him for leadership.

"Let's all be seated," Randolph said. "First, I'd like to get the casualty report from the attacks on L.A. and New York city," he said, nodding to General Christian Germaine, who cleared his throat twice before beginning.

"Sir, at the moment, we don't have an exact casualty number, given the situation on the ground in both cities, but we're estimating around three and a half million in L.A. and upwards of six million in New York city."

"However, we expect those numbers to go up as the situation on the ground becomes clearer and radiation begins to impact the surrounding areas in the coming days."

"And what about rescue efforts?"

"Sir, we're scrambling all available emergency services in the surrounding areas of both cities including EMS, firefighters, police, and national guard, but, with all due respect, this was a nuclear attack. There's only so much that they can accomplish given the destruction that it's already caused."

Randolph leaned forward over the polished mahogany table, his chin resting on his tented hands. He would've asked about the radiation, but he knew that while the presence of first responders would certainly be welcomed by any survivors, there was very little to be done about the radiation and the wave of illness in the surrounding areas that would result from it.

He turned to General Joseph Hartson, the head of the national guard. "What's the situation in Chicago?" Hartson briefly consulted a thick manila folder that had been handed to him several moments ago by one of his aides.

"Mr. President, we have all national guard forces mobilized on the ground, but so far, they've been unable to contain the rioting. A roadblock on South Michigan

Avenue Street was overrun by a large crowd armed with automatic weapons about fifteen minutes ago. At the moment, the situation is completely out of control."

"Is there any expectation of containment in the near future?" Randolph demanded, even though he already knew the answer.

"No sir, at the moment, it looks unlikely."

"And in Phoenix?" Randolph asked with a hint of apprehension, privately dreading the answer.

"Mr. President, there have also been riots of a similar nature in Phoenix. At the moment, we're estimating casualties in the hundreds, although those numbers are likely much higher by now, as the situation appears to be getting worse by the minute. The contingent of national guard troops is doing its best to contain the situation, but we're talking about a couple hundred troops trying to control an entire city of over one and a half million people. With all due respect sir, the task is impossible."

Randolph, a small voice in his head telling him that it was pointless growing stronger with each iteration, listed off over a dozen major cities to General Hartson, and received the same response every single time: out of control rioting, hundreds, if not thousands of casualties, national guard contingents overwhelmed or outright killed in the streets, no reasonable expectation of containment in the near future. Slowly, the president recognized that he had completely lost control of his country. After several hours of discussing possible responses, he could see that they had no choice. At 3:07 am, President Randolph gave the order to send troops from the U.S. army into major U.S. cities to quell the violence. When a nervous Hartson asked the president if this was a declaration of martial law, Randolph responded with a grave nod, unable to look the General in the eye as he did so.

CHAPTER 10

Benjamin Alrite shot up in bed, drenched in an icy sweat. He sat there for a minute, breathing hard, trying to collect himself. The nightmare had woken him up again. It had been the same thing for the last several months. He was alone in a dark water-filled cave, screaming uselessly as the frigid water rose above his head. He knew immediately that something was wrong. He swung his legs out of bed and began to pace back and forth in front of the bed, running his hands nervously through his short cropped brown hair. His wife, Jennifer, stirred, but he barely noticed as he wandered over to the bedroom window, his anxiety increasing considerably when he noticed a lightning-shaped crack on the windowpane.

As he looked out the window, to his eyes, everything seemed completely normal. In fact, the sleepy suburban neighborhood with its perfectly manicured lawns, large oak trees, new cars lining every driveway, and endless rows of large light gray cape cod-style houses, seemed especially peaceful this morning. He found himself unable to rationalize the sudden grip of fear that had seized him, but he found himself unable to dismiss it either. He felt his wife approach him from behind, her wonderful long fingers brushing his bare shoulders.

"Honey, what's the matter?" she asked. "You look like you've seen a ghost."

He brushed her off, running a slightly shaking hand through his light brown crew cut. She gave him a worried look. Throughout their twelve years of marriage, simply hearing her voice and feeling her gentle touch always brought him at least some measure of relief, until today.

"I need a smoke," he muttered and hurried out of the bedroom, rubbing his temples agitatedly as if he had suddenly developed an intense migraine.

Jennifer Alrite stood rooted in the middle of the room, totally dumbfounded.

"Need a smoke, what the hell was that?" she thought. Her husband Ben had not touched a cigarette in over eight years, ever since she'd gotten pregnant with their daughter Grace. She glanced out the bedroom window, feeling a small twinge of discomfort at the sight of the cracked windowpane that had been in perfect condition when they'd gone to sleep last night. She suddenly noticed the neighborhood was entirely too quiet, even for this time of morning. The usual sounds of small children playing in their front yards, car engines starting as parents left for work, and paperboys tossing newspapers into driveways were all missing.

She sat down on the bed, her cool hand pressed to her forehead, lost in thought. She looked up as her eight-year-old daughter Grace, clad in her favorite bright red footie pajamas, wandered into the room, smiling joyfully.

"Hi, mommy!" Grace said enthusiastically, bouncing over to the bed and jumping up next to her mother. Her jubilant smile faded when she saw her mother's face. "What's wrong, mommy?" she asked.

"I don't know, honey," Jennifer replied, hugging her daughter close to her chest. She could've told her it was daddy, that he was in big trouble, but she knew even then that wasn't quite it. Like Ben, she could tell from the moment she'd woken up that something was terribly wrong. She hugged Grace tighter, squishing her into her chest.

"I'm sorry baby, but I just don't know right now."

Ben wandered into the spacious living room, searching for the pack of cigarettes he kept on the mantelpiece, before he suddenly recalled that he hadn't kept any up there for almost nine years. Cursing under his breath, he started for the front door, the migraine growing steadily worse with each passing minute,

Ben walked out onto the porch, grateful for the cool morning air.

"Hey, you okay?" came Jennifer's voice.

He turned to face her. She was frowning. Ben sighed and shook his head.

"Something's wrong," he said, turning back to the street. It suddenly occurred to him that an eerie silence had gripped the neighborhood overnight.

Jennifer followed his gaze, her anxieties increasing as it slowly dawned on her how empty the neighborhood had suddenly become. Nearly every driveway, as far as they could see, was empty. Every house up and down the street was dark, many of them with their windows boarded up. There didn't seem to be a single living person anywhere. Jennifer suddenly found herself clutching her husband's arm.

"What's going on?" she asked nervously.

Ben shook his head.

"I don't know, honey. But whatever it is, it's not good."

CHAPTER 11

Michael Swezenko, who had been busying himself with rearranging a few of the liquor bottles behind the counter of the Sunoco station convenience store, looked up as Ben Alrite walked in the front door, his expression haggard.

"Hey old buddy," Michael said at the sight of his good friend, smiling his gap-toothed grin. "You look like hell."

"Feel like it too," Ben replied exasperatedly. "You got a pack of Marlboros back there somewhere in that mess of yours?"

Mike's grin faded.

"Um…sure…" he said hesitantly, reaching behind the counter for the cigarettes.

Ben snatched them from his friend's hand without thanking him and immediately lit up. Mike watched him, his brow furrowed. Like Jennifer, he was well aware of the fact that Ben hadn't smoked a single cigarette since his daughter had been born. The last time Mike had seen him do it was when his both parents had been killed in a car accident.

"Didn't know you still had that thing," Mike remarked, gesturing to the silver cigarette lighter and trying to keep the nervousness out of his voice.

Ben took a long draw on his cigarette before replying, the fumes wafting up to the ceiling aimlessly.

"Didn't know either until about ten minutes ago," Ben replied, his mood noticeably improved now that he had the cigarette. "Was lying in my glove compartment. Completely forgot I left it there."

Mike nodded as Ben took another draw on the cigarette. Anyone who knew Mike could tell you it took a lot to make the fifty-four-year-old former convict nervous. But seeing his good friend Ben acting like this made him very nervous. He'd sworn off alcohol, cigarettes, pot, the whole damn thing ever since he'd gotten out of prison almost twenty years ago. It brought back too many bad memories of growing up on the rough streets of inner-city New York. In spite of what his black leather biker jacket, full "Hell's Angel" patch on his left bicep, and scraggly salt and pepper beard might suggest, that was not him anymore. And it certainly wasn't Ben.

"Does Jennifer know you're smoking again?" Mike asked as Ben tossed his cigarette on the floor and stamped it out with the toe of his sneaker. Ben didn't reply.

"C'mon man, what's going on?" Mike prodded.

Ben took a deep breath before replying.

"Did you see anybody when you came in to work this morning?" he asked.

Mike, suddenly noticing that Ben looked almost as worried as he was, thought for a moment before responding.

"Actually, no," he said, suddenly realizing this fact for this first time. "I mean, you know me, I ride in doing about seventy-five," he said, gesturing to the black Harley Davidson sitting out in the otherwise empty parking lot. "But no, there was no one around. I figured everyone was in church or something."

Ben smiled weakly. He knew well that Mike was a die-hard atheist who'd largely abandoned his faith in God after nearly being killed in a prison riot when he was serving time. It was also this fight that was responsible for the gap in his front teeth.

"Surprised that cycle is still running," Ben joked. "Assuming my calculations are correct, it's older than you!"

Mike laughed heartily.

"Well, you're an actuary, if I'm not mistaken, so some poor souls better hope they're correct!" causing them both to chuckle.

Ben recalled privately that the motorcycle was actually in excellent condition despite its age.

"Besides, you know I take better care of that motorcycle than I take care of myself," Mike said with a hint of amusement. "She's all I've got in this world!"

"Well, you know how it is to have a wife then," Ben said, and they both cracked up.

Mike grinned, a deep sense of relief washing over him as Ben tossed the cigarette aside.

"Get much business this morning?" Ben asked.

"No, not a whole lot, in fact. Sun's barely up, but normally that don't stop people from showing up and at least using the pumps. And Lorenzo would normally be in here for his morning Gatorade right about now. Haven't seen him yet."

Ben furrowed his brow. Lorenzo Robinson, a physician at the Mountainside Medical Center up in Montclair, in spite of attaining the ripe old age of 63, always ran four miles before going into the office every day like clockwork and nearly always stopped to pick up a Gatorade at the Sunoco station on his way to work.

"I could give him a call," Ben suggested.

Mike nodded. A wide-awake Lorenzo Robinson picked up the phone on the second ring.

"Hey Ben, what's going on?"

"Hey, Lorenzo, you good?" Ben asked.

"What, you think an old man can't take care of himself?" he said jokingly. "I'm sixty-three, Ben, not one-hundred and three."

"Alright, alright," Ben said placatingly, a hint of amusement coloring his voice. "It's just that when I came into the Sunoco this morning, Mike said you hadn't come around, and it worried us a bit."

"Yeah, if you're wondering, no, Serena didn't convince me to stop doing my runs," Lorenzo said with a hint of pique, stealing the words right out of Ben's mouth. "As I've told her many times, I will run 4 miles every day until the day I die, and if it kills me, I'll die a happy man."

Ben smiled.

"Anyways," Lorenzo continued, "I was meaning to give you a call anyway, because there's something you should probably know. Is Mike there?"

"Yeah, he's here," Ben replied. "Put it on speaker, you both need to hear this."

Ben, feeling slightly apprehensive, set the phone to speaker and placed it on the counter where both he and Mike could listen.

"I was driving out to the dog park in Arlington around 6 o'clock this morning," he continued, "but I was stopped out by Laurel Avenue, you know, where that old Roman Catholic church that looks like it belongs in medieval England is?"

"Yeah, I know the one," Ben replied.

"Wait, hold on a minute," Mike interrupted. "You were stopped by the cops? What for?"

"Well, that's the bizarre part," Lorenzo continued. "You see, cops don't normally wear full combat gear and camouflage or block the street with Humvees."

Both Ben and Mike sat in stunned silence for a moment.

"They were military?" Ben asked.

"Looked like it," Lorenzo replied.

"Did they say what they were doing there?" Mike asked, and Ben swore he'd heard his voice shake, just a little. Hearing fear creep into the voice of Michael Swezenko scared him almost as much as whatever the hell was going on out in the streets that would require military presence.

"Well, like I said," Lorenzo responded, "I'm driving along Kearney Avenue, when I run into two Humvees just sitting in the middle of the street surrounded by what look like soldiers in full battle dressed toting M16 rifles. One of the soldiers walks up to me and says that the street is inaccessible right now and that I need to turn around and start driving in the other direction. When I asked him what the hell was going on and why were there Humvees blocking the street, he tells me he's not going to ask again and if I don't get the hell out of here now, he'll use force. So, I obviously get scared and drive away, because, I'll be honest, he didn't look at all like he was kidding."

Ben exchanged a look with Mike, who now looked almost as worried as he felt.

"There was something else though," Lorenzo said suddenly. "When those guys were yelling at me, they sounded angry, no question about it. But there was something else, too. Something in their eyes. They looked scared, Ben. Like they were afraid for their lives."

They sat in stunned silence for a moment before Ben hung up the phone.

"What the hell was that about?" Mike asked finally.

Ben shook his head. "I need another smoke," Ben muttered.

"Make that two," Mike added.

CHAPTER 12

Ten minutes later, Ben and Mike were sitting in Ben's white Porsche Cayenne, crawling their way through the deserted streets towards Laurel Avenue and the aforementioned military roadblock. Unnoticed by Ben, a Ruger LCR revolver was sheathed in Mike's black leather waistband holster. He hoped it wouldn't get any use today, but, as his WWII veteran grandfather had been fond of saying, always have an umbrella ready in case of a shitstorm.

"What do you reckon happened that would get the military blocking cars on the street?" Ben asked as they passed a deserted Old Navy with an ugly department store mannequin waving to them from the window.

"I don't know," Mike replied a little too quickly, although Ben took no notice. Actually, Mike did have an idea. When his grandfather had been shipped off to the pacific theater, his grandmother had written him dozens of letters from Hawaii about how scared she'd been after they'd instituted martial law on the island, several of which Mike had discovered in his mother's attic when he was a kid. "I'm scared Samuel, they arrested my neighbor in front of his family yesterday and dragged him off, what if they come for me next?"

"He looked like he might actually shoot me..."

Those had been Lorenzo's words. It seemed to fit perfectly with his grandmother's description of military rule.

"What the hell..." Ben gasped, shaking Mike from his thoughts.

He noticed that the Porsche had come to a stop. He looked out the windshield and immediately echoed Ben. Vehicles, well over a thousand of them, many of them having collided with those in front or behind them, were piled into the narrow street bumper to bumper for the next several blocks. A defunct midnight blue FORD-F150 had smashed through the storefront window of a Whole Foods and now hung half in the store and half in the street, the driver having long abandoned it. Many people had abandoned their damaged or stalled vehicles and were now standing in the street. As they exited the vehicle, carefully moving their way through the tightly packed crowd towards something in the distance that appeared to be the source of the backup, they could hear pleading mixed with children's distressed cries. It took them nearly twenty minutes to make their way to the front of the crowd, during which time it seemed to swell further with the arrival of more demonstrators. Finally, they saw the source of commotion. Two identical Humvees clearly meant to form a blockade sat stationary in the middle of Laurel Avenue, surrounded by a company of soldiers in full battle dress, touting black M16s whose chrome glinted in the bright September sunlight.

As they approached the soldiers' position, they could see that the soldiers were raising their weapons threateningly and sweeping the line of protesters that were pressing ever closer to the line of Humvees.

"This is an illegal gathering, disperse immediately or we will open fire," declared one soldier that appeared to be the unit's commander into a bullhorn, but his declaration fell on deaf ears. If anything, the shouting only seemed to be increasing in intensity. The unit commander, a twenty-five-year-old well-built marine named Brad Slater, wiped the sweat from his brow with his gloved hand that, despite the heat of the day, was more the result of nervousness than anything else. He had been shouting those exact same words for over two hours now, refusing orders from command to open fire. He had fifteen men at his command, and a hostile crowd over a thousand strong opposing them. Firing a shot would be signing his own death warrant as well as those of the men around him. But as the crowd continued to press in on them, he knew he was running out of time and options.

"Hey," came a man's voice from somewhere in the crowd, causing Captain Slater to instinctively turn his weapon on Ben and Mike, both of whom were growing angrier with each passing minute.

"You mind telling me what the hell's going on here?" Ben demanded. Slater tightened his grip on his M16. The men were now within a few feet of him, firmly in the no man's land formed between the gathering crowd behind them and the soldiers.

"That's close enough!" he barked. "Step back, or I will fire!" It was enough to stop the men's progress, although they did not back away.

"What the hell are you boys doing out here?" Mike demanded.

"Keeping the peace," Slater replied, although Ben could tell the young man was nervous.

"Oh, damn fine job you're doing," Mike retaliated. "What authority do you have to keep American citizens caged in here like animals?" he demanded.

Slater didn't reply, his attention now focused on the crowd behind Mike, several members of which were now following the two men into no man's land. The whole crowd seemed to be inching forward almost too slowly to be noticed.

"Who gave you the authority to shoot innocent civilians?" Mike continued. "How many kids have you fuckers killed in the name of..."

His speech came to an end as a twenty-three-year-old marine named Reginald Lawson, a close friend of Slater's who had served with him in Afghanistan, smashed Mike in the head with the butt of his M16 rifle, sending Mike sprawling on the asphalt. The barrel of the rifle was now squarely over Mike's forehead.

"One more word," Reginald growled. "I'm warning you, asshole, one more word out of you, and I'll shoot you like a mongrel."

"Sir, please," Ben pleaded, causing Reginald to refocus his weapon over Ben's heart.

"We just want to know what's going on."

Slater considered him for half a second before saying, "We're not at liberty to..."

Slater suddenly stopped mid-sentence. He doubled over as a sudden spasm of pain gripped his stomach. He fell to his knees, retched, and then vomited.

"Get the hell out of here, now!" Reginald demanded, hitting Ben in the chest with the barrel of his rifle.

For a moment, time seemed to slow down. Ben didn't move, and judging by the look on Reginald's face, Ben could've sworn he was about to fire, when an old man with fraying white hair in a dark green polo burst out of the crowd, panting heavily and holding his stomach. Reginald's attention snapped away from Ben in time to see the old man stumble up to him as if drunk and grab the front of his uniform with both hands. Taken completely by surprise, Reginald stumbled and nearly lost his grip on the rifle. The old man clung to him like a drowning sailor clinging to a life buoy, spittle flying from his mouth in his rush to speak.

"Sir, please, please help me..." he gasped, struggling to breathe.

Reginald, whose rifle now lay on the ground, backed away from the old man furiously as if he might be contaminated, but the old man hung on ferociously, his legs dragging across the asphalt as they moved in a kind of twisted, weirdly mesmerizing slow dance, Reginald thrashing and shouting at the man to get off of him the entire time.

The man bent over and vomited all over the front of Reginald's uniform. Another soldier, his eyes wide with panic, grabbed the old man by the back of his shirt and threw him to the pavement away from Reginald. Reginald, his fear replaced by a sudden fiery anger, pressed the barrel of his M16 into the back of the man's head, and, ignoring the scream of "No!" from Slater, fired. The man's head flopped onto the pavement like a ragdoll and remained still. The whole world went silent, apart from the faint ringing in Ben's ears, as the crowd and the soldiers stared at the motionless body of the old man. Then, after an eternity that lasted no more than thirty seconds, Slater broke the silence.

"What the hell have you done, old buddy?"

CHAPTER 13

Reginald opened his mouth to reply, then closed it again without taking his eyes off the body, his expression far away. Slater crossed over to Reginald and shook him by the front of his uniform, finally tearing his gaze away from the body.

"WHAT THE HELL HAVE YOU DONE?" he screamed.

Reginald stared into the face of his friend, horror dawning on his own as he slowly realized what his friend had known since the moment the crowd had begun to gather in the street several hours ago. Unnoticed by any of them, Mike had risen to his feet, his expression a mask of cold, ruthless anger. In slow motion, he withdrew the 9mm from its holster and leveled it at Reginald Lawson's head.

Ben noticed a second too late and threw his hands out to deflect the gun, missing by no more than six inches. The gun fired, the bullet striking Reginald Lawson square in the temple, killing him instantly. Ben tried to grab the gun from Mike, who threw him to the ground, overwhelmed by uncontrollable anger. He turned the gun on a completely stunned Slater, and a second from death, Slater was saved by his comrade, who caught Mike in the shoulder holding the gun with a bullet, sending the gun tumbling to the pavement along with its owner, who lost consciousness before he hit the pavement.

Through a haze of pain, Mike felt a pair of hands lift him off the pavement by the back of his shirt and drag him to some unknown destination, the world around him a whirlwind of screams, shouts for blood, automatic rifle fire, orders being barked in every conceivable direction, explosions, and the dreadful sound of bones being crushed under the unrelenting stampede of the crowd advancing on its oppressors. And then, through all the chaos, a far-away voice:

"Hang in there, Mike, hang in there, buddy, stay with me, stay with me."

Slater, upon seeing Mike fall to the pavement, stood stock-still in shock for a brief moment, before one of his men grabbed him by the front of his uniform and shouted for him to snap out of it. He sprinted into the turret atop the lead Humvee and got a single shot off from the machine gun before a stray bullet struck him in the chest, sending his lifeless body to the pavement where he lay still.

Ben dragged Mike's limp body into the nearest empty alleyway, trying to ignore the large blood stain growing by the second underneath Mike's t-shirt.

"C'mon Mike," he muttered under his breath. "Stay with me damnit, stay with me, c'mon!" In the street, Ben saw that the crowd was now surging forward towards the soldiers' position, brandishing pistols, butcher knives, and a few automatic rifles openly that had been concealed only moments before.

"Had to kill him, boss..." Mike muttered deliriously. "Little fucker pulled a knife on me..."

Ben laid Mike with his back up against the alley wall.

"I'll be back in a minute," he explained quickly. "I'm gonna see if I can get us a ticket out of here." Mike grinned in response.

"Don't worry boss, I'll be right here," he said. A few seconds later, he passed out again.

The armed rioters that had converged on the squad of marines stationed at Laurel Avenue did not let their oppressors go peacefully. Slater, having died almost instantly after a stray bullet ripped cleanly through his aorta, and Reginald, who died just as quickly as his comrade, turned out to be the lucky ones. The scene left behind at Laurel Avenue was a gruesome one. A 22-year-old marine named Jonas Tearson who had only finished his final tour overseas less than two months ago was held down in the street while a middle-aged man wearing a black sleeveless t-shirt applied a handsaw to his leg until it severed, lying in the street like a defunct car tire. He howled in pain for nearly twenty minutes before finally bleeding out.

Two brothers, Larson and Prentice Clearwater, were strung up by a rope hung over a streetlight and were left to asphyxiate to death. Several of the marines' throats were cut, and two had their hands removed while they were still alive. The brutal crimes committed against the marines did not go unpunished. Less than an hour later, when the crowd approached the Belleville turnpike, they were approached by a contingent of four Humvees supported by two Blackhawk Sikorsky UH-60 helicopters. There was no hesitation this time. Immediately upon contact, all four turrets on the Humvees, as well as the Blackhawk helicopters, unleashed hellfire on the crowd, most of whom fled back down Kearney Avenue for their lives with a few choosing to fight back with automatic rifles. Finally, after ten minutes of fighting, when no more than a dozen of the initial three-hundred or so fighters remained standing, the Blackhawks unleashed their four air-to-surface missiles in rapid succession, eliminating any remaining resistance to military authority in Kearney, NJ.

CHAPTER 14

"**G**et me a pair of tweezers," Lorenzo barked out, sliding a pair of latex rubber gloves over his age-knotted hands.

As if on cue, Ben immediately returned from the bathroom, a full fitted first aid kit in hand. He quickly handed the tweezers to Lorenzo, whose face was already shining with sweat.

"Get his shirt off," he ordered Ben and another middle-aged man named Jason Morandez, a physician's assistant who had worked in the surgery department with Lorenzo for the last several years.

When the shirt had been tossed to the floor, Jason squatted down next to the handsome brown English Arm Roll sofa where Mike was lying unconscious and examined the small hole in Mike's shoulder for a moment before turning back to Lorenzo.

"He got lucky, bullet missed the brachial artery. It's still lodged in there, but from the looks of it, it's still in one piece, so we should be able to remove it without any problems."

Lorenzo nodded but privately thought that Jason's assertion that removing the bullet would be "no problem" was quite ludicrous.

"So he's gonna make it?" Ben asked urgently, turning to Jason.

"Yeah, he'll be alright," Jason said distractedly, reaching for a bottle of isopropyl alcohol that had been left on the coffee table. "Shock's knocked him out for now, but he'll live." Jason's most pressing concern right now was the potential for infection. Often when proper clinical care was available, he wouldn't have even removed the bullet, at the risk of causing further bleeding and tissue damage. However, without any proper clinical care available, the risk of infection was too great to leave the bullet alone. Isopropyl alcohol would delay that for now, but given the situation in the streets, proper clinical care would be a long time coming, if ever, so it was up to him and Lorenzo to keep the wound clean as best they could with whatever they had available.

"Alright, Jason, sterilize the wound."

Jason nodded and uncapped the clear plastic bottle. He poured a generous amount over the hole in Mike's shoulder, creating a faint hissing sound. Mike's mouth twitched a little in his sleep, but he did not wake up. Lorenzo squatted down next to Jason, bearing the pair of tweezers, while Ben, his wife, Jennifer, who had sent their daughter Grace out of the room along with the other children, Lorenzo's wife Serena, along with a few other families from the neighborhood that had remained behind stood around them in a semi-circle, watching them anxiously.

"I'll give you as much room as possible," Jason said, although he did not sound hopeful. He placed both thumbs and forefingers in a circle around the wound and then spread them apart as far as he could to expose the bullet.

Mike stirred in his sleep, muttering something about teenagers, but he didn't wake up.

Lorenzo carefully slid the tweezers in between Jason's outstretched fingers into the bullet hole, praying that Mike didn't wake up in the middle of the procedure.

"If he wakes up and starts thrashing around while I've got the tweezers in him, this whole thing's gonna turn into a bloody nightmare," Lorenzo thought. He got the tweezers clamped firmly around the bullet and hadn't moved more than a single inch before that nightmare became a reality.

Mike's eyes shot open, causing the whole room of onlookers to gasp in surprise. For a split second, Mike sat perfectly still, his eyes wide with shock. And then he let out a braying howl and jerked his arm away from the source of the pain, causing the tweezers to tear out of his arm with a splatter of blood.

"Hold him down, damnit!" Lorenzo shouted at the unmoving crowd behind him.

Immediately, Ben, Jennifer, and another man named Tyson walked towards Mike, now staring in shock at his bleeding arm and pinned him down by all four limbs. Mike thrashed about, struggling to get free, but they managed to hold him still enough for Lorenzo to get the tweezers back into the hole with Jason's help. This time Lorenzo was less careful and slid the blood-drenched bullet out of Mike's arm as fast as possible, causing Mike to howl with pain and another splatter of blood to rain down on the floor. For a moment, Mike stared at his persecutors, wide-eyed with shock and anger that made Ben feel a small stab of guilt before passing out on the sofa.

"Well, poor guy's been through a lot today," Jason said, applying more isopropyl alcohol to the now bleeding wound and wrapping it with a gauze bandage. "Can't blame him for being upset, just wish he'd waited until after we were finished."

Despite his long and brutal day that left him feeling physically and emotionally more drained than he could remember being in a very long time, Ben couldn't help but chuckle at the remark. He clapped Jason on the shoulder and smiled dazedly.

"You need a drink, my friend? I could go for one."

Jason returned Ben's smile.

"Sounds lovely."

A few minutes later the four of them were sitting around the table in Lorenzo Robinson's oversized kitchen, nursing bottles of hard lemonade that Lorenzo had dug out of his fridge. Many of the families had gone home with their children after Mike had passed out, but a few remained in the living room, chattering nonchalantly about work, concerts they wanted to go see, or concerns about childcare, seemingly any casual subject that would temporarily distract them from the elephant in the room that Ben knew would be brought up eventually. He was quietly dreading that very moment. Ben could sense the tension in the room, could see the way his friends stared down at the kitchen floor and grasped their bottles with such force that their knuckles turned white, and Ben was afraid they might shatter. Eventually, Jason managed to break the silence.

"So, Mike's gonna make it," he said. "Just needs a few hours rest and he should be good to go."

"Go where, exactly?" said a tall, well-muscled African American man named Tyson, and every head in the room turned in his direction.

"Look man," Jason said, "after what happened today with the military trying to keep us here like animals in a cage, is it really a good idea to just sit around and wait and see what happens?"

No one answered him at first.

"I mean, look what they did to Mike, or better yet, go out to Laurel Avenue and look at all the people they murdered. Who's to say they won't come marching through the neighborhood one of these days, shooting anything that moves?"

"Alright, alright, let's just calm down for a second," Ben said finally, slamming his bottle on the table rather harder than necessary. "Those people were trying to break through a military blockade, obviously there was a reason it was there in the first place. We'll be a lot safer if we stay put for the moment and figure out what the hell is going on here than if we march out there all half-cocked up to a squad of fully armed marines and demand that they move aside."

There was no argument, and Lorenzo nodded at Ben.

"Has anyone bothered to turn on the news in the last 24 hours?" came a voice from the doorway.

They all turned. Mike was standing in the doorway, a gauze bandage clearly visible on his upper arm, a shot glass of whiskey in his hand. Ben smiled at the sight of his good friend.

"Yeah, I had to get off my back. My arm," he said grimacing, "was fucking killing me, so I figured a pick-me-up sounded like a damn good idea!" He drained the shot glass and slammed it rather harder than necessary on the table. "And before you ask," he said, turning to Lorenzo, "no, I don't need anything for the pain."

They all laughed except Lorenzo, who managed a halfhearted grin. "Sorry about that man," he said.

Mike waved his hand dismissively. "Now, back to my original question, has anyone bothered to turn on the news the last 24 hours?"

They all shook their heads.

"You want to pull it up, Lorenzo?" Mike asked, gesturing to the small TV set mounted on the kitchen wall.

Lorenzo nodded and switched on the TV.

Their immediate impression was that the remote control simply hadn't worked and that the TV remained off. It took them all a moment to realize the channel they were on simply wasn't running any programming.

"Weird," Lorenzo muttered, flipping to the channel guide. But what he found next was much stranger.

Every single channel on the TV guide had had its scheduled programming removed, leaving them staring at an empty black void on the screen.

"What the hell," Mike muttered.

"Your TV is working right, Lorenzo?" Tyson asked.

"Was working this morning," Lorenzo replied, scrolling down through the guide and coming up empty.

With each passing second, Ben was growing increasingly nervous. His mind flashed back to the scene that morning, and the terrified look he'd seen in Reginald's eyes when the sick old man had grabbed him.

"They looked scared, Ben. Like they were afraid for their lives…" Lorenzo's words echoed through his mind.

"Stop," Ben said suddenly. Lorenzo paused with his finger on the scroll button. "There's nothing there."

"What do you mean?" Lorenzo asked nervously.

His question was answered a few seconds later as the blank TV screen suddenly blared to life. They all abruptly turned to see a middle-aged man with close cropped gray hair dressed in a crisp two-piece black suit adorned with two gold buttons and a matching tie. Several medals were pinned to the front of his suit, along with miniature flags representing over two dozen nations. The man was standing behind a large ornate wooden desk placed in front of three tall bay windows. A pair of white curtains had been drawn to reveal an enormous lawn sprawling behind the building. In the distance, Ben could make out an enormous crystal-clear reflecting pool turned bright orange in the setting sun, and a large, triangular stone pillar he recognized almost immediately as the Washington monument. The man's expression was very grim.

"Hello," he said. "To those of you who do not know, my name is General Christian Germaine of the United States Army. I have interrupted your regularly scheduled broadcasting to deliver you a message from the Oval Office."

None of them even looked up as Serena, Jennifer, and Alison, Tyson's wife, entered the room, their faces filled with worry. The eight of them stared, dumbfounded, as General Germaine continued.

"Over the last 24 hours, we have suffered a series of nuclear strikes from the Russian military in several major U.S. cities. The attacks have touched off a wave of mass unrest all across the country that the National Guard has failed to contain. For this reason, President Randolph has declared a state of martial law nationwide and has asked me to oversee this operation."

"Son of a bitch!" Mike roared, throwing the shot glass furiously at the TV screen.

The glass missed by inches, shattering on the wall to the right of the screen and sending brown streams of whiskey dribbling down the wall.

"As you may have noticed, contingents of U.S. soldiers have established roadblocks on streets, highways, and other avenues of transportation. These measures are intended to keep you safe. By order of the U.S. military and the oval office, you are to shelter in place until further notice, and I have authorized the military to maintain the quarantine with force if necessary. We will get through this crisis, but we must work together and ensure cooperation. Thank you."

The screen immediately went dark, leaving only a heavy silence to fill the empty space. It was several moments before any of them spoke again.

"We've got to get the hell out of here," Ben said, grabbing his wife's hand and starting for the kitchen door.

"Wait," Mike said, causing them to pause. His grandmother's words echoed through his mind. "I'm scared they're going to come for me next…"

"If you go out there right now, they're going to tear you to pieces."

"No Mike, he's right," Tyson interjected. "We can't just sit here and do nothing."

"Those soldiers are just as scared as we are," Serena said. "Maybe they can be reasoned with."

Lorenzo shook his head.

"They might be scared, but they're still soldiers. They follow orders. What happened today is proof of that." He cast a dark look toward Mike.

"So, what do we do then?" Jennifer asked nervously, still clutching her husband's hand.

No one answered her. Suddenly, Grace burst through the kitchen door, causing them all to jump. Her warm brown eyes were wide with fright.

"Grace!" Ben exclaimed, immediately hurrying over to her. "What's wrong honey?" Grace's lower lip began to quiver, and within seconds, she was crying uncontrollably.

"I don't know, I don't know," she gasped. "Marianne, she's…"

"She's what?" Tyson demanded, jumping up from his seat.

"We were listening from the living room, and she just…" The rest of her words were lost in a flood of crying.

Serena immediately rushed into the living room. Jennifer picked her daughter up and held her while she sobbed her heart out on her mother's shoulder. Within seconds, Serena burst through the kitchen door, looking every bit as frightened as Grace.

"Lorenzo, you'd better come quick," Serena said hurriedly. "Marianne just collapsed."

Lorenzo burst into the living room along with the others only for his heart to sink at the sight before him. Alison was on her knees on the floor, bent over the unconscious body of her little girl. The distressed look Alison gave Lorenzo as he entered the room reminded him unpleasantly of a mother confronted with the death of her child.

"Please, help her," Alison pleaded, her face shining with tears.

"When did it start?" Lorenzo asked, getting down on his knees next to Alison.

"About five minutes ago," she replied. "She was perfectly fine before, it seemed like it just happened out of nowhere."

Behind them, Marianne let out a very wet cough that sounded like it came from somewhere deep in her chest and expelled a fresh wave of mucus and yellow vomit that looked suspiciously like stomach bile onto the floor.

"Mommy," she whimpered. "My head hurts. I'm so dizzy."

"I know baby, I know," Alison soothed, stroking her daughter's burning forehead. "It's alright, it's alright baby, mommy's here."

Lorenzo, who had been about to suggest that the girl might simply have food poisoning, suddenly paused. Headaches were a possible symptom of food poisoning, but dizziness?

All at once, Marianne collapsed on her back onto the floor, causing both of them to jump. For a brief moment, both Lorenzo and Alison were completely frozen, neither of them taking their eyes off of the little girl who had gone completely rigid on the hardwood living room floor. Lorenzo, whose mind flashed back to his days in the hospital, was fairly sure he knew what was happening. He grasped Alison's hand as she reached out towards her young daughter's face and held her back. Alison gave him a quizzical look, but he was too focused on Marianne to notice. Marianne's warm dark brown eyes had glazed over, as if someone had pulled an extension cord that supplied electricity to her brain. Alison let out a scream of surprise as her daughter's torso suddenly spasmed six inches off the floor. Her arms shot rigidly out to her sides and began jolting in all directions as if struck by lightning.

Her head thumped against the floor twice in rapid succession. Alison, whose eyes were welling up with tears, reached down to grab her daughter, but Lorenzo quickly pulled her away.

"No, no, don't, she's having a seizure, you'll hurt her!"

But the woman, driven half mad by the sight of her daughter losing control of her body, screamed, "Get off me!" and struggled in Lorenzo's grasp.

Lorenzo, hating himself, shoved her against the wall to keep her away from Marianne, taking blows from the woman desperate to get her daughter, a part of him feeling as though he deserved every one of them.

"Listen to me…" he started to say, but pausing abruptly as Alison struck him again.

It was no use. Even if she weren't screaming over him, she was half out of her mind with fear for her nine-year-old daughter; there was no reasoning with her. Alison went to smack him again, and Lorenzo finally managed to grab hold of both her arms.

"There's nothing you can do for her, I'm trying to help!" Lorenzo shouted, and Alison immediately stopped screaming.

Lorenzo relaxed, realizing he had finally broken through to her. She slumped against the wall, tears running freely down her face now. Tyson, who had been held back by Ben and Mike, suddenly stepped forward, and Lorenzo became very aware of the SIG P226 holstered to his belt. The momentary rush of fear when he saw the concerned expression on Tyson's face. Jason entered behind him and immediately went to Lorenzo.

"You alright?" he asked. Lorenzo nodded.

"What's wrong with her?" Tyson asked Lorenzo while holding a sobbing Alison.

Lorenzo considered his words carefully before replying.

"When I was just getting out of medical school, I joined a team that was heading to Ukraine to provide aid in a hospital in Chernihiv. I was working in the ER. A lot of my patients were in Chernobyl and the surrounding towns when the meltdown happened. Can anybody guess what the number one thing they came in for was?" He wasn't sure he could've brought himself to say it allowed.

Jason, who had been watching Lorenzo almost as intently as Tyson, suddenly started. "Acute radiation syndrome. Lorenzo, are you suggesting…"

"I'm not suggesting, I'm stating a fact," he said assertively, cutting Jason off. There was a trace of carefully concealed fear in Lorenzo's voice that Jason almost missed. "That soldier Ben saw fall ill, he had acute radiation sickness. That old man begging the soldiers for help, he was dying of acute radiation sickness."

Tyson picked his unconscious daughter up off the floor and rested her head against his shoulder.

"That's impossible," Tyson said, almost angrily. "If she has radiation sickness, how come the rest of us don't have it too?"

"We will, soon enough," Mike said, almost too quietly to hear. Privately, he was hoping that was, in fact, the case, but his hopes were dashed when every head in the room turned towards him.

"Mike," Lorenzo said, "what are you saying?" although he already had a pretty good idea.

"Sometime last night, according to the U.S. government, the Russians finally hit the big red button and successfully detonated one if not multiple nuclear weapons on U.S. soil. And if that truly is the case, we have a giant cloud of radiation blowing in our direction."

For a moment, no one spoke. Everyone in the room stared off blankly into space as if they were hypnotized. Marianne shivered in her sleep. She looked sickly and was as pale as a ghost. Jason felt a rush of sympathy for the poor little girl, knowing that, with medical care unavailable, she likely only had weeks to live. Tyson finally broke the silence.

"I'm not just gonna sit around here and wait for my family to die. I'm leaving." He started towards the bathroom door.

Jason grabbed his arm.

"Tyson, what good would it do? There are soldiers blocking the roads, you wouldn't make it out of town."

Tyson brushed him off angrily.

"No, there's hospitals out there, they have to help her, I'm not just gonna let her die!" They could all see that he was fighting not to cry.

Alison laid a hand on his arm, her eyes welling up with tears.

"Babe, there's nothing we can do."

"Yes, there is!" Tyson insisted. "We have to at least try."

And without another word, Tyson walked out of the bathroom, carrying Marianne and holding Alison's hand.

"Tyson!" Mike called, a note of panic in his voice.

"Let him go," Ben said, resigned. He knew there was no hope of stopping him. A moment later, they heard the front door of Lorenzo's house swing open and snap closed again. What Ben didn't realize at the time is that by allowing them to leave, he had just condemned Tyson, Alison, and Marianne, who had less than an hour to live, to their deaths.

CHAPTER 15

Marianne drowsily opened her eyes and was immediately confronted by a beautiful, cloudless, starry night sky. The black Mercedes Benz had just exited Kearney and was now heading down Route 7 towards the Belleville turnpike. Marianne yawned and smiled up at the wonderful, twinkling stars. Her mother used to tell her that grandma and grandpa lived up there in the stars, smiling down on her. Even in her exhausted and sickly state, this thought still made her smile. Tyson was beginning to have hope that they would get out of this okay. Laurel Avenue had been deserted, and so far, they had not run into a single soldier on the road. Even if the first hospital they came to was deserted, he could simply walk in and take what they needed. Marianne was going to be okay, he was steadily growing surer of it with every passing moment that they were not stopped by a military blockade.

He heard a faint cough from behind him and realized that his daughter was awake.

"Hey, baby," he said quietly. "How are you feeling?"

"I feel sick, daddy," Marianne replied, and to his dismay, Tyson saw in the rearview mirror that she was clutching her stomach in pain.

"Daddy, am I going to be okay?"

"Yeah baby, don't worry," he said. "Daddy won't let anything happen to you. I'm gonna keep you safe."

Marianne smiled weakly. Her daddy had always kept her safe because he was big and strong and nothing could ever hurt him.

"Get some rest, baby, you'll feel better in the morning."

Marianne lay back on the seat and stared out at the beautiful starry night sky. The thought of grandma and grandpa watching over her and daddy from somewhere up in the sky, smiling their wonderful smiles, caused to experience a swell of happiness that momentarily obscured the pain in her stomach. She finally closed her eyes and started to drift off.

"Hey, daddy?" she said softly.

"Yeah, baby?"

"I love you."

Several thousand feet above them, the Blackhawk Sikorsky UH-60 was almost perfectly camouflaged against the black velvet curtain of the night sky. Manned by a crew of four U.S. marines who had orders to obliterate anything that moved and packing a six-barrel electrically operated gatling gun as well as four heat-seeking air-to-surface missiles, the helicopter was a well-oiled killing machine, so effective that it was patrolling this stretch of highway alone without any immediate backup. At least, that's what the pilots were told by their CO, and given the show it had put on earlier in the day, they didn't have a hard time believing it. However, the CO in question was more aware of the deteriorating chain of command and lack of warm bodies than the pilots, and he intended to keep it that way.

The Sikorsky was making another pass over the turnpike when the spotter, a twenty-two-year-old African American man named Colton Merandez, who had been almost to the point of dozing off after nearly fourteen hours of nonstop back and forth over the deserted stretch of highway, suddenly snapped awake as a moving object came into the periphery of his night-vision binoculars.

"Hey Mitch!" Colton called out to the pilot over the roar of the helicopter rotors. "We've got something moving along route 7, looks like a vehicle."

For the Sikorsky's pilot Mitch Cranston, who had been struggling to fight off the encroaching fog threatening to overwhelm his exhausted brain for the last several hours, the news was better than an oversized shot of adrenaline.

"Alright, I'm going in for a closer look."

There was a small scramble behind him as Cetan Aung, the Sikorsky's gunner, Colton, and another young African American man named Wayne Trotsky bolted for their seats and quickly secured themselves into their harnesses as the helicopter took a sharp dip left, bringing within less than a thousand feet of the highway below.

"Yep, it's definitely a vehicle, Mitch," Colton called out.

"You know the drill," Mitch shouted back. "Anything that moves gets fired upon."

Colton and Wayne didn't hesitate. The second the helicopter leveled out from its dive, they both scrambled to their stations. Cetan, however, didn't move at first. His eyes were glazed over, and even a casual onlooker would've been able to tell he was lost in thought. His parents had been killed trying to escape a brutal military regime in Myanmar when he was only ten years old.

Now, with what they were about to do, they were no different than the soldiers who had killed his parents, cold-blooded murderers who had gunned down innocents in the name of national security, or whatever the hell his CO had determined it to be. He felt a hard clap on his shoulder.

"C'mon man, let's go!" Colton shouted.

Feeling strangely weightless, Cetan jumped up from the seat and repositioned himself behind the electrically operated six-barrel gatling gun.

"I've got eyes on the target," Wayne called out. "Heading straight in our direction, ETA, about thirty seconds."

For Cetan, everything was moving unusually slowly, as if he were underwater.

"ETA, about fifteen seconds." "Cetan, be ready to fire on my signal," Mitch barked from the cockpit.

Cetan positioned hands that did not feel like his own in the firing position, a right index finger he didn't recognize sliding inside the trigger guard.

"Fire!" came Mitch's voice from somewhere far off.

Only he was not Mitch anymore.

A black top hat and magician's cloak had replaced his army uniform. He had no face. Where his face should've been there was a black hole that led into the abyss.

The temperature in the helicopter had suddenly dropped ten degrees. Wordlessly, the thing that had once been Mitch nodded to Cetan, grinning wickedly, revealing long, bone-white incisors that looked sharp enough to rip him to shreds. Cetan did not think twice. He slammed down on the trigger, sending a fine spray of fiery lead raining down on the black Mercedes Benz cruising along route 7 below. It swerved wildly as a stunned Tyson lost control, barreling across three empty lanes before toppling over into the center divider, where it came to rest with the driver's side door pinned in the dirt.

"Well done, Cetan," came a voice from the cockpit. But the voice no longer belonged to Mitch. It was a baritone, rough, gravelly sound that sounded like it had emerged from the darkest depths of hell. The thing smiled wickedly at him with its enormous incisors. And then it began to laugh cruelly.

CHAPTER 16

T he following is a situation report from the local base command in Newark, NJ to secretary of defense Preston Grace at the White House in Washington D.C. The envelope was labeled URGENT in red block letters by the sender:

FROM: Major Dennis Applewhite, United States Marine Corp Base Command, Newark, NJ

TO: Office of Secretary of Defense Preston Grace, White House, Washington D.C.

RE: Situation in Kearney, NJ

Situation in Kearney currently out of control. Blockade established on route 7 was destroyed less than an hour ago by large protesting crowd, which was put down using force. Blockade on route 21 was destroyed by large protesting crowd at around the same time, put down with force. Not enough warm bodies to sustain effective blockades at many points around the city, and large numbers of troops are rapidly falling ill to acute radiation poisoning, stretching already thin blockades to breaking point. Over a hundred men under my command have also deserted their posts. Requesting immediate reinforcement ASAP

The following is an inter white house memo sent from Secretary of Defense Preston Grace to the president's desk:

FROM: Office of Secretary of Defense Preston Grace

TO: Office of President Aaron Randolph

RE: Operation Olympus

Situation is currently stable in cities of Chicago, Phoenix, and San Francisco with additional troops sent in to suppress protests and authorization to use force if necessary. Local commanders report that majority of citizens have retreated inside of homes following armed confrontations with soldiers. Situation still tenuous in other cities including San Diego and Madison. Troop numbers and resources are stretched thin, and large groups of citizens are arming themselves and challenging blockades. Upon your request, I have relayed to local commanders that soldiers are authorized to use lethal force in these instances. Overall, situation is still very dangerous, and there is little prospect of regaining total control at the present time with nearly every resource already in play.

Three candidates for Operation Olympus have already relayed their concerns to me through their local contacts, and I am receiving more of these messages by the hour. The situation for the candidates appears to be rapidly deteriorating, as they and their families are becoming the target of violent mobs in many major cities, and soldiers tasked with guarding city borders and keeping peace can only offer minimal assistance. My office is already making plans to set Operation Olympus into motion. At the present, all the necessary preparations have been made, and we are ready to begin the operation on your order.

CHAPTER 17

Originally constructed in 1791 under the direction of U.S. army Major Pierre Charles L'efant and intended to serve as an arsenal and garrison for the U.S. capitol, Fort McNair army base in Washington D.C. is home to a wide variety of military operations. In addition to housing the 1st battalion of the 3rd U.S. infantry regiment, the base acts as headquarters for the Army's military district of Washington, acts as an official residence for the Vice Chief of Staff of the U.S. Army, plays host to two historic military universities, the NDU and IADC, as well as the U.S. Army Center for Military History. It is easily the largest U.S. army base in the D.C. area., standing on 28 acres of peninsula overlooking the Potomac River. To the average tourist or casual onlooker, however, there is nothing especially eye-catching about the base on the surface.

However, several miles beneath the surface is a different story entirely. If you were to enter the fort, which is closed to the public, walk down the tile hallway lined with pictures of famous military figures including George S. Patton and Omar Bradley, to the office of Major General Bryce Kranston, who is in charge of all operations on the base, go to the back left corner of his office, you would find a large, oak bookshelf decorated with various career achievements and old novels such as "The Art of War" that the general occasionally reads in his limited spare time. If you were to move this bookshelf you would find a hidden steel trapdoor, beneath which you would discover an engineering marvel.

The underground survival shelter, aptly named "Olympus," had begun its construction in late November of 1962 in the aftermath of the Cuban missile crisis. The shelter looked more like a luxury resort than a fallout bunker. Complete with luxury apartment buildings, Olympic-sized swimming pools, gymnasiums, restaurants, paved streets, parking facilities, sidewalks, agricultural greenhouses, livestock, a mass water purification system, cell phone towers, and every other convenience imaginable that the affluent enjoy in their day to day lives, the shelter was constructed specifically with these affluent in mind. There had been a running joke ever since its construction among those few who were privy to its existence that the name was appropriate, given that its intended occupant's position in life would be more prevalent than ever as the world above them was burned to the ground by whatever disaster had set "Operation Olympus" in motion, and taking those billions not fortunate enough to be granted access with it.

The fact that the construction and maintenance of the shelter had been funded with over two trillion taxpayer dollars, siphoned from the same taxpayers who would be left out in the cold to perish when the end of the world came, never seemed to bother any of the presidents or congressional committees who quietly approved the diverting of taxpayer funds for its continued construction and maintenance year after year. In the words of an unknown member of cabinet in 1983, because of Operation Olympus, "humanity will go on long after the world has ended." And today, the day had finally come for the operation to go into effect.

CHAPTER 18

Henry Alsten straightened his blood red tie in the large mirror hanging off the wall in the CBS studio's large dressing room and wiped a few droplets of sweat from his forehead. He couldn't remember ever feeling so nervous before a news broadcast, and he had covered the evening news on 9/11.

"Then again," he thought, "even on 9/11, the military wasn't in charge of the country. And politicians, as much as we hate them, are much less likely to break into the studio and start shooting the minute we say something they don't like."

Henry nervously ran his thumb over a patch of blush on his cheek, smearing it and barely noticing. The knowledge that what they were about to report would not be appreciated by the military brass did not help his overwrought nerves. If a soldier, or God forbid, an entire battalion of soldiers, marched into the studio with their rifles and demanded an audience with him and Tracy, it was unlikely they would stop and listen to his long-winded explanation on why they were legally protected under the 1st amendment. With a small shudder, Henry also realized that any soldiers sent here to stop the broadcast would probably shoot first and ask questions later.

"Sir," came a woman's voice from the doorway. "You're on in two minutes."

Henry quickly straightened his tie and walked towards the dressing room door, still unsure of what he was going to say and not say during the broadcast. He had his hand on the doorknob when his cell phone began vibrating in his jacket pocket.

"Hello?"

"Am I speaking with Henry Alsten of CBS news and world report?" came an urgent man's voice.

"Speaking," he replied. "Who is this?"

"Listen to me. Before you address the American people in a few minutes, there's something you should know."

Henry felt a trickle of sweat slide down the back of his neck.

"Who the hell is this?" Henry demanded.

"We don't have a lot of time," the man barked. "Now, when you go on for the broadcast, there's something you need to discuss. It's a top-secret government program called Operation Olympus."

Henry, dumbfounded, felt a cold sweat beginning to break out on his forehead.

"Look, I'm out of time here," the man said. "When you go on, let the viewers know that Operation Olympus is a top-secret government program involving an underground disaster shelter meant for politicians and ultra-wealthy businessmen and their families. The shelter is located beneath the U.S. Army Center of Military History, run by their director of operations, General Bryce Kranston. I've gotta hang up now…"

"Wait a moment," Henry said, and the man on the other end paused momentarily. "Why are you telling me this?"

"Because I can't stand the thought of the elites in this country living happily ever after while the rest of us are being gunned down by battalions of soldiers. The people at least have a right to know."

Henry Alsten hesitated before replying.

"I'll include it in the broadcast," he said finally.

"That's all I ask," the man replied. "The people can do with it what they want, but they at least have the right to know."

Henry was about to reply, when a sudden pounding followed by what sounded like the phone hitting a carpeted floor emerged from the other end. Henry heard several muffled yelling voices, followed by the splintering of a wooden door, more shouting, automatic rifle fire, and then dead silence.

CHAPTER 19

Henry sat down opposite his co-host in one of several large plush gray armchairs on the stage. Tracy Edgemont pushed her wiry eyeglasses up the bridge of her nose and put on a very forced smile that Henry did not return. He felt strangely numb. Just beyond the stage standing behind a large black Sony TV camera mounted on a tripod, a cameraman held up all five fingers to indicate the five seconds until they were live. Henry felt a little sick to his stomach, and he had half a mind to tell the cameraman where he could stick his held-up fingers and to not start the damn broadcast at all. But then sounds of shouting and gunshots ringing through the phone flashed through his mind, and his resolve stiffened. The broadcast would go on.

"We're live!" came the shout from the cameraman, and for the first time all day, Henry managed a wry smile.

Tracy straightened her glasses and crossed her legs on the armchair, trying to appear as relaxed as possible in spite of her nervousness.

"So Tracy," Henry said, turning towards his attractive co-host. "How has the situation developed since the military took control?"

Tracy shifted nervously in her seat and wet her lips, her thoughts drifting momentarily to her husband and their little boy, currently sheltering in their two-bedroom apartment a few streets away.

"Well, I'll tell you Henry, they have definitely not had a positive relationship. Not only have they sequestered terrified civilians in their homes, but they have used deadly force as the primary solution when these orders have not been complied with. Here's a clip of what appears to be a military helicopter and armored vehicles gunning down rioters along route 7 near Kearney, New Jersey."

Another clip played on the TVs of those at home of the scene that had occurred earlier that day along route 7 in Kearney.

"Well Tracy, as it turns out, these soldiers are not just killing innocent civilians, but informants and journalists as well."

As he said it, he saw Tracy shudder.

"Our viewers are likely not aware of this, but our CBS correspondent in Los Angeles Brian Falsten's body was found by armed soldiers who had broken into his office in an attempt to stop him from warning onlookers about an impending nuclear attack targeting the city. Rumor has it that when his body was found, soldiers threw it out a fortieth-story bay window as a warning to anyone watching."

Henry shuddered as the realization dawned on him of what he was about to do.

"The words of the military might be loud, but there are orders from your government that are not meant for your ears," Henry said gravely, noticing the brief flash of surprise in Tracy's eyes and realizing that he had not told her about the phone call.

"Minutes before we went on the air, I was informed by an anonymous source about a top-secret government program called 'Operation Olympus.'"

There was a sudden loud banging on the locked heavy metal studio door.

"Open up in there!" came a shout. "By order of the adjutant general, stop what you're doing immediately!"

Henry's face broke out in a cold sweat. Tracy let out a low moan.

"If you didn't catch that," Henry continued, struggling to keep his voice as steady as possible while silently motioning the small team in the studio towards the back door, "I've just been ordered to end this broadcast by members of the United States military. I am refusing this order due to the importance of the information that I am about to tell you." He paused for a couple seconds before adding: "information that a man gave his life for."

The banging on the door became louder.

"Sir, this is your final warning. Open the door and stop your broadcast immediately, or we will break it down ourselves."

Tracy looked at him, her eyes wide with fright behind her glasses. The studio felt eerily empty now that it was only the two of them. He leaned over the seat of his armchair just enough so that she could hear him.

"Go," he whispered. "I'll finish this."

She smiled gratefully, got up from the chair, hugged him briefly, and scurried out the back door of the studio after the departed studio team. As Tracy disappeared down the hallway, he heard the banging on the door intensify.

"Open the door now, or it's coming down!" the soldier shouted.

Henry began to speak more hurriedly.

"Operation Olympus is a cold-war era classified taxpayer funded program in which your government quietly diverts funding from other public government programs to fund the construction and maintenance of an underground disaster shelter meant to house politicians, ultra-wealthy American businessmen, and their families. While American citizens are being gunned down in the streets under orders from the U.S. government, dying of radiation poisoning, or being wiped from the face of the Earth by Russian nuclear weapons, America's elites are being sheltered from harm by your government. I have been informed by my source that this shelter is located below Fort McNair army base in Washington D.C."

At that moment, the door to the studio finally broke down and a battalion of U.S. marines rushed through it, M16s all pointed in Henry's direction.

"Sir!" shouted the soldier from before. "Stop this broadcast immediately or we will open fire!"

One of the soldiers shoved the TV camera off its tripod, shattering the screen against the tile floor.

"A battalion of U.S. marines have just broken down the door to the studio and are aiming their rifles at me with intent to kill me if I do not stop broadcasting this story," Henry said, suddenly feeling strangely calm. "They have attempted to stop me by breaking my camera, but my microphone is still in perfect working order, so the broadcast will continue."

"Sir, this is your last warning!" the marine shouted, bringing the barrel of his rifle within two feet of Henry's face.

"For those of you who still have the strength," Henry continued, "I encourage you to stand up against the tyranny of your government. Stay strong out there and be safe. This is Henry Alsten, with CBS news, signing off…"

He barely finished when the crack of the soldier's rifle rang out through the small studio. Henry sat rigid for a split second, before his lifeless body slumped to the ground.

"Alright," the battalion commander who had killed Henry said gruffly. "Get his body up, we're gonna make an example out of this asshole."

He looked at his subordinates, who did not move. "What are you shitheads looking at, get his damn body up and get it outside, now!"

One of his men reluctantly stepped forward and bent down to retrieve the body. It happened so fast the commander barely even saw it. One moment, the young marine was squatting down to retrieve Alsten's body. The next second, he had gone completely rigid, his mouth open in shock. Then he collapsed lifelessly to the ground, a spreading pool of blood forming at the base of his spine. The commander looked up in time to see three rifles pointing straight at his head.

"HAVE YOU FUCKING LOST IT YOU STUPID LITTLE…"

He was cut off as the rifle's shots echoed off the studio walls, sending him catapulting backward off the stage. He was dead before his body hit the ground. Anyone still listening to the broadcast's audio would've heard shouting, more gunfire, glass shattering, screams of the dying marines on both sides, several explosions in rapid succession, and silence.

CHAPTER 20

Dylan Teryon wandered aimlessly into the tiny apartment kitchen, his stomach already beginning to complain from hunger. He wondered vaguely if there might be food in the fridge that morning. He tried to recall the last time his mother had said she would go to the grocery store but came up empty. He'd only been home for a few weeks, so it was probably sometime before that. He closed his eyes in anticipation and popped open the door to the small refrigerator, praying for a miracle. He was confronted with a half-used bottle of ketchup and a nearly empty bottle of milk that had developed an unpleasant looking yellow hue. His stomach gave another loud groan at the sight of it, and for a moment, he thought he might actually be sick. He slammed the refrigerator door shut hard enough to rattle it on its hinges.

"Don't get angry, don't get angry..." he thought even as he stomped over to the kitchen wall with its peeling white paint.

He drew back his arm, his face burning with shame.

"Don't do it, remember what the therapist said, take a deep breath, take a deep breath..." But it was no use. With a strangled cry of bitter frustration, Dylan slammed his closed fist into the crumbling plaster, which collapsed in on itself, leaving a hole in the wall the exact size of the skinny eleven-year old's small fist.

Dylan, panting hard, felt a brief note of grisly satisfaction as he observed his handiwork. As his brief anger subsided, however, fear quickly overwhelmed him.

"When mom comes home, and she sees what I did..."

The rest of the thought was lost as he turned his gaze to a small section of the stovetop that had been badly blackened by a couple of burnt eggs. His mind flashed back to his mother's enraged screams, followed by the intense pain and his own useless cries as she'd walloped him over and over again until he lay on the floor curled in a ball on the floor. He cried hard that day, but silently, for fear she might hear him and decide to return. It was a skill he'd learned after he had drawn her ire several times for daring to cry out loud. Of course, she always calmed down later. She would hold him on her lap and hug him and kiss him and tell him how sorry she was and how she'd never do it again. She even cried sometimes. These moments almost made the beatings worth it. They reminded him that despite the alcohol and the drugs, in spite of the strange men she'd taken to bringing around the house after dad had passed away, in spite of sending him off to that terrible orphanage while she'd served time, his mother still loved him.

Dylan Teryon flopped down into the old ratty beige armchair his mother had found on the side of the road when he was a kid, staring aimlessly up at the ceiling, wondering if his father might appear there. He had tried this many times, and it had never worked, but he kept trying anyway. In the eerie silence of the small, rundown apartment, Dylan felt tears brim in his dark eyes.

"Dad," he whispered through choked sobs. "Oh dad, why'd you have to go away?"

Preston Teryon, a firefighter for the CFD, had passed away when Dylan was four years old when a burning house he'd been working to get a little girl out of had collapsed on him. There had been no beatings when his dad had been alive, no strange men, no drugs, no police coming to the door to take him away from his mother and sister. Their lives had been perfect when his dad had been around. He still remembered his father's last words to him, on the morning of that fateful day:

"Dylan, I won't be around forever, son, so you've got to be the man of the house. You've got to look out for your mother and sister, you understand?"

"Yes, sir," Dylan had replied, his four-year-old self not really understanding the weight of the task given to him.

Preston picked up his son and spun him around while he laughed in a way he had never laughed since.

"I love you son."

"I love you too, dad."

Dylan began to cry harder.

"I'm sorry, dad," he whispered, casting a glance around the decrepit apartment.

"I'm sorry I couldn't protect mom like I said I would. I couldn't keep her out of jail, I couldn't keep her off the drugs, I couldn't keep us living in a decent neighborhood. I don't know what to do dad, I wish you were here, PLEASE COME BACK TO US!" he wailed, a flood of tears pouring out of him, momentarily obscuring his view of the dilapidated apartment.

Dylan looked up as the apartment door flew open and his mother stumbled in, her expression haggard. From the way she was swaying back and forth, Dylan could tell she'd been drinking. He braced himself, ready for the beating that would surely come. To his total surprise, Josephine Teryon took no notice of her son as she hurried into her children's shared bedroom.

"Damnit," she hissed when she saw that Dylan's sister Anette wasn't there.

He tensed again as his mother hurried back into the living room.

"Dylan?" Josephine asked softly, keeping her voice as level as possible, "have you seen Anette?"

Dylan turned to his mother, his expression blank as he struggled to recall what it was Anette had told him when they had been riding home on the school bus yesterday.

"I think she got off the bus yesterday with her friend," he said after a moment of thought.

Josephine instantly looked panicked.

"Shit, shit, shit," she muttered, practically flying into her room and throwing open the small closet. Dylan followed her into her room and silently watched, slightly confused, as his mother began to throw clothes onto the floor and stuff them haphazardly into a weathered dark gray canvas satchel that had fallen off of one of the shelves.

61

"Mom, are you okay?" he asked, wondering if the landlord was after them again.

"Yeah, baby, mommy's okay," Josephine muttered absentmindedly as she threw articles of clothing seemingly at random into the bag.

"Baby, could you go into your room and put some of your clothes into your backpack?"

Dylan continued to stare at her confusedly as if he couldn't comprehend what she was saying. She shooed him away absentmindedly with her hand as she pulled a few more things from the depths of the closet. He didn't react, so concerned with his mother's strange mood that he'd forgotten about the possibility of a beating coming his way.

She grabbed his hand and dragged him towards the front door of the apartment.

"Where are we going, mom?" Dylan asked, now more confused than ever.

"To go get Anette, honey, just to get Anette," in that strange, faraway voice that she had adopted over the past several minutes.

The reply didn't reassure Dylan. In fact, he was becoming more and more certain that his mother had completely lost her mind, and he had half a mind to break from her grasp and run in the opposite direction as fast as possible. Josephine, figuring her daughter was out with one of her friends, turned to Dylan.

"Baby, do you remember where your sister said she was going after school?" Dylan screwed up his face in concentration as he struggled to remember.

"A girl with glasses and her shoulder-length white-blonde hair in a ponytail...pink backpack bearing a unicorn from a cartoon he didn't recognize...her voice, it was squeaky..."

"Mouse Myrtle!" he blurted out suddenly.

The name came from a school assembly where Myrtle "Mouse" Forsin, as she was now referred to, had read a poem in front of the whole school on Veterans Day. Personally, Dylan had thought it was quite nice, but one of the older boys had stood up and shouted, "you sound like a squeaky little mouse with that voice of yours!" The whole auditorium had started laughing, driving Myrtle quickly to tears, and Dylan couldn't help but feel bad for her anytime someone came up to her in the hallway and used the cruel nickname "Mouse Myrtle" on her. Josephine, who knew about the incident and also felt bad for the poor girl, recognized her immediately and quickly pulled her street address from memory. It was only a few blocks from their apartment.

CHAPTER 21

Ten minutes later, Josephine Teryon's rusted out beater pulled up in front of the two-story, gray-shingled stucco house standing behind a stone-paved sidewalk with an enormous, jagged crack running through the center like a bolt of lightning. In the distance, Josephine could hear the near-constant cacophony of hundreds of shouting voices occasionally split by a bullhorn or the crack of a rifle. Josephine shuddered as an explosion rang out a few blocks away and a small plume of black smoke rose into view. She turned to her son, who was staring out the window, his eyes wide with fear.

"Dylan, honey, I need you to stay right here while mommy goes and gets your sister, okay?" Josephine said.

Dylan nodded silently, never taking his focus off the smoke rising from the street a few blocks from where they were. Josephine slammed the rusty car door, careful not to catch her skirt on the exposed chunks of metal hanging off the bottom, and hurried up the walk towards the house, feeling a hint of admiration in the way the lawn was so neatly cared for.

"Helps to have a man around the house, I suppose..." she thought, and quickly pushed the thought away, unwilling to get caught up in old, painful memories.

She was hurrying up the porch steps when the ripped screen door retracted, revealing a thin young blonde woman in a sunflower-yellow house dress and brown open-toed sandals. Laura Forsin smiled wearily when she saw Josephine. She had met Josephine a few years ago at a parent's night at her daughter's elementary school. It was how their children became friends. Josephine hugged the shorter woman.

"You've heard the news, I assume?" Josephine asked.

"Yeah, we've been listening all day," Laura replied.

"That reporter at CBS...Josephine," she stuttered, her voice rising slightly. "They killed him live on the air. How can they do that, how can something like that happen in America!?" she cried out, near tears.

Josephine shook her head, unable to produce an answer. In the distance, the shouting and bursts of rifle fire were getting closer.

"Is Anette here?" Josephine asked.

"Yeah, she's in the backyard playing with Myrtle," Laura said, turning back into the house and letting the screen door swing closed behind her.

"We were going to call you right when you showed up," she continued. "We want to get out of the city as soon as possible with the situation being what it is."

Josephine nodded, feeling the same way.

"We would've called you last night when she was sleeping over, but we didn't hear the news until pretty late, and we figured it was safer for her to stay here than risk going out in the street."

Josephine privately disagreed but merely nodded, too exhausted to argue. Laura pulled the back screen door and stepped out onto the weathered stone porch that was cracked in several places.

"Myrtle! Anette!" she called. No response. Josephine, standing directly behind her, quickly scanned the small backyard devoid of child's toys other than a small, wooden swing rigged to the lone large oak tree with two fraying ropes. Laura, feeling her blood pressure tick up a notch, took a few steps into the yard.

"Anette!" she called. "Your mother's here, c'mon out," trying to hide the panic in her voice from Josephine, who was also beginning to feel increasingly nervous.

In such a barren backyard, there were only so many places two little girls could hide.

"Anette!" Josephine called out. "Anette, stop fooling around and come out!"

Nothing moved except for the slight sway of the swing in the late morning breeze.

"Roy!" Laura shouted into the house. "Roy, where are the girls?"

A tall, gangly man with a well-trimmed black goatee wearing a "Peanuts" t-shirt emerged from the adjacent hallway, bending over to avoid hitting his head on the sloping doorway.

"They're in the backyard, right where I left them," he said matter-of-factly, quickly glancing around as if to confirm this for himself. He cupped his hands around his mouth and called, "Anette, Myrtle, come inside!" A flash of surprise crossed his face when he received no response.

"Where the hell did they go?" he muttered under his breath. Josephine, on impulse, stepped out into the grass, slowly lowered herself down onto her belly, and pressed her head down into the grass so she was able to look in the thin space under the porch. No kids, but a small, dirty, gray kitten hissed when it saw her and scurried out from under the porch. Josephine stood up to face Roy and Laura, who now looked extremely worried. She shook her head in dismay.

"Shit!" Laura exclaimed.

CHAPTER 22

Cetan Aung stumbled through the deserted street in a drunken daze, his military uniform discarded, his M16 slung over his shoulder. Ever since he had stepped out of the helicopter around one in the morning, he had felt a bizarre sense of disembodiment, as if he were watching another person live his life. He was a mere spectator as he listened to Mitch, Colton and Wayne joke around casually as they landed, the events of the evening completely forgotten. A few minutes later, as he changed into his civilian clothes, he first heard the voice.

"Cetan..." in the voice Mitch had used in the helicopter when he had no longer been Mitch, but something else entirely.

It persisted all the way to the deserted main street bar where Mitch had suggested that if the world was ending, they might as well help themselves to some free booze. Perhaps strangest of all, the alcohol had done nothing to silence the voice. After five beers, he was so tipsy he could barely stand up straight without grabbing onto the table for support. However, he could still hear the voice as though he was fully sober. In frustration, he'd thrown and shattered a large vodka bottle against the wall, prompting Mitch to cut him off from the alcohol, which did nothing to improve his mood.

He watched wordlessly, his gut twisting more and more violently with anger as he watched his friends drink themselves into a stupor, their laughter and idiotic jokes ringing in his ears while the scene in the helicopter replayed over and over again in his head. Finally, after several hours, he couldn't take it anymore. He locked himself in the men's bathroom, barely reaching the toilet before he vomited up the remains of his lunch. While he was still leaning over the toilet bowl, his sweaty shaking arms barely supporting him, the voice spoke again.

"She was just a kid, Cetan. Just like you."

A little girl's bloodied and broken face swam in front of him. He knew instantly that this was the person they'd murdered that night, along with her entire family. Faintly, he could hear the raucous laughter coming from the bar, causing a rush of pure hatred to burn in his gut.

"They did this to me, Cetan," the little girl whispered.

"I know," Cetan replied, hanging his head shamefully even as his voice shook with anger. "I'm so sorry."

For a moment, there was silence. Even in death, the little girl didn't look down on him with disdain. There was no anger in that gaze. Only pity.

"Then kill them," she whispered. "Kill the bastards."

He suddenly became aware of the presence of his sidearm still strapped to his waistband.

"Kill them," she whispered again.

Cetan stood up slowly, feeling the weight of the pistol against his side. Wordlessly, he wandered casually back into the bar, where his friends were laughing at some joke Colton had just told.

"Hey Cetan, where you been?" Wayne asked without looking up. He leaned back in his chair and downed half the bottle of beer in his hand in one gulp.

Cetan had stood stock still, the rage building inside of him at a furious pace, before casually pulling his pistol and shooting the three of them dead.

He walked casually over to Mitch's body and turned his still wide-eyed face over with the toe of his boot.

"Nothing but a jingoistic sick son of a bitch," he thought disgustedly.

"Just like your parent's killers," the voice whispered.

Cetan had looked up to see the thing had been pretending to be Mitch back in the helicopter standing in the corner, grinning at him with a mouthful of razor-sharp incisors.

"It's human nature, Cetan. The only way to purify humanity is to slay all of it."

For a brief moment, the broken bodies of his dead parents flashed before his eyes, and he realized this thing, whatever it was, was right.

"The human sickness must be purged," the Puppeteer said coldly. "And you will help me purge it. Your parents will be so proud of you."

Cetan had smiled back at the monster.

"You're right," he thought savagely. "They will be."

At first light that morning, Cetan had wordlessly disassembled and cleaned his rifle with what rags he could find in the garbage. As he walked out into the cool breezy August morning, the rifle strapped over his shoulder, the image of the dead little girl flashed through his mind, along with his teammates, who were standing over her, laughing. A surge of white-hot anger coursed through him. He let out a feral roar and fired a lone shot from his rifle into the air. He stood in the middle of the street, breathing hard. For a second, a sudden sense of grief threatened to overwhelm him, and he fell hard onto his knees. His mother and father's faces swam in front of him, and tears came to his eyes when he saw them.

"We love you, son," they said. "Make us proud." And then they were gone.

Cetan rose to his feet, all feelings of grief gone, replaced by a cold, steely determination. As he wandered down the deserted street, still a little tipsy from the previous night, he looked down at the M16 rifle clutched in his grip, and he laughed maniacally, the terrifying cacophony echoing off the tall office buildings surrounding him as if hundreds of people were laughing along with him. Oh yes, he would avenge them today, and they would be very proud indeed.

CHAPTER 23

"**C**'mon, c'mon!" Myrtle exclaimed cheerfully, pulling her reluctant friend along by the hand through the semi-dark rubbish-strewn alleyway.

Anette gasped for breath, struggling to keep up with her energetic friend.

"Where...are...we...going..." Anette gasped.

"I want to show you something cool!" Myrtle replied, grinning broadly.

Anette, still confused as ever, hurried to catch up with Myrtle as she rounded the corner and came to a stop outside of a small corner liquor store christened "Matt's" on a large neon sign hanging slightly lopsided above the double glass front doors.

"Seriously, Myrtle," Anette begged, pulling on her friend's t-shirt sleeve. "What are you trying to..." She froze as her gaze fell on the body lying next to the double doors.

He was clad in a dark green wool hat, a black sweatshirt covered in stains that were clearly visible despite the color, and dark blue jeans that were somehow more stained than the sweatshirt. He was badly in need of a shave and even more in need of a shower and a laundromat based on the smell reeking off him. An empty beer bottle laid next to his right hand, and his head slumped over onto his shoulder. Anette's first impression, apart from the smell, which made her pinch her nose in disgust, was that the man was dead. She mentioned this to Myrtle, who tittered happily in response, as though a dead homeless man lying in front of the liquor store next to an empty beer bottle was the funniest thing she'd ever seen.

"Uh, duh! Of course he's dead, he wouldn't be any fun if he were still alive!"

Myrtle picked up the beer bottle and chucked it at the wall of the liquor store, causing Anette to let out a little scream as it shattered against the wall of the liquor store. Myrtle made a pouty face at Anette, who was now cowering slightly.

"C'mon Anette, don't be a stick in the mud!" Myrtle complained, grabbing Anette by the arm and dragging her over to the dead homeless man. Myrtle looked expectantly at Anette, hands on her hips.

Anette cowered in front of the body, too nervous to move any closer. She glanced down at the ground, unable to meet the man's gaze anymore. She saw the man's middle finger twitch out of the corner of her eye. It was only a minute twitch, nothing more than a millimeter or two, but for a second or two, she was sure it had moved. Annette let out a small scream and jumped back. Myrtle socked her playfully on the shoulder.

"You're such a scaredy cat," she teased. "Watch this!" She approached the body, squatted down at his level, and reached into the man's breast pocket.

Although Myrtle, in her excitement, was oblivious to it, Anette heard something in the distance that sounded like a gunshot from not far off. She grabbed Myrtle by the shoulder and shook her.

"Myrtle," she hissed, "We need to go, now!"

"Anette, don't be a baby," Myrtle said, now sounding slightly irritated. She continued fishing through the man's pocket, and after a moment, withdrew it, a small plastic bag full of white powder clutched in her closed fist.

"Look at this, Anette," Myrtle exclaimed happily, throwing her the bag so abruptly that Anette nearly dropped it. "What do you think it is?"

Another gunshot, this one closer now, made her jump. The bag of white powder fell to the ground and burst open on the ground, spilling its contents all over the sidewalk.

"Look what you did!" Myrtle pouted.

Anette frantically grabbed Myrtle's shirtsleeve as a man emerged from an alleyway from a few hundred feet away, dressed in blue jeans and a midnight blue sweatshirt. Anette slowly realized to her horror he was wielding a pistol. Abandoning all regard for her friend, Anette turned and sprinted down the street away from the gunman who was now running at them.

"Anette, c'mon," Myrtle pleaded, completely oblivious to the danger. "It's just a…" She cut off suddenly.

Anette looked over her shoulder to see Myrtle standing stock-still in the middle of the street, a small pool of blood slowly spreading from the middle of her chest. Then she fell forward as the gunman practically vaulted over her, his dark eyes blazing with sick, frenzied glee. Big fat tears splashing from her eyes onto the pavement, Anette sprinted down the street for all she was worth. She ducked into another dingy alleyway at the last second as a shot rang out behind her, smashing the brick and mortar where she had been a split second before. From somewhere behind her, she heard a deep, bellowing laugh that sounded like it came out of the deepest pit of hell.

Anette sprinted through the alleyway and ducked behind an industrial-sized dumpster as another shot rang out behind her. She sank to her knees behind the dumpster, struggling to catch her breath, unable to run anymore. She whimpered helplessly as the deep, rumbling voice emerged, not from the man chasing after her, but from somewhere inside her own head.

"Anette…" it growled. "You cannot run from me…"

She barely noticed the beat-up brick-red pickup truck pulled up beside the alleyway. She only looked when her mother threw open the door and sprinted towards her, arms wide open, preparing to embrace her daughter. Anette sniffled and raised her shaking arms to her mother. It happened in the span of less than a second. One moment, her mother was running towards her, arms outstretched. Anette blinked, and the shot rang out from somewhere to her right.

Josephine fell to the ground, twitching uncontrollably, a small pool of blood spreading from the base of her neck. Anette screamed, her scream intermingled with the screams of Laura and Roy Forsin.

"Mommy!" she heard her brother wail in terror.

Her mother lay still on the pavement, blood pooling on the ground underneath her. Anette was deaf to Laura's distressed cries begging her to get in the truck. Whimpering, Anette reached out a shaking hand to her mother's body and cried out in pain as a booted foot crushed her hand against the pavement. Anette slowly looked up into the face of the gunman, his wild dark eyes blazing with triumph.

Laura and Roy were yelling somewhere behind him, but Anette was deaf to their calls. The man raised his hand into the air as if clutching an invisible ball. Anette screamed as she was hoisted into the air as if by an invisible rope. Her hands closed around her throat as she choked, struggling to breathe as her windpipe was crushed by the rapidly tightening noose. The man stared up at her with those black eyes that absorbed any speck of light that entered them. Anette screamed soundlessly as his nightmarish voice entered her head.

"Anette…" Anette wailed in terror as the images came rushing at her like a giant unstoppable freight train. Millions of dead, broken bodies lying in the street, blood pooled so thickly around them that it was running into the gutters in a river…her childhood home destroyed, the entire roof and part of the top three stories missing, the lawn in front charred and blackened…cities flattened, clouds of light gray smoke floating listlessly through the air, the pavement covered in a layer of glass…the images coming at her faster and faster, so fast she had no time to process what they were…

Laura screamed and buried her face in her husband's chest as Anette's eyes rolled back into her head to reveal only the whites of her eyes. There was a loud crack, and her lifeless body collapsed to the ground.

"Anette!" Dylan screamed, hot burning tears stinging his eyes.

The soldier loomed over her, grinning at his handiwork. Then he turned slowly around and looked straight at Dylan. Dylan screamed in terror at the sight of those soulless eyes boring into his own.

"Kill him!" the Puppeteer screamed in Cetan's ear.

Cetan Aung raised his pistol, ready to purge the evil bastards from the face of the earth. Roy hammered the gas pedal in the old pickup truck at the last second, speeding away down the street, gun fire echoing from behind them. Dylan screamed and threw himself on the floor of the pickup, covering his head with his hands and cowering behind the driver's seat. He remained there even after the repeated crack of rifle shots faded behind them, fresh hot tears pouring from his eyes that resulted as much from terror as the realization that his mother and sister were dead, finally came crashing down on him.

CHAPTER 24

As the mid-morning September sun gradually rose high above the D.C. metropolitan area, causing the high rise aluminum office buildings to shimmer in the heat like a sort of strange desert mirage, a powerfully built, well-dressed, middle-aged man exited the quadruple automatic glass doors of the Cambria hotel just down the street, shielding his eyes against the bright morning sunlight as they adjusted. He crossed the street in a hurry, anxiety clouding his mind. There was no need to satisfy his caffeine addiction that morning. Not after the CBS broadcast that he had woken up to.

He'd woken up to a block letter CBS headline from his favorite newscaster, Henry Alsten, declaring that the world was ending. He'd been strangely deaf to most of what Alsten had said as he sat in front of the hotel TV, dumbstruck. But there was one point that had stood out: Operation Olympus. Alsten hadn't managed to deliver many details before a battalion of marines had broken into the studio, but what he had given Veranda had been more than enough.

He had turned off the hotel TV, unable to watch anymore as the image of Michael Pines dressed in a sharp three-piece black suit flashing him a shit-eating grin on the steps outside of the Superior Court of the District of Columbia slowly emerged in his mind like a helium balloon being slowly inflated to full mast. The drug-dealing scumbag who had ruined his daughter's life was going to live happily ever after in an underground bunker funded by his taxpayer dollars while his victims were brutally massacred. David shuddered in spite of the heat of the day.

Michael Pines was the very worst possible combination of a trust-fund baby, a narcissist, and a sociopath. He had been raised by his ultra wealthy senator father to believe that he could have what he wanted when he wanted it. David was so distracted, he nearly ran into a homeless man stumbling along the street, rambling something about Jesus and judgment day. He jerked away as the man tried to grab his shirt lapels.

"JUDGMENT IS COMIN' FOR ALL THE SINNERS'!" he screamed. "CHARIOT'S A-COMIN' AND YOU DON'T WANT TO BE LEFT BEHIND, SON!"

As David was running down the street in the opposite direction, not necessarily scared of the man but nevertheless wanting to put some distance between them, he wondered vaguely where the soldiers were this morning. He had seen plenty on the streets from his hotel room the previous evening. Now it seemed like most of them had abandoned their posts. "Chariot's a-comin'…" The thought suddenly turned his bubbling fear into a hard-boiling pot of rage. The chariot was fucking coming all right, but not for him, or his wife, or his two beautiful daughters, one of whom would probably never come home. It wasn't coming for the millions of others who had unwittingly helped to build it.

As he passed the James C. Dent House, the dark windows with their drawn curtains seemed to mock him. His thoughts drifted to his eldest daughter. It had been less than five years since Lilly had been on top of the world. Valedictorian, accepted to MIT, loved by everyone. He wiped a single tear from his eye. God, he and Anna had been so proud of her. And then she'd met Michael Pines. Within three months, she'd developed a methamphetamine addiction, dropped out, been tossed out onto the street, and ended up in a psych ward, where she was still condemned, after a series of suicide attempts. The lawsuit he'd brought against Michael had been abruptly thrown out by a judge that owed his appointment to Michael's father, Senator Roger Pines. Thinking about it was enough to make the extremely mild mannered and calm David Veranda smash his closed fist into the nearest available object.

David began to pick up the pace, knowing his wife and youngest daughter were at home, anxiously awaiting his return. He pulled out his cell phone to text Anna that he was okay and discovered to his mild annoyance that he had no cell service.

"No surprise," he thought, quickly shoving the phone back in his pocket. "World's ending, phone service should be the last thing on anyone's mind."

Still, the idea that he couldn't communicate to his wife and daughter that he was fine and coming home soon bothered him greatly. His thoughts turned to Maria. The only thing worse than what had happened to Lilly was seeing the effect it had on her younger sister. At first, she'd broken down and cried nearly every day, and that had been bad enough. But the coldness and indifference towards nearly everything that came after was worse. She stopped coming home after school. Her grades slipped. The swim coach called and said she'd been skipping practices. There were many nights where she simply hadn't come home at all.

It had made David feel even worse to hear about these things from his wife, as he knew he hadn't been there for either of them, consumed by work he'd piled on himself to block out the terrible memories of what had happened to Lilly. They used to own a cabin up north next to a small river back when Lilly and Maria were little kids. They'd played in the river for hours, laughing and splashing one another. They hadn't visited it in years. David sighed heavily. Those were the best days. As he passed an abandoned used car lot, the few cars that remained sporting crow bars through their windshields or missing tires, David made a silent promise to take Maria and Anna up to the cabin. All of them, and Maria especially, needed a break from the chaos at home.

David stopped suddenly. He heard something from far off in the distance. Only these weren't the gunshots and occasional explosions he'd heard last night from his hotel room. This was shouting that sounded as though it were coming from hundreds of people, occasionally mixed with what sounded like someone speaking through a bullhorn. After a moment, he could make out what the person using the bullhorn was saying

"This is an illegal gathering. Disperse immediately, or we will open fire!"

"Probably some poor souls protesting in front of a military blockade," David thought. He started to turn away, deciding it would be safer to head back down 2nd street and take Potomac Avenue. Then he paused suddenly, the words of the newscaster flashing through his mind: "A survival shelter exclusively for politicians, celebrities, ultra wealthy businessmen and their families, rumored to have been built directly beneath Fort McNair military base in the DC area."

David looked up the street. Fort McNair was only a couple of blocks away. As he listened, considering, the protest seemed to grow louder. It took David a moment to realize that they were chanting the same short phrase over and over again: "Death to tyrants!" A part of him wanted to leave it alone, to get home as quickly as possible, to be with his wife and daughter. But something held him back. The face of Michael Pines flashed through his mind again. That disgusting, shit-eating grin he'd worn as they'd exited the courthouse. David started to turn away again. And that's when he heard it. The voice that sounded as though it had emerged from the deepest pit of hell.

"He's there, you know."

David didn't have to ask who or what the voice was referring to. Immediately, David could feel the rage building inside him, his face already swelling with the heat of his anger.

"He deserves it, David. Make him pay."

"Oh, he will," David thought furiously, his normally mild and carefully controlled manner abandoned. "The little shit won't be getting off this time, he can be sure of that."

And that was why, rather than walking the other way towards his neighborhood and the house where his wife and daughter, their things already packed, anxiously awaiting his return, David Veranda began walking in the direction of the shouting. The Puppeteer, invisible to him, watched him from the opposite side of the street, grinning wickedly, knowing his quarry would shortly arrive at Fort McNair military base on that cool morning in August, setting off a chain of events that would turn David Veranda's world upside down.

CHAPTER 25

As David Veranda approached Canal Street and the gates of Fort McNair military base came into view, he saw a crowd numbering at least a hundred gathered outside a low wooden building with a white roof to match the solid white trim circling the roof. A gold-embossed block-letter logo over the door read "U.S. Army Center of Military History." Standing between the crowd and the building was a picket line of stoney faced men in full battle dress armed with M16 rifles standing guard over a tall, gray-haired man in well decorated officer uniform toting a bullhorn. As David moved closer to the crowd, he heard a cacophony of confused shouting and wailing overshadowed by the same repeated message emitted from the bullhorn over and over.

"Stand back!" the officer bellowed. "This is an illegal gathering. Disperse immediately, or we will open fire!"

The crowd, however, seemed undeterred, and as David got to within a hundred feet of the crowd, their cries only seemed to grow louder with each reiteration of the officer's threat.

"What the hell is going on here?" David muttered as he pushed past a woman holding a little girl. David Veranda had served in the marines for eight years and the thought of opening fire on unarmed civilians was incomprehensible. The people in this crowd were unarmed, and, as David was beginning to notice, many of them were begging for the marines' protection as they were holding their small children.

"They won't let us in, that's what's happening," someone shouted back. David shook his head. He never would've believed that kind of conduct could come from marines if he wasn't seeing it for himself.

As David continued to push through the crowd, he saw the line of marines standing in front of the stone steps of the center suddenly part to allow a black limousine to pass through. David watched as one of the marines opened the door of the limousine, and a tall, thin, dark-haired woman carrying a designer purse over her shoulder emerged. Almost immediately, a thin, pallid scowling, young man emerged behind her, and David caught a glimpse of his face. Their eyes locked for a fraction of a second, and the man smiled at David. David felt his blood boil. He would've recognized that self-indulgent, shit eating grin anywhere. And suddenly, David heard the voice again.

"Kill him, David…He deserves it…"

For a moment, David stood still, sweat pouring down his face, suddenly feeling hot and cold at the same time. And then, as Michael Pines followed his mother up the steps toward the museum, he heard a high, cold, cruel laughter that echoed off the sides of the surrounding buildings as if hundreds of voices were laughing together.

David began pushing his way towards the front of the crowd where Michael and his mother were being escorted inside of the U.S. Army Center of Military History by the uniformed officer with the bullhorn. As he moved closer to the front of the crowd, David began to hear more clearly what was being said to the stone-faced marines:

"Please, my son is dying, why won't you help me!?"

"How can you do this to American citizens!?"

"I have a baby, how can you turn us away!?"

"I don't want to die out there, officer, please!"

Every beseeching request was met with the same repeated, almost mechanical response: "This is an illegal gathering, disperse immediately, or we will open fire."

David felt his jaw clench. Finally, David emerged at the front of the crowd of the no man's land between the line of marines and the crowd, oblivious to the two marines who had their M16s trained over his heart.

"Stop right there!" one of the marines shouted at David, who ignored him.

The officer glanced down at the commotion and raised his bullhorn.

"Sir, you need to step back immediately, or you will be fired upon." He said it in the same mechanical tone that caused David's blood pressure to tick up a notch each time he heard it.

"You took an oath, just like me!" David shouted. "You swore to always be loyal not just to your fellow soldier, but your fellow American!"

"Sir, you need to leave now!" the officer roared back, the bullhorn forgotten.

"You have a duty to these people!" David shouted, advancing closer. "What the hell are you doing blocking access to a survival shelter to people who are in desperate need of help, many of whom have children?"

"Sir, you need to leave now!" the officer fired back.

David saw his hand reach for the holster in his waistband, but he refused to back off.

"I have children too!" David pleaded, ignoring the marines whose attention was now fully focused on him. "And I'm trying to keep them safe! That's why I became a marine! To protect people who couldn't protect themselves! That's our duty!"

For a brief moment, David swore he saw a flash of emotions cross the officer's face.

"Do your duty, sir! Give these people a chance!"

The officer paused, but only for a second.

"I'm sorry sir," he said, withdrawing his pistol, "but I can't help you."

The barrel came to rest over David's heart. But the officer had allowed David to get a little too close. In an instant, David's training kicked in, and the officer blinked in surprise as the weapon was slapped from his hand, the barrel now coming to rest directly between his eyes.

"Shoot!" his brain screamed. For one second, David Veranda hesitated. And that was enough. He felt a hard metal object slam into the side of his head. He fell to his knees as stars began to appear in front of his eyes. And then he heard the shot.

CHAPTER 26

L ight gray smoke wafted from the barrel of Heckler & Koch special clutched in Mack Morgan's right hand. As the crowd surged forward all around him and the marines began to open fire in response, he slowly felt the weight of what he had just done crash down on him, sending him painfully to his knees. For a split second, his eyes met those of the man he'd just saved, which were wide with shock.

"Thank…you…" David stammered, neither man able to move even as the crowd charged forward around them, threatening to trample them into the asphalt.

Out of the corner of his eye, Mack saw the barrel of an M16 swing towards him. Mack, with every last bit of fight drained from him, prepared to die, closed his eyes, only to have them shoot open again as the barrel swung past him to come to rest on David, still on his knees on the pavement.

Mack raised his own weapon, knowing a split second before the shot rang out that he was too late. A gunshot echoed to Mack's left. David's attacker went rigid for a split second, then dropped dead on the pavement. Mack turned to see another marine with his rifle still trained on David's would-be killer. Both Mack and the marine quickly trained their weapons on each other. Mack, with his finger firmly on the trigger, suddenly hesitated. The man's brow was covered in sweat and had a scattering of pimples that resembled many of Mack's high school classmates on the tail-end of puberty. His eyes were as wide as a deer caught in twin headlights at night, and Mack realized with a start that he couldn't have been older than nineteen years old.

Mack hesitantly lowered the pistol to his side. The marine kept his rifle up for a moment, but his hands were shaking so badly, Mack was sure this man had no intention of shooting him. David, momentarily stunned by this exchange, slowly rose to his feet and approached the marine, who turned his focus to David.

"That's far enough!" he shouted, but both David and Mack heard the slight break in his voice.

David raised his hands above his head.

"Look man, we're on the same side. We both want the same thing here," David said. "I was in the service, just like you."

Slowly the young marine lowered his rifle to point at the pavement as a look of recognition crossed his face.

"Semper fi," David said.

"Semper fi," the young marine echoed him, managing a nervous smile.

Around the small, still island with its three inhabitants, the storm raged violently. The marines had been driven back inside the center, hundreds of the protestors drawing concealed weapons.

"I'm Jack," the young marine said, extending his hand. David shook it in reply, managing a smile of his own.

Jack started to say something else, but his words were lost on David as a wall of bodies suddenly swept him in the direction of the center like a raging tidal wave. David fought to keep his balance as he was pushed along, knowing that losing it in the middle of a charging crowd could easily be fatal. Mack and Jack quickly became swept up in the crowd along with David. As they entered the center, David glanced around and noticed that the group of marines defending the center only consisted of a little over half of the original members that had formed a line outside of the center. Then a smile crossed David's face as he noticed out of the corner of his eye two marines firing from cover behind two doric marble columns in the direction of the retreating group of marines. David ducked behind a large wooden bookcase just a glass case shattered to his right, spraying glass in every direction.

"Semper fi!" he shouted.

One of the marines turned to him and flashed a wry grin.

"Semper fi!" he echoed.

Jack and Morgan entered the building behind him and had taken cover on the other side of the room behind a large glass case filled with old military rifles. The air was filled with the continual sound of gunfire from pistols and automatic rifles. After a few minutes of shooting, David was coughing on the smoke choking the air in the building as well as the sulfurous smell. But the more the fighting raged on, the further into the building the marines were forced to retreat. As David ducked behind a doorway as one of the marines released a spray of lead in his direction, he heard a shout from somewhere up ahead: "Get into the trapdoor, there's more weapons in the shelter!"

The image of Michael Pines and his shit-eating grin reemerged in David's head like a bad nightmare.

"Kill him David..." urged the voice.

The marine had him pinned down, and David suddenly realized he was out in the open, slowly advancing on him, rifle raised. In one swift motion, he launched himself onto the open floor of the hallway, catching the marine by surprise, and before he recovered, David had scored a direct hit right between the marine's eyes. He collapsed to the ground and did not move again. David lay on his side for a moment, trying to catch his breath. Around him, he noticed that the constant crack of gunfire had nearly vanished, and shouts were now echoing throughout the building, each demanding to know where the location of the shelter was. David got to his feet and headed back down the hallway in the direction of the main gallery of the museum. He walked slowly up to a shattered glass case and selected a civil-war era style bayonet.

"Kill the little bastard," the voice whispered, and David could almost picture the thing's grinning face.

He smiled as he observed the well-polished steel and how perfectly it reflected the mid-morning sunlight streaming through the overhead skylight. His smile was not that of a human. It was that of a hungry reptile.

CHAPTER 27

Because the roof of the underground shelter was soundproofed, Roger Pines and his family, along with all the additional inhabitants of "Olympus," were completely oblivious as to what was happening above them in the U.S. Army Center for Military History. A group of teenagers, including Michael Pines and the attractive fifteen-year-old daughter of an extremely wealthy real-estate tycoon with whom he had become fixated with were hanging out in the outdoor spa just off the Olympic-sized swimming pool, getting to know one another and debating how this strange new world they now inhabited compared to the lives they were used to back home. Several middle-aged men and women including Roger Pines were at the fitness center, taking advantage of the treadmills and the occasional bench press.

A very attractive redhead woman in her early thirties wearing a sports bra that was more revealing than necessary named Marina had caught the eye of Roger, who had had more one-night stands than he could possibly account for over the course of his long and distinguished career first in international law and then in U.S. politics. He was busy chatting up Marina while they ran on adjacent treadmills, while she laughed at things she didn't find funny in the slightest and smiled at him indulgently, all thoughts of her sixty-five-year-old billionaire husband whom she admitted shamelessly was nothing more than a very small, non-functioning penis with a very large wallet, forgotten.

As they chatted casually enough while privately sizing each other up, Roger Marina's sizable rack and firm buttocks, Marina Roger's well-toned thigh, bicep, and ab muscles that could point to his potence, they were each blissfully unaware that David Veranda was walking up the underground street, bayonet in hand, flanked by Mack and Jack, still in full battle dress and toting his M16. David's expression was as black as midnight, and a crowd of over a hundred men and women who had survived the firefight were behind him, including several of the marines tasked with protecting the center. The first man to notice them, a well-dressed insurance executive in his early 40s and already graying, had been walking to the grocery store, canvas sack in hand, and barely had time to let out a panicked shout before Mack put a bullet through his heart, killing him instantly.

A number of others out on the street turned towards the source of the disturbance, all annoyance dissipating when they saw the well-armed crowd marching towards them. Terrified screams echoed throughout the street from every direction, followed by people dashing madly in every direction, scrambling to get into the perceived safety of their electronically locked apartment buildings. Large portions of the crowd veered off from the main road and began firing their weapons at the bulletproof windows and door panels of the luxury apartment buildings. David, however, stormed up the road towards his target, who was sitting in an outdoor spa next to a girl who didn't look any older than fifteen.

As David grew closer to his quarry, his expression burning with hatred, he saw the eyes of several of his companions widen with fright as they saw the bayonet he was brandishing. He heard a girl scream, and suddenly they were jumping out of the outdoor spa and running like scared chickens for the apartment buildings down the street. All except Michael Pines, who was standing in a bright blue bathing suit in the middle of the spa, his eyes wide, paralyzed with fright. David, who had planned to kill his quarry with the bayonet, casually tossed it aside.

"Too humane," he thought savagely.

Michael glanced at it, a flash of confusion crossing his face, that immediately disappeared when David grabbed Michael with both hands by his scrawny neck and shoved him forcefully under the hot foamy water.

Michael struggled against David, his hands slapping uselessly against the water. After about ten seconds, David yanked Michael, coughing hard, out of the water. He pressed his face inches from Michael's, who looked infinitely more vulnerable from the arrogant little boy who he'd seen walking out of Superior Court of the District of Columbia several months ago.

"Do you know who I am?" David growled.

"You're...Lilly's...dad..." he sputtered.

"Yeah," David said coldly, and slammed Michael's face into the concrete, squashing his nose like an overripe tomato and spewing hot blood onto the concrete.

"That's me," David said. "The father of the girl whose life you destroyed," and shoved Michael underwater again.

He held him under for almost a minute before dragging him back up. Michael smiled, causing David's already boiling blood to burn even hotter.

"I remember that girl," he muttered listlessly. "Real nice body on her. Cute face, too. You raised a good one, Mr. Veranda. Best sex I've had in years, and it's always better when they're into it the way she was..."

David, who had barely kept his fiery temper under wraps up to this point, finally snapped. He shoved Michael Pines underwater one last time, and this time, he did not let him up again. He held him firmly under the foamy, hot spa water for about two minutes before his struggle finally ceased. David stood up, breathing hard, watching the lifeless body of Michael Pines float lazily just underneath the surface of the water.

"Well done, David," the voice whispered.

It certainly didn't feel that way to David. He did not feel any pleasure at the sight of that body. He had become strangely deaf to the screaming and gunfire erupting all around him. He sat down on the stone edge of the hot tub, his head hung in defeat. His entire body had gone strangely numb. He thought of Maria.

"I'm sorry..." he whispered.

From somewhere far off, he heard the voice break into a fit of cold, gravelly laughter.

CHAPTER 28

Jody Razitsky opened her eyes. Bright late afternoon sunlight streamed down on her through a gap in the trees. She groaned and sat up, her sore, aching body protesting each move she made. She was in a small clearing scattered with fallen leaves in the midst of a dense thicket of enormous oak trees. It slowly dawned on her that she was no longer an adult, but a child who couldn't have been older than about ten or eleven years old based on her size.

"C'mon Jody, up here!" came a child's voice from somewhere above her head.

She looked up and saw her childhood friend, a petite brunette girl with thick eyeglasses named Kaitlyn who couldn't've been older than about ten, sitting on a thick tree branch about twenty feet off the ground.

"Kaitlyn!" she heard herself hiss. "Get down from there, you'll hurt yourself!" remembering the near-constant scoldings from her friend's mother about not climbing too high.

Kaitlyn giggled in reply. Jody reluctantly began to climb the tree, muttering something the entire time about how much trouble Kaitlyn would be in if her mother ever found out about this. Far below, a small boy with sandy blond hair that stuck out from his red and black "Atlanta Braves" baseball cap ran through the clearing, his bright blue eyes darting around the surrounding trees.

"He'll never find us up here," Jody whispered in Kaitlyn's ear.

Kaitlyn let out a fit of high-pitched laughter in reply, causing the boy to stop and look up into the trees.

"Found you!" he called out.

"You have to tag us!" Kaitlyn called out, causing both girls to burst into a fit of giggles.

"Oh, c'mon you guys, that isn't fair!" the boy whined. Jody laughed along with her childhood best friend, their shrieks echoing through the trees. Jody had half-forgotten the memories she had shared in the woods with her childhood friends all those years ago, when she'd been nothing but a carefree little girl with a belly full of laughter and a heart full of fire. Jody sighed. What had happened to those days?

"What's wrong?" Kaitlyn asked.

Jody turned to her best friend. She was peering at Jody intently through her enormous eyeglasses, all hint of delight suddenly gone. Something had shifted behind those eyes that went deeper than her expression. She looked more grown-up somehow, as if a much older, more emotionally mature version of her childhood best friend had suddenly taken the wheel. Jody shook her head.

"I don't know, I just..." she continued to shake her head, struggling to find the right words.

Kaitlyn continued to watch her, her brow furrowing slightly.

80

"Kaitlyn, what happened to me?" Jody asked finally. "Just playing with you now, I feel so..." she paused, her lower lip trembling.

"Carefree?" Kaitlyn offered. Jody nodded, her lower lip quivering.

Kaitlyn wrapped Jody into a hug as she started crying.

"I just feel so...empty..." Jody sobbed. "Even when I should feel happy, there's just nothing, like I'm not capable of feeling anything at all! Everything I do, it's meaningless, I wake up every day not knowing why I'm even still alive!"

Kaitlyn held her best friend close, stroking her dark hair, shushing her the way a mother might shush a crying baby.

"I'm sorry, I just..." Jody stammered, wiping her eyes. "I've been living on inertia these last few years, and I don't know how much longer I can do it."

"There's a numbness, isn't there?" Kaitlyn said, staring pensively down at the little boy who was now pacing in the clearing down below, throwing them a spiteful look every once in a while.

Jody nodded. Kaitlyn sighed heavily, and Jody was shocked to see that tears were forming in her eyes.

"We were afraid this would happen, after you left," Kaitlyn said. "You don't even remember this place, do you?"

Jody opened her mouth indignantly, about to insist that she had never forgotten this place or any of the people, Kaitlyn included, who made it special for her, until the truth slowly dawned on her. Jody sighed and slowly shook her head.

"I didn't think so," Kaitlyn replied, and it occurred to Jody that her voice had suddenly become much deeper, more sonorous.

"I almost hoped that was the case," Kaitlyn went on. "With what you went through here, I was worried if you remembered..."

Kaitlyn paused, shaking her head. Jody felt the hair on the back of her neck stiffen at these words.

"What happened?" Jody asked, her voice quavering a little. The image she'd seen that night on the mountain of her father's dark eyes, blazing with hatred, flashed through her mind suddenly, causing her to shiver in spite of the heat of the day. Kaitlyn shook her head, tears streaming down her face.

"I can't tell you," she sobbed.

"Kaitlyn please," Jody begged, feeling tears form in her eyes. "Please just tell me. I have to know."

Kaitlyn suddenly grabbed her and held her tightly, her small face buried in Jody's chest.

"I love you, Jody," she whispered. "I don't want to hurt you anymore."

"I know," Jody whispered. "But I have to know the truth. If you love me, please, tell me what happened."

Kaitlyn broke away from her, wiping the tears from her eyes.

"Are you sure?" she asked nervously.

Jody took a deep breath.

"I have to know," she repeated. "No matter how much it hurts."

Kaitlyn sighed.

"Take my hand," she whispered, her hand trembling as she extended it.

Jody closed her own firmly around it and closed her eyes.

"I'm ready," she whispered.

She heard Kaitlyn murmur something under her breath, and felt the branch disappear beneath them as they hurtled through empty space.

"Good luck," Kaitlyn whispered in her ear, and then she was gone.

CHAPTER 29

J ody woke up in an unfamiliar bed, surrounded by peeling, dark green wallpaper, a moth-eaten shag carpet, an old, wooden chest of drawers with a small lamp set on top of it that had been extinguished, and a tiny walk-in closet on the opposite wall, the type that small children always imagined monsters were hiding in. She glanced out the window and was met with an enormous blood red moon silhouetted against a starry strewn night sky overlooking a vast coniferous forest dwarfing Jody's small backyard. Smiling at the beautiful sight, Jody slipped out of bed and walked over to the window, gazing up at the sky filled with bright evening stars overhead. She felt more at peace than she had at any point in the last decade. Her smile slowly faded.

"I don't want to hurt you anymore, Jody..."

She suddenly felt an icy sweat break out on her forehead. Something was coming, something that was powerful and twisted enough to completely shatter the peaceful scene in front of her.

"But what happened?" she asked nervously. She found she had no answer.

Jody nearly jumped in fright as something crashed downstairs followed by a series of shouts.

"They've never argued in their life..." she thought, shocked at the realization.

In the ten or eleven years of life she had lived up to this point, she had never witnessed a fight between her parents. She pressed her ear to the door, straining to hear what was going on. She slowly realized that the screaming was being done almost exclusively by her mother, whose voice was steadily rising with each reiteration. A shiver passed up Jody's spine.

"What the hell is going on down there?" she thought nervously. She started to open the door, then recoiled suddenly as if she'd been burned as a scream erupted from downstairs. Jody shuddered. Her mother no longer sounded angry. She sounded panicked. Jody began to tremble as a heavy silence gripped the entire house.

Jody waited, silently begging for the shouting to begin again, but all remained quiet. Suddenly, heavy footsteps began to thud their way up the old creaky wooden staircase. She practically threw herself across the room and dove into the closet just as the door to her bedroom flew open and slammed hard into the wall behind it. Her father entered the room, and although Jody couldn't see his face, his tense posture suggested that he was extremely angry about something. The sight made Jody extremely nervous. Her father was normally an unusually calm man, and rarely became angry at all, much less to the degree that he appeared to be now.

Edward Razitsky stalked into the room, his shoulders bunched so high they nearly brushed against his jawline, every muscle in his face tensed into an expression of burning malice. Jody stifled a whimper as he wandered over to her bed and threw the threadbare sheets onto the floor with such force that they made contact with the opposite wall before coming to rest on the wooden floor. His dark eyes swept the room, coming to rest on the closet door where Jody was hiding. Jody clapped a hand to her mouth, barely stifling a terrified cry, when she saw his eyes. She had known her father's warm, coffee-brown eyes that always radiated intelligence and seemed to dance with light whenever he laughed. What she saw now was two soulless black holes that seemed to fall endlessly into the abyss. For an eternity that lasted no longer than thirty seconds, he stared through the crack in the closet door directly into Jody's deer-in-headlights light brown eyes with those twin black holes where her father's beautiful, comforting gaze should have been, his lip slowly but steadily curling back over his front teeth in a sneer.

Through her bottomless well of terror, she felt a flash of searing warmth somewhere close to her heart. It lasted less than a second, but she knew it had been real.

"Firelight..." she whispered. Her tears had stopped.

From somewhere far off, she heard the monster whisper, "I will extinguish this little spark."

The voice that didn't belong to her father was no longer angry, but a dead, cold, calm spray of frigid black ice and snow across her heart. But there was something else in her heart, something that could penetrate through any snow, ice, or...

"Or darkness," she whispered.

And then the closet door flew open, and the monster was upon her, bringing the meat cleaver already drenched in her mother's blood down on her again and again, each time spraying hot blood onto the floor and walls of the closet. Jody, now lying prone on the floor, her abdomen a jagged crisscrossing of slashes, glanced at the windowsill. The moon, the beautiful stars. They all seemed to be infinitely far away now. She allowed her heavy eyelids to slide close as the monster brought the blade down one last time, rupturing her diaphragm and immediately halting her shallow breathing.

The monster, feeling a sense of satisfaction at the sight of the girl's lifeless blood-soaked body, tossed the meat cleaver aside indifferently and turned to leave, sure that the girl was dead. When he reached the door however, he found the doorknob wouldn't budge. He began pounding on the door with his fist, and when that made no difference, he drove his shoulder into it repeatedly, but still, it refused to budge. As he continued his furious assault on the door, Jody, through a haze that had enveloped her brain, felt a stab of heat just below her breastbone that slowly traveled downward in a straight line like a welding torch being applied to a severed pipeline, and then disappeared almost as soon as it had appeared. She let out a long slow breath with the help of her cauterized diaphragm. Jody, suddenly feeling wide awake, turned her focus to the bedroom door as the monster continued in vain to throw itself against it.

"That's right," Jody whispered. "I am the spark."

The monster slammed itself against the door one final time and was thrown back across the room as the door exploded inward with a blast of heat strong enough to singe Jody's hair.

Flames raced up the tinder-dry wooden door frame towards the ceiling, curling and blackening the old dark-green wallpaper as they went, igniting the wooden floor, bathing the closet doors in their light, curling their way out of the door frame into the hallway beyond. The monster stared at the spectacle, half confused, half horrified. A part of it couldn't rationalize what was happening, how could it possibly not have seen...

"The girl..."

The flames quickly crossed onto its side of the room, and it could feel their heat now. It moaned in agony at the approach of the flames, its entire body searing with unbearable pain as the flames licked up and down its body, the skin of its vessel curling black. Jody, her eyes now open a crack, surrounded by flames but not bearing a single burn on her entire body, saw the approaching monster, the skin on its face now as black as its eyes as the body it inhabited was slowly consumed by the raging flames, and turned her focus to the closet doors.

The thing was almost upon her, just outside the burning closet doors, when they blew outward in a burst of flames, sending the creature backward into the opposite wall above the bed where its head slammed against the wall. It slumped onto the bed and did not move again. Jody approached the monster, knowing it could hear her in spite of its stillness.

"Why'd you do it?" she whispered, her voice trembling with fury.

It didn't reply.

"WHY'D YOU DO IT?" she screamed. "WHY'D YOU KILL MOM? WHY DID YOU RUIN MY LIFE?"

"I'm sorry, kid," the voice echoed in her head. Her father's voice. His real voice.

"Dad..." Jody stammered.

"I'm so sorry, kid. I couldn't stop him."

Jody stared at the lifeless body of the monster who had once been her father, her lower lip quivering as she struggled not to cry.

"You can't let the pain control you, Jody," her father said. "You have a life out there, and people who love you. You have to escape this place. Go, go now!"

"Dad!" Jody screamed as the room began to fade around her. "I love you!"

For a second, as her consciousness faded, she wasn't sure he would answer.

"I love you too," he said finally.

Jody allowed her eyes to slide close, tears silently streaming down her cheeks as the air in the room caught fire and the resulting flashover ripped through the room, destroying everything, innocent or malevolent, in its path.

CHAPTER 30

Tyson Saunders heard the beating rotors of the Blackhawk Sikorsky UH-60 military helicopter seconds before it unleashed a spray of lead on the black Mercedes. Marianne cried out in surprise as the rear window exploded, sending a rain of fine glass shards onto the seat behind her.

"Marianne, get down!" Tyson roared as the Sikorsky unleashed another barrage.

Marianne threw herself into a tight ball onto the floor, shielding the back of her neck with her hands as bullets pierced the leather seat where she'd been only seconds before. Alison snapped awake at the sound of her little girl's cries.

"Tyson, what's going on?" she exclaimed.

Tyson, caught in a blind panic, jerked the wheel to the left to avoid another strafe from the helicopter, barely managing to correct it before they went head over heels into the ditch below.

"Daddy!" Marianne screamed, terror gripping her voice.

The minigun went off again, sending bullets flying over Marianne's head, several of which became lodged in the back of Tyson's seat.

"What the hell do we do?" Alison screamed.

Tyson jerked the wheel again to avoid another round of bullets, but this time, he was less lucky. The Mercedes spun out of control, heading straight for the ditch strewn with abandoned vehicles at the side of the road. Alison and Marianne both screamed, their screams merging into a single high pitched note while Tyson fought in vain to regain control of the vehicle. The wheels left the pavement, and for a split second, the three of them were suspended in midair. Then the illusion imploded as the Mercedes landed face first in the ditch, crumpling the front bumper like a candy wrapper and shattering the windshield into a thousand pieces. Tyson threw up his arms to protect himself and felt shards of glass slice into his outstretched arms. The vehicle remained momentarily upright on its front bumper before gravity took over and tilted it forward, sending it slamming into the earth with a heart-stopping crash.

"Marianne..." Tyson thought a second before his head smacked into the ceiling, causing him to lose consciousness.

Tyson woke up to his daughter crying softly somewhere behind him.

"You okay honey?" he asked.

"Daddy, help me!" Marianne wailed, tears spilling down her face.

"I'm here, I'm here baby," Tyson gasped as he reached her. "We're going to get out of here, okay?"

Tyson, rolling onto his back, kicked a few stubbornly hanging shards of glass from the broken passenger side window.

"Okay, baby," he said, turning back to Marianne. "I need you to crawl out the window now, okay? I'll be there in a second."

"I'm scared, daddy," Marianne whispered, tears streaming down her face.

Tyson, still on his stomach, clumsily wrapped an arm around her shoulders.

"You'll be okay, baby, just do what I say, okay?"

Marianne nodded.

Tyson watched nervously as she crawled toward the broken window on her hands and knees, carefully avoiding shards of glass strewn everywhere. He heard her suck in a breath before launching herself through the broken window, landing in the grass on the other side.

"You okay, honey?" Tyson called.

Marianne, rubbing her aching shoulder, nodded.

"Alison," Tyson gasped, crawling painstakingly towards the passenger seat.

"Alison, you okay, honey?"

No response.

"Alison?" he called, a hint of panic entering his voice.

"You okay?"

"I'm here, love," came his wife's faint reply.

Tyson, beginning to panic, quickly closed the remaining distance to the passenger seat. Alison's eyes were half closed. Her face and clothes were dotted with blood and glass.

"Alison, Alison," Tyson whispered, urgently unclasping her seat belt.

"You're gonna be okay, you're gonna be okay."

He sounded as though he was trying to reassure himself as much as his wife.

"Tyson," Alison murmured.

"Honey, stay quiet, conserve your energy," Tyson murmured, reaching behind him and kicking out a few shards of glass from the windshield.

"Tyson, look," she said, glancing down at her arm.

Tyson followed her gaze, and what he saw caused his heart to drop to his toes. Alison's right arm, streaked with blood, was pinned beneath the roof of the Mercedes.

"Okay listen," Tyson said, panic fully setting in now.

"Tyson," Alison whispered. "Forget it."

"No, no," Tyson stammered. "We'll call the paramedics, we'll get an ambulance, you're going to get out of this!"

"Tyson, we both know there are none of those left," Alison groaned. "There's no way out of this."

Tyson shoved his hands beneath the roof, feeling shards of glass slicing into his hands and not caring, fighting with all his strength to remove the metal object that had condemned his wife.

"Tyson," Alison whispered. "Tyson, stop."

"I can't leave you here," Tyson pleaded. "I won't!"

"Baby, listen to me," Alison whispered, placing a blood-streaked hand against Tyson's cheek. "Marianne needs you, now more than ever. You have to be strong. For her. Do you understand me?"

Tyson, the realization finally dawning on him, hung his head in defeat.

"I love you," he whispered. "I love you so much."

He reached down and kissed her, feeling the unpleasant taste of iron on his lips and not caring.

"Go," she whispered, her consciousness fading. "Save our child."

Tyson, hating himself, crawled out through the broken windshield, feeling more glass slice into his broken body and finding he didn't care. He landed on the grass at the bottom of the ditch, gasping from the effort. For a moment he lay still, struggling to catch his breath.

"Daddy?" Marianne asked nervously. "Where's mommy?"

Tyson didn't reply.

"WHERE'S MOMMY?" Marianne screamed, tears blurring her vision.

Tyson forced himself to his feet, throwing his arms around his sobbing daughter.

"It's okay, it's okay baby, we have to go," he said, fighting the urge to cry himself as he hauled his sobbing daughter up out of the ditch as she pounded her fists against his back, screaming hysterically for her mother.

CHAPTER 31

Benjamin Alrite was walking alone down main street, headed for the place where Mike had been shot a few days ago, every line of his face etched with stone-faced determination, a Smith & Wesson 500 that he had taken from the abandoned gun shop back on Columbia Avenue carried openly at his side. Although he gave off a vibe that suggested the first person to get in his way would be executed on the spot, Ben found that he was extremely nervous. From his sheltered childhood in a pleasant suburban neighborhood where groups of kids played street hockey on Saturday mornings, to graduating Kellogg business school with his MBA, to working a comfortable office job as an actuary, to settling down in a neighborhood similar to the one he'd grown up in with his wife and child, nothing in his life could've prepared him for the situation they were in now.

He found his eyes darting back and forth between the different alleyways he passed, as if he expected someone to step out of the dark and shoot him where he stood. As if to underscore the point, as he approached Laurel Avenue, he was greeted with a sight so disturbing it nearly brought him to his knees with fright; the mutilated bodies of over a dozen marines, noticeably decomposed after several days in the late summer sun, were strewn throughout the street.

Two had been hung by a rope to a lamp post and were swinging gently in the breeze about twenty feet above him.

"Jesus..." Ben whispered as his eyes darted from one body to the next, taking in the carnage.

Two severed hands that had rotted enough to expose the bones beneath the flesh lay in the street, their owners lying several feet away. A severed leg lay not too far away from the hands, its owners face a mask of unbearable pain. Dried blood coated the street so thickly it looked like a child had spilled several cans of red paint everywhere. Ben turned away, unable to bear the sight for another second, dry heaved twice, then vomited up the remains of his breakfast. Ben stood up shakily, wiping his mouth with the back of his hand.

"Is it safe up there?" Mike called from about a block away, where the group was huddled in the lobby of an abandoned hotel, awaiting Ben's "all clear" signal.

For a moment, Ben didn't reply. There were children in the group, they had no business seeing the brutality committed against these marines, who had by no means been innocent, but were nowhere near deserving of such a fate. After a moment, just as Mike was becoming sure that something had happened to Ben, he called back

"Yeah, it's safe, just..." he paused to think for a minute, wondering about what sort of scars such a scene would leave on his own little girl, or any of the other children, for that matter. "Just don't bring the kids this way," he finished.

"What do you mean?" Mike replied.

"Just trust me," Ben said. "Bring them around on Magnolia Avenue and tell them to meet us outside the embroidery. You'll understand when you get here."

He got no further argument from Mike, who did as Ben instructed, privately wondering the entire time what had prompted Ben to avoid sending the children through the area, but having a very bad feeling that he hoped was proven incorrect that he probably knew already.

Expecting to see the bodies of civilians, Mike was all the more aghast when he and Lorenzo met up with Ben, who was silently glad Lorenzo had sent his wife, Serena, in the group with the children to spare her the sight of the grisly scene on Laurel Avenue.

"Jesus," Mike muttered, echoing Ben's sentiment.

The sight sent shivers down Lorenzo's spine, and he didn't consider himself a sensitive man. Lorenzo squatted over and nearly vomited himself. He'd worked in a surgery department for over two decades, and had seen more disturbing cases than he could recall, and yet this was the only scene he could recall brutal enough to bring him to his knees.

They began to walk silently towards Magnolia Avenue and the embroidery, none of them particularly inclined to discuss what they'd seen, where the rest of the group was already waiting for them.

"If this cycle of violence continues, what are we looking at here?" Ben asked, although he already knew the answer.

"A giant shitstorm," Mike replied matter of factly.

"Essentially," Lorenzo said, "what we just saw is going to happen all over the country wherever there have been confrontations between the military and civilians who are going to be boxed in and pissed off about it just like we saw a couple of days ago. This will continue until we either exhaust ourselves, someone with a louder bullhorn than the military takes control, or we kill enough that we can avoid coming into contact with each other."

"And based on what we've just seen, I'm guessing the third option is the most likely scenario," Ben muttered.

Lorenzo nodded.

"Unless someone gets a louder bullhorn," Mike said. "Any idea who that might be?"

Neither Ben nor Mike gave any ideas. They were approaching the group now.

"We don't mention this to anyone, agreed?" Ben muttered just before they were within earshot. Mike and Lorenzo silently nodded. Jennifer immediately went to her husband as he approached.

"What happened out there? What weren't we supposed to see?"

Ben glanced down at Gracie, who was watching them, wide-eyed.

"Nothing, honey," Ben said dismissively, still looking at his daughter as he said it more to her than his wife. "Nothing important."

Jennifer nodded. Although she didn't believe that whatever Ben was hiding from her wasn't important, she trusted him enough to know not to pry.

"What's the plan?" Serena asked.

"If there's radiation coming in from New York city, we need to get as far away from Kearney as possible," Ben replied.

"On foot?" Jason asked, a little incredulous. "We won't get far, even without those marines blocking our path."

Mike glanced down the road and noticed a black Toyota Corolla parked on the shoulder and pointed at it.

"We might not have to stay on foot for long if I can hotwire that thing," he said, a small smile crossing his face.

Half the group, Ben and his family along with Mike, piled into the small Toyota Corolla while the remaining four selected a white Chevrolet SUV they stumbled upon a little further up the road. They drove in silence until they were approaching the turnpike, when Mike noticed a black shape approaching them on the horizon through the windshield, along with the faint sound of helicopter rotors. Both Ben and Mike, while they had not seen the massacre that had occurred several days prior near the turnpike, immediately assumed the worst at the sight of the approaching helicopter. Ben pulled the Corolla over to the shoulder of route 7, startling Jennifer and Grace, both of whom had been near sleep.

"Ben, what's going on?" Jennifer asked nervously as Ben stopped the car on the shoulder.

"No time to explain now, honey, just trust me," Ben said quickly.

The underlying note of fear in his tone of voice made the point very clear that there was no time for an explanation. Jennifer immediately threw open the door of the Corolla and quickly shooed Grace out. Mike breathed a huge sigh of relief as he saw the Chevrolet pull off onto the shoulder a few hundred feet in front of them and its passengers scramble out onto the road. Ben, Mike, and Jennifer hurried over to join the rest of the group, Jennifer holding her daughter's hand in an iron grip to make sure she kept up.

"You saw it, too?" Lorenzo asked as soon as Ben was within earshot.

Ben nodded, glancing nervously up into the sky. The dark gray, heavily armed helicopter, which was undoubtedly military, was no more than ten miles away and heading straight in their direction.

"Shit," Mike muttered as he noticed how close the helicopter was now.

Jennifer had seen it too, and she threw her arms around her daughter protectively, and picked her up off the ground in a fireman's carry.

"Ben…" Jason muttered, not even able to finish the question due to the fact that his tongue seemed to be sticking to the roof of his suddenly extremely dry mouth.

"What do we do?" Lorenzo asked, finishing it for him.

Ben, whose gaze had been transfixed on the helicopter, which seemed to be approaching them with unnatural speed, glanced down the road in desperation, and his eyes suddenly fell on the Belleville turnpike up ahead.

"Head for the turnpike!" he called out. "We can take cover underneath it!"

The seven of them sprinted for the turnpike, Jennifer lagging slightly behind the rest of them as she was burdened with Grace. Ben, who had noticed Jennifer struggling, took Grace in his arms, and they both hurried to catch up with the group. Mike, shielding his eyes against the harsh mid-morning sunlight, glanced into the sky and saw that the helicopter was now no more than a few miles away.

"Hey Ben, Jen," Mike called, both of whom were still lagging behind the group, "better get your asses moving, that thing's almost here!"

Both Ben and his wife got the point and began pumping their legs even harder as the helicopter came into clear view above them. The seven of them made it under the turnpike without a second to spare. The helicopter's six-barreled gatling gun came into range no more than five seconds after they had taken shelter under the turnpike. They stood panting, most of them bent over with their hands on their knees as they watched the helicopter glide past the turnpike down the road.

"Quick thinking, Ben," Mike said after he'd caught his breath.

Ben just nodded weakly, still struggling to catch his own breath.

"That helicopter's gonna be back soon enough," Lorenzo said. "We should get off the highway before it does."

Ben nodded, and the rest of the group silently agreed with him. They waited until the helicopter was out of sight and then resumed walking down the shoulder of the highway, the sun beating relentlessly down on them, but no one seemed to have the courage to go back and get the vehicles. As they walked down the road in the direction of North Arlington, based on the road signs, Ben's thoughts wandered back to Tyson and his family.

"You think Tyson made it out okay?" Ben asked Mike as they walked side by side. Mike considered for a moment before replying.

"I sure hope so man," he replied. "Tyson's a smart guy, and he has a wife and daughter to protect, so if he did run into a blockade somewhere down the road, he would've found a way around it."

But even as he said it, Mike felt even less sure than he sounded, which wasn't a high bar to begin with.

"I keep thinking about the little girl," Jason chimed in as he caught up with them.

"Think she's alright?" Mike asked, although he was fairly sure he already knew the answer.

"She was real sick," Jason replied grimly. "And with the state of the country right now, most hospitals are going to be closing their doors, and even if they weren't, I don't know how much they could do for her anyway." He paused for a moment. "Her father's a good man though, and he seemed pretty determined, so maybe he'll find something,"

Jason added, although he didn't sound very sure. Ben nodded. He'd known Tyson for years, and he admired him both for his ability to rise from a difficult upbringing in an inner city ghetto neighborhood, and how tender he had always been with his little girl, Marianne. He was a good man and certainly deserved better than to watch his little girl suffer such a painful and inhumane fate. As Lorenzo pointed out an exit for North Arlington just up ahead, they exited the highway just as the sun slipped past the midpoint in the sky, signaling that morning had melted away into afternoon, Ben only hoped that Tyson was having better luck than they currently were.

CHAPTER 32

nna Veranda was never one to get nervous about a minor illness. While she had absolutely no problem comforting a crying three-year-old after they had fallen and skinned their knee on the sidewalk, she loathed the type of hypochondriac parent who would rush their child to the ER after they developed a mild cough overnight. She had a less euphemistic term to describe that type of parent: loony. She'd been telling herself all morning she was being dramatic, that her symptoms were nothing more than a minor cold. She had vomited up her insides twice already that morning, she had been coughing non-stop, accompanied by a constant nausea that had already put her on her knees in front of the toilet several times in the last hour alone. While David often insisted that she needed to take better care of herself, she could never bring herself to explain to him the origin of her conditioning. Her father had been a petroleum engineer, and the demands of his job meant he was more often than not absent from the house, leaving young Anna with her mother.

Patricia Veranda had been very fond of reminding Anna from the time she could walk that she was the result of an accidental pregnancy and a father who didn't believe in abortion while she sat in front of the TV smoking cigarettes. She also became very angry with her young daughter if she ever inconvenienced her mother with a small problem such as a broken arm while she was watching a particularly important episode of "Gallagher Girls." Anna had one very vivid memory when at nine years old, she'd stepped on a nail in the garage. She'd gone crying to her mother, who'd proceeded to scream at her for getting blood on her precious white carpet and tossed her onto the porch. She'd bawled her eyes out for around twenty minutes before a neighbor had come outside and rushed her to the ER. Recalling those days still caused Anna, even at the age of thirty-eight, to visibly shudder.

She sighed and hugged herself while she lay against the bathroom wall next to the toilet, where she'd been driven after the nausea had threatened to overwhelm her. She hoped David would be home soon from his overnight business trip, see her in this state and would, as he had done on many occasions, tell her that he was driving her to George Washington University hospital and that he would accept no argument from her. While, at least outwardly, she acted as if she resented him each time he had done this, deep down, she was grateful that she had a man who loved her enough to see through her childish games ("Big girls don't cry, Anna!") and get her the help she needed. Still, with every passing moment she did not see a car rolling up the driveway, her anxiety worsened. He'd called her last night after he'd landed to let her know he was staying at a hotel for the night and that he'd be home by nine the next morning. By now, it was quarter to noon.

Suppose he'd gotten caught up in one of the riots downtown? An unnerving image of her husband being trampled by a stampeding crowd swam into her mind. Anna shuddered and quickly pushed the thought from her mind. David Veranda, a 6'4" former marine and a Lieutenant for the SWAT division of the D.C. Metropolitan PD, was the toughest man she'd ever known. The thought of him being disarmed, much less killed, was unfathomable to his wife. She'd recently asked him while they were lying in bed one night what she would do if he ever left her. He smiled and said, "Never gonna happen, love. Marines don't die without permission." The memory made Anna feel a little better.

"Hey mom, you're going to want to see this," came her daughter Maria's voice from the kitchen.

Anna immediately turned away from the master bedroom where she had planned to lie down and instead headed towards the kitchen, her head aching in protest. She put on as bright a smile as she could muster as she entered the kitchen and embraced her wonderful seventeen-year-old daughter, Maria. Once they pulled apart, she stood still for a moment, taking in her daughter's vibrant face. She had had success in the genetic lottery, combining the best features of her and David, her curly chocolate brown hair and dark eyes inherited from her father, her high cheekbones, pert nose, and light scattering of freckles coming from her mother.

"You okay, mom?" Maria asked, frowning.

"Yeah, sweety, I'm fine," her mother said distractedly, walking past her into the spacious kitchen. She laid a hand down on the kitchen countertop and stared at it blankly without really seeing it at all.

Maria sighed. She'd seen her mother like this many times before, ever since Lilly had been taken away. It caused Maria a slight sense of guilt, given how absent she'd been lately. She'd busied herself with school, the swim team, dumb teenage boys, anything to keep her mind off her sister or the bastard who'd gotten her hooked on meth. Still, the worst memory was the one she had to work the hardest to block out. She'd come home from practice one evening to find the house empty. She'd gone into Lilly's room, only to find her lying passed out in her bed, her mouth filled with vomit, a large empty bottle of pain pills lying next to her. It still brought tears to Maria's eyes to picture her sister's lifeless body as the paramedics worked desperately to revive her. Still, if she pushed herself hard enough in school and at practice, running from one activity to the next until she was too tired to think, she managed to outrun the terrible pain brought on by these memories. Anna suddenly looked at Maria with a dazed look in her eyes as if she'd just noticed her daughter was there.

"What did you need, sweetheart?" Anna asked.

Maria shook herself mentally, forcing herself to come back to the present.

Maria had nearly forgotten the reason she'd called for her mother in the first place.

"Mom, I just saw something on the news you're going to want to see," she said, pulling the iPad down from the wooden shelf it usually sat upon next to the finely carved kitchen cabinets. Anna watched her daughter with distracted interest as she

94

pulled up a video feed on the screen titled "General Christian Germaine addresses the nation following attack on U.S. Army Center for Military History." Anna's eyes widened when she saw the title of the recording.

"There was an attack on the military history center?" she asked. "That's less than an hour from here." Maria nodded as she opened the recording.

"You don't think your dad…" Anna began and cut off abruptly as Maria held up the finger to silence her as the clip began playing.

A tall, gray-haired man wearing a two-piece black suit was standing behind an ornately carved wooden desk flanked by three tall bay windows with the white curtains drawn.

"This is General Christian Germaine reporting from the Oval Office. I am addressing the nation today following an attack on the U.S. Army Center for Military History by a large, armed crowd that as far as law enforcement can tell us is still in progress and casualty estimates are already in the hundreds and authorities expect those numbers to increase throughout the day."

The general kept talking but by now, Maria and Anna, watching stony-faced, had tuned him out. A clip of the U.S. Army Center for Military History, surrounded by hundreds of people, many of them shouting and a few openly carrying weapons, blockaded only by a thin picket line of no more than two dozen U.S. marines, began playing in the background. As they watched, their eyes traveled to the right side of the screen, where a black limousine had just entered into view and appeared to be headed for the entrance. But it was the sight of the thin, pallid, scowling young man that emerged from the limousine a moment later that made Anna Veranda's heart skip a beat. The face that had haunted her nightmares ever since they'd taken Lilly away. Maria, who wore an expression so icy it was almost unnerving, followed Michael's gaze, and what her eyes landed on nearly caused her to jump back in surprise.

"Mom, look!" she exclaimed, pointing to the man on the screen now talking to a uniformed officer carrying a bullhorn.

When Anna saw what her daughter was pointing at, her eyes widened with shock. It was David. Even with the blurry footage shot from hundreds of feet away, she would recognize her husband anywhere. As they stared, transfixed, all hell broke loose as the crowd stormed forward, sweeping David and the officer up with them. And then the footage cut out completely. The general said something else about the attack, but neither Anna nor Maria heard her. They looked at each other, and Anna saw tears brimming in Maria's eyes. Anna held her tightly as she began to cry.

"Baby, baby, look at me, look at me!" she commanded, and Maria obliged. "Your father is the toughest son of a bitch I have ever met in my entire life, and he is not going to die on us today. We're going to bring him back to us, do you understand me?"

Maria sniffed and nodded. "M-marines don't get to die without permission," Maria choked, and the ghost of a smile crossed her face.

"That's right, baby," Anna whispered as she reached for her car keys, almost smiling herself. "That's exactly right."

CHAPTER 33

David Veranda exited the U.S. Army Center for Military History in a daze. The sea of blood and bullet-riddled bodies he had waded through in the center spilled out into the street. He left the center surrounded by a throng of members of the victorious army. Except there was no sense of comradery among this victorious army, even as they walked side by side in the street through the sea of destruction and death surrounding them. There were no proclamations of their supposed victory. In fact, the only thing that could be heard in that place a few minutes past noon on that day in late August was a cold, empty silence, punctured only by the thudding footfalls of soldiers that had suffered a terrible defeat. Because David Veranda, like the rest of them, had lost that day. They'd all lost, and while their wounds might not be visible in the way that a bullet through the shoulder or a piece of shrapnel pierced through the leg might be, they would all bear those wounds for what remained of their lives. As David aimlessly followed what remained of the crowd away from the center on 4th Avenue SW, the image of the lifeless body of Michael Pines floated through his mind.

For the last several months, Michael Pines had been David Veranda's obsession. He could think of nothing else during the day, which had drastically affected his performance at work. He was nearly always angry and short with everyone he came into contact with, even members of his own family, and he'd nearly been removed from the S.W.A.T. division of the D.C. Metropolitan P.D. after getting into a shouting match with his boss about a simple mistake he'd made when writing up a new protocol. Even in his sleep, he found himself unable to escape the constant torment, as a smiling Michael Pines had become the constant subject of David Veranda's nightmares. However, he would've suffered through thousands of those nightmares rather than face another day in the real world. Because the worst part about the whole thing was the feeling of helplessness. He had been reduced to a mere spectator as his eldest daughter had been confined to a mental hospital, his youngest daughter had gradually withdrawn from the family, and his wife spent most nights bawling her eyes out in the bathroom while he lay in bed, wanting to go to her but not knowing how to help.

Now David was angry again, not at Michael Pines, but at himself. All the anger he'd built up and been forced to stew in for the longest several months of his entire life had meant nothing. To lay his hands on the little turd, to beat him bloody, to drown him with his own bare hands must mean something, must trigger some sense of closure. Because he had won, he had conquered when it seemed like his every effort was doomed to fail, he had done something, damnit. HE'D DONE A HELL OF A LOT, IN FACT! He glanced to his right at a seemingly abandoned gas station. He rubbed his aching temples, grunting irritably. After considering for a moment, he figured no one was around to stop him from breaking in and poaching a few Ibuprofens. He shambled toward it away from the small crowd in the street, his heavy footfalls punctuating the empty stillness around him that resembled his present emotional state. Because there had been no closure when he'd watched Michael's dead body floating in that hot tub. There hadn't been anything. Just total silence, as if the world were shunning him for what he had done. As David reached for the double glass doors, surprised to find them unlocked, the boarded-up windows seemed to stare at him accusingly as he entered, silently whispering amongst themselves about the terrible crime he had committed just hours ago.

David wandered aimlessly down a few aisles, most of their contents having already been ransacked by previous intruders, until he found a solitary bottle of Ibuprofen lying on the floor mostly hidden beneath one of the shelves. He fumbled with the child-proof cap for a moment, then dry-swallowed two of the pills, his craving to relieve his now pounding headache outweighing his dislike of dry-swallowing pills. When he came to the last aisle, he stopped dead in his tracks. A pair of legs clad in blue denim overalls were sticking halfway out of the bathroom door. Suddenly convinced he was no longer alone, David instinctively shot a glance over his shoulder, but the store remained as quiet as a grave. Slowly retrieving the Beretta Px4 he'd taken off his long-ago friend Bryce Kranston, he nervously approached the bodiless pair of legs, his gun hand trembling slightly. Every few seconds, he would shoot another glance over his shoulder, convinced that at any second, a masked gunman would round the corner and put a bullet between his eyes. After what felt like an eternity, he finally reached the bathroom door, and looked down at the dead body of a grizzled man in his golden years who, judging by the name tag pinned to his denim overalls, was the manager of the gas station.

David stared down at the lifeless body of the old gas station manager, suddenly feeling slightly sick to his stomach. The man's eyes were wide with fright, as if he'd been surprised by his attacker, probably just after leaving the bathroom. David knelt down beside him, and slowly slid his eyes closed. It was then that David noticed the coagulated blood that had trickled in a thin stream from the man's open mouth. His eyes moved down the man's lifeless body, until he found the source of the blood: a bullet hole just above his navel filled with coagulated blood. Even though David had closed the man's eyes, David couldn't help but feel weirdly that the man was still watching him, accusing him.

He could almost hear the man saying, "Hey David, how's it going, old buddy? Have a good day today? Nah, didn't think so, but if I could hear you, you'd probably say it was great, you killed that little fuck Michael Pines, right? Did the world a big goddamn favor, right?"

Absurdly, David felt himself nod at the last remark.

"Yeah, you did the world a big fucking favor, David. Feel better now, David? Everything's going to go back to normal now, right? You'll get on good terms with your boss, you won't have to yell at Maria about getting a couple of damn B's anymore, no sir, that right David?"

"Shut the hell up," David muttered, but it kept right on going.

"Anna will stop spending every night crying and start touching you again the way she used to, Lilly will be back home where she belongs, and Maria can stop staying out all night because she can't stand the sight of you or her mom, that right, David?"

David turned away and vomited up a mess of hot bile coupled with an unpleasant burning sensation from the aspirin. As he sat on his hands and knees, shaking all over, sweat pouring over his brow, he felt the hot, stinging tears start to well up in his eyes. There had been no closure, because killing Michael Pines hadn't been about getting revenge, David knew that now. He didn't want revenge, he wanted things to go back to normal, he wanted his loving wife and daughters, both of them, to be at his side as long as he lived, but killing Michael…hadn't brought them back to him…Lilly was gone…and Anna and Maria would be following pretty soon, he was sure of it. He began to cry even harder at the thought of Anna leading Maria by the hand out the front door and slamming it behind her, leaving David standing alone in the kitchen of the empty house that no longer felt like his own.

"I want my life back," he whispered between broken sobs. "Please god, just give me my life back."

CHAPTER 34

When Anna Veranda saw her husband break from the crowd and enter the gas station on 4th street SW, she'd parked the car on the curb and pulled Maria by her hand through the crowd of people that had gathered in the street. As Maria hurried to keep up with her mother, she glanced around at the people in the street. No matter where she looked, they didn't so much walk as shamble along, and they all carried a dull, empty expression on their faces that reminded Maria unnervingly of photos she'd seen of longtime Botox patients whose facial muscles no longer function. Doing her best to ignore them, Maria hurried after her mother towards the gas station. When they reached the twin glass doors, they were as surprised as David had been to find that they were unlocked.

As they entered the building, Maria startled a little as she saw the state of the store, the shelves either having had their contents ransacked or spilled out in chaotic piles all over the tile floor. The cash register had been ripped off of the counter and thrown six feet across the room, where it lay inside of a freezer case behind a completely shattered pane of glass. Immediately, the sight made her want to get out of that store as quickly as possible. She almost jumped out of her skin when she heard what sounded like someone sobbing in the aisle next to her. Instinctively, she backed up so fast she collided hard with the shelf behind her, sending a small bottle of contact lens fluid that had been hiding under the shelf rolling into the middle of the aisle.

Maria nervously turned the corner into the next aisle, her hands shaking worse with every step she took. When she saw her father, leaning over what looked like a body lying on the floor and sobbing uncontrollably, she froze, unsure of how to react.

"Dad!" she cried out, tears of joy leaking down her face as she ran towards her father, arms extended, ready for him to sweep her into his powerful embrace. Suddenly, Maria froze. Her broad smile faded almost instantly. The image of a dead body, floating just above the surface of a pool of water, flashed through her mind. It took her a moment to recognize the body.

"Michael…" she whispered. A tall, powerfully built man she instantly recognized as her father approached the body. Maria shuddered. Her father was carrying a long, gleaming blade in his right hand. There was no hint of emotion in his expression. His gaze was colder than she had ever seen it. Maria shook herself.

"It's impossible…" she whispered. "I don't believe you, you're lying." But the image remained tattooed to the inside of her eyeballs, forcing her to look upon what her father had done. From somewhere far off, she heard a high cold, cruel laugh that echoed off the walls as if a hundred people were laughing all at once.

Maria screamed, and then the image was gone, and she was back in the gas station, her entire body rigid with fright.

Her father looked up, his eyes tear-stained and bloodshot, his hands shaking uncontrollably, and Maria drew back slightly, suddenly very afraid. She looked up as her mother approached from the other side of the aisle, her mouth dropping open when she saw her husband. She immediately went to him and knelt down by his side. Maria's brain began to scream danger, and she had the crazy urge to tell her mother to get the hell away from him. She tried to reassure herself that this was her father, but in that moment, it didn't seem to matter to her who he was. The only thing that mattered was the sight she'd seen a few moments ago: her father's remorseless gaze as he stared at the lifeless floating body of his victim. She had to work increasingly hard to repress the urge to scream at her mother to get the hell away, to drag her away from that man, to scream that he was a killer, to demand to know how she could be so fucking blind!

By now, David had stopped crying, and his gaze met Maria's.

"Maria, come here," he said calmly, reaching the arm out to her that was not holding her mother. Maria stared at him unmovingly, not backing away, but refusing to get any closer. She shook her head almost imperceptibly. Almost. David's small smile faded when he saw that headshake. His already overwrought brain began to work furiously, the image of Anna dragging Maria out of the house by the hand returning to haunt him. His thoughts almost immediately drifted to Michael Pines.

"She knows," he thought. "Somehow, she knows I killed Michael, I can see it written all over her face, and you did this, David, every damn bit of it, was killing Michael Pines worth losing your daughter, tell me, David, WAS IT FUCKING WORTH IT?"

Maria, meanwhile, saw the expression on the man's face fall flat, and then she did take a step backward, fear now consuming her thoughts.

"He knows, he knows I know what he did, and now he's angry, he's concealing it right now, but he won't later, not when he's pointing that handgun at you and mom, and that's what he's going to do, oh yes, maybe not right now, but one of these days, he's going to kill both of you …"

Then her father and mother were getting to their feet and walking out of the store, her father's arm draped over her mother's shoulders. At first, she didn't follow, staying rooted to the spot. Her mother shot her a quizzical glance as they turned the corner towards the doors. Her father appeared not to notice. Finally, Maria relented, and began to follow them out of the store, realizing the irony of the silent promise she'd made to herself that morning that she'd never forgive God if she lost another family member to Michael Pines.

CHAPTER 35

Tyson Saunders was driving a navy blue Ford F150 down Ridgewood Avenue in Glendale, following the signs for the Mountainside Medical Center. The truck had been abandoned by the roadside on route 7 with the back window blown out and several dozen shell casings littering the back seat and bed of the vehicle. Tyson had tried not to think about what might have happened to the family that had abandoned it in the first place as he'd driven it down route 7, Marianne dozing in the passenger seat beside him while he kept one eye on the road and one on the sky above him in case the helicopter came back, but it seemed to have disappeared, along with any military blockades that had undoubtedly littered the road at some point in the last few days. Now, piloting the Ford down Ridgewood Avenue, an outsider might've found it strange that Tyson hadn't shed a single tear for his dear wife.

Tyson had always been a prototypical tough guy, the type of six-foot-four, well-muscled, stoic, expressionless man you'd be more likely to find bouncing outside of a nightclub in a rough urban neighborhood than raising a family in a quiet suburb in southwestern New Jersey. But tough was what you had to be growing up on the gritty streets of Englewood, Chicago, where kids as young as eight years old were beat up or shot at for having nice shoes, getting caught reading at school was grounds for a few lost teeth, and park basketball games all adhered to the "no blood, no foul" rule. Crying well, crying was something you did if you wanted the kids beating you behind the school to go on for an extra fifteen minutes just to prove a point. He had never cried in front of Alison in all the years they'd been married, even in moments when he'd been invited to. It was not that she would love him any less. In return for her love, he'd made a silent agreement to always be strong for her and for Marianne. Between the circumstances of his childhood and his marriage, Tyson had become so used to suppressing his tears that he found that by now they simply wouldn't come.

As Baldwin Street melted into Walnut Crescent, he glanced over at Marianne, still asleep in the passenger seat. She turned over in her sleep, and Tyson felt his nerves stir up at the sight of his little girl's unnatural paleness. She still looked like she hadn't eaten in days, and there were dark circles under her eyes that reminded him of their wedding day when Alison's mother had been a little overly generous with the eyeshadow. She'd been mostly asleep for the last few days and even when she'd been awake, she'd barely spoken a word, her silence broken only by occasional fits of crying. Several times, Tyson had been forced to pull the Ford off the side of the road and hold her hair back while she vomited into the ditch at the side of the road. Tyson was growing increasingly nervous with each empty town they passed on their way to Montclair. He knew that if he couldn't find a doctor in

101

a hurry, there was a good chance that she would fall asleep one last time and never wake up again.

The Mountainside Medical Center came into view on his right as he hung a right onto Bay Avenue, and his strung-out nerves relented a little. They had arrived at the solution to all their problems, the medical center. There would be a doctor here who would be able to help Marianne, there had to be, how else could they be helping all those poor people who were brutalizing each other out in the streets, they wouldn't just leave them out in the streets to bleed to death, of course they wouldn't, it simply wouldn't make any sense. This is what Tyson told himself as he turned into the parking lot of the medical center. In his excitement to be arriving at the source of Marianne's salvation, he failed to notice the lack of additional vehicles in the parking lot, or the darkened windows in the hospital, or the total silence that seemed to surround the place like a dense fog.

Tyson glanced over at Marianne, who let out a tiny, pained moan in her sleep. Her complexion was ashen. Tyson shook her lightly by the shoulder. She slumped over in her seat like a ragdoll and slept on. Tyson carefully picked her up and slung her over his shoulder in a fireman's carry.

"You'll be okay, you'll be okay," Tyson whispered, stroking his daughter's hair as they walked through the double automatic doors to the ER department, trying to convince himself as much as his poor child. "I'm going to keep you safe, I promise," Tyson whispered, and just for a second, he swore he could feel a spectral hand on his shoulder.

When Tyson entered the Emergency Room at the Mountainside Medical Center, Marianne still asleep in his arms, he was greeted by a scene that was the stuff of nightmares. The overhead fluorescent bulbs had gone dark, meaning the room's only source of light was the sunlight filtering through the small, dust-covered windows, several of which had had their panes shattered near the ceiling, but it was enough for Tyson to take in the devastating scene. The floor was strewn with a chaotic mixture of broken glass, medical instruments, discarded hospital scrubs, and dried blood.

Added to that were hospital sheets, which had been stripped off of the beds and thrown wildly in every direction. The blood, in addition to staining the floor in various places, had splattered onto the stripped-down beds and onto the whitewashed walls. An IV machine had been thrown on the floor, spilling morphine from a clear plastic bag onto the floor. Several of the beds had been flipped over, dozens of blood-soaked scalpels protruding from the mattresses. A pair of legs stuck out from under one of the overturned hospital beds, the rest of the body having been crushed underneath the bed's girth. Only when Tyson entered the emergency room did he notice that the entire medical center was as quiet as a grave.

Although a part of him was screaming at him to turn and run in the other direction as fast as he possibly could and not look back, he continued to walk gingerly into the semi-dark room, feeling vaguely as if he'd been drugged. He wasn't quite in control of his own body, he certainly must've had some control, but it felt closer to a simulation than reality, like he was watching someone else's feet slowly make their way past the overturned hospital beds and pools of blood in the semi-darkness rather than doing those things himself. He glanced down at Marianne, who looked smaller and more helpless than ever, her ghostly complexion visible even in the poorly lit emergency room. So, Tyson, against his better judgment, walked through the emergency room and into the equally deserted waiting room beyond it.

He swore in frustration when the waiting room greeted him with a scene similar to the emergency room. The entire room looked like it had been through a tornado. Several of the windows had been shattered, two computer monitors that had once been stationed behind the receptionist's desk had been thrown halfway across the room, chairs had been overturned and scattered this way and that, magazines and broken glass were strewn across the floor, the corpses of half a dozen colorful tropical fish lay on the floor next to an overturned, bone-dry fish tank with a giant hole punched through the glass. But what disturbed Tyson most was the blood. There was easily enough to have filled three people between all the droplets and splatters that lined every surface, including the floor, overturned furniture, and the walls, and it was so widespread through the entire room that it could've easily belonged to a dozen or more people. As he walked slowly through the room, taking care to avoid the broken glass and sharp medical instruments littering the floor, he tried not to think about how badly a person would have to be hurt to spill that much blood both on the floor and halfway up the walls.

"God, what the hell happened here?" Tyson thought, his hands trembling a little as he slowly opened an office door labeled "Dr. Allen Bennicker" and peered inside.

The office was still in working order, but the papers and family picture frames littering the floor as well as the blue glow from the computer monitor that hadn't been switched off suggested that its occupant had left in a hurry. Swearing again, Tyson slammed the office door shut and continued down the hall. Marianne stirred a little in her sleep at the sound of the door slamming, but she didn't wake up. Tyson was becoming increasingly nervous with every empty office door he opened, and every semi-dark hallway strewn with blood and broken glass he walked down. Tyson squeezed past a gurney occupied by a sheet-covered corpse.

"There is something here," Tyson insisted. "There has to be."

But even as he said it, he didn't really believe it himself. The hospital was a dead end and he knew it, but he couldn't bring himself to leave, not yet, because if the hospital couldn't help Marianne, he didn't know where to turn next. It might even be the case that there simply was nowhere left to turn, but that was not a prospect that Tyson was willing to confront. Tyson peered into another abandoned hospital room with an overturned IV machine leaking a purple fluid all over the floor.

"We should leave, there's nothing here," Tyson thought, sounding resigned. He shook his head angrily as he threw the door open to another empty room where the bed had overturned.

Becoming increasingly angry with every empty room he entered, Tyson stormed through the hallway towards a large set of double doors marked "Surgery." Tyson threw an empty gurney that was in his way halfway down the hall, where it banged to a stop against a half-open door to another hospital room that Tyson was already sure was empty. Tyson threw open the doors to the surgery department and walked down another empty hallway. Marianne stirred in his arms but still did not wake up. Tyson could feel his anxiety beginning to spike again. A dull pounding was developing over his right temple. Tyson glanced into a surgery room, swore when he saw it was empty, and kept walking. He was doing his best to ignore the alarm bells going off in his brain. Another room, empty. Another room, torn to pieces and empty. Empty, empty, empty, EMPTY, EMPTY, FUCKING EMPTY! Tyson swore under his breath and threw a tray of surgical instruments across the room before storming out.

"Daddy, stop."

The voice made him stop dead in his tracks. He glanced down at Marianne. She was wide awake, staring up at him, her warm brown eyes wide with fright.

"There's nothing here."

Tyson stared blankly at his daughter, his mouth opening and closing uselessly as he struggled for words.

"W-what do you mean?" Tyson stammered.

"We have to leave this place, now," she said, her voice suddenly much stronger. Tyson stumbled backward in shock, nearly tripping over his own feet and sending them both sprawling.

"We have to go to Virginia, daddy," she continued. "There's someone there who can help me. I dreamed about her."

Tyson, barely conscious of what he was doing, found himself running in the direction of the ER doors to where they had parked the Ford.

"Sweetie," he stammered, "who is this person?"

"Jody," Marianne replied softly, her eyes starting to close again. "She's trying to heal, just like me. I think we can help each other, daddy."

Tyson, barely comprehending what his little girl was telling him, threw open the passenger door of the Ford and set Marianne gently down in the passenger seat, who immediately curled up into a fetal position.

"Daddy?" she whispered as Tyson started the engine.

"Yeah, honey?" he replied, quickly pulling the Ford out of the parking lot.

"I love you."

CHAPTER 36

I f Ben had previously had any semblance of hope that leaving behind Kearney would leave behind the violence and destruction that he had witnessed in the last several days, that hope went up in smoke when he saw the state that North Arlington was in as the group left the exit ramp of the highway near sundown and began walking through a residential neighborhood, or at least what was left of it. The street was completely empty, save for a few defunct cars scattered aimlessly along the curb, their occupants having long fled. The windows in all the houses were dark with the shades drawn, giving the houses a haunted look. Many of the windows on the houses had been shot out, either partly or completely. The front doors of several of the houses had been blown clean off their hinges, and from what little Ben could see of the inside, furniture had been broken and overturned indiscriminately.

He saw a dining room table with two of the legs snapped clean off that was sitting overturned on the front lawn not far from a shattered bay window that it appeared to have been thrown through. One of the houses had a giant hole in the second-story wall and room, as if someone had thrown a grenade at it. Grace, who was walking just behind Ben and holding her mother's hand, tugged on her mother's sleeve.

"Mom, where'd everybody go?" she asked, her expression suggesting that she was genuinely curious.

Jennifer opened her mouth, closed it again, repeated the gesture, then just shook her head, unable to find the words that would explain to her nine-year-old daughter why all the people had disappeared.

Jason caught up with Lorenzo, who had Serena clutching his arm tightly, her eyes wide with fright as she took in the scene around them.

"Do you really think Tyson's here?" Jason asked.

Lorenzo took a minute to reply as they passed a cul-de-sac off to their right.

"No," Lorenzo said. "He had a doctor and a PA at his disposal who had access to basic household medical supplies, the only reason he would've left in the first place would've been if he thought he was going to find a functioning hospital somewhere."

Jason nodded.

"Do you think there's one out there, honey?" Serena asked.

"A functioning medical center?" For an answer, Lorenzo gestured to the derelict surrounding houses and shook his head.

"It's possible," Jason said. "But it wouldn't look like what we think of as a traditional hospital, like the kind of places we worked in back in the day," he said, turning to Lorenzo.

105

Lorenzo gave Jason a quizzical look.

"Think about it," Jason said. "The rule of law no longer exists, for the moment at least, we have to assume that, agreed?"

"Agreed," Mike said as he caught up with them, thinking about the old man being thrown down into the street and shot in the head by soldiers.

"So, if we assume the rule of law no longer exists, who are the most powerful people in society?" Jason asked the three of them.

"The people with the biggest guns, that's how it's been since the beginning of time," Mike said immediately.

"Well, partially," Jason replied. "The people with the biggest guns certainly have the most power, but the other group with a significant amount of power are the people who can help the people who've been harmed by those guns, i.e. medical professionals like myself and Lorenzo," Jason said.

"What's your point?" Mike asked. Lorenzo, his hand rubbing his chin thoughtfully, was fairly sure he already understood Jason's point.

"My point is that medical care, like every other modern commodity, will continue existing, for the right price," Jason said. "Think about it, Lorenzo. Someone comes to your door with a bullet through their forearm begging for help. You haven't eaten in three days because there's almost no food, and what food there is has been contaminated with radiation or mold. What do you do? Obviously, you tell them you can help in exchange for a little food. Word spreads. Suddenly, you've got ten people at your door the next morning with similar problems. What do you do? The exact same thing you did the previous day, if you're smart."

"So, if there was a group of people doing the same thing you're suggesting, would they form a kind of primitive hospital?" Serena asked.

"Exactly," Mike replied, finally understanding what Jason was getting at. "It's the law of supply and demand. It doesn't matter if they're operating out of a trailer, a house, or an abandoned storefront. If there's a high demand for their services, which there will be, no doubt, they suddenly become the most powerful people in society."

"In other words," Jason said, "the idea that a lack of a hospital would stop Tyson from finding a doctor around here is bs," he said matter-of-factly, kicking a crushed Pepsi can out of their way into the grass.

"What about commodities other than medical care?" Serena asked. "Could something similar happen?"

Lorenzo thought for a moment before replying.

"Again, it depends on supply and demand. Demand is often dependent on the social fabric of a society. What's the average income? What's the standard of living? How widely available are those commodities, i.e. the phenomenon of keeping up with the Joneses."

"So, in other words, given that the world has gone to shit, demand for TVs is going to be pretty low these days," Mike said.

"Right," Lorenzo said. "A lot of modern comforts are going to disappear for a long time until society as a whole is able to get to a point where basic survival needs are essentially taken for granted, which is where we were until the shit hit the fan a few days ago. Right now, everything is going to be about those basic survival needs."

"Hell, there's only one non-survival related quantity that's been around since the dawn of time," Mike added somberly. "Power."

All six of them, even Grace, turned to look at Mike.

"He's right," Ben said after a moment of quiet. "One of the most important consequences of eliminating the rule of law that we haven't considered yet is the power vacuum that is created in its absence. Assuming the U.S. government is even still operating, they've completely destroyed their legitimacy, so they're symbolic at best."

"What about the military?" Jennifer asked. "The government willingly handed power over to the military, so where does the concept of a power vacuum come into play?"

"That's true," Jason said, "although there are two caveats to that. First, no one supports this new military government, and the only method of maintaining control that they have thus far demonstrated is murder. Just like the government, their power is symbolic, but for different reasons. I assume most of you have heard of General Sherman's march to the sea."

Everyone besides Grace nodded.

"It was based on a very interesting concept. An army can only stand with the support of the people. Strike at the people, and the army falls apart."

"Except they've done the striking for us in this case," Mike said.

Jason nodded in response as the group approached a road sign signaling that they were entering Canterbury Avenue. Grace tugged on her mother's sleeve.

"Mom, when can we stop? My legs are getting tired."

"Soon honey, real soon," Jennifer murmured soothingly, although privately, she was pretty sure that was not the case.

"If no one's in support of this government, and everyone is rebelling against it, we can assume, at least for now, that they are irrelevant in this power struggle, agreed?" Mike asked.

No one responded. They didn't have to.

"Hence," Mike continued gruffly, as they entered Canterbury Avenue. The scene they encountered was similar to the one on 4th Street. "We have a situation where the seat of power remains empty. We currently have an unknown number of candidates who will rise up to try and fill it."

"The problem is," Ben added, "there's no telling who the people will turn to first. Somehow, I don't think their first concern will be the social welfare of their fellow man when it does happen, and history would agree with me."

"What do you mean?" Jennifer asked, her grip on her daughter's hand tensing slightly.

The rest of the group watched Ben intently as he pondered his reply.

"Well, history tells us that when a society as a whole is miserable or is failing in some way, their first instinct is to find someone to blame. Oftentimes this reduces the appeal of more moderate leaders who try to fix the problems gradually and gives way to more extreme leaders who will use manipulation to rile the people up against another group they can blame their problems on. The best example is probably Nazi Germany, but expulsion of the Jews during the Middle Ages and the Armenian genocide during world war I also fit the equation."

"So, who's going to get blamed for the downfall of human civilization when all the normal scapegoats have gone extinct?" Lorenzo asked.

"Who says he has to blame one group in particular?" Ben said as he walked alongside his wife. "A leader with the right mix of charm and charisma might have a different scapegoat for every person he comes across."

"I mean, that sounds great in theory," Serena said, "but to get in the heads of that many people who are as spread out and terrified as they are right now, you'd have to be Hitler, Mao, and Pol Pot rolled into one, with an IQ of about two hundred to make that work. I just don't see it."

No one responded to that. The truth is, no one wanted to, because they were all thinking the same thing. A week ago, they had all been leading their normal, quiet lives, quite content with the way things were going. To have that all turned on its head in the span of a few days the way it had been, it wasn't such an unreasonable stretch of the imagination to think that what Serena had just described would indeed happen, and much quicker than anyone could've expected. As they approached Third Street, Grace could feel her legs starting to give out from underneath her.

"Mommy, I'm so tired!" she whined. "Can we stop soon, please?"

Jennifer, still holding her daughter's hand, looked up at Ben.

"It's not a bad idea," he said, glancing around at the abandoned houses surrounding them. "We could stay in one of these houses for the night, almost all of them are deserted." He looked around at the rest of the group, all of whom looked exhausted.

"I've got no complaints," Mike said, drawing his Smith and Wesson and walking in the direction of a small bungalow with light blue siding and a large front room bay window on the other side of the street.

"Why the gun?" Jason asked, hurrying to catch up with him, the others following in their wake.

"Better safe than sorry," Mike said, peering intently at the darkened windows. "If we go in there and it turns out not to be abandoned, I'm guessing the residents won't exactly throw us a welcoming party."

Jason nodded, drawing a Beretta from his own waistband.

"We'll clear it first before we all go in," Mike called back to the group as they crossed the front lawn. "Make sure it's safe."

Ben nodded.

"Hang on," Serena said as Mike and Jason started toward the front door, guns poised. "There's a safer way."

Lorenzo threw his wife a quizzical look while Mike looked slightly annoyed. Serena bent down and picked up a fist sized rock from the small garden standing in front of the porch. Before anyone could ask what she was doing, she hurled the rock through the front room window of the house.

Several of them jumped in fright as the rock punched a hole through the window and dropped soundlessly onto the living room carpet, accompanied by the tinkle of breaking glass. Jason started to say something, but Serena held up a hand to silence him, straining to listen for any signs of movement. After a moment, a smile spread slowly across her face.

"It's abandoned," she said matter of factly.

"How do you know?" Ben asked.

"If someone threw a rock through your window," Serena said, "wouldn't you be running for the front door with your gun drawn?"

Ben glanced at his daughter, who was staring at Serena with a hint of awe, and nodded.

"Exactly," she said, clearly satisfied with herself. Serena pushed past Jason and Mike as she started for the front door.

Mike shot Jason a quizzical look, who gave him a look that clearly said, "what are you going to do?" before they both hurried after her, Lorenzo, Ben, Jennifer, and Grace in tow.

CHAPTER 37

Dylan Teryon stared out the window of the pickup at the darkening sky and passing farm fields with a childlike curiosity that didn't extend deeper than his facial expression. In fact, no emotion whatsoever extended deeper than his face. His emotional landscape was similar to the dark cloudy sky he was staring at out the window of the pickup: dark, expressionless, and exuding a bone-deep coldness that blanketed everything like a black bridal veil. This coldness had not gone unnoticed by Roy and Laura, the latter of whom had been turning around to check on the little boy every couple of minutes for the last several hours, her concern growing every time she asked him "you ok, honey?" and receiving no response in return.

Roy, although his concern for the boy was just as great as his wife's, had told her several times to leave him be, knowing that the constant badgering was not helping his emotional state, a request which Laura had ignored. As Roy stared out at the darkening, two-lane farm road, trying to concentrate on his driving in spite of the dull pounding developing under his right eye due to the dizzying circles his mind had been spinning in for the last several hours, he felt Laura tug on his shirt sleeve.

Resisting the urge to shout at her, Roy instead calmly asked, "What's up?"

"Roy," Laura whispered urgently, "Dylan hasn't said a single word in the last several hours, I'm really worried about him."

Roy sighed, trying to conceal his growing frustration that wasn't being helped by his steadily building headache.

"Laura, you should really give it a rest…"

"Roy, do you remember when we first started dating?" Laura asked irritably, cutting him off.

"Yes, I remember, Laura…" he said exasperatedly, knowing the exact speech she was about to go on and finding he didn't have the energy to head it off. He loved Laura more than life, but when she built up a full head of steam, it was almost impossible to cut her off.

"The night I told you that story about what my childhood was like, remember that?" Laura rolled on.

With every word, Roy could feel the pounding in his head steadily building.

"Did I need to be left alone then?" Laura said indignantly, her voice rising a little with every word.

Roy sighed, running a hand over his now pounding forehead.

"No, I didn't need to be left alone," Laura admonished, ignoring the fact that he hadn't replied. "I needed to be held, I needed to be touched, I needed to be soothed, you held me all night and stroked my hair and told me you loved me…"

"You needing something doesn't mean every person in the world needs the same damn thing! Grow up!" Roy snapped, not really meaning to yell but unable to contain his frustration anymore.

Laura sat back in the passenger seat, and Roy heard her choke back a sob, but he didn't care in that moment. The kid didn't deserve to be constantly badgered on top of seeing his sister and mother killed in front of him, and if he needed to yell at his wife to get her to leave him alone, he was perfectly fine doing that. He returned his focus to the road, switching the headlights of the pickup on as the road grew dark around them. As his anger subsided, however, he felt a sense of guilt creep in. He hadn't been fair to Laura, and he knew it. She was only doing what she thought was best for the kid, and she clearly cared about him. He glanced in the rearview mirror at the kid. He hadn't moved in the last several hours.

He was still staring out the window of the pickup at the passing fields and occasional modest farmhouse with a gravel driveway housing a pickup truck or mammoth brick-red barn housing pigs, chickens, horses, or some combination, and Roy wondered vaguely how many of those animals would starve to death because their owners had picked up and left after hearing the news that the world was ending, or been shot by soldiers or street thugs looking to pick up some loose change.

"Or just for the fun of it," he thought with a shudder, Anette's horrible, bloodied face swimming into his mind.

"Poor kid," Roy thought, glancing back at Dylan. Roy ran a hand through his close-cropped light brown hair, suddenly feeling horrible about his stupid and utterly meaningless outburst in the midst of the situation they were in. He turned to Laura to apologize and saw with a start that she was crying silently into her hands.

"Laura, honey..." Roy said soothingly, wrapping an arm around his wife.

"Roy, oh Roy," she sobbed, laying her head against his shoulder. "I'm sorry, Roy. I haven't even thought about her the last few hours. Our daughter is dead, and I'm fighting with you about...about..." Her sobbing buried the rest of her sentence.

Roy felt the tears welling up in his eyes now too. He had been in such a state of complete shock over the last several hours that somehow Myrtle had slipped his mind, but there she was again. His wonderful, sweet, energetic little girl, his pride and joy, the girl he'd promised to love and cherish forever as much as his beautiful wife the day she was born, was gone. Roy, unable to keep the truck steady with a rain of tears now blurring his vision, turned off into the gravel driveway of a farmhouse, and embraced his wife as she sobbed her heart out on his shoulder.

They held each other tightly, supported each other as their emotional states turned as cold and empty as the night sky above them. Roy rocked his wife back and forth slowly, stroking her long honey-blonde curls, meaning to soothe himself as much as he meant to soothe his wife.

"It's alright baby, it's alright," he whispered, knowing deep down that it wasn't alright, hell, it was probably never going to be alright again as a matter of fact, but he still said it. Although he hadn't noticed, he might've found it strange that Dylan hadn't moved a muscle throughout this whole exchange. He stared blankly out the window at the dark corn field to their left, the image of his sister's eyes rolling into the back of her head as her body twitched uncontrollably three feet off the ground, then crashing to the ground like a dropped dinner plate replaying over and over again in his head.

Roy nearly jumped back in surprise when he heard a tap on the window behind Laura. A short, stocky man, probably late fifties to early sixties based on the white stubble beard and considerable wrinkles he was sporting, wearing a plain white t-shirt and dark gray cargo shorts was standing outside the window, peering in at them through the glass. Roy leaned behind him and hit the button on the driver's side door to roll down the window.

"You folks alright?" he asked with a low, Texan accent that reminded Roy of Sam Elliot. He was toting a double-barreled shotgun, but he didn't seem to think the three of them were worth using it on.

"Yeah, we're alright," Laura said, who had by now untangled herself from her husband. "I'm Laura, this is my husband, Roy, and the kid's name is Dylan."

"Nice to meet you, my name's Eric Chandler," the man said, stretching out his hand to Laura, who shook it heartily. "What are you folks doing out here?"

"Same thing as everybody else," Roy replied, stepping out of the car. "Getting away from the cities."

Eric nodded solemnly, even though from the look of things, the mobs hadn't caused him any problems.

"Looks like you've been alright though," Roy said, nodding to the house free of any broken windows or bullet holes in the walls. Eric nodded in reply.

"Yeah, I've got my own little slice of heaven out here with my wife and two girls. My two girls moved to Chicago after they finished high school, told me they were bored with country life."

"We just came from there," Laura said, who had gotten out of the truck as well. "Bet they don't think this place is so boring after the shit they saw last night," she said, eliciting a belly laugh from Eric.

"They just got in last night actually," Eric said. "Luckily, they got out before the real shitstorm started. Like you said, they ain't in no hurry to get back." Eric looked out into the distant night sky at nothing in particular, his expression careworn. He ran a hand through his short white hair and sighed heavily.

"Well, if you're looking to get away from the end of the world, you've come to the right place," he said. He sighed again. "It's honestly sad what happened out there. Hell, everyone's saying Petrov ended the world, but he didn't, those crazies out there shooting people in the street and blowing up houses, started doing that the minute the news got out. Hope the people figure that out and decide to do something about it before it's too late if it isn't already."

Roy shook his head slightly, privately thinking that there wasn't a chance in hell that would happen, not after what he'd seen today. He saw the bloody face of Anette again, and he visibly shuttered.

Eric noticed.

"Look," he said. "I've got a spare bedroom upstairs. If you folks want to stay the night, I'd be fine with that."

112

Roy looked at Laura, who would've been too tired to argue even if she wanted to. To both, the offer sounded like a gift from the Gods after the day they'd had.

"We'd love to, sir," Roy said, managing a weak smile.

Eric smiled in return, and clapped Roy on the back.

"Happy to have you," he said.

Laura opened the back door of the pickup and saw that the back seat was empty. She was about to turn around and ask Roy if he'd seen Dylan get out when she noticed him standing on the far side of the gravel driveway, staring out into the cornfield. Shooting her husband a quizzical look, and receiving a shrug in return, Laura walked towards the little boy she'd only met that day but still cared about as if she were her own, both men on her heels.

Dylan didn't turn around as she approached. Laura gently laid a hand on his shoulder.

"Dylan, this nice man has offered to let us stay here the night," Laura said calmly.

Dylan didn't respond, didn't even blink. The lines on Laura's face stretched with the worry that had been growing steadily over the last several hours.

"Dylan," she said, a note of pleading in her voice. She shook him lightly by the shoulders.

Nothing. The boy's deadpan stare never wavered for a second. Laura felt Roy's hand on her shoulder.

"C'mon honey, we should let him be, he'll come in when he's ready," Roy said soothingly, wanting to believe it was true.

Laura, wanting to protest, instead calmly nodded, and followed Roy and Eric back towards the house.

"He's out there you know," Dylan said in a stone-cold voice completely void of emotion so unlike his own.

All three of them turned at once, staring at Dylan, who now turned away from the cornfield. His expression was unreadable.

"He's here right now, watching us." A strange smile that was somewhere between a joyful little boy and a hungry dog sizing up a fat rabbit crossed his lips. Laura let out a terrified scream at the sight of it.

Dylan lay in the guest bed next to Roy and Laura, who had fallen asleep spooning. It had taken Laura a long time to fall asleep that night. She tried to reason that he was only a little boy, and the anxieties of the day really must be getting to her if she believed he was a threat to her own as well as her husband's safety. But something about the boy's behavior simply didn't add up. While it had seemed reasonable that the boy might be in a bit of a state of shock given the traumatic events he had been through that day, following that up with a strange declaration that hadn't made any sense to her but chilled her to the bone nonetheless after not having spoken a single word all day didn't sit right with her. And then there was the way he smiled. It made her shudder just thinking about it. It reminded her of a rabid dog infected with rabies that had terrorized a small town in some old movie she'd seen a long time ago with Roy.

As much as she tried to convince herself that she was being dramatic, that any boy would act strangely after watching their sister and mother get gunned down in the street one after the other, a small nagging feeling that refused to retreat from the forefront of her mind would not allow her to dismiss her anxieties so easily. Even with Roy right beside her, she had lain awake for over an hour, watching Dylan stare unblinkingly up at the old wooden ceiling of the guest bedroom the way a college girl walking alone late at night will keep tabs on a perfectly harmless fellow male student walking down the street behind her, and privately wishing she'd had the good sense to insert Roy between herself and the boy. Finally, when she decided she couldn't take it anymore, she silently crawled out of bed and into the small bathroom adjacent to the guest bedroom, where she'd left her black canvas backpack on the floor next to the white linoleum bathtub.

She dug around in her bag until her hand closed around a small, white, plastic bottle which she removed from the canvas backpack with trembling fingers. She stared at the bottle for a long time, considering it as intently as one might consider a life-altering surgery, which was an apt metaphor for the decision she was about to make. The bottle in her hand was labeled "Midazolam" in large bright-red block letters. The nightmares had started when she was 17, a few months after she'd run away from home. Always the same. It started with her hiding under the bed, a hand clapped to her mouth to keep from crying out as the bedroom door slowly creaked open to reveal a faceless man wearing a blue Dodgers baseball cap identical to her father's. He'd drag her out from under the bed while she screamed for help that never came. And then the pain, like a red-hot ball of lead, would explode in her groin as the monster tore her clothes off, forcing himself inside of her, his laughter audible even above her high-pitched screams.

She would lay in her bed for hours after she'd woken up, crying silently to herself so as not to disturb her roommates. It had gone on like this for around six months, until one night she'd woken up in a psychiatric hospital after a suicide attempt. She'd been there for a couple of weeks until they'd found the right cocktail of drugs that had "stabilized her emotional state," in their words. The only important one in her opinion, however, was the Midazolam. It kept the nightmares away. The last time she had touched this bottle was over a decade ago, around the same time she and Roy had started sleeping together regularly. His warm, safe body, snuggled tightly against hers, had been as effective at keeping away the nightmares as the pills had been. She'd kept the bottle in the back of the medicine cabinet ever since she'd stopped taking them, hoping to God she'd never need to look at it ever again.

Laura sighed heavily. She knew it was irrational, but the way Dylan had smiled at her earlier. It reminded her eerily of the way her father had smiled whenever he'd come into her room at night. The same cold hungry look of a large predator eyeing a fat rabbit. Laura shuddered and shook herself mentally.

"He's just a boy," she reasoned. "He can't hurt you." She glanced into the bathroom mirror. Her blond hair was tousled and her whole face seemed to sag from exhaustion. It suddenly dawned on her how tired she was. She quickly dry-swallowed two of the pills and crept back into the guest bed beside Roy. Feeling drowsiness begin to overtake her, she snuggled close to her sleeping husband, laying her hand gently on his bare chest. With help from the pills, she'd drifted off to sleep, but although her usual nightmares stayed away that night, her dreams were plagued with moonlit eerily silent cornfields that she would enter and become hopelessly lost in and tall, dark, faceless men that stalked her as she frantically ran through the endless rows of corn, desperate for a way out.

CHAPTER 38

Dylan remained awake long after the others had fallen asleep. He hadn't noticed the anxieties of any of the adults, or much of anything else over the past several hours. He had entered his own, private world. The magic man was watching him. He had first seen the magic man chasing Anette in the alleyway before he'd killed her and his mother. As Dylan had watched, the magic man had looked him straight in the eyes and flashed him his signature wicked grin. After that, they had driven away, but the magic man hadn't been left behind. Dylan had nearly screamed aloud when he'd seen the magic man standing on the side of the road next to a defunct Toyota Prius, grinning at him, but some invisible force had glued his jaw shut, and he'd been unable to do so. Somehow, Dylan knew the magic man had done it. Screaming would've alerted Roy and Laura to his presence. The magic man was for Dylan's eyes, and Dylan's eyes alone. He appeared again half an hour later in front of a gas station as they idled their way through a small town in northwest Indiana, still grinning wickedly at him. Dylan had averted his gaze, not wanting to look at him, but he could feel the magic man's icy gaze burning into the back of his skull as they drove past. He'd seen him a few other places that they'd driven past, always casually leaning against some inconspicuous object, grinning like a Cheshire cat.

Dylan had always averted his eyes, but it made no difference when the magic man's gaze penetrated his skull as effectively as a surgeon's drill. Because the magic man wasn't content with simply following Dylan to the various places they passed by. Even when Dylan had closed his eyes to try and block out the magic man, he could see him as if he were painted on the inside of Dylan's eyeballs, his cape billowing behind him in a high wind that mysteriously didn't seem to affect his black top hat, smiling at Dylan. But this smile was no longer gleeful. It was as cold as a dark, moonless night in the dead of winter, and just as unforgiving. Unable to scream, he immediately threw his eyes open again to avoid looking at that terrible face, but there it would be again, posing casually somewhere outside another gas station or truck stop or highway sign. He began to cry in helpless, silent, pleading sobs as night began to fall, begging the magic man to leave him, to let him be free of his terrible smile on a face that was otherwise a bottomless pit of darkness. The magic man's grin seemed to grow wider at the sound of these pleas. And Dylan knew, without the magic man even having to tell him, that no one else could hear his cries.

Now as he lay in bed, staring blankly up at the dark ceiling, he'd given up trying to beg the magic man to leave him alone. He lay on his back, completely stone-cold and devoid of all emotion. The existence of the magic man became another fact of life for Dylan. He felt completely numb, as if the faucet that supplied the cocktail of hormones that governed his ability to feel had been turned off for the lack of paying the enormous bill Dylan had racked up on it over the past several hours. He waited ambivalently for the magic man to come and steal away with him into the night. His overwrought nerves had stretched his ability to fear so thinly that he no longer registered their signals. The way the shadows danced across the dark ceiling in a strange sort of tango with the faint moonlight filtering through the small bedroom window above the oak wooden dresser on the opposite side of the room produced a series of objects on the ceiling above Dylan, none of which particularly interested him.

He saw a shadow dog, a shadow peacock, a shadow orangutang, and a few others, each passing by as aimlessly and meaninglessly as the last. Dylan could feel himself beginning to drift off when another animal appeared at the edge of his vision. Only it wasn't an animal this time. It was a man, or what might have passed for a man, but Dylan knew better. The magic man twirled on the ceiling, his cape billowing out behind, and ended it with a bow, bringing his top hat down over his chest like he had performed a fantastic magic trick for a large crowd. But the magic man needed no large crowd for his magic tricks. Dylan Teryon was all the audience he had in attendance for tonight's show, and that was all he would need.

"Hey kiddo," said the shadow on the ceiling that was the magic man, and Dylan flinched.

The magic man spoke in the voice of his father. The magic man's black cape and top hat vanished, replaced by his father's plaid work shirt and cargo shorts, along with a navy-blue Yankees baseball cap.

"D-dad?" Dylan stammered, sitting up in bed, his mouth hanging openly slightly in shock.

The shadow on the ceiling that had become his father hung its head as if it were ashamed.

"Dad!" Dylan cried, feeling tears stinging his eyes. "Dad, I've missed you so much!"

His father remained silent, staring down at his shadowy hands. Dylan stared at the shadowy figure, his lower lip quivering, willing his father to pick him up, to hug him, to tell him everything would be okay. Instead, his father shook his head in disappointment.

"Dylan," his father said, struggling to keep his voice steady. "Do you remember the last thing I ever said to you the morning of my death?"

"O-of course," Dylan stammered. "You told me to be a man, to protect mom and Anette."

"And did you?" Dylan went silent, suddenly feeling less sure of himself.

"Have you done as I asked?" his father repeated.

"I..." Dylan stammered, struggling for words. "I don't..."

His father shook his head again, and Dylan fell silent.

"I always knew you weren't up to the task," his father said, all the warmth in his voice suddenly gone.

Dylan stuttered, desperate to say something, anything, but there was nothing to say.

"I always knew you were weak!" his father exploded, suddenly jumping to his feet.

Dylan recoiled, whimpering. He'd never seen his father angry before.

"They're dead Dylan, THEY'RE FUCKING DEAD!" he screamed.

"I'm sorry!" Dylan cried, tears spilling down his face. "I'm so sorry, dad!"

"You disappoint me, son," his father muttered, pacing angrily back and forth. "You disappoint me so much, I just..."

He paused, and Dylan held his breath, silently begging his father not to say whatever he was about to say. His father shook his head.

"I cannot have a spoiled child that breaks down when things get difficult," he said coldly.

"Dad, I'm not..." Dylan pleaded.

"Someone who destroys his mother's things when he is angry," he plowed on ruthlessly, and Dylan fell silent, the image of the hole in the kitchen wall flashing through his mind.

"Your mother and I, we have put up with a lot from you. Even when you were taken away, your mother fought like hell to get you back, but you are just out of control, and I..."

"Dad," Dylan whispered. "Dad, please, don't leave me."

"You are no son of mine," his father said coldly.

Dylan threw himself back onto the bed, sobbing his eyes out while his father watched, no hint of sympathy in his gaze.

"I tried Dylan. I really did," he said. "Goodbye." And with a tiny pop, he was gone.

"Dad!" Dylan wailed, sobbing uncontrollably. "Dad, I'm so sorry, I'm so sorry..." Dylan sobbed, the mattress stained with his tears.

The magic man, concealed in the shadows in the corner of the room, grinned at his handiwork. He pulled a large silver coin from his jacket pocket and held it up to the faint moonlight streaming the window, examining it.

"Wanna see a magic trick, old buddy?" the magic man whispered in Dylan's ear.

"No," Dylan choked out, turning away from the voice. "I don't want anything from you,"

The Puppeteer's smile quickly faded. Suddenly, Dylan cried out in pain and grabbed his ear as a painful, prickly, burning sensation erupted just beneath his earlobe. He heard a soft thump on the mattress, and the pain died away as quickly as it had come. Lying on the mattress was a bright, round, shiny U.S. quarter that looked as new as if it had just come hot off the coin press. Dylan stared blankly at the coin for a few seconds before he realized that it was not George Washington staring up at him from the heads side. It was his father, standing next to his mother and sister in front of the house they'd lived in before his father died. Only they all had their backs turned to Dylan, refusing to look at him, their expressions cold and emotionless.

"FUCK YOU!" Dylan screamed, tossing the coin across the room where it struck the opposite wall and landed soundlessly on the carpet. "FUCK YOU, FUCK YOU, FUCK YOU!" LEAVE ME ALONE, LEAVE US ALL ALONE!

THEY'RE GONE, THEY'RE FUCKING GONE AND I COULDN'T SAVE THEM!" Finally exhausted, Dylan collapsed back onto the tear-stained mattress. He curled himself into a fetal position, crying silently to himself. But no matter how many hours Dylan Teryon spent after that lying awake, silently begging for forgiveness, it made no difference. His family was gone.

CHAPTER 39

Cetan Aung stumbled drunkenly down the deserted, rubbish-strewn city street, his M16 strapped over his shoulder, his expression unreadable. His eyes glanced lazily at the body of an old African American man lying with his back against the bricked side of an old laundromat, an expression of horror permanently frozen on his weathered face, a river of dried blood extending from a bullet hole that punched cleanly through his neck. Cetan smiled bemusedly at the sight. More of his master's good work, he had no doubt. Another human cockroach wiped from existence before it could bring any more suffering to the world. As he continued down the street past an abandoned hotel, he saw the lifeless bodies of two twin girls wearing matching sky-blue party dresses, stained with blood, lying in the entryway.

The face of the smaller one rested on the shoulder of the older one, her eyes closed. The older one's eyes were open, glaring accusingly at Cetan. There was a pistol lying in the older one's hand. He smirked at the sight. Whichever servant had killed them (and Cetan was aware, even then, that he could not be the only one) had done the world a great service. They would've undoubtedly joined THEM otherwise, toting rifles of their own and gunning down his master's servants in dark alleys when their backs were turned. Cetan sighed as the memory of his parents' deaths flashed through his mind. But there would be more, no doubt. The human race was like a plague that never stopped, blighting everything in their path until there was nothing more left. Cetan was nervous.

His master had warned him that THEY were everywhere. The human race bred like rats, multiplying by the millions to inflict their pain and suffering on the world. Even now, he was sure they were watching him, savoring his fear. He shot a nervous glance over his shoulder. It always paid to be alert to your surroundings. The marine corps, as well as his parents, had taught him that very well. Cetan bared his teeth. It would be all the more satisfying to see the stunned looks on their faces when he and his master struck first, spilling their blood and organs before them, laughing as the light slowly left their eyes while they bled to death in the street. And he wouldn't have to wait long. His master had assured him of that. His master had a plan, and he was nearly ready to set it into motion.

He stopped beside a small local post office, suddenly feeling very alert. He gazed up into the sky, an expression of serenity rolling slowly over his face like a gentle breeze. He heard the voice. His master's voice.

"Cetan…" it growled. He smiled joyfully at the sound of that voice. It filled his belly with a warm glow, the way his mother's hot soup used to.

"Cetan, I have an assignment for you," his master growled in his ear.

120

"I'm ready, master," Cetan said, grinning broadly like a child opening a large box on Christmas day.

"Good," his master replied, and Cetan could sense that his master was grinning down at him from somewhere high above.

"There is a woman, Cetan. A very important woman named Jody Razitsky."

Cetan nodded to show he understood. As if on cue, an image of a tall, physically fit, brunette woman in her mid to late twenties swam into view in front of him. Cetan stared at it intently.

"Now Cetan, listen to me very carefully," his master continued. "This woman is very important to me, but she is also very dangerous. You see, she is the one who controls THEM."

The instant his master mentioned THEM, Cetan immediately became hyper alert, all sense of dazedness vanished in an instant.

"She is going to lead an army of THEM against me, Cetan, and I need you to stop her."

Cetan nodded, slinging his rifle over his shoulder, and holding it up to the darkening late afternoon sky to show he was ready.

Cetan stared into the face of the young woman, his grip on the rifle tightening, his face slowly turning red with anger.

"She killed my mom and dad, didn't she?" Cetan said. It wasn't meant to be a question. He knew. THEY had killed his parents, the cowards who shot people in the back down dark alleyways, the same ones who had ordered him to murder innocent civilians. The sickness that was the human race, the one he and his master would soon purge for good, by murdering this Razitsky woman. Cetan turned his face to the sky and let out a feral roar that howled through the empty streets and shook the window panes on nearby buildings. Cetan, breathing hard, holstered the rifle, knowing it would be put to good use later. Because that Razitsky woman was going to be staring the business end of the rifle's barrel soon.

The Puppeteer, standing nearby, watched Cetan stalk out of the alleyway, rifle slung over his shoulder, murder written on his face, and grinned wolfishly.

CHAPTER 40

Maria Veranda stared out the passenger side window of the Chevrolet Equinox as it rolled down interstate 70 through West Virginia, passing by endless rows of empty rolling farm fields, the animals having long fled. Maria had spent the entire day pointedly refusing to look her father in the face and hating herself for it. The glassy eyed expression she wore as she stared at the empty landscape concealed the violent tropical storm battering at the wooden pillars that held her mind together. Her two most fundamental instincts, her undying love for her father and her need to protect herself and her mother had been fighting all day, tearing her mind apart in the process. She had loved her father to death from the moment she was born, and she had always been his sweet baby girl.

No one in the world had done more throughout her seventeen years on this Earth to love her, care about her, or dote her on, even on things as stupid as middle school crushes. But as she stared aimlessly at the twinkling stars in the cloudless night sky, those things seemed to be a million miles away, pushed into some dark closet of her brain and forgotten about. And the only thing that remained was that terrible image of her father standing next to the hot tub, staring impassively down at the lifeless body of Michael Pines. A small voice had been speaking in her ear on and off all day, telling her to grab her mother and run. She had pushed it from her mind, knowing it was irrational, but it persisted, growing a little more persuasive with each iteration.

Lying across the back seat of the Chevrolet, to Maria's great relief, her mother had managed to enter a seemingly peaceful sleep. She'd complained about a headache a few hours ago, about an hour after they'd left D.C. behind them, so Maria had reluctantly switched seats with her. Thankfully, her father, who seemed to be concentrating on his driving, hadn't spoken a word to her. At first, she'd felt a little pinch of sadness, sitting there next to him but feeling as though she were a million miles away, but then the image of Michael's dead body flashed through her mind, and the feeling had immediately died. Now, several hours later, she was just praying he would leave her alone. She kept shooting nervous glances at the gun holstered in her father's waistband, a little voice whispering in her ear each time that he would surely turn it on her. She remembered the look she'd seen in her father's eyes back in the gas station in D.C. It had been a look of recognition.

"He knows," the little voice whispered in her head. "Somehow, he knows that you know about the murder." The thought was enough to cause Maria to shudder violently.

She turned around to check on her mother and was a little taken aback at her haggard appearance. All the lines on her face appeared to be stretched beyond recognition, making her look as though she had aged thirty years. She also seemed unnaturally pale, like all the color in her face had been washed away. Dismissing it as a trick of her imagination brought on by her own exhaustion, Maria settled back into the passenger seat and returned her gaze to the densely packed pine trees passing by on either side of them. She closed her eyes, doing her best to push the thoughts of her father's gun from her mind. David, for his part, was concentrating all his might on keeping the car steady on the uneven road in front of him, doing his best to forget the terrible events of the day. Neither of them noticed when Anna let out a low moan of pain from the backseat.

About an hour later, they pulled into the empty parking lot of a deserted Holiday Inn in the small town of St. Clairsville, Ohio. David was unperturbed by the darkened windows or the shattered double glass door panels that had once functioned as automatic doors but now resembled a pair of dead, haunted eyes staring out at the nonexistent street goers. He figured if anything, the fact that the place was abandoned meant it was safe for them to sleep there, at least for the night. As they exited the car, Maria watched as her mother, now paler than ever, stumbled drunkenly out of the back seat, and Maria had to grab her to keep her from falling over onto the pavement. She gasped when she felt her mother's icy hands. Anna smiled at her daughter and straightened up.

"Thanks baby, it's nothing, just tired is all," she said as cheerily as she could manage.

Maria managed a small smile, but privately, she thought her mother sounded far more than merely tired, and her haggard appearance only added to Maria's worries.

David stood with his hands on his hips, gazing up at the hotel and around the parking lot for signs of life, completely oblivious to the interaction between his wife and daughter.

"Alright, looks like we should be safe here for tonight," he said matter of factly, turning to Anna, who managed a weak smile in response. He turned hesitantly to Maria, unsure of the reaction he was going to get in response. He had spent the last several hours turning what happened at the gas station over and over in his mind, and with every single turn, he managed to loop back to that look Maria had given him when he had held out his hand to embrace her. It was about the worst look a father could ever imagine receiving from his daughter: an acidic mixture of revulsion and fear, as if she'd caught him with another woman in their house. Somehow, she knew he'd killed Michael. He didn't know how, but the thought that she might be afraid of him because of his actions chilled him to the bone.

He shook his head, irritated. There would be a time and place to talk to Maria properly, but right now, standing out in the chilly night air in front of a near-perfect sanctuary, if only a temporary one, was not that time or place.

"Maria, get your mother inside so she can lie down," he said as evenly as he could muster. "I've got to take the car back out to see if I can refill the gas tank."

Maria stared at him coldly, and for a moment, David actually thought she was going to refuse, when she wordlessly took her mother by the arm and walked her towards the broken glass panel doors. David watched them go for a moment, hating the way Maria refused to meet his gaze but knowing at the same time that he deserved it, nonetheless, and got back in the Chevrolet, throwing one last look at the pair of them as he drove away. Maria didn't return it.

Maria Veranda half carried her mother, who was leaning heavily on her the entire time, into the lobby of the Holiday Inn, and laid her down as gently as she could manage on a sturdy-looking, brown, leather couch that sat in the middle of the room. Her mother, despite the surprising stiffness of the couch cushions, laid down on her back gratefully, smiling weakly at her daughter.

"Thanks, kiddo," she murmured.

Maria laid a cool hand against her mother's forehead and jerked it back in surprise as if she'd accidentally touched a hot griddle. Her mother was running a high fever, at least one hundred and two degrees in Maria's relatively conservative estimation (some small part of her still wanted to believe this was nothing more than a passing bug, a notion the larger, more rational part of her rejected).

Her mother must've seen the worry etched in her face, because after a moment she dismissed it with a small wave of her hand, saying, "I'm fine, baby, I'm fine, don't worry about me, I just need some sleep that's all, I'm just a bit tired."

This did not mitigate Maria's anxieties, who heard what her mother was really saying in her tone of voice: "I'm sick baby, I'm sick real bad and I need help, and I need it real bad."

But no help was coming, and Maria knew it, not with the state the world was in. She hung her head, ashamed, tears beginning to well up in her dark brown eyes. She felt as helpless as she'd been when she was seven years old and her mother had forgotten that school let out two hours early, and she'd stood crying on the school playground, abandoned by the other children who had already gone home, until the principal had come out and taken her into his office.

In that moment, she felt like that young child crying loudly on the school playground. She wanted nothing more than to curl up into a ball on the floor and allow the tears to overwhelm her, the same way they had back then. But then she saw the dreadfully exhausted look on her mother's face, and it was suddenly the present day again, and she remembered who she really was. She fiercely wiped away the tears on her face, knowing they had no business there. She rested lovingly against her mother's burning cheek, trying her best to feign a smile.

"It's alright mom, I'm right here," she said, doing her best to keep her voice from shaking. Her mother returned a strained smile.

"I know, love," she murmured, rubbing her forehead with a grimace. "I'd love to just sleep it off, but my head's killing me."

"I'll go find some Tylenol," Maria said quickly before her mother could ask.

Anna smiled.

"You're a good girl Maria, you know that, right?"

Maria smiled.

"I know mom." But even as she hurried away, she felt that little girl on the playground creep back into her memory, who didn't understand why things happened the way they did, who asked, "Mommy, why did this happen?" in her high-pitched little girl's voice. Glancing back at her exhausted and sickly mother, present-day Maria privately asked the same question.

About an hour after Maria had finished administering Ibuprofen to her mother that she had found left behind in one of the medicine cabinets, David Veranda pulled the Chevrolet up to the front doors of the hotel, sweaty and exhausted, but the kind of exhausted where you know you had gotten that way by some important accomplishment like a runner after winning a 3200M relay at a state track meet. In the trunk of the Chevrolet lay two full, brick-red, five-gallon gas cans. He looked at the dark windows of the hotel, many of them broken, peering down at him like a crowd of half-starved Roman citizens hungrily anticipating a gladiator match, and felt a shiver pass down his spine. But it would have to do at least for tonight. When David entered the hotel lobby, he saw his wife passed out on the couch opposite the concierge's desk, and Maria was sitting in an armchair by the extinguished electric fireplace, reading an old paperback she'd taken off the concierge's desk. Not wanting to disturb his wife, David removed his trainers and walked across the tile floor in his socks.

When he sat down in the second armchair next to Maria, her eyes glanced at him briefly, and then immediately to a novel emblazoned "Anne of Green Gables" on the front cover in black block letters. Maria was trying with all her might not to look at him, but it did almost no good, because she could still sense him there, looming over her like a tall shadow a small child might mistake for a demonic presence on their bedroom wall. She shot a nervous glance at the gun clasped to his waistband and quickly looked away, refusing to allow herself to dwell on what he might do with it. They both sat in silence, staring at the cold, empty fireplace, neither of them knowing what to say to the other. Finally, Maria stood up quickly and strode out the room, the paperback under her arm. David knew better than to follow her.

CHAPTER 41

Tyson Saunders sat stiffly behind the wheel of the Ford-F150, doing a steady sixty-five down the four-lane highway that was route 78 through Northeastern New Jersey. They swept past a sign that read "You are now entering Lebanon." Sweat dripped steadily down his face. His facial muscles were so tense that the skin on his face appeared to be pulled taut over the bones, giving him an almost skeletal appearance, which was helped by the fact that he was also extremely pale, and had been for the last several hours. Every few minutes, he glanced in the back seat at Marianne, who was again unconscious. His lip quivered at the sound of that terrible word. What made it worse was the fact that she'd barely been conscious at all the last several days.

She'd faded in and out of consciousness several times the previous night, when they'd stayed in a unit at an empty apartment building nearby. Tyson had stayed awake by her beside the entire night, with no regard for his own desperate need for rest. He glanced back at Marianne again. She looked smaller and more helpless than ever, and he felt his anxiety tick up another notch.

"There'll be something real soon," he muttered under his breath as they passed a Sonic franchise with almost all the windows blown out. "Real soon, baby." As they passed by an exit sign advertising a Marriott hotel just off the main road, he heard a small cough from the back seat.

He glanced in the rearview mirror and saw that Marianne was slowly sitting up.

"Hey baby, you up?" Tyson asked, feeling the massive weight of anxiety raise itself from his shoulders. Marianne rubbed the sleep from her eyes, and glanced out the window at the large white farmhouses they were passing.

"Daddy, where are we?" she asked. Her voice sounded a little stronger now, to Tyson's relief.

"Hopefully somewhere good, baby," Tyson said, glancing around as they passed through the surrounding town in search of a hospital or even a small medical clinic. Marianne let out a series of small, very dry coughs from somewhere deep in her chest. Every single cough felt to Tyson like a stab with a hot poker to his stomach. He opened up the glove compartment, and to his great relief, a pair of unopened plastic water bottles stared back out at him. He handed one back to Marianne, who began to suck on it gratefully.

"Feel better?" he asked after a minute.

Marianne smiled weakly at him in the rearview mirror in reply, which Tyson cheerfully returned. She collapsed back onto the seat, exhausted, staring out the window thoughtfully as they passed by a small church with an American flag posted out front. As they made their way down main street, Tyson's worry slowly began to return. The more they saw of the town, the surer Tyson became that they were going to have to keep moving. Apart from not seeing anything resembling a functioning medical facility, Tyson hadn't seen a single living person in the street or in any of the buildings they'd passed, all of which had their shades drawn and their windows dark. Marianne yawned and slumped further into the back seat as they approached a sign that read "Now leaving Lebanon township."

Tyson had to restrain himself from slamming the steering wheel with the heel of his hand in frustration as they approached it. Yet another hope dashed. They must have passed through at least half a dozen small towns exactly like this one over the last several hours, and the result had been the same each time: boarded up businesses, dark windows, empty streets, completely abandoned. How far would they have to travel before they found a living soul, let alone one that could help Marianne, and would she even make it that long? He glanced back at her nervously. She was slumped against the seat, staring off at the barren, empty countryside in the distance. Her eyes, which bore the beginnings of dark circles underneath them, were half-shut. As Tyson turned back to the road as they were pulling out of Lebanon, his mind flashed back to the terrible destruction they'd seen at the Mountainside medical center, and he felt his blood pressure tick up a few notches. The odds of them finding a functioning medical facility seemed to be growing longer with each passing minute. He glanced nervously at his daughter in the rearview mirror, who had fallen asleep.

"God, what am I going to do?" Tyson thought, running a hand over his aching forehead in exasperation.

They drove in silence for about an hour after that. Marianne watched the small towns and road signs of Northwest New Jersey come and go out the window, fading in and out of consciousness every few minutes. When she came to, a light sweat was always plastered to her forehead.

"Daddy," Marianne murmured so quietly that Tyson almost didn't hear her as they passed by a sign announcing they were entering the town of Clinton. "My stomach hurts."

Tyson sighed heavily as they passed a large, white-tiled building labeled "YMCA." He rooted around in the glove compartment with his free hand for a bottle of Ibuprofen or Advil. No such luck.

"Drink some more water," Tyson said, knowing it wasn't much but not seeing any better options. "We're going to get you some help soon, I promise," he said, more to himself than to her as they passed by a sign that announced that they would reach Reading, Pennsylvania ten miles down the road.

"Okay, daddy," Marianne whispered, curling up into a ball in her seat.

Tyson sighed, praying she wouldn't start crying. Any strength he'd had in his beyond-exhausted muscles had vanished like a candle flame that had been snuffed out, and he was no longer sure he even possessed the strength to comfort her in the event that she broke down. Somewhere behind him, he heard Marianne gasp sharply as if she'd had the wind knocked out of her. She leaned over the seat and vomited the remains of a half-eaten bagel she'd eaten cold out of a stranger's fridge that morning all over the floor. She moaned in pain and wiped her mouth with the back of her sleeve.

"Daddy?" she asked, and the nervousness in her voice was perhaps the worst part of all this for Tyson. "Am I going to be okay?"

It was the question he'd dreaded having to answer, but he hadn't known just how much until it came rolling out of her mouth like a great ball of rock blasted out of a cannon at the walls that were holding his sanity together. He opened his mouth to reply, then closed it again. He wanted to tell her something, anything to relieve the terrible fear he saw in her dark eyes she'd inherited from her wonderful mother, but there was nothing he could say. Tyson stared out at the road ahead, unable to meet his daughter's wide-eyed gaze. It was the worst possible thing he could've done. She stared at him for several minutes longer before it finally dawned on her what his lack of response meant. Very slowly, as if she were a caterpillar crawling into a chrysalis, she curled up into a ball in the back seat, her arms surrounding her knees, her whole body shaking with dry, heaving sobs. Tyson felt his lower lip tremble at the sight.

CHAPTER 42

Jody Razitsky woke up in an unfamiliar yet comfortable bed, an oval-shaped light fixture affixed to a whitewashed ceiling, bathing the entire room in soft golden glow. Outside the bedroom bay window, the bright, mid-morning sunlight smiled back at her through the white linen curtains slowly fluttering in the slight breeze filtering through the open window. Jody sat up slowly, rubbing the sleep from her eyes, wincing slightly as her aching muscles groaned in protest. She felt as though she had run an entire marathon the day before and had collapsed into bed while forgetting to stretch or ice properly. As if in agreement, her stomach grumbled irritably. She glanced around the bedroom, hugging her knees up to her chest like a small child who is resisting his parents' repeated demands that they get out of bed. A small night table still laden with artifacts from the former owners of the house stood to her left, tucked under another smaller bedroom window draped with the same style of white linen curtains.

A large dresser sat in the corner next to the bay window, several of the drawers hanging open with their contents scattered aimlessly on the hardwood mahogany floor. A large ornately framed mirror hung on the wall above the dresser. A child's lime-green foam football lay on top of the dresser along with a scattering of personal items that had been left behind. The room gave off an air of tranquility, as if it had been cut off from the madness that had taken over the outside world over the last several days, and Jody felt a sense of comfort cradled on this bed that had been absent from her life since she was a small child sleeping in her parents' loving arms. This was a common occurrence at the end of family movie nights, especially on the weekends when she usually managed to convince her parents to let her stay up until the end of the movie on the basis that there was no need for her to wake up for school the next morning. She would sit between her mother and father on their old yet exquisitely comfortable sofa, and stare at the soft glow of the television screen, her expression a sense of wonder that is only possible to achieve in childhood, when the bittersweet realities of the world have not yet set in.

"Hey," came a little girl's voice.

Jody sat up in bed, coming face to face with Kaitlyn. She was wearing her favorite pink Hello Kitty t-shirt and black slacks. Her dark hair fluttered around her head in the breeze blowing in through the open window. She smiled nervously, but Jody could see that her brow was furrowed with worry.

"You, okay?" she asked.

Jody lay back on the bed, the image of her father's savage gaze flashing through her mind as he raised the knife already stained with her mother's blood. She slowly shook her head.

129

"Yeah, didn't think so," Kaitlyn said, sitting down on the bed next to Jody and wrapping an arm gently around her shoulders.

Jody laid her head on childhood best friend's shoulder. They sat in silence for several moments before Kaitlyn spoke again.

"I'm sorry," she said.

Jody shook her head sadly. A single tear slid down her cheek.

"It doesn't make sense," she said, wiping her eyes dry. "It just doesn't make sense."

"I know, kid," Kaitlyn said, pulling Jody closer to her. "I know."

The room blurred around Jody as tears began to stream freely down her face.

"Why would he do it?" she wailed. "How could he kill mom? HOW COULD HE LEAVE ME LIKE THIS?"

"A lot of people have monsters inside," Kaitlyn said, gently stroking Jody's hair. "Your father, he..." Kaitlyn paused, choosing her words carefully. "He went through a lot at an age where no child should have to see the things he did. He chose Mauvilla to raise his family because it was quiet, secluded, and there was a good community there, three things he'd never had before. He left that life behind."

"So, then what happened?" Jody asked, wiping the tears from her face. "Why is my mother dead, Kaitlyn?"

Kaitlyn shook her head, struggling for the right words.

"Why, Kaitlyn?" Jody begged. "Please, I have to know."

Kaitlyn hesitated.

"There's something here, Jody. Something dark."

Jody's blood immediately ran cold. The look in Leo's eyes, the look in her father's eyes, flashed through her mind.

"He is taking them, Jody. I don't know how, but he's..."

"I was born sick, Jody..." Leo's words echoed in her mind.

Jody knew Leo's backstory.

"He saw his mother," Jody whispered. "The night she threw him out into the street. Kaitlyn, he's using their worst nightmares against them. That's why they're doing these things. That's why...my dad..." Jody broke down into another fit of hysterical sobbing.

Kaitlyn remained silent, comforting her best friend while she sobbed her heart out on Kaitlyn's shoulder.

"You can't let it control you, Jody," Kaitlyn whispered.

Jody looked up, tears still blurring her vision.

"What?"

"Your trauma," Kaitlyn said. "You can't let it control you. Your father succumbed. Leo succumbed. But you can't. You are strong, Jody. More than that you have strength of character. He can't control you easily."

Jody stared at her best friend, speechless. Kaitlyn suddenly looked more grown up than Jody had ever seen her.

"You are their last hope, Jody. You are the last candle flame in an otherwise dark world." Kaitlyn took Jody's hands in both her own, smiling wanly at her best friend.

"Kaitlyn..." Jody started to say.

Kaitlyn held up a finger to shush her.

"You have to find the others, Jody. You have to take them to the river and carry out the ritual. It's the only way."

Kaitlyn leaned over, so that her mouth was next to Jody's ear.

"You are the firelight, Jody. Spread it. Show this world how to find their way again. You are the best hope they have. Make them trust you."

Jody closed her eyes, embracing her best friend, and when she opened them again, Kaitlyn was gone.

Jody curled up into a fetal position on the bed, suddenly feeling more than alone than ever in the deep silence that had settled over the room. Suddenly, a stimulus cut across her mind like a bolt of lightning. A wild, terrified scream. The feeling of ice-cold water invading her mouth and nose, suffocating her...Jody whimpered and squeezed her eyes shut until the feeling faded. Despite the warmth of the late summer sun streaming in through the large bedroom window, Jody felt cold all over, as if she'd been submerged in ice cold water in real life and not merely in her imagination.

Barely realizing what she was doing, Jody threw herself off of the once comfortable bed that now felt to her like a rock-hard, piss-stained jail cell mattress and stormed out of the room, throwing the bedroom door open hard enough to bang it against the opposite wall. Suddenly, her feet had carried her into the small bathroom down the hall from the bedroom, and she was leaning over the sink, staring into its depths with a pensive expression on her face. She looked into the mirror above the sink. She gave off the air of a woman who hadn't gotten any sleep the previous night. There were dark circles underneath her eyes, and her dark hair was mussed. The image of a knife held by an unseen hand flying silently through the air towards her flashed through her mind, and she tore her eyes away from the mirror, breathing hard, a thin sheen of sweat breaking out on her forehead.

"Immergo..."

A horrible feeling of dread suddenly gripped Jody like a vice. She'd heard the word before, she was sure of it. Jody shuddered violently. The temperature in the room suddenly felt as though it had dropped twenty degrees.

"Immergo..."

Jody let out a cry that was cut off instantly by the feeling of water forcibly invading her mouth and nose, as if she were experiencing waterboard torture.

"Jody..." came Kaitlyn's voice suddenly. "The ritual must be performed. It's up to you."

Jody hung her head, unable to look at herself in the mirror. She was gripping the marble countertop so hard her fingernails left small white scratches.

"Don't you see?" she thought miserably. "I can't stop him. No one can."

"That's what he wants you to think!" Kaitlyn replied, more urgently this time.

"You know what you have to do, Jody."

"Immergo..."

A sudden rush of anger overtook her. Jody threw her head back so that she was looking up at the ceiling, where she knew Kaitlyn was hiding, invisible to her but nonetheless present.

"I DON'T FUCKING KNOW WHAT YOU WANT!" she screamed. "I DON'T FUCKING KNOW HOW TO STOP HIM! HE DOESN'T JUST HAVE THE DARKNESS ON HIS SIDE, HE IS THE FUCKING DARKNESS, DON'T YOU GET IT! HE'S A DEMON, AND WE'RE JUST HIS PLAYTHINGS! I CAN'T STOP HIM AND NEITHER CAN ANYONE ELSE, SO STOP FUCKING SENDING ME THESE FUCKING MEMORIES AND BULLSHIT WORDS, I DON'T FUCKING KNOW WHAT ANY OF IT MEANS AND I DON'T FUCKING CARE!"

She collapsed onto the floor, shaking with anger, tears blurring her vision. Kaitlyn was silent, as if she were choosing her next words very carefully, and Jody prayed Kaitlyn would just stay quiet and leave her alone.

"You got my father killed," she whispered under her breath. "You fucking got my father killed because you couldn't just let me have a normal life, no, god forbid, you sucked me into your goddamned power struggle, now everyone I know and love is dead because of you, so just leave me the fuck alone."

Kaitlyn said nothing. Jody Razitsky curled up on the floor of the small bathroom into a fetal position and cried soundlessly.

CHAPTER 43

Benjamin Alrite was nervous. Although he tried his best to conceal this fact from the four others in the vehicle who had come to depend on him as their rock, their sanctuary from the living nightmare they were all in the midst of, he had become uncannily aware of the tremor in his hands that had steadily worsened the further they'd driven along Interstate 95 through southeastern New Jersey into Philadelphia, past the defunct cars that littered the shoulders, and occasionally spilled out onto the road itself like something out of an apocalyptic horror film, their window panes lying shattered on the asphalt below, bullet holes littering their rusting metal corpses. More than once, Ben had been forced to take the SUV very carefully onto the shoulder to squeeze around traffic jams, sure that each time, the vehicle would roll over into the ditch and kill them all, but thankfully, he had barely managed to keep it upright each time. Jason's black Volvo idled along just behind them with Lorenzo and the others.

But even with the apocalyptic horror show that had been Interstate 95, it wasn't until they'd entered downtown Philadelphia that Ben, his knuckles white on the steering wheel as they idled past a 711 with most of the window panes thrown out into the street, where they lay in tiny, glittering fragments in the late afternoon sunlight, had begun to notice the bodies. They seemed to be everywhere, so numerous that they appeared to have rained down from the sky in some places, some still sitting upright in the driver's seats of abandoned vehicles, bullet wounds still leaking blood from their foreheads, some flung out into the roadway, a few hanging from the bridges they passed under by nooses. Ben had tried to tear his eyes away from these awful sights, but he could feel their cold, empty eyes on the back of his head, as if they were glaring at him and demanding that he acknowledge their presence. Now, passing by a UPS office with the front door torn clean off its hinges and one side of the building completely destroyed from what looked like a grenade, Ben saw the nearly toothless corpse of the old postmaster behind the shattered front bay window, grinning at him from behind the counter, a pair of bullet holes dried shut with congealed blood protruding from his light blue crewneck. Ben could imagine the man asking him politely what he could help him with today, and the thought sent shivers racing up his spine.

He felt a familiar comforting hand on his shoulder and didn't have to turn around to know it was his wife's. Even her gentle touch did little to soothe him.

"Ben, are you alright?" Jennifer asked, her voice laced with concern.

Ben didn't trust himself to reply. He forced himself to concentrate on the road as he maneuvered the SUV around an overturned tractor trailer, its cargo, an old, rusted John Deere tractor, buried halfway into the brick wall of a small local bank across the street. Jennifer, after waiting for nearly a full minute for any sort of response from her husband, finally lay back against the seat in defeat, feeling useless. Grace, who hadn't said a single word for the last several hours, seemed to sense her mother's nervousness.

"Mommy, are you okay?" she asked, her voice trembling nervously.

"I'm alright, baby," Jennifer murmured, embracing her only child. "Everything's gonna be alright." Jennifer, as she gently stroked her daughter's hair, privately wondered if she believed the sentiment herself.

Serena woke up with a jolt as Jason brought the Volvo to a sudden halt. She looked out the windshield, only to see Ben exiting the SUV, which had pulled over in front of them. Jason and Mike exchanged a look somewhere between worry and confusion. They could see Ben leaning on the driver's side door of the SUV, rubbing his sweaty forehead as if he were developing a bad migraine, a deep sense of distress etched into his expression.

"Think he's alright?" Jason asked. Mike didn't answer right away. He knew that look. It was the same look he'd worn that time he'd shown up at Mike's door one night after a fight with Jennifer, at the time pregnant with Grace, who had told Ben point blank he had to do something about the cigarettes, or she was going to leave him.

"I'll go talk to him," Mike said finally, opening the passenger side door. Jason watched Mike nervously approach Ben. Ben, who was staring helplessly up into the rapidly darkening evening sky, turned as Mike approached. His gaze was immediately drawn to the grip of Mike's Desert Eagle poking out of his waistband, and Ben found himself wishing desperately that he had a gun of his own.

"You alright, man?" Mike asked as he approached Ben, the shadow of an abandoned office building that had lost nearly all its windows on the first three stories and sported large holes in the walls in several places looming over them. The corpse of a bullet hole-riddled young man clad in a sharp black business suit lay in front of the concierge's desk, a sight that Mike remained transfixed by for a full ten seconds before finally managing to tear his eyes away. Ben continued to stare wordlessly at the concierge's rotting corpse, shaking his head sadly.

"You know what this is, old friend?" Ben asked, gesturing to the ruin in front of them.

Mike didn't reply. He didn't need to. They were both thinking the same thing.

"This is the end. Not just the end of law and order like you said earlier. It's the end of the whole goddamn world, and we're the lucky ones who get to stand here and watch it fucking happen." On the word "fucking," Ben's voice took on a note of defeat that struck a chord of raw, unbridled fear in Mike.

Had it not been for Ben's unwavering determination to push on the last several days, Mike had no doubt that he would've hung himself by now, and the others would've almost certainly done the same. Ben, intentionally or not, had been their rock in the midst of the unrelenting nightmare they were trapped in. To hear that quavering note of hopelessness in Ben's voice now was profoundly disturbing and created an array of possibilities that Mike was almost certain he couldn't afford to face.

"You're right," Mike said, gazing up along with Ben at the dark, hollow windows, many of their panes lying shattered in the street. "This is the end of the world, old friend."

Ben nodded slowly.

"You notice something else?" Mike asked. "We're the only ones here to witness it. Listen."

Ben obeyed and realized that the only sound he could detect was the faint gusts of wind blowing back and forth along the street.

"We're really alone," Ben said after a moment.

Mike nodded.

"All of civilization gone, just like that."

There it was again. That note of utter defeat that chilled Mike to the bone. Ben slowly removed the Smith and Wesson 500 from his waistband, and gazed at it like he was sizing up an overly large pill his doctor had prescribed him. Mike shot it a nervous glance, briefly considering the possibility Ben might be thinking of using it on himself.

"This is all it took," Ben said, suddenly sounding angry. He brandished the gun at Mike, who recoiled slightly. "This is all it fucking took to destroy civilization. A few bullets. How fucking ridiculous is that?"

Mike, for his part, didn't find it ridiculous at all. He had suddenly become very aware of the jagged scar racing across his neckline that had resulted from a knife wound he'd received during a prison riot. When he'd woken up in the ER, the doctor had told him the blade had missed his aorta by millimeters. Seven people, including two guards, both of whom had children at home, had died that day. Mike, without saying a word, carefully slid his way through the double doors rife with gleaming shards of broken glass that marked the entrance of the former office building.

Ben watched as his best friend walked over to the dead body of the concierge, carefully laid him flat on the ground, and slid his eyes closed as gently as a mother putting her newborn to bed.

"Maybe we're here for a reason, old friend," Mike said as he carefully walked back through the broken glass doors towards Ben, who was staring at him with something almost like awe. Mike smiled and clapped him on the shoulder.

"Maybe we're meant to fix all this shit." He looked back at the building, a pensive expression clouding his face. "You never know," he said under his breath. "Even I could maybe put some good out into this world."

Ben glanced behind them at the late-afternoon sun that was quickly disappearing behind a tall office tower a few blocks away.

"We should get out of here," Ben said, tugging on Mike's shirt sleeve. "It'll be dark soon."

"You're right," Mike replied, "we can't stay in the city tonight. We should at least get to the outskirts before the sun goes down. But there's a lot of potentially useful resources here. Food, water, gas, maybe even weapons. I say we camp on the edge of the city tonight and then come back tomorrow and take whatever is left."

Ben nodded.

"I saw a Walmart a few blocks up the road," Mike continued as they started back in the direction of the vehicles. "We can bring back some supplies for tonight if we hurry."

After letting the others know the plan, and leaving Jason Ben's Smith and Wesson in case any problems arose, they hurried off down the road in the direction of the massive blue and white sign sitting just above the horizon in the distance, unaware that the series of events they were walking into would change the fate of the world forever.

CHAPTER 44

Jody Razitsky had spent the last several days walking a long road to nowhere, which had slowly deteriorated into a half-shuffle, half-stumble like a walking corpse in one of those old black and white zombie apocalypse films, which wasn't far from the state she was in at the moment. The hours and days had begun to blur together for her so that the only remaining indicator of the amount of time that had passed had become the rising and falling of the sun. As she wandered her way aimlessly through the war-torn streets of Philadelphia, each stumble step threatening to spill her onto the blood and glass-soaked ground beneath her, she thought she heard a child laughing from somewhere far off. She glanced around at the broken buildings and heaps of rubble lying in the street around her on top of a blanket of broken glass, blood, and body parts, as if hoping to see the culprit standing in the midst of the anarchy, smiling and motioning for Jody to come join her. As she sauntered along, she began to wonder vaguely if the child had been real or not and quickly found that she didn't give a damn. As her body broke down and her resistance deteriorated, she found she was coming to terms with the fact that none of this mattered at all.

The body of a small boy, probably not any older than ten or eleven, lay in the street in front of her, coagulated blood staining his t-shirt, a shard of glass still clutched in his bloody hand. Jody stared at the body blankly for a few seconds before giving it a small kick with the toe of her trainer. The boy didn't acknowledge her. She stared down at his lifeless form impassively for another moment before wandering on, forgetting him almost instantly. A brick fell from the mostly destroyed second story of an old machine shop up the street and clattered loudly to the pavement, the echo sounding like cannon boom in the stillness. As she wandered up the deserted street, Jody glanced around dispassionately at the bodies scattered haphazardly about. A middle-aged man wearing a UPS uniform with a bullet wound through the center of his forehead. A young woman in a knee-length yellow house dress missing one of her arms from the elbow down. An elderly man covered in bloody glass propped up against the remains of an old bakery on the corner. She glanced at their lifeless faces, an expression of mortal terror permanently frozen on each one, and found she no longer had the strength or the will to be angry at the sight of the terrible slaughter.

"Why'd he do it?" she muttered, her father's dark eyes, gleaming with savage triumph, flashing through her mind. "Why the fuck did he do it?" she asked again, a note of pleading in her voice.

There was no reply.

Jody's shuffling footsteps slowly ground to a halt, and she was almost shocked to feel tears brimming in her eyes. In slow motion, she fell to her knees, cutting her legs painfully on shards of glass littering the asphalt and not caring.

"You have to keep trying," Kaitlyn's voice whispered in her ear. "You have to keep going, I promise, it will get better."

"I..." Jody choked out, tears flowing freely down her face, as much for herself as they were for the people surrounding her that had died as needlessly as she soon would. "I...can't..." she sobbed, burying her face in her hands. "I just...can't...not anymore..."

"Jody..." Kaitlyn whispered, and Jody could almost feel her best friend's arms slide around her.

Jody shook her head violently, bitter tears of frustration erupting out of her. All the memories and the terrible pain she'd sequestered the last several years came flooding back in a rush. The night her father had tried to kill her. Waking up in the ER only to learn that her parents were dead and her childhood home had burned to the ground. Her foster parents throwing her out onto the street the day she turned eighteen. Leo, the man she'd fallen in love with, stabbing her that night at the hospital, his soulless gaze bearing down on her as her life puddled out on the floor around her.

"Just...leave me alone. Please..." Jody whispered. "I just want it to stop. I can't take the pain anymore. Just...let it end..."

A dark shadow fell over her suddenly, and she looked up to see the Puppeteer standing over her. Only he was no longer faceless. The face of her father stared back at her, grinning at her like a wolf eyeing a fat rabbit. His black, soulless eyes glittered like black opals.

"C'mon baby, don't you want to watch a movie?" he said in her father's voice, extending his black gloved hand out to her.

She glanced around at the dead bodies and destroyed buildings surrounding her, and out of the corner of her eye, she saw the hungry grin widen as she did. Jody lowered her head in defeat. Because she had lost. She'd lost before she'd even been born. Leo had been right. They were sick. Every single one of them.

She looked up into those glittering black eyes, at that moment, the last of her resistance finally broke down. She slowly extended her trembling hand out to her father. The Puppeteer's grin widened as she did.

"Finally," he thought as his hand came within inches of his quarry's. "It's complete."

Suddenly, his gaze refocused on something approaching them from down the street. All the confidence of his imminent victory evaporated in an instant, replaced by a cold, alien feeling of imminent doom. Suddenly caught in an inexplicable web of panic, the Puppeteer vanished. Jody stared at the spot where her father had been, her tear-filled eyes glazed over, as Ben Alrite and Mike Swezenko ran towards her.

CHAPTER 45

When Ben Alrite and Mike Swezenko had first come upon the woman lying on her knees in the blood-drenched street, Ben was sure she was dead. Had it not been for Mike's whisper of "holy shit," he might've walked right by her without a second thought. In spite of the heavy bags they were shouldering, Ben and Mike sprinted towards the woman, glass and rubbish crunching under their feet. The woman didn't acknowledge them as they approached. She was staring unmovingly at a spot directly in front of them, her eyes as blank as marbles.

"W-we can't..." she whispered, her voice trembling, as Ben squatted down beside her. She turned her face toward Ben's, and Ben drew back slightly when he saw her haggard appearance. She was cut in several places, the dark circles under her eyes suggested she'd hadn't slept in days, and her whole face seemed to sag as if her muscles no longer had the energy to keep it upright.

"We can't beat him," she whispered, and Ben winced as she grabbed his wrist suddenly. Her touch sent a shiver up Ben's spine.

"Don't you get it?" she asked urgently. "We can't beat him. This," she whispered, gesturing at the destroyed buildings. "This is it. This is how it all ends."

In slow motion, the woman's eyes rolled up into the back of her head, and she fell forward towards Ben, who caught her just before she hit the ground. Ben glanced nervously at Mike, who suddenly looked terribly frightened. They were both recalling what Serena had said days earlier: "To get into the heads of that many people, you'd have to be Hitler, Mao, and Pol Pot rolled into one, with an IQ of about 200 to boot..." Wordlessly, Ben and Mike slung both of the woman's arms around their shoulders and carried her in the direction of the vehicles, the image of a faceless man with the traits of charisma and intelligence Serena had described haunting both men the entire way.

Jason, who had been close to dozing off at the wheel of the Volvo, immediately snapped awake at the sound of Ben and Mike's running footsteps. Jason turned to Lorenzo, who had dozed off in the passenger seat beside him and shook him awake.

"Oh shit," Lorenzo murmured as he caught sight of them. "Looks like they're in trouble."

Jason turned to Lorenzo.

"Get the SUV started."

Lorenzo nodded and threw open the passenger side door. Jason gunned the engine as his friend sprinted back toward the SUV, his right hand poised over the gear shift. Ben and Mike were now within a few hundred feet of him. When he noticed what they were carrying between them, he immediately jumped out of the vehicle, all thoughts of a quick getaway from some unknown assailant gone.

"Oh my god, what the hell happened?" Jason asked, his eyes glued to the unconscious woman whose legs had been sliced to ribbons. Somewhere behind him, he heard Lorenzo throw open the door of the SUV.

"She was out in the road," Ben managed between gasps, struggling to catch his breath. "We found her like this. We thought she was dead at first."

Lorenzo gasped when he saw the state the woman was in.

"She's lost a lot of blood, get her into the back of the SUV," he ordered. "Jason, grab her shoulders. Mike, get a sleeping bag out of your pack."

Jason and Lorenzo carefully transferred the woman between them, allowing Mike to remove the backpacking backpack from his shoulders. After a moment, Mike emerged, a dark blue thermal sleeping bag clutched in his hands.

"Lay that down in back, set her down on it to keep the debris out of her wounds," Lorenzo ordered.

Grunting, Jason and Ben helped Lorenzo heave the unconscious woman up into the back of the SUV on top of the thermal sleeping bag. Mike, straining, heaved the two heavy packs up into the back after her.

"Did you pick up any first aid supplies?" Lorenzo asked Ben, jumping into the back.

"The stash was pretty picked," Ben replied. "I got some gauze, band-aids, rubbing alcohol, scissors, basic stuff like that, not a whole lot."

"I got a few things myself," Mike said, hauling his own pack into the back after Lorenzo. "Do what you can."

Lorenzo nodded.

"Jason, you're up here with me. You guys drive, we need to get her to a safe location as soon as possible."

Jason jumped up into the back of the SUV after Lorenzo, while Ben ran around to the driver's seat. Mike took the wheel of the Volvo. As they sped away from the deserted street corner, Ben could hear Lorenzo giving urgent orders to his former PA from the back of the SUV, and he felt a pang of sympathy for the young woman. The sight of her lying on her knees in the street, covered in blood and half out of her mind, just about broke what little sanity Ben had remaining. Still, as they sped their way towards the city limits of Philadelphia, the shattered windows of the surrounding buildings stared down at them with their hollow, dark eyes, silently judging them, he couldn't shake the woman's terrified words from his mind: "We can't beat him. He is all..."

CHAPTER 46

A few hours later, the seven of them had pitched the four tents Ben and Mike had brought back from the Walmart in a small meadow a few miles outside of the city. They had managed to scrape together a small pile of firewood from the scant supply around them, and Ben had put his cigarette lighter to good use. The resulting fire provided a small amount of warmth to the exhausted group as they huddled close to each other on the ground around it. Ben glanced in the direction of a small orange tent pitched a few feet from where they were sitting. Grace, without saying a word to either of them, had disappeared into the tent as soon as it was pitched about an hour ago, and hadn't emerged since. Jennifer, looking worried, had gone in after her a few minutes ago, and he'd seen neither of them since. Ben's brow furrowed as he watched the tent for any signs of movement. The more he thought about it, the more Ben realized that he'd heard little from his normally cheerful daughter all day. Trying to distract himself from his worries, Ben turned to Jason. A few feet away, Serena could feel herself slowly dozing off as she stared pensively into the flames.

"How's our girl doing?" Ben asked, casting a glance at the red tent pitched a few feet away where she was sleeping.

Jason cast a worried look towards it.

"Lorenzo's with her now," Jason said. "We stabilized her in the SUV, but she's in pretty bad shape."

"Think she'll make it?" Ben asked, immediately regretting the question.

Jason didn't reply for a moment, and Ben was privately hoping he wouldn't just before he did.

"If she were in a fully functioning hospital with the proper medical equipment, absolutely. But out here," Jason glanced around at the tall dark grass surrounding them on all sides. "Without proper help, there's no guarantees."

Ben nodded, knowing Jason was right. All three of them looked up from the fire as the tent flap zipped open and Lorenzo emerged, his face looking grim. Fearing the worst, Ben hailed Lorenzo as he approached the fire.

"How's she doing?" Ben asked, fearing the answer but needing to know nonetheless.

Lorenzo sighed and ran a hand through his rapidly graying hair.

"She's stable, but she's lost a lot of blood, and she's badly dehydrated. I'm going to let her rest for tonight, but we need to get some fluids in her the moment she wakes up."

Both Ben and Jason breathed a massive sigh of relief in unison. Lorenzo sat down next to Jason, who was staring aimlessly into the crackling embers with a haunted expression.

"How are you holding up?" Mike asked Lorenzo.

"I'm alright," Lorenzo replied quickly, but even Mike could tell he was lying.

Deciding it was better not to pry, Mike returned his gaze to the dying fire.

"So, about tomorrow…" Mike started to ask.

"We're already here," Ben interrupted. "Might as well go back if there's anything left worth taking," although it was the last thing he wanted to do.

Mike nodded, understanding exactly how Ben felt as the images of the dead bodies strewn about in the streets flashed through his mind. He shivered.

Ben turned to Serena, who had woken up, dreading what he was about to say next, but knowing it had to be said.

"Serena," he said.

"What was it you said a few days ago back in North Arlington? About a potential leader of the masses?"

Serena thought for a moment before answering.

"Ben, I'm not sure that's even possible, let alone realistic. To bring all these people scattered all over the country who've just experienced a nuclear holocaust together doesn't seem like something a human being could achieve, at least for now. Just think about the amount of charisma and careful planning that would take, at a time when all anyone can think about is making it to the next day alive."

Ben almost bit his lip to prevent himself from saying what he was about to say next. Almost.

"When we found that woman on the street earlier…" He glanced at Mike, who averted his gaze, but didn't stop him.

"She said something that scared the shit out of both of us."

Suddenly, everyone's full attention was on Ben, all traces of sleep instantly vanished from their faces. Ben paused for a moment, unsure of whether he should continue. The fire crackled impatiently as if telling him to get on with it.

"She thinks that there is a leader out there somewhere," Mike said finally. "And from what she said, it doesn't sound like he intends to get the country back on its feet."

Everyone sitting around the fire recoiled noticeably. Serena looked especially shaken.

"But if she was in as bad of shape as you said she was, couldn't she have just been babbling?" Serena asked hopefully.

Ben was about to say that it was possible but then stopped himself. As much as he would've liked to believe that it had been nothing more than mindless babbling brought on by life-threatening dehydration and blood loss, he knew deep down that it wasn't true. Judging by the gaunt look on Mike's face, he was thinking exactly the same thing. But neither of them seemed to be willing to express this thought out loud. Everything was quiet for a moment that seemed to go on far longer than it actually did. Finally, Serena spoke up.

"Look, it was a throwaway comment. We can't get all worked up just because a woman we found on the street made another comment that sounds vaguely like it might suggest that there was some truth to what I said. It just doesn't make any sense."

But suddenly, despite the deafening silence that had enveloped them, everyone seemed to be very worked up.

The nervous energy hung around the dying campfire like a gathering storm cloud. No one seemed to be under the delusion that what Serena had said was just a "throwaway comment," not even Serena, who shifted uncomfortably in her seat.

"Let's say this is true," Mike said. "Let's say this woman isn't crazy. If that's true, what the hell are we dealing with here?"

No one answered him. They didn't need to. While the pictures that each of them were forming in their minds might have differed slightly, each was too terrible to express out loud. The silence spiraled horribly.

Mike stood up and said, "Look, if we want answers, we need to talk to the woman."

Lorenzo looked up at Mike as he started for Jody's tent.

"We can't right now."

"Why the hell not?" Mike said, sounding irritated. "If some sick fuck is out there, watching us, waiting for the perfect moment to leap out of the dark and cut our heads off, we need to fucking know about it right now!"

Now it was Lorenzo's turn to stand up.

"Not now," he said firmly. "We can wait until morning. The more we badger her, the longer it's going to take her to recover, and the longer we're stuck here."

Mike, although he would've liked nothing more than to keep arguing the point, calmly nodded and sat down again. He had a great deal of respect for Lorenzo, even if he was firmly convinced he was wrong in this instance. Lorenzo remained standing.

"We can't lose our heads now," he said. "Whatever this woman might or might not have said doesn't matter right now. The only thing we need to be worried about right now is staying alive and finding a permanent shelter. So everybody go get some rest, and we can figure out whatever the hell this business about a demon man is in the morning when my patient has had a good night of sleep and her wounds have closed up."

Ben glanced around the mostly burned-out fire at the worried and strained faces of his compatriots, but to his surprise, no one argued with Lorenzo. Serena yawned and got up to go to bed. Jason followed her.

Over the next few minutes, the rest of the group followed him, until it was just Mike and Lorenzo sitting next to Ben on the ground, staring into the few dying embers that remained from the fire. Their expressions looked haunted.

"You think that was the right call?" Ben asked Lorenzo. "Just telling them to wait until the morning for answers isn't going to make them sleep any better."

Lorenzo thought for a moment before responding.

"Look," he said. "When I told you she'd lost some blood and was a bit dehydrated, I left something out. She woke up when I was in the middle of applying rubbing alcohol to her injuries." Lorenzo looked Ben in the eye. "Ben, she didn't react at all. I've had some patients practically screaming in pain from doing the exact same thing, to much smaller wounds no less, but she didn't even flinch. I didn't even notice she was awake at first."

"When I finally noticed, I asked her how she was feeling, and she didn't even look at me. She just stared blankly up at the ceiling the whole time like I wasn't even there."

"What's your point?" Mike asked.

"My point," Lorenzo said, "is that there's a lot more wrong with her than just the cuts on her legs. And when you told me what Serena said, I just…" Lorenzo trailed off.

Ben felt his stomach twist into a knot when he realized what Lorenzo was saying.

"I mean, what could've fucked her up so badly she didn't even react when I poured rubbing alcohol into an open wound? What could scare a person that badly?" Lorenzo asked, sounding as though he were pleading for an answer.

Neither of them had an answer. The faceless man swam back to the front of Ben's mind, only he was leering at Ben now, as though he were listening to their every word.

"Why didn't you tell the rest of the group this?" Mike asked. He no longer sounded the slightest bit annoyed.

"C'mon Mike," Lorenzo said, "didn't you see their faces? They're scared out of their minds as it is."

Ben, who privately thought it would've been a better idea to tell them up front, regardless of their reaction, said, "Look, it's like you said Lorenzo. We'll have better luck trying to work this out if we do it after a full night's sleep. We all need some rest after the day we've had."

Although neither Mike nor Lorenzo looked particularly happy about it, they both nodded and went to their tents, both of them too tired to argue. Ben didn't follow. He sat with his knees pulled up to his chest, staring at the scant pile of logs they had gathered from the meadow as the last surviving ember in the fire smoldered and died, leaving Ben sitting in complete darkness.

Ben removed the cigarette lighter from his pants pocket, along with a small pack of Marlboros he'd snagged when he and Mike had taken their field trip to Walmart. He had made a point of hiding them from the others, especially Jennifer, who would've undoubtedly been pissed if she knew that her husband was back on the nicotine high. In truth, he was a bit ashamed of it. Ben considered the cigarette lighter for a moment. He flipped it open and closed a couple times but couldn't get it to light. Annoyed, he was about to give up, when he saw something that caught his attention. A bright blue flash of light. It lasted for only an instant, and Ben almost believed he'd imagined it. Then he heard the voice. A deep, cool, rich voice that barely spoke above a whisper.

"Immergo."

Ben stared at it, dumbfounded. Through his confusion, a strange thought emerged: the word was familiar somehow. He couldn't quite place where, but he'd definitely heard it somewhere. He felt as though he was seeing a childhood friend again for the first time in years but couldn't quite remember who they were.

Suddenly, an image flashed through his mind like a thunderbolt. He was surrounded by a giant body of dark water that tossed and turned brutally as if a storm were taking place. Ben waved his arms above his head, struggling to stay afloat, but it was no use. A giant swell swept over him, sending him into the depths, his scream cut off as water filled his lungs. He heard it again just then. The same whispering voice, the exact same word.

"Immergo."

Ben stared blankly into the darkness, completely speechless. While the image certainly terrified him, a small part of him also felt a spark of curiosity.

"Immergo," he thought, a shudder running through him that had nothing to do with the cold. "Immergo…"

CHAPTER 47

A navy-blue Chevy Sedan wound its way silently down the deserted, twisting route of the U.S. Interstate 80 through western Pennsylvania, small piles of leaves and rubbish whispering out of its way. The man behind the wheel wore a dark blue sweatshirt and black sunglasses he'd picked up at a ransacked clothing store back in Allentown, where he'd spent the previous night in a small motel just off the interstate. Despite the near fourteen hours of driving he had put in that day with only a small break for lunch at midday, Cetan Aung lay back comfortably against the smooth leather passenger seat, a bemused smile plastered on his face. Cetan was in a good mood, the events of a few days ago back on the street in Kearney a distant memory.

He steadily piloted the sedan around a tractor trailer that had jackknifed in the middle of the highway, not bothering to slow down as he did, even when it wobbled dangerously as it hit the gravel on the side of the road. Cetan calmly turned the wheel left even as the car threatened to plunge off the side of the road into the yawning ditch below and easily righted it back onto the asphalt. His master would allow no harm to come to him, not at such an important moment. While Cetan's memories of the events back in Kearney were a bit fuzzy, he was perfectly clear on one thing: his master was planning something, and Cetan would play a great role in that plan, oh yes, he dared even say that he would be acting as his master's general in arms.

Cetan was filled with a strange, elixir-like confidence that flowed through his veins as effortlessly as his own blood, not necessarily in himself, but certainly in the man (thing) who guided him forward to his unknown destination. The fact that he didn't know precisely what that destination was had not occurred to him, and it wouldn't have bothered him even if it had. His master would guide him. Cetan was confident of it. He guided the sedan around a tight corner, narrowly avoiding a large black pickup truck with the back window shattered that had been abandoned in the middle of the road. There were some very important people waiting for him in a small town just up the road. They were believers, sent by his master to help him accomplish the mission. Cetan smiled at the thought. Soon, the bastards who had killed his parents would be purged from his master's world. He was sure of it.

An observer might have noticed Cetan hadn't bothered to turn on the sedan's headlights, even though the road was nearly pitch-black in the cloudy, moonless night. There wasn't any need to have them on. It was yet another thing he was confident of. Cetan glanced out the window at the dark night sky, almost believing he could see his mother and father's faces somewhere up there among the stars, smiling down at him.

"I love you mom and dad," Cetan whispered as he swerved to avoid a black Honda Civic and white Toyota that had crashed head on in the middle of the road. "You'd be so proud if you were here right now."

Around daybreak, just as a thin line of blazing red-orange early morning sunlight began to peek over the horizon, Cetan Aung pulled the dark blue sedan off Ohio route 314 and on a back road just outside the small village of Chesterville, Ohio. Several free-roaming farm animals gave him a curious stare as he piloted the sedan carefully down the cracked asphalt. Once or twice, Cetan hit a pothole, sending him flying off his seat, and both times, he barely blinked, completely unfazed. Finally, he pulled the sedan off the road onto a narrow gravel path that barely accommodated the entire width of the car. He continued down the path for a few minutes before it opened into a wide clearing. The grass was overgrown, and several farm animals were wandering about, the old wooden fences meant to keep them confined having long been breached. A dark red barn with the shingles falling off the roof in several places towered over the scene. Cetan stared up at the weathervane on the roof of the barn tilting lazily back and forth in the breeze, a feeling of ice-cold determination pouring into his veins as effectively as adrenaline from an epi-pen.

A broad smile broke out over his face at the sight of the abandoned farm. This was exactly where he needed to be. The men sent by his master were here, he could feel their presence somewhere in the barn. Feeling a heightened sense of purpose, Cetan stepped out of the vehicle and walked towards the barn, not bothering to notice that a light had been turned on in the upstairs window of the small farmhouse next to the barn. He tried the barn door, but it didn't budge. Cetan then noticed the padlock bolting the door shut. He strolled around the side of the barn, wondering if there was another way in. He turned at the sound of approaching footsteps, and before he knew what was happening, the business end of a double-barreled shotgun was being shoved in his face by a broad-shouldered, red-faced man in a red and black-checkered shirt and light blue overalls.

Cetan didn't flinch. He stared calmly up into the face of the taller man. The man's angry expression slowly faded as he stared into Cetan's calm visage, his grip on the shotgun slowly loosening as he realized who he was looking at, and Cetan smiled as the realization came to him: his master had told the man that Cetan was coming. The man tentatively lowered his shotgun as if he wasn't sure whether Cetan was a threat or not. Cetan stepped toward the man and calmly pushed down the twin shotgun barrels so that they pointed at the ground. The man, whose name suddenly appeared to Cetan as Rick Goldson, didn't resist. Rick, seemingly convinced that Cetan didn't pose a threat, smiled broadly and stuck out his large, callused hand. Cetan returned the smile and shook the man's hand heartily. Wordlessly, without needing to ask why Cetan was there, the man turned and walked around the barn to the barred front doors. He rapped hard on the wood. Cetan watched curiously, expecting to hear a knock from the inside in return, but all was quiet inside the barn. Then, Cetan felt his spine stiffen at the sound of his master's voice.

"Enter..."

A moment later, Cetan heard a bolt slide back from the other side of the door. Evidently, the men in the barn had no trouble understanding his master's message either. Rick pushed open the barn doors, allowing a sliver of moonlight to penetrate the pitch-black space inside the barn. Rick, toting the double-barreled shotgun, motioned Cetan forward. As he entered the barn, Cetan saw the outlines of two more men, both of them toting what looked like rifles, hidden in the darkness just beyond the moonlight filtering in through the open barn door. Although they hadn't spoken a word to Cetan, he was aware that their names were Jacob Armiston and Kane Lewellyn, both former military who had abandoned their posts when the world had turned upside down. But they hadn't been afraid. They'd been called, just as Rick Goldson had been called. Just as he himself had been called.

Rick entered the barn behind Cetan. Normally, as a former soldier, Cetan would've hated the thought of turning his back on a man with a gun. But he was perfectly calm in spite of this. There was nothing to fear in Rick Goldson. He was a true believer. He posed no threat to Cetan. Rick didn't close the door behind him. They would need the moonlight. As Cetan approached them, Jacob and Kane stepped fully out of the shadows. Kane, the taller and lankier of the two, sporting a well-trimmed black goatee, smiled broadly and shook Cetan's outstretched hand. Cetan then turned to Jacob, who was shorter and stockier than Kane and sporting a tattoo which read "Semper Fi" on his bulging left bicep and shook his hand as well.

"Good to have you..." Kane started, but Cetan quickly held up a hand to silence him. The hair on the back of his neck suddenly stiffened. Something was wrong.

"Are we alone?" Cetan asked, carefully concealing his sudden nervousness.

"Yep," Rick replied. "You're the only living soul we've seen since we ditched our posts a few weeks ago."

Cetan remained silent, his dark eyes darting around the barn.

There was an intruder here. And they needed to be taken care of. Wordlessly, Cetan drew his pistol and wandered deeper into the barn out of reach of the thin sliver of moonlight that had penetrated through the cracked barn door. His comrades exchanged quizzical looks.

"Cetan, what's wrong man?" Kane called.

Cetan didn't reply. With each passing second, he could feel the rage building in his chest, along with a steadily deepening sense of dread. Something was terribly wrong here, and as determined as he was to find the intruder who had somehow penetrated into their midst, a part of him dreaded what he would find when he actually caught them. He stormed over to the abandoned cow pens, brandishing the pistol in front of him, suddenly overcome with anger. He threw open the door to the last pen at the back of the row, aiming the pistol, every muscle in his body tensing as he prepared to shoot the interloper that had dared encroach on their territory, and immediately froze.

A little girl, no older than ten or eleven, was cowering in the corner of the pen, her knees pulled up to her chest, her dirt-streaked face concealed in her arms. Her clothes were torn in several places, and so dirty that the colors were almost

148

impossible to distinguish. Cetan stared at her, dumbfounded, the pistol hanging forgotten at his side. The little girl raised her head at the sight of him, her face streaked with tears.

"Please, mister," she whispered, her voice shaking. "Please don't kill me."

Cetan said nothing. He didn't know what to do. She was no older than he had been when his parents had been killed. She'd probably lived in this place with her parents, taken care of animals, eaten dinner around their dining room table as a family every night. Just a normal kid who'd never hurt anyone in her life. Cetan slowly approached the huddled little girl, bending down to embrace her.

"NO!" came a little boy's terrified scream, causing Cetan to jump back with fright. "DON'T MAKE ME GO BACK IN THERE, PLEASE!"

"GET BACK IN THERE YOU LITTLE SHIT AND SERVICE YOUR CLIENT AS YOU ARE TOLD!" a woman roared angrily.

A hard smacking sound, followed by a series of weak sobs, echoed in Cetan's ears. Cetan stood rooted to the spot, dumbstruck. It took him a full minute to understand what he'd just heard. The little boy's voice...it had been his own. And the woman had been...Cetan gasped. The little girl was gone. And in her place, a middle aged overweight dark-skinned woman wearing a flowing velvet nightgown and numerous golden bracelets on her wrists...the woman who still haunted his nightmares even years after he'd escaped her...Cetan felt a burst of white-hot rage erupt inside him as the madame of the brothel in India he'd been sold to after his parents had been killed grinned up at him.

The memories, which he'd sequestered after he'd finally escaped the brothel at the age of sixteen, came flooding back to him in a rush as he stormed over to the little girl and dragged her up by her hair, oblivious to her terrified cries as the scene in front of him and the scenes flashing through his mind blurred seamlessly so he could barely tell which one was really happening. The gunshots and the little boy's screams as his parents' lifeless bodies collapsed to the ground, their killers standing feet away in their military camouflage, rifles still poised. Dragging the little girl by the hair over the rough barn floor back towards the barn door, still oblivious to her screams. Being discovered hiding among the cargo on the boat by the two Indian dock workers. Dragging her into the moonlight, noticing neither the shocked faces of his comrades or the girl's continued screams begging him for mercy. Crying uselessly as he was ordered to enter the room where a naked old man was already lying poised on the bed, only to be struck hard enough to send him crashing to the floor by the madame.

Throwing her wordlessly to the ground, aiming the gun at her head, tears spilling down his face as the gun trembled in his hand. Stabbing the madame with a shiv he'd sharpened from a toothbrush. She'd died that night, he'd watched it happen. But she was not dead. She was right here in front of him, mocking him with her continued existence. From somewhere far off, he could hear the yells of his comrades as they stormed out of the barn after him, none of them fully understanding what was happening but knowing it had to stop.

"Cetan, stop!" Rick roared. Without evening noticing, he had aimed the barrel of his M16 rifle directly at Cetan's head. "This is sick, man!"

Cetan, who was oblivious to the three rifles aimed at him, paused suddenly. For a brief moment, the image of the madame faded, and he saw the little girl again, curled up into a ball on the ground, wailing uselessly, preparing for death.

He felt the gun slowly lower to his side. Rick, Kane, and Jacob, all of whom had been preparing to shoot, slowly lowered their rifles, breathing hard. Cetan slowly bent down to comfort the little girl, his brain working furiously trying to understand what had gotten into him.

"Cetan, what the hell…" Jacob began.

But the rest of the man's words were lost to Cetan. He saw the image of the little boy cowering at the feet of the madame, his nose bent at an unnatural angle and oozing blood, tears spilling down his face as he silently begged her not to send him back into that room again, anything but that. And then he heard it. Laughter. High, cold cruel laughter echoed off the walls of the narrow hallway so that it sounded as though a hundred people were laughing at him all at once. Only the laughter was no longer coming from the madame, the woman who only existed inside his head. It came directly from the little girl.

Only she was no longer a little girl. The madame had returned. She was lying on the ground exactly where the madame had been, mocking him, daring him to shoot her, daring him to finish the deed he had failed to carry out as a scared, helpless teenager.

"YOU FUCKING BITCH!" Cetan roared, brandishing the pistol.

The girl screamed, Rick, Kane, and Jacob all yelled, "NO!" in unison, both of which were drowned out by the sound of the gunshot. A final pitiful moan of pain escaped the girl before she slumped to the ground and lay still. Rick stared wide eyed at the little girl's body, his lips moving soundlessly. Jacob and Kane, unable to bear the sight, averted their gaze. Cetan stared impassively down at the little girl's lifeless form, breathing hard. He raised the still smoking gun again and emptied the magazine into her dead body.

"Bitch," he muttered, shoving the pistol into his waistband.

"Fucking sick, every single one of them." Without another word, he stormed off in the direction of the farmhouse.

Jacob and Kane, unable to bear the sight of the little girl's bullet riddled body, retreated into the barn, slamming the door shut behind them. Rick, now alone, collapsed to his knees in front of the dead little girl.

"I'm sorry," he whispered, his voice shattering into a thousand pieces. He reached out and brushed his callused hand across the cool skin on her cheek. "I'm so sorry." Rick closed his eyes, silently reciting a prayer that had once been spoken at his mother's funeral.

In the morning, before Cetan had woken, Jacob and Kane returned with shovels from the barn. Together, the three of them wordlessly buried the little girl whose name they had never learned.

CHAPTER 48

Dylan Teryon lay wide awake on the hard ground inside the small two-man tent Roy had pilfered from a long-abandoned department store, the small navy blue sleeping bag lying in a heap beside him. Ever since his first encounter with the magic man, Dylan had been trapped in a perpetual daze. His life had slowly played out before his eyes as if he were watching a movie of someone else living his life rather than living it himself. Only two things had kept Dylan Teryon tethered to reality since that night; the first was the coin lying in his pocket that felt as though it weighed a thousand pounds instead of a few grams as it should've. Many times, Dylan had wanted to toss it out the window of the pickup, or into the tall, dark woods that the clearing they were camping in that was surrounded by trees on three sides.

But he knew it wouldn't do any good. He could drop it in the middle of the Pacific Ocean, and he would still wake up the next morning with it lying next to him. The second was the terrible, sickening feeling of constantly being watched. It no longer mattered whether Dylan saw the magic man standing at the side of the road, or in front of an abandoned gas station, or anywhere else. In fact, he hadn't actually seen him anywhere for several days. But it didn't matter. Because he was always there. Always watching with those soulless black pits that led directly into the abyss…

Sometimes, the coin would grow hot in his pocket as if someone had applied a branding iron to it, and these were the worst moments of all for Dylan. He barely kept himself from crying like a helpless child whenever he felt the burning hot press of the coin through the seat of his trousers. The coin was not merely lying inanimately, its impossible weight lying on his heart like a dropped dumbbell. It was calling him, beckoning him to service. To his service…Dylan moaned softly and squeezed his eyes shut. The magic man wanted him for something, Dylan understood that much. His understanding didn't stretch to what task it could possibly be, but he knew intrinsically that it was a dreadful one, and a part of him didn't want to know, couldn't bear to know what the magic man wanted (would make) him to do.

Dylan wailed pitifully as the familiar burning sensation grazed his thigh. It was calling him again. He could feel those terrible eyes watching him, growing more insistent with every passing second as the nightmarish creature's patience slowly ebbed away. Dylan rolled over and felt around in the pitch-dark for the sleeping bag. The coin was growing hotter now, scalding his flesh, demanding to be acknowledged. Dylan curled up into a ball inside the sleeping bag, his hands squeezed over his ears, trying to ignore the increasingly painful feeling that was now traveling up his leg. He whimpered in pain as it passed over his stomach, spreading slowly into his chest, onto his arms, and into his neck, until it felt like his entire body was filled with molten lead. He screamed in pain and thrashed about inside the sleeping bag, his internal temperature steadily rising past one hundred and three degrees. Then the laughter began. A cruel baritone chortling that seemed to underline the helplessness of his plight, building to a crescendo until it was inside Dylan's head, practically screaming its vicious ostentatious refrain now, louder, louder, louder...

Dylan screamed and threw the sleeping bag off of him, all hope of resistance gone. He threw the tent flap open, the cool night air an ice-cold oasis in the desert of his burning pain. He turned his face up to the sky and howled his terrible bottled-up grief, pain, and red-hot fury at the moon, tears sliding freely down his face as he screamed for his father, for his sister, for his mother, but none of them came. For the first time, Dylan Teryon realized with a certain finality just how alone he was. He collapsed against the side of the tent, his tears cutting lines in the dirt streaking his face. He cried for what felt like hours before a sharp voice broke the silence.

"Shut the fuck up."

Dylan looked up, his vision still blurry through a haze of tears, his eyes darting around for the source of the voice.

"Dylan, just shut the fuck up."

Without fully understanding why he was doing it, Dylan removed the coin from his pocket. Only to discover that the head of George Washington had vanished. In its place was a narrow hallway that perfectly matched the silver of the coin's surface but would have sported peeling moss green wallpaper and ugly brown shag carpet. A little boy was cowering at the feet of a thin, middle-aged woman that also perfectly matched the silver of the coin. Dylan however, remembered her wearing a flowered apron and black slacks, as well as her short graying hair that was pulled back into a severe bun. She wore an expression that suggested something unpleasant had been shoved beneath her nose. It took Dylan a moment to realize what he was looking at.

Shortly after his father had died, his mother had begun bringing strange men into their apartment every few nights. This had gone on for several years. One of these men had not taken kindly to Dylan and decided to discipline him by beating him into a bloody pulp after he'd broken something of his mother's. Social services had been called when Dylan showed up to school the next morning covered in bruises. The woman who was standing over his eight-year-old self had run the orphanage he'd been sent off to after his mother had temporarily lost custody of him. Dylan stared, transfixed as the images that were now etched into the coin's face began to move like a bizarre old black and white film. He saw his eight-year-old self stand up, his face stained with tears.

"I want my mom," the little boy whimpered.

"SHUT THE FUCK UP!" the old woman screamed and slapped him hard across the face. "YOUR MOMMA AIN'T HERE NOW! AND IF YOU KEEP CAUSING ME TROUBLE, I'LL MAKE SURE YOU NEVER SEE HER AGAIN!"

Dylan threw himself against the side of the tent and howled pitifully up at the dark sky like an animal suffering great pain. His own terrible cries mingled with the magician's booming laughter until Dylan squeezed the sides of his head against the terrible sound, sure that he would be forced to scream his pain for all the world to hear or die. And then all at once, it ended, leaving only a terribly cold empty silence that seemed to stretch on endlessly. Dylan began to tremble, a tiny part of him even wishing the cacophony would resume. Somehow, the cold, deep, dark, empty pit of silence that had filled his mind in its place was worse. Much worse. A sense of ice-cold dread filled Dylan. He wasn't alone. He could feel the magician lurking nearby, watching, waiting, anticipating whatever atrocity he would soon force Dylan to commit on his behalf. Then another memory flashed through Dylan's mind, this one only a few days removed from the scene that had appeared in the coin. He saw himself approaching a much larger boy named Gary who, along with his friends, had beaten Dylan since the first day he'd arrived. Gary was laughing and saying something to his friends about Dylan being a fag, unaware that the smaller boy had a butcher knife from the kitchen concealed behind his back.

Dylan screamed as his younger self drove the knife deep into his tormentor's stomach, Gary gasping as blood spurted from the wound, puddling on the floor around him. Other kids were yelling, Dylan was screaming, and the magic man was laughing. But even through his terror, Dylan couldn't fail to notice something else. His younger self was standing triumphantly over Gary, who had collapsed to the floor, an ice-cold grin plastered on his face as he watched his tormentor's body spasm helplessly. That grin...it looked exactly like the magic man. As Dylan watched, petrified, the smaller boy began to laugh cruelly. High cold cruel laughter that echoed off the walls of the cafeteria. The magic man's laughter. Coming out of his younger self as if the two had swapped bodies. Whimpering, Dylan threw the coin deep into the woods and threw the sleeping bag over his head, crying silently into the thick nylon.

Dylan woke up several hours later, his entire body drenched in an icy sweat. His dreams had been a nightmarish blur of blood, broken glass, and kitchen knives swinging in his face. His eyes darted from shadow to shadow as if he expected to see someone lurking in one of the dark corners of the tent. He pressed a cool hand to his burning forehead, shivering in spite of the heavy sleeping bag, which he quickly threw off of himself. Dylan flung himself out of the tent, dead leaves crunching loudly under his feet as he stormed towards the woods, not thinking about where he was going and not caring, wanting nothing more than to get as far away from that place as possible. Then he noticed something out of the corner of his eye that made him stop dead in his tracks. It was Laura, walking quickly away from him into the forest, her arms folded protectively over her breasts, her head down as if she were trying not to attract attention.

Dylan stood rooted to the spot, staring after her quizzically. Finally, after she had nearly faded from view through the dense trees, Dylan began to follow her, although every fiber in his being was screaming at him to run as fast as possible in the opposite direction. Laura was hurrying along, and she had much longer legs than Dylan, so he practically had to run to keep up with her. In his struggle to keep her in sight, Dylan failed to notice the racket he was making, but luckily for him, Laura, who was muttering something under her breath Dylan couldn't quite make out from this distance, seemed too preoccupied to notice. She stopped abruptly at the edge of a small clearing illuminated by the moonlight coming through the relatively thin overhead tree cover. Thinking he had been spotted, Dylan quickly ducked behind a large oak tree, his ragged breath catching in his chest. After a moment of silence, he gingerly peeked out from behind the tree. Laura hadn't made a move towards him or given any other indication that she had noticed his presence.

In fact, she hadn't moved at all. She was staring at something in her hand that Dylan couldn't quite make out, and he realized with a start that her hands were shaking. Laura Forsin sank to her knees, a shiver passing through her entire body that had nothing to do with the cold, her curly blond hair blowing about her tear-streaked face in the cool September wind. The tear-splattered bottle of sleeping pills clutched in her trembling hands seemed to stare back at her, mocking the terrible agony of her continued existence. Her father visited her again tonight. Roy had kept him away for many years, even after she'd given up the pills. He was the man who had taken her away from her pedophile father for good. He'd told her constantly that he was the only man for her, that she would never belong to any other man whenever he would touch her inappropriately or climb into bed with her at night. This aspect of the grooming, more than anything else, had kept her isolated for many years. Roy had been the one to finally break the hold that had been placed over her when she was only a child.

A sob escaped Laura, her knuckles turning white from gripping the pill bottle so hard. But now he was back. He'd violated her again tonight, bringing back all the pain and humiliation of those years in a rushing river that threatened to break the dam of her sanity and send her plunging into its depths. She twisted the cap off the bottle and emptied half of a dozen small white pills into her trembling hand. Her isolation was total. She couldn't wake Roy. There was nothing more he could do for her. For the first time since she'd met him many years ago, she didn't feel safe. She felt vulnerable, disgusting, worthless. She couldn't bear it another second. The whole thing had to end right now. Slowly she raised the handful of pills to her open mouth, her hand shaking so badly she nearly dropped them, tears cascading silently down her face.

"It's done," she whispered. "It's finished."

CHAPTER 49

Dylan, who had remained motionless while watching the spectacle unfold, nearly jumped in surprise as Roy Forsin's thunderous footfalls suddenly came crashing through the underbrush. Quickly concealing himself behind a large oak tree, Dylan watched as Roy knelt down beside his unconscious wife, looking panicked. Even from a distance, however, Dylan could hear Laura's shallow, but steady, breathing, her chest rising and falling with each rasp. After a moment, this observation seemed to strike Roy as well, and Dylan saw him breathe an enormous sigh of relief. Seeming not to notice the open bottle of pills lying on the ground next to her, Roy scooped up his wife and hurried back towards the tents, never noticing Dylan hiding just a few feet away. For Dylan's part, he barely noticed the pair of them leaving. His gaze remained transfixed on the open bottle of pills lying in the now empty clearing, several of the capsules scattered on the ground around it. Dylan shook his head, wanting nothing more than to turn away and run, but something held him back.

He was suddenly able to remember the things Gary, his foster home bully, had done to him more clearly now. Dumping milk on his head in the cafeteria while everyone around him laughed. Jumping him in the hallway during break, usually with a group of his friends. Pantsing him while he was brushing his teeth. Stealing his things and convincing the staff Dylan was a liar whenever he told them. Dylan squeezed his eyes shut, his hands balling into fists. The knife might've seemed crazy to most, but to Dylan…it had seemed only fair. The little bastard hadn't died that day, but he'd sure learned a good lesson. And, if Dylan was honest with himself…

"How did it feel?"

Dylan gasped audibly. The magic man was back.

"You remember, don't you?" the magic man asked. Dylan stared up into the starless night sky. He could almost picture the magic man somewhere up there, grinning coldly down at him. And for the first time, Dylan found he was no longer afraid of the magic man. His voice was almost a comfort, like having his father back.

"How did it feel, Dylan?" the magic man asked again.

"Good," Dylan thought, and although he hadn't said it aloud, he knew the magic man had heard him. "It didn't just feel good," Dylan continued. "It was the best damn feeling in the world!" Dylan hesitated for a moment before saying his next words. "The bastard got what he deserved."

The magic man remained quiet, but Dylan could somehow sense his grin widening.

"But…" Dylan hesitated, his father's furious expression flashing through his mind.

"Your mother and I put up with a lot from you Dylan…" his father's voice echoed in his head. "Dad wouldn't want me to do this, he…"

Dylan was cut off suddenly as though an invisible force were crushing his windpipe. His arms were yanked painfully out to his sides as if by invisible ropes, which slowly began to hoist him into the air by his wrists and ankles.

"They abandoned you, Dylan…" the magic man hissed. "They left you in that place. They don't love you."

Dylan cried out soundlessly as his mother, father, and sister appeared before him, their expressions grim.

"I'm sorry Dylan," his father said. "But you've crossed the line. We're done."

They turned without another word and began walking into the distance, Dylan's mind screaming silently, tears spilling down his face as their figures grew steadily smaller until they vanished completely. All at once, the ropes holding Dylan broke, and he collapsed to the forest floor, crying out in pain as he landed hard on his right shoulder.

"SHUT THE FUCK UP DYLAN!" came the old woman's scream. Dylan, whimpering, curled up into a ball on the ground as blows from hundreds of invisible pairs of feet began raining down on him from all directions, the screams of the old woman mixed with the jeering laughter of his fellow foster children.

"DAD!" Dylan screamed as the invisible feet kicked at him relentlessly. "DAD, PLEASE, HELP ME DAD!"

But the blows continued to rain down on Dylan unabated, his father, along with the rest of his family and anyone else he'd ever loved gone. He was all alone.

Finally, after what felt like an eternity, the beating stopped. Dylan, curled up in a ball on the ground, cried silently into his hands. After a few moments, he managed to climb shakily to his feet, his whole body trembling as his feet carried him soundlessly towards the place where the pill bottle still lay on the ground, along with a second one, outwardly identical to the first, that hadn't been there a few moments before.

"I'm so sorry, dad," he choked out, reaching for the second bottle that appeared to belong to Laura Forsin.

The bottle his master had left there especially for him so that he could accomplish the horrific act that he now finally understood in its full, terrible entirety.

"I'm so sorry."

CHAPTER 50

M aria Veranda lay awake on the hotel bed, fully clothed, staring up at an empty spot on the dark ceiling, the day's events playing over and over again in her mind. The crowd outside the museum back in Washington, wandering the streets like a pack of zombies, their eyes lifeless and cold. Her father knelt over the lifeless body of the old gas station manager, the handgun clearly visible within his waistband. The feeling of touching a hot griddle as she gingerly laid a hand on her mother's burning forehead, then practically having to feed her the two small ibuprofen tablets as she was too weak to do much more than open her mouth and swallow with obvious effort. The feeling of her father's dark eyes boring into her whenever he thought she wasn't looking. There was no love in that gaze. Only hunger, like a ravenous wolf eyeing a limping fawn. For the first time in as long as she could remember, Maria Veranda felt truly vulnerable.

She wanted nothing more than to shut her eyes and forget the god-awful events of the past few days, if only for a few hours, but her frazzled nerves seemed to have their own selfish agenda. Her mind drifted to the medicine cabinet where she'd found the ibuprofen tablets. She was fairly certain she'd seen an additional bottle labeled "Melatonin gummies," and she found herself longing for a few of the small red sweets to help take her mind off of things. She got off the bed, her anxiety easing a little at the thought of pleasant sleep, and her hand was on the doorknob when she paused suddenly. She pressed her ear against the door, listening intently. Nothing but dead silence. It might've been unnerving if she hadn't been utterly terrified of the noises that could've replaced it.

She went to open the door again, and then jerked away suddenly, as if she'd been burned.

"He could be out there..." a voice murmured in her ear.

"Shut up," she thought irritably, although she could feel herself trembling slightly.

"Right outside the door with his gun, just waiting for you to come out, so he can, you know..."

Unfortunately for Maria, she did know, and the thought was enough to make her back slowly away from the door, half expecting it to burst open at any moment with a cacophony of screams and gunfire.

"Just like he did to me," the voice whispered.

It took Maria a moment to realize it was the voice of the old gas station manager, although she couldn't have explained how she could possibly know that.

"What happened?" Maria whispered, her voice trembling, still staring wide-eyed at the closed bedroom door. She heard the old man sigh heavily, as if he were recalling a particularly painful memory.

157

"It all happened so fast," he replied after a moment. "I was just coming back to see if I could salvage anything useful from the store, when your father walked in. I figured it was just another robber, so I hid in the bathroom, figuring he would just take what he needed and go away."

Maria shuddered at the thought of her father, a man she'd once loved and respected, stalking through the abandoned gas station, gun drawn, his devilish eyes sweeping chip bags and energy drinks scattered across the floor and shelves.

"I became terrified that he would find me hiding in there and what he might do to me if he did. I tried to make a run for it, but he caught me as I left the bathroom. For a moment, we just stared at each other, neither of us sure what to do. There was something in his eyes, something not human...like...like..."

"Like an animal," Maria whispered.

"Yes," he replied after a moment. "Like a hungry lion eyeing a fat antelope."

Maria shuddered again, remembering that same look in her father's eyes.

"I begged him to let me go, but he'd made up his mind. That terrible hungry look in his eyes, that was the last thing I ever saw before he killed me," he finished, his voice trembling. Maria sat down heavily on the bed, her entire body shaking.

"How..." she whispered. "How could he..."

"I never met your dad before all this shit went down kid, but the person you loved and respected is gone. What I saw wasn't a loving husband and father like you knew. I saw a monster."

"No," Maria whispered insistently. "He's not a monster, I know he's not, he's my father for Christ's sake. A person can't just turn into a monster overnight, that's not possible!"

She was nearly screaming now, suddenly oblivious to the fact that her father might hear her.

"He's not a monster, he's not a monster, HE'S NOT A GODDAMN MONSTER!" she screamed, tears pouring down her face.

"It's possible," the voice replied solemnly, and although Maria barely noticed it, it was considerably deeper than it had been before. "It's in our nature. When we are left alone in the dark with nothing but our own hatred, pain, and fear for company, we often find that such changes are not only possible, but inevitable."

Maria shook her head violently.

"Shut up, shut up, SHUT UP!" she screamed. But the voice was boring into her like a whirring drill bit.

"And right now, with the world going to shit, everyone is scared, everyone feels alone, so what do you think happens to people, Maria? They start murdering gas station managers over energy drinks. Hell, your dad didn't even kill me over something as stupid as that, seems like he enjoyed it. If that's the case, it probably won't be the last time he kills, and he still has the gun, you know..."

Maria shot a terrified glance at the bedroom door, which had remained undisturbed.

"W-what do you want?" she whispered shakily.

"To show you the truth," the old man replied. "To show you what your father has become."

158

And then, for the second time, the terrible image of her father advancing on a stunned Michael Pines, a gleaming steel blade clutched in his fist, flashed through her mind. Maria watched, dumbstruck, as her father, in slow motion, cast the blade aside, grabbed Michael by the shoulders, and shoved him beneath the surface of the water.

"10 seconds…20…30…"

"Don't dad, please don't, don't do it, don't fucking do it!" Maria silently pleaded as she watched Michael's struggles gradually weaken.

Then, slowly, they died out altogether. Her father stood up, breathing hard, staring coldly down at the lifeless body of the man Maria had once hated so much. She began to tremble.

"How could he…" she whispered.

But the rest of the words died in her throat. A broad, predatory grin spread across her father's face. Maria let out a low moan. This man was not her father. He couldn't possibly be.

"No…" Maria whispered. "No, no, no, you're lying, it's not true, IT CAN'T BE FUCKING TRUE!" She could feel tears pouring down her face and found that she didn't care.

"I'm sorry kid." It was the voice of the old janitor again. "But your dad is gone."

Maria felt her legs give out from beneath her, and she collapsed to the carpeted floor, her head hung in defeat.

"Daddy…" she whispered, crying soundlessly. "I don't understand…"

"Maria," came her father's voice, and she had to clap a hand to her mouth to keep from screaming. It took her a moment to realize the voice was only in her head. "I was born sick, baby girl, just like you," he said calmly. "We're all sick, but he's coming to end the sickness. That's why all of this had to happen."

Maria, her vision blurred by tears, threw herself down onto the bed and squeezed her hands over her ears.

"You're lying…" she whispered. "You're not my dad, I don't know what you are, but my father is a good man."

"There are no good men, Maria," the thing pretending to be her father hissed. "You'll understand soon."

Then the thing that had once been her father vanished. But not before Maria had seen his eyes. She curled into a fetal position on the bed, feeling fresh tears welling up in her eyes. There had been no light behind her father's eyes, none of the usual cheerfulness and intelligence she'd grown up with. They were like a pair of black holes, consuming every ounce of light that touched them.

CHAPTER 51

M aria didn't sleep that night. She lay on top of the sheets fully dressed, her hands clasped over her stomach, staring up at the strangely dancing shadows cast by the faint moonlight on the dark ceiling, the night's events torturously replaying in her head over and over again. She wasn't even aware that the sun had arisen over the sprawling hills in the distance until she heard shuffling footsteps in the hall just outside the door. Her breath caught in her throat, her whole body suddenly awake. She shot up in bed, her gaze darting towards the hotel room door. She held her breath as the footsteps approached the doorway, cold sweat suddenly breaking out over her entire body. The image of her father shoving Michael Pines underwater flashed through her mind. She didn't dare breathe until the footsteps retreated down the hallway out of sight.

Maria, breathing an enormous sigh of relief, collapsed back onto the bed, running a hand distractedly through her long curly dark hair. After a minute, she forced herself to get up and go to the bathroom.

"Well, I look like shit," she thought sardonically as she observed herself in the mirror. Her dark hair was mussed and hung limply about her face. Her eyes were slightly bloodshot from tiredness, and her whole face seemed to sag slightly, as if her facial muscles had given up trying to support it. Somehow, the absurdity of the whole situation combined with her haggard appearance almost brought a smile to her gaunt face.

Maria walked out into the hotel lobby about ten minutes later to find her mother sitting in a leather armchair next to a cold, dark, empty fireplace, her eyes half closed. She turned at the sound of Maria's footsteps, and Maria's heart sank when she saw that the night's rest had done little to improve her mother's emaciated appearance. She smiled weakly at Maria as she approached, her face contorting with the effort.

"Mom," Maria gasped, sitting down beside her.

Anna laid a hand comfortingly on her daughter's shoulder.

"I'm fine baby, don't worry about me," she said softly, although truthfully, she felt anything but fine.

Maria nodded. She didn't want to waste what little energy her mother had arguing, although she would've liked to very much.

She reached over and brushed a loose strand of hair off her mother's sweat-laced forehead, her nervousness growing at the heat radiating off her mother's forehead. It didn't appear that her fever had improved since the previous night.

"Your dad's bringing the car around," Anna said weakly.

Maria didn't trust herself to respond. "Said he didn't want me to walk too far in my state," Anna said, a wan smile crossing her face.

"Your father's always acted like I'm made of glass, you know that baby? Even when we were first married, he'd always come home with a bottle of aspirin if I so much as sneezed. I know it's only because he cares, but I wish he wouldn't sometimes. It stresses him out."

Maria squeezed her eyes shut, fighting back tears. The thought of her father coming home from work and embracing her mother, bouncing her and Lilly on his knees, her mother crying and hugging him after he convinced her to go to therapy, the thought of the man her father had once been, was almost more than Maria could stand.

A moment later, the Chevrolet appeared in front of the shattered hole in the wall that had once been the twin glass doors. Maria supported her mother as she hobbled to the car, refusing to look her father in the eye as they approached, trying her best to block out the wonderful childhood memories of her father that were doing their best to resurface, forcefully reminding herself over and over.

"It's not him, he's gone, it's not him, he's gone…"

CHAPTER 52

Several hours after they had left St. Clairsville behind them, Maria glanced out the window of the Chevrolet to see that they were passing by a road sign that announced they were entering the city limits of Springfield, Ohio. Her father hadn't said a word since they'd begun the drive, but even so, she could feel his eyes on her, the gun protruding from his waistband like a large black python. The thought made her shudder. David Veranda knew something was wrong. He'd known since the day his wife and daughter had discovered him in that gas station, bent over the body of the dead station manager. He'd seen the look in Maria's eyes. She was afraid. At first, he'd tried to tell himself that it had nothing to do with the scene she'd encountered in the station, there was no possible way his youngest daughter could think her strong, supportive, loving father killed that man, it simply didn't make any logical sense.

But her silence over the last several days, combined with the fact that she was avoiding eye contact with him, made the notion increasingly difficult to dismiss. He'd tried to speak to her the previous night, but she'd gone to bed before he got the chance. He stared at the seemingly endless line of asphalt in front of him, spinning different possible ways he could explain to Maria what she'd seen in the gas station, each feebler than the last. Finally, after about an hour, he gave up.

"Maria," he said, struggling to keep his voice steady.

She didn't answer.

"Maria, I didn't kill that man. I would never do something like that, you know that," he continued, a note of pleading in his voice.

She said nothing. The image of Michael Pines' body floating lifelessly in the outdoor hot tub while gunfire and Molotov cocktails exploded all around them flashed through her mind, so that she barely heard her father's meaningless words.

"Maria," David said again, turning to look at her as they crawled along a residential street dwarfed by abandoned vehicles and small suburban-style homes that had fallen into disrepair.

Maria watched the houses slowly move past, refusing to look her father in the eyes. She could feel the eyes of the python clipped to her father's waistband staring up at her hungrily, and she could almost feel him fingering it, debating whether to draw on her or not.

"Maria," David said again, a note of anger creeping into his voice, sending alarm bells screaming off in Maria's brain. "I did not kill that man."

But Maria barely heard him. Her eyes darted up the street to a small two-story house with light blue siding and white trim positioned at the far end of the street. If she went right now, could she make it in time? The Chevrolet was moving slowly enough that she could jump out without being seriously injured. Her thoughts moved to the gun. She couldn't hope to outrun him while he had it. He'd shoot her in the back before she made it ten feet.

She glanced quickly down at the gun. Buried deep in her father's holster. Could she get to it fast enough? If she could get the gun…David followed his daughter's gaze, which had flickered to the gun clipped to his waistband.

"Shit…" Maria thought, her breath catching in her throat. All rational thought ceased, her brain screaming at her to move now.

"Maria," David began again.

It all happened in less than a second. In one swift motion, Maria's right hand lashed out and clasped around the grip of the Beretta, forcing it from its concealment within the holster. David's eyes widened in surprise as he noticed too slowly what she was doing. Maria threw open the door of the moving vehicle and jumped, hitting the pavement hard as she landed. David slammed on the brakes as his daughter sprinted for the house at the far end of the street, the gun swinging wildly in front of her.

Maria burst through the front door of the house, eyes wild, her pounding heart threatening to burst free from her chest. Her hand shaking, she parted the living room curtains. The Chevrolet had stopped in the middle of the street. Her breath caught in her throat when she saw him running up the street towards the house. She took several shaky steps back from the front door, aiming the gun at the spot where he would come bursting through in a few seconds, her shaking fingers already applying pressure to the trigger.

"Hey, what are you doing!?"

The voice destroyed Maria's last thin shred of sanity. Without hesitation, she spun on her heel and fired at the source of the voice. The bullet missed Roy Forsin's temple by no more than two inches and punched through the drywall next to him, leaving a small hole. Maria cried out in terror and fired again, nearly striking her target for a second time.

Roy, completely bewildered, took shelter behind the old-fashioned large metal stove in the kitchen.

"Hey!" he called out. "Hey kid!" It struck him at that moment the absurdity of the situation, and that it was in fact a kid who was shooting at him. "Listen," he continued. "Let's put down the weapons and…"

The rest of his sentence was lost as another round punched through the drywall just above his head, followed by a howl of raw fury from the other room.

"Shit," he muttered, his gaze flickering to the gun clutched in his right hand. "Shit, shit, shit!" Roy threw himself into the kitchen doorway and fired, his shot striking the wall behind the dark-haired teen.

Undeterred, the girl fired her own weapon, her shot whizzing within inches of Roy's head. Roy fired again, his shot grazing the teen's left shoulder, drawing a spray of blood. The girl cried out in pain and fell to her knees, clutching her wounded shoulder, the gun clattering to the floor. Roy threw his own gun aside and hurried to her side.

Fresh blood was already soaking through the girl's shirt. Roy removed his own shirt and pressed it over the wound, trying to stem the bleeding. The girl gave him a look that was somewhere between gratefulness and inquisitiveness, and Roy now saw that she couldn't have been older than fifteen or sixteen years old.

"Who are you?" she asked.

"Just a guy trying to survive," Roy replied, relieved to see that the bleeding was lessening. "How about you?"

Maria paused for a moment before replying.

"Same here," she said finally.

"Sorry I shot at you."

"Sorry I shot you," Roy replied, lifting the shirt slightly to check the wound. He was pleased to see it was shallower than he'd initially thought.

"No hard feelings," Maria said, and she saw the ghost of a smile cross Roy's face.

"I'm Roy," he said.

"Maria," Maria replied, breathing a sigh of relief at the sight of her shoulder, where the bleeding had been halted by the beginnings of a callus.

"You alright?" Roy asked, although his worry had mostly dissipated by now.

"I'll be fine," Maria replied, smiling. The man was rather handsome, cool, intelligent, dark eyes, muscular, close-cropped black hair, the kind of guy girls would giggle about behind their hands in the hallways. Disarmed by the older man's good looks, Maria couldn't help but wonder why she had shot at him in the first place.

Roy looked up as a door opened gingerly at the top of the stairs, and a young woman with curly blond hair took a tentative step out into the hallway, followed by a small boy dressed in a dirty navy-blue sweatshirt and long black athletic pants. Maria felt a small stab of guilt when she caught sight of the scared look on the woman's face.

"It's alright Laura, just spooked her is all," Roy said, almost jokingly.

The woman's eyes darted from Roy to Maria and back again. Maria tried to force a smile but only managed a half-hearted sort of grimace.

The woman looked away uncomfortably, unable to meet Maria's gaze. Maria turned her focus on the little boy and was a little taken aback. In contrast to the woman Maria assumed to be the boy's mother, the boy didn't appear nervous at all. Their eyes met briefly, and Maria pulled her gaze away with a shudder. There was no light behind those eyes, as if they were the entry to a bottomless pit. They looked just like her father's had the previous night. She shook herself, sure she had imagined it. Even so, she felt herself tense as she felt the little boy's dark eyes observing her curiously, although his eyes didn't look curious at all, they looked…empty, as though the soul they were supposed to be the window to was mysteriously absent.

"H-hello," the woman said nervously, interrupting Maria's thoughts. "I'm L-Laura, and this is…"

Before she could finish, the front door exploded inward with enough force to crash into the opposite wall, causing the four of them to jump. David Veranda, panting, his face shining with sweat, burst into the room, gun drawn.

His dark eyes swept the room, coming to rest on Maria, still sitting on her knees on the rough hardwood floor. Their eyes met, and Maria felt her entire body tense like a spring ready to explode outward and destroy everything in its path. Then she heard that terrible voice again.

"Do it..." the old gas station manager hissed.

Without even knowing how it had gotten there, the gun was back in her hand and pointed directly over her father's heart. Then came another voice. Her sister's.

"Oh god Maria, please help me, oh god, he's going to kill me, don't let him kill me!"

Maria turned to see her sister, her shirt torn and covered in fresh bruises, lying helplessly on the floor, her father's gun aimed directly at her head. Laura screamed and threw herself over Dylan. Roy stared, his mouth hanging open stupidly. The man looked almost relieved to see Maria, even with the gun pointed in his face, the weapon holstered harmlessly at his side.

"DON'T YOU TOUCH HER!" Maria screamed, the gun trembling in her hand.

Her father turned, and Maria screamed as if in agony when she saw his eyes, a pair of large glittering black opals lodged in a face she no longer recognized or wanted to recognize. David took a step toward her, completely bewildered.

"Maria..." he said placatingly.

"Who are you?" Maria whispered, her voice shaking. "WHAT ARE YOU!?"

David stared at his daughter, slack-jawed, not knowing what to do. The gun trembled so violently in her hand that she had a better chance of hitting the floor or ceiling than her actual target, who was now frozen in place.

"Let it fly, Maria," the gas station manager whispered encouragingly. "Let it fly."

The voice no longer originated in her own head, but rather from somewhere directly behind her. But she didn't move. Her finger remained on the trigger of the trembling gun, but she didn't fire.

Despite every nerve in her body screaming at her to fire, every muscle desperately squeezing to apply that final 1/2 of pressure to the weapon's trigger, she didn't fire. Something was wrong. Her sister was fading away, the vibrant bright red hair slowly fading to a dull, ghostly gray until she was as transparent as a ghost. Her father's eyes were changing, the lightless black opals morphing back into their normal cool, intelligent, dark brown. The gun he held was fading into nothing, and she could see the outline of the same weapon holstered to his hip. And then the little boy was standing next to her, close enough to touch her.

Only he was no longer a little boy. He wore a tall black top hat, a black cape like something you'd see on a magician, black gloves, and tall black boots. His eyes were identical to her father's, lifeless black orbs.

"DO IT!" he screamed, wrenching her gun hand upward to point towards her father, whose face was a mask of shock, his hands held up in a gesture of surrender, his gun hanging uselessly at his side.

Maria screamed as the gun fired, her father collapsed, and her vision slowly faded to soothing darkness.

CHAPTER 53

R oy Forsin heard the shot, and for a split second, he was sure that David Veranda had been hit. Then he blinked, and realized that David was still on his feet, staring dumbfounded at Maria, who swayed once, twice, then slumped to the floor, the gun skidding away into the corner. A small hole marked the spot in the plaster where the bullet had punched through.

"Jesus," Roy whispered, staring at Maria's lifeless body. "Jesus." It took him a moment to register his wife's muffled cries coming from the foot of the stairs.

Cowering, she held Dylan tightly to her, her tears wetting his hair. Dylan gave no notice. He stared intently at the lifeless body of Maria Veranda, his dark eyes flashing angrily. The pure, unbridled hatred radiating off the boy in waves was so fierce that Roy felt himself shudder, his wife's sobs echoing from somewhere far off. Roy blinked and the expression was gone, replaced with a distressed expression nearly identical to his wife's, the boy's eyes shining with tears. Roy shook himself, sure he had imagined what he'd seen only a second before.

Both Roy and David jumped as the door crashed open, Anna Veranda silhouetted in the shadow cast by the bright autumn sunlight, her expression wild and frightened.

"David, David…" she stammered, "David, I heard a shot, I…" She froze halfway across the room, her gaze falling on her unconscious seventeen-year-old daughter lying sprawled on the floor.

David caught his wife as she collapsed to her knees, throwing her arms around her husband's neck as she collapsed into him, sobbing her heart out on his shoulder.

"Oh my god…Maria…is she okay?" she gasped.

"She'll be alright," Roy said, hooking the unconscious girl under the armpits and dragging her onto the posh navy-blue sofa positioned underneath the large bay window perpendicular to the front door.

"Has she been shot?" Anna asked, looking up at Roy.

"Just grazed. Most of the shots came from her. Guess I scared her."

Anna suddenly looked unnerved. She moved over to the couch, brushing a strand of Maria's sweaty dark hair out of her eyes.

"It's the stress," she said softly. "I think we're all a bit on edge these days."

Roy nodded, not satisfied with the explanation but unwilling to cause the woman any more distress.

"Mind if we stick around?" David asked Roy.

"Make yourselves at home," he replied. "Not like we have any claim to the place anyway. And the company would be nice, for the boy at least," Roy said, turning to Dylan, who had moved away from Laura and was crouching in front of the banister, staring pointedly at Maria. There was an intensity in his gaze that Roy didn't like, but he was too exhausted from the whole ordeal to worry about it now. He turned to David.

"Mind if we talk?" he said in a hushed tone so that Anna, who was still tending to Maria, wouldn't hear.

"Sure," David said, looking slightly apprehensive.

Without another word, they turned and walked into the kitchen, closing the door behind them.

"Last time I was stressed, I didn't pull a gun on anyone," Roy said in a whisper as soon as the door was closed.

"Look, the truth is," David began, "she's been behaving a bit strangely lately, but nothing like this."

"Strangely how?" Roy pressed.

David considered his words carefully.

"Well, she's just been a bit distant. She hasn't said a word to me in days, she's been eyeing me when she thinks I'm not looking, like I'm a poisonous snake raising itself up to attack or something."

"Just you?"

"Just me. With her mother everything is normal. It's been like this since..." David paused.

"Since what?"

"Since I found the body of that janitor at the station back in D.C." David replied slowly.

Seeing Roy's startled look, David replied quickly, "I didn't kill him, I just found him like that. Looked like some guys broke in, windows were all smashed, stuff was scattered everywhere, you know, typical end of the world kind of stuff."

Roy nodded slowly, as if he were considering whether to believe him or not.

"But to pull a gun on you..."

"I know, I know," David said. "And the stuff she was screaming, it was totally out of whack."

Roy looked back towards the closed kitchen door and shook his head slightly.

"I don't know man. Guess we can't do much until she wakes up."

CHAPTER 54

It was several hours later before Maria Veranda would regain consciousness, by which time dusk had arrived. Dylan had shut himself in one of the upstairs bedrooms and refused to come out, despite prodding by Laura. Roy and David had made a run into downtown Springfield and returned an hour later with two large brown paper sacks filled with food scavenged from a local Trader Joe's. With what they had managed to find, Anna was able to mix up a decent meal of spaghetti noodles mixed with tomato sauce, although to the four of them, none of whom had eaten so well in what felt like years, the meal was divine. For the first time since the news of the attacks had reached his ears, sitting around the enormous yet unornamented oak dining room table next to his wife, whose face was flushed as she enthusiastically chatted up Anna, Roy felt hopeful. He talked with David about their old lives, shooting the shit like they were both back in college, neither they nor their wives minding in the slightest the crude humor sprinkled into the conversation.

Anna even cracked up when Roy suggested that the way he always remembered Laura's birthday was by reliving the memory of the one time he'd forgotten it. Laura, laughing but looking slightly embarrassed, mumbled something about checking on Dylan, and left the room.

"By the way, Roy," David started. "Have you heard the story about a naked woman robbing a bank..."

He was cut off by the sound of Laura's excited voice coming from the other room.

"She's awake!"

David started to get up, but Roy cut him off.

"Let me go and talk to her first," Roy said. "She's comfortable with me, and last time she saw you, she tried to kill you. There's a better chance she'll open up to me about whatever's going on with her."

David nodded slowly and sat back down, hating himself for doing so but knowing Roy was right.

Roy entered the room, closing the door softly behind him. Laura was on her knees beside the sofa, eye-to-eye with Maria, who looked like a scared rabbit caught in headlights, her dark eyes wide with fright and darting around the room as if she expected a masked killer to be lurking in one of the semi-dark corners. Laura turned as her husband approached.

"She's alright Roy, the bullet didn't do any lasting harm. She's just...freaked out."

As if to illustrate the point, Maria threw herself off the sofa and marched towards the front door, head down, breathing hard, muttering something under her breath that Roy couldn't make out. Roy quickly stepped in front of her to block the door.

"Maria…"

Maria, without looking at him, moved to shove Roy out of the way, and he grabbed her by the shoulders, shaking her slightly.

"Maria," he said insistently. "No one is going to hurt you here, you're safe."

Maria shook her head violently, struggling against Roy's grip, shooting frequent glances at the stairs. Roy followed her gaze and felt his blood run cold. Dylan was standing at the top of the staircase with his left hand on the banister, his form masked in shadow, except for his eyes, which glowed dark red like flaming coals. Maria let out a piercing scream and Roy pressed himself against the wall beside the door, his entire body shaking. As he stepped into the faint sliver of sunlight cast by the setting sun however, the glowing light faded from Dylan's dark eyes, and the shadows surrounding him lifted, revealing the baggy t-shirt and cargo pants he'd occupied for the last several weeks.

"Is she okay?" he asked, landing lightly on the living room floor, and approaching them tentatively.

Roy let out an exasperated sigh, shaking himself. He badly needed some rest; the chaotic state of the world was clearly getting to him.

"Y-yeah," Maria said shakily, taking several deep breaths to calm herself down. "Yeah, I'm alright." Still feeling very uncomfortable, she made a point of not looking Dylan in the eyes as she sat back down on the sofa.

Roy sat down on the sofa next to Maria, whose hands were twisting nervously in her lap. Her brow was plastered with sweat. She stared pointedly down at a spot on the floor, avoiding Roy's eyes.

"My dad, he…" Maria paused, unsure whether she should continue.

Roy glanced at Laura, who was eyeing Maria nervously. Dylan had retreated up the staircase into his room, the door shutting with a brisk snap behind him.

"I-I saw him do something. Something terrible."

Roy and Laura looked at each other anxiously. Laura laid a hand on Maria's shoulder.

"Honey, did your daddy do something to you?"

Maria shook her head indignantly.

"No, no, nothing to me. He killed this bastard who got my sister hooked on drugs a few years back. Drowned him in cold blood."

"I'm so sorry you had to witness that," Roy said, unsure of what else to say.

Laura was now staring uncomfortably at the floor.

"Well, I-I…" Maria paused again. "That's the worst part. I didn't witness it."

Both Roy's and Laura's gazes snapped back to Maria.

"Well, I didn't exactly witness it. He, he…." She wet her lips nervously. "He showed me."

Roy, now looking very worried, opened his mouth, but Maria beat him to the punch.

"Dylan showed me. I know that probably sounds insane, but I saw him there. And I-I saw..." Maria closed her eyes, fighting back tears. "I saw Lilly. I thought...I thought..."

"You saw Lilly?" They all turned to see David Veranda standing in the open doorway, his expression a mask of shock. "You saw her?" He didn't sound as if he believed it himself.

"Daddy," Maria moaned, her eyes filling with tears. "She was here, and you were gonna...he made me think...I thought...I thought..."

The rest of her words were lost in a flood of tears. David crossed the room in two strides and pulled his sobbing daughter into a fierce embrace.

"It's alright pumpkin, I've got you," he whispered. "No one's gonna hurt you now, you're safe."

"No daddy, I'm not safe," she whispered, gazing up into his great, bear-like bearded face. "I'm not safe here, none of us are." And silently, she turned to look up at the closed bedroom door that Dylan Teryon had vanished through moments before. "No one is safe here anymore."

CHAPTER 55

Anna Veranda wiped a string of vomit from the corner of her mouth with a shaking, sweaty hand, the knuckles white from gripping the rim of the toilet seat so hard. Her whole body was drenched with a cold sweat. Her eyes were rimmed with dark circles, and her head felt as though it weighed at least a couple hundred pounds. She forced herself to turn away from the chunky green-brown mess filling the toilet bowl and dragged herself across the tiled bathroom floor to the sink. She nearly broke the handle off in her rush to get the water running, cupping the flow into her open mouth like she was dying of thirst, the wonderful, cool substance soothing her burning throat and washing away the pervasive taste of vomit. She gripped the sides of the sink, struggling to catch her breath. She was well aware that she was no longer "just a little tired," that much had become clear over the last several days, which had passed by for her in a blurry haze as though she'd been drugged.

She leaned heavily over the sink and was overcome by a deep coughing fit. She spat up a large, wet blob of phlegm, and felt her anxiety rise when she saw the spider's web of blood mixed with the phlegm. She rested her forehead against the sink, the cool marble soothing her burning fever a little. Whatever she had, it was much worse than a simple head cold, as she'd initially told herself, and, to make matters worse, it seemed to be progressing. The vomiting had started a few days prior when they were still on the road, at first only once every several hours, but by now, it was almost constant. The fever had taken hold of her in the last several hours, along with a terrible nausea that had made the simple act of making it to the bathroom before the vomiting began again a dizzying ordeal.

A knock on the bathroom made her jolt upright.

"Anna, you alright?" came a concerned woman's voice.

Anna sighed. Evidently, she had woken Laura up with her antics.

"I'm fine," she replied in a croaked whisper.

Unable to hear her, Laura waited another moment before opening the door to find Anna lying on her side on the cold bathroom floor, moaning in pain, her entire body shaking.

"Oh Jesus, Anna," Laura gasped, hurrying to her side.

Anna sat up and tried to smile at her new friend, although she only managed a pained grimace, and her sunken appearance only served to trouble Laura further. She hurried to the sink to get Anna a glass of water, which she accepted gratefully. Laura sat down next to her with her back against the cupboard underneath the sink.

"You look terrible," she said after a moment's silence, unsure what else to say.

Anna managed a pained smile.

171

"You think I look terrible now, you should see me when I'm woken up before eight on a Sunday morning."

Laura smiled at that.

"Maria okay?" Laura asked.

"Yeah, she's alright," Anna replied. "Just shaken up."

"She ever do anything like that before?"

"No," Anna replied firmly. "She's a good girl, she's just…" She wracked her brain for the right word to describe what exactly her daughter was, but nothing came to her. *Scared enough to almost shoot her dad…* she thought.

"We're all a little messed up right now," Laura said. "I mean God, who wouldn't be, look at the state of the world right now. If someone wasn't messed up by it, especially someone her age, I'd be shocked."

Anna nodded, not comforted in the slightest.

"Messed up is locking yourself in your bedroom after school every day and crying all afternoon," Anna said weakly. "Shooting your dad is something else."

Laura merely nodded, unsure of what to say.

"David told me what Maria said after she woke up," Anna continued. "He looked pretty shaken up about it."

Laura peered at her intently.

"She said she saw David drown someone with his bare hands. She said that…" she paused, not even sure how to explain what she had heard to Laura.

Laura was now looking very worriedly at Anna.

"What did she say, Anna?" Laura prompted, a feeling of cold dread creeping into her stomach.

"She said that Dylan…"

But whatever Anna had been about to say about Dylan was lost in another vomiting fit, and the momentary bubble of fear that had risen in Laura's throat at the mention of Dylan was lost as she rushed to hold Anna's hair back as she spat up the remains of her lunch into the white marble bathroom sink.

"God, I need to sleep," Anna gasped when it finally stopped, wiping spittle from the corner of her mouth. "Even just a few damned hours, I'd feel so much better."

Laura, who doubted very much that a few hours' sleep would do her friend much good but had no idea how else to help her, said:

"Hang on, I've got something."

She left the room, leaving Anna shaking and sweating while she leaned over the bathroom sink, waiting for the nausea to pass. She returned a moment later, and Anna saw she was carrying a small white medicine bottle in her hand, which she placed on the bathroom counter in front of Anna. Anna gave her a quizzical look.

"Look, if you need to sleep, I've got some pills that you could try. I usually save them for when I have nightmares, but I think right now, your need is greater than mine."

Anna removed the cap on the bottle and shook a few of the small round white pills into her hand. She contemplated them for a moment.

"I usually take two," Laura said, starting towards the door.

172

"Wait," Anna said suddenly, causing Laura to pause. "Did Dylan ever act…strangely when you were on the road? Like he might be hiding something?"

Laura thought for a moment, not sure how much she should reveal.

"Get some rest," she said finally. "I'll come find you in the morning and we can talk."

Anna nodded. Laura started towards the door.

"Thank you, Laura," Anna said, smiling.

It was the first time Laura had seen her smile without looking like it caused her any pain to do so. Laura smiled back.

"Sleep well, kid," Laura said, and vanished through the door.

Anna watched her leave. unaware that it was the last time she'd see her alive.

CHAPTER 56

Anna Veranda snapped awake in bed, breathing hard. Her entire body was drenched in a cold sweat.

"Bad dream," she thought. She seemed to be having a lot of those lately. She reached over to shake her husband awake, then remembered he was in the other room with Maria. She'd wanted to be in there with them, but David had insisted that it was better if she slept alone, as in her condition, she needed her rest.

"Well, so much for that," she thought. She groaned as a sudden sharp pain pierced her stomach. She could feel the bubble of vomit rising in her throat. She made a move to get up off the bed, but her muscles didn't respond. She lay still, a sudden vice-like grip of fear rising in her throat. She suddenly felt very weak all over. She tried again to get off the bed, but she didn't even have the strength to lift her arm. Now beginning to panic, she tried to cry out for help. She only managed a weak rasp before the vomit rose into her mouth and nose, cutting off her airway. Panicking, she thrashed about, trying desperately to turn herself over, but her muscles refused to obey. She was sweating profusely, her body temperature rising at an alarming rate. She sputtered and choked, desperate for air. The room began to spin in front of her.

"Help me," she coughed weakly. She twisted her head violently from side to side in a desperate attempt to clear the vomit from her airway, her efforts gradually weakening as the room faded to gray around her. Then she heard it. From somewhere far off, a deep throaty chuckle that sounded as though it had emerged from the depths of a deep mineshaft. Then she saw him. He was sitting in the corner of the room concealed in the shadows, his black magician's cape billowing behind him despite the lack of a breeze, his black top hat held at a slight angle on top of his head. He beckoned to her with a gloved hand, grinning wickedly. His dark eyes slowly reached out to meet her as the room faded to black around her, and she saw that there was nothing behind those eyes except inky blackness, a dark, empty hole spiraling into infinite nothingness. Anna tried to scream but no sound came out. The world faded to black, and she lay calmly back against the pillow, perfectly still.

CHAPTER 57

Laura woke with a terrified scream, the ghastly image from the first night her father had climbed into her bed burned in front of her eyes even as the dream faded around her. She took several deep breaths to calm herself down.

"You're not back there," she murmured to herself reassuringly. "He can't hurt you now. You're here with Roy, he's here to protect you, you're okay, you're okay..."

She glanced over at her husband, who was still sound asleep. She thought about waking him but decided against it. She knew he'd want to hear about the dream, she knew he'd want to comfort her, but she couldn't bring herself to disturb his sleep after he'd nearly been shot less than twelve hours ago. She glanced over at the bedside clock radio, then remembered that it was dead.

"Guess the end of the world will do that," she thought dryly.

She hugged herself, her arms folded protectively over her breasts. She thought longingly of the sleeping pills. It was a dangerous path to wander down. She'd once attempted suicide by swallowing half a bottle of the pills shortly after meeting Roy. He'd discovered her lying unconscious on her bathroom floor and rushed her to the hospital. Only when she later regained consciousness did she finally confess to him the horrors from her childhood that had haunted her into adulthood.

Through the years of therapy, medication, and nightmares that followed, Roy never left her side. Eventually, the need to take the pills had subsided. At least it had, until the world had gone to shit and the nightmares that had stopped years ago had begun again. She swung her legs over the edge of the bed. She glanced back at her sleeping husband. She could wake him up. He'd hold her and tell her everything was okay, and she would never have to touch the pills again, everything would be alright then. She shook her head.

"Yeah, everything will be alright until the next time," she thought. "You have to make it stop, whether you like it or not. And right now, this is the only way."

She couldn't argue with that. She got out of the bed and walked across the hall into the bathroom. Guided by the faint moonlight shining through the tinted overhead window, she opened the battered medicine cabinet, expecting to see the small, white bottle. The cabinet however was empty. For a moment, Laura stared perplexedly at the empty space where she'd left the bottle. Then she realized Anna had never set the bottle back when she'd given it to her. She must've taken it back with her into her room.

Taking a moment to recall what room Anna was sleeping in, Laura walked back out into the dark hallway, the moonlight guiding her in the direction of Anna's room. It felt strange to Laura, not having the power working. She tried not to think about it too much, as it was only another reminder of the unfortunate situation they were in.

"Unfortunate," she thought, smiling. "If by unfortunate, you mean the entire world woke up from a night of drinking doing ninety on the freeway, you probably got a point," she thought in the voice of Richard Pryor, managing a laugh.

She knocked on the door of Anna's room. No response. Not wanting to frighten her, Laura gently pushed open the door to the bedroom. Anna was lying on her side in bed, her face turned away from the door.

"Anna?" Laura whispered.

Nothing.

"Anna?" Laura said, a little louder. Still no response.

Figuring she should just let Anna sleep, Laura went to the bedside table and began opening drawers, searching for the bottle. She came up empty. She glanced back at Anna, who still had not moved despite the noise. Laura felt a small twinge of anxiety creep through her but ignored it. Laura bent down and felt under the bed, wondering if it had fallen underneath it. No luck. She turned to the closet, and saw it was closed. Now feeling slightly perplexed, Laura turned back to Anna, who still hadn't moved. She felt that small twang of anxiety creep through her once more, a little stronger this time.

"Anna?" Laura said, prodding her shoulder gently.

No response.

"Anna?" Laura tried again, shaking her a little. Anna remained completely limp. A shiver raced up Laura's spine. She suddenly had the irrepressible feeling that something was wrong.

Laura grabbed Anna by the shoulders and shook her hard.

"Anna!" she shouted.

Anna didn't stir. It suddenly occurred to Laura that Anna wasn't breathing. Had she taken too many of the pills? Laura swore she'd only told Anna to take two, but maybe she'd misheard…Panicking, Laura shoved her right middle and index finger deep into Anna's neck, feeling desperately around for a pulse. Nothing.

"Anna!" she screamed, shaking her hard by the shoulders.

From somewhere far off, she heard doors opening and running footsteps. She rolled Anna over, positioning her hands above Anna's chest for compressions. Only to feel her insides dissolve as she stared into the wide-open terrified eyes of Anna Veranda, her face blackened from asphyxiation, her tongue lolling out the side of her mouth uselessly, her entire mouth filled with dark green vomit. Laura screamed as Roy burst through the door, managing to catch his fainting wife before she hit the floor. He felt a wave of deep nausea pass over him as he caught sight of Anna's lifeless body.

He turned as the door opened again. Dylan stood in the doorway, partially hidden in shadow. Although Roy couldn't see his face entirely, he could tell the boy was looking directly at Anna's body, and judging by the lack of a reaction, the sight didn't trouble or even surprise him in the slightest. The thought unnerved Roy.

"He did this…" Roy nearly jumped with fright at the sound of the voice in his head.

176

Dylan stared at the body in the bed impassively, seeming to not even notice Roy. "He did this..." The words terrified Roy.

It was ridiculous, impossible, his mind was playing tricks on him, that was all. Still, the way Dylan was staring unblinkingly at Anne's lifeless body, his eyes blazing in a way that badly frightened Roy, he seemed almost...angry. Then the spell was broken as the door flew open again as David crashed into the room, followed by Maria.

"Roy, what the hell..." David exclaimed.

He froze when he saw the body, the blood draining from his face.

"Anna?" he whispered, his voice trembling.

Maria pushed past her father, slowly approaching the dead body of her mother. Her legs failed her, and she dropped to her knees.

"M-mom?" she whispered, the room blurring in front of her as the tears filled her eyes.

"MOM!" she screamed, sobbing into her hands.

For several minutes, the hushed audience members stared uncomprehendingly at the strange spectacle that lay before them, the silence broken only by the wails of the girl who now felt the destruction of civilization was finally complete.

CHAPTER 58

Kaden Versantos lay awake on top of the sleeping bag, staring up at the "x" the crossed tent poles made at the point where they converged directly above his head. His father, sleeping a few feet away, snored loudly, but Kaden didn't notice. He was used to his father's snoring. He hadn't slept much in the last several weeks, although he never felt the slightest bit tired, as if he were perpetually being injected with stimulants. His father hadn't said anything about it. Kaden knew he was worried about him, which he didn't mind, so long as he kept believing it only had to do with his mother dying of radiation sickness. This of course was part of it, and he thought of little else during his waking hours. However, at night, Kaden's thoughts turned to other, more pressing matters. He didn't have a name for the state he was in during the times he normally would've been asleep, including this moment. He had effectively shut out the outside world and confined himself to a small room in his head, which functioned as a sort of radio station. He could get a general sense of what was happening on whatever channel he'd tuned into tonight, which appeared to be somewhere in the Midwest, possibly in Ohio, but he couldn't be sure.

What he really would have liked to do was enter the mist, so that he could have a clearer picture. His anticipation had been steadily building throughout today in preparation for whatever important event tonight would bring. Unfortunately, entering the mist required a bathtub or at least a body of water. He'd wanted to ask his father if they could stop somewhere near a river or a stream but had avoided doing so for fear he would start asking questions. He wasn't sure how his father would react to learning his son had some bizarre form of telepathy, especially with all the stress the last few months of being on the road had brought. Since leaving home, they'd avoided the cities and populated areas. His father explained that they were too dangerous, and the odds were that anyone they ran across would be a threat.

Kaden knew he was right, but the approach meant they also couldn't scavenge from abandoned houses and grocery stores, which meant their diet consisted of a half a dozen types of wild berries his father could identify as safe, and small game roasted over hastily constructed campfires. Kaden hadn't complained, knowing it would do no good, but his ever-increasing hunger was making it difficult to concentrate during times like these when he needed more than ever to see into the mist. The nuclear holocaust hadn't been an accident. He'd known that almost as soon as it had happened. Something was pulling the strings, a dark presence whose malevolence was terribly great. Kaden had shielded himself from this monster for the time being, but he could feel it poking around in the dark corners he concealed himself in, searching for him. And it was getting closer every day.

Moving from place to place didn't seem to deter its progress at all, leading Kaden to believe that the monster, like himself, could access the mist. Whenever he worked up the courage to ask himself what the monster intended to do with him if (when) it found him, he thought of the vision he'd had on the night he nearly drowned. The little boy with the glittering black eyes. The way he'd plunged a knife into that poor little girl, over and over again...it hadn't been human. Couldn't've been human. Somehow, the monster had acted through the little boy. Could it be that he still was? Kaden refocused on the place in Springfield, Ohio, trying with all his might to see through the thick static clouding his sight, needing to know if the little boy was there.

And then he froze. He felt it then. The same dark shadow he'd felt when the little girl had been rising into the air on invisible strings. He was there. In that house. Kaden strained to see more, but he couldn't get a clear picture without the bathtub. He was on the move. There were others moving around the house too. Two women, they were talking about something. One of them was very sick.

"The pills...to stop the dreams..."

The thoughts were flowing in randomly now, disconnected, arriving so fast he barely heard one before the next overtook it. What he did know, though, was that they were plotting something. He heard a woman's scream, then a deep, cruel laugh. Kaden jumped out of his sleeping bag, his entire body drenched in sweat, trembling all over. His father stirred.

"Kaden, go back to bed," he muttered sleepily, rubbing his aching forehead.

He turned to his father, who had rolled over in his sleeping bag, ever muscle tense.

"Dad, we need to get to a river, now."

He wasn't sure it would do any good, but it was the only thing he could think of now. He had to get back into the mist if there was any chance of the stopping the demon from hurting the people in that house.

His dad mumbled something incomprehensible and rolled over again. Kaden bent down and shook his father hard by the shoulders. His father swatted at him sleepily, muttering irritably.

"Kaden, go back to sleep," he said irritably. "I'll talk to you in the morning."

"Dad," Kaden insisted. "In about five minutes, a woman is going to die."

The words came tumbling out of his mouth, startling even himself with their purposefulness. His father sat up suddenly, gazing at Kaden with a mix of curiosity and astonishment. He still hadn't gotten used to his son's sudden ability to speak after he'd gone sixteen years without saying a single word.

"Kaden," he started.

"Her name is Anna Veranda. She's about thirty-five years old, and she has a daughter named Maria. They're sheltering in a house in Springfield, Ohio with a couple named Roy and Laura. They brought a little boy with them named Dylan, and I think the magician is possessing him."

Kaden's father stood up and laid his hands gently on his son's shoulders.

"Kaden, look, I'm sorry if you had a nightmare. We can talk about it in the morning."

179

Kaden stared at his father incredulously. In the back of his mind, he could feel the monster moving closer, preparing to spring on his unsuspecting target.

"Damnit," Kaden thought. "He's not going to listen, damnit, what do I do?"

The answer became clear a moment later. Kaden slowly stepped backward, feeling around for the tent flap behind.

"Kaden what are you doing?" his father asked, his brow furrowed.

"I'm sorry, dad," Kaden said, zipping the flap open. "But I have a job to do."

Without so much as a backward glance, Kaden sprinted off into the dark woods, ignoring his father's alarmed shouts, feeling thorns and branches cutting into his bare feet and not caring. He could sense the monster moving closer to Anna. It was almost on top of her. There wasn't much time left.

Kaden felt his lungs burning as he pushed himself to run harder, trees flying past him on both sides, small animals scattering as he approached. He kept glancing off to either side of him but was met only with a solid wall of trees. From somewhere far behind him, he could hear his father's heavy running footsteps chasing after him through the thick underbrush.

"Gotta find water," he thought desperately.

The monster was on top of Anna now. It was starting. He nearly fell as a large bramble pierced deep into the ball of his foot. Blood marked his every step now. A wail of pain pierced the night air.

"No, no, NO!" Kaden screamed, searching around desperately for a nearby body of water.

Nothing. He could hear Anna's heart beating out of sync with his own as he ran. It was rapidly fading away with every passing second.

He gasped, nearly tripping over his own feet as a small lake emerged in the center of a wide-open clearing less than 100 feet away. Kaden sprinted toward it like a man dying of thirst in the Sahara Desert. He heard his father crash out of the underbrush somewhere behind him as he plunged head-first into the freezing water, knowing Anna wasn't dead yet, but not knowing how much longer she had. Ignoring the cold searing like fire through his entire body, he closed his eyes, his feet coming to rest on the muddy bottom. His heart rate slowed; his brain waves lengthened. And then the world was gone, replaced by a small dark bedroom, moonlight filtering through the open window to his left. Kaden, standing in the corner, surveyed the room. Anna Veranda was lying in the bed next to the window, gently being prodded by another woman who was standing beside the bed. Kaden started towards the two women, then felt his heart drop like a stone. The woman in the bed was lying on her side, her eyes open, dark green vomit leaking from the corner of her mouth. He was too late.

He fell to his knees, watching her still face blankly as the other woman began shaking her lifeless body, screaming at her to wake up. Kaden shook his head, feeling the tears stinging his eyes. He'd failed. Anna Veranda was dead. A man, presumably the woman's husband, burst into the room, catching his wife just as she fainted. And then someone else entered the room. Kaden's blood ran cold. It was a little boy. The woman's husband stared at him quizzically. The boy was glaring at the dead body on the bed. Kaden moaned in terror as he saw the little boy's eyes. They were as black as midnight.

The vision faded as a pair of strong arms grasped Kaden under the armpits, ripping him from the bottom of the lake and pushing him towards the surface. Kaden, his entire body feeling limp, didn't resist. Kaden sputtered and coughed as his face broke the surface. A second later, his father emerged beside him, dragging his son towards the shore. Kaden splayed out in the grass next to the lake, coughing weakly. His father lay down next to him, spitting out lake water onto the grass.

"Kaden," he gasped. "Kaden, what the hell..."

"She's dead," Kaden said hollowly.

His father said nothing.

"Dad, this may be hard for you to hear, but I'm not crazy," Kaden continued.

"Do you remember the night I told you about the magician? Before all of this started?"

Kaden's father nodded, unsure what else to say.

"He's real. He started all of this. He controls people somehow. I'm not exactly sure how he does it, but there's a little boy. His name is Dylan. The magician has a hold of him, and he used him to kill Anna."

Kaden's father shook his head weakly, wanting to believe his son but unable to process what he was hearing.

"Dad, even if you don't believe any of this, can you do one thing for me?" Kaden's father, who had his head clasped in his hands as if he were having a migraine, took a moment before replying.

"Sure, son," he said weakly. "What do you need me to do?"

"We need to go to Fairfax, Virginia. There's a group of people there that needs our help."

CHAPTER 59

The sign announcing his arrival on interstate 495 passed by much slower than it should have as the Ford-F150 rolled smoothly along. In another time and place, Tyson Sanders wondered vaguely whether he had inadvertently slowed the truck down or whether he had reached such a state of exhaustion to where his perception of time was slowing. He sighed and rubbed his eyes for what felt like the hundredth time in the last ten minutes. In his current mental state, it could've been either, and he had no desire to figure out which it was. For Tyson, the odds had never been more against him. The world around him that he'd known was gone. He'd driven through every town they'd passed, first along route 78 through southwestern New Jersey, then route 76 into Maryland, and finally route 270 into southern Maryland where the abandoned and in many cases heavily damaged skyline of Washington D.C. became visible just over the horizon.

Even from a distance, the city looked as though it had personally been through its own nuclear holocaust. He'd crawled through suburban streets, banged on front doors, ran through abandoned hospitals calling out desperately for help. Not one answer had come. He was all alone with his poor, sick child, whom he could not help, whom he had failed, who…(would die soon). Tyson glanced back in the rearview mirror at her tiny sleeping form as they passed by a massive farm field. A lone pair of cows raised their heads and stared curiously after the truck as it passed.

In truth, Marianne had not stirred for the last several hours, and she'd barely spoken at all in the last several days. Tyson had convinced her to eat some cold meatballs he'd scrounged out of a basement freezer back in Emmitsburg, but that had been almost a day ago, and since then, she had not begged for anything more. He'd spent the last six hours trying to ignore the terrible leaden feeling of dread growing in his gut that combined with his dull pounding in his temples to reduce his vision to a pair of slits that barely provided enough coverage to see the road in front of him. But he pressed on anyway. He ran a shaking hand over his scruffy black beard, a new addition to his once handsome features that he had not been able to shave in several weeks. He would find help soon; he was sure of it. Then he would wake Marianne up, and they would go see the doctor, and they would help her get over this thing.

Yes, she'd knock back a few pills with names far too complicated for him to ever remember, and they'd get on with their travels. Yes, that's all they were doing right now, just a father and daughter road trip vacation, they'd had a little hang-up, that was all. Mommy couldn't come because she was too busy at work and couldn't get time off, that's why she wasn't there with them, Alison would see them when they got home, the home they would be going back to in a few days when they ended their trip, might to have end it a little early for Marianne's sake, she really seems quiet lately, probably just a stomach bug, nothing to worry about, nothing a little water and bed rest couldn't fix, everything would be fine, just…perfectly…fine. He glanced back in the rearview mirror at Marianne as they passed another abandoned farmhouse on their right. She hadn't moved.

He had quit knocking on doors at some point. He didn't exactly remember when. It had to have been more than a day ago because they hadn't stopped driving since then. He hadn't stopped to find food. His appetite seemed to have deserted him, along with the hope that he would find some stranger still in their home who could help Marianne. So he'd continued the drive south while Marianne slept, struggling to keep his eyes open but somehow managing to do so, not so much to see the road in front of him as to see any living human being if by some miracle one emerged, preferably one with a medical degree and clinical experience, but he felt content to fulfill the first criteria that they had a pulse. Even if they couldn't help Marianne, the presence of another living human being might help keep him sane for a little while longer.

Although, come to think of it, he might already have gone beyond the point of no return in that regard. Automatically, he shifted the steering wheel to the right. For a brief moment, he thought his better judgement might've finally decided they were both beyond saving and was trying to end it quickly but then saw that he'd turned off on an exit. A small dark green road sign emerged on his right, announcing that he was entering the city of Fairfax, population 24,387. This thought brought him no joy. To Tyson, it made no difference where he was. Cities were meant to be bustling metropolis' where thousands of real, living, breathing people pushed past each other on overcrowded sidewalks on their way to work, honked their horns incessantly at one another, nearly getting flattened in crosswalks while they were on calls with their bosses, and big teenagers in ripped muscle shirts beat up eight-year-old kids for wearing nice shoes. In this brave new world, those places had ceased to exist.

As they pulled away from the exit ramp and cruised towards what looked to be downtown, a strange feeling came over Tyson. He no longer felt like he was driving the truck… as though he was some strange ghost that was spectating the events unfolding in front of him rather than participating in them himself. The ghost had no control over the events that were taking place, just as he had no control. It might have troubled him under normal circumstances, but his nerves were so shot by this point, he'd probably lost the ability to feel troubled by anything days ago. As the two-story office buildings and small business storefronts rose up on either side of them, Tyson became aware of the fact that the world around him had gone perfectly silent, as seamlessly as if he'd slipped a pair of noise cancelling headphones over his ears. Not even a bird chirping merrily. The entire world seemed to have passed away, leaving only him and the sick little girl sitting in the backseat to fend for themselves.

"Fairfax, Virginia…" he thought absurdly. "The last bastion of civilization."

Under normal circumstances, it might've struck him as funny. Now however, the only thing it made him want to do was cry. But Tyson did not cry. He would not break down and cry if there was still a chance he could save his little girl. He turned at a corner marked by a small local grocery store. A block later, he entered a neighborhood. He scanned the houses as they passed by without much hope of seeing one with any life. Boarded up doors. Dark and broken windows. Cars piled up haphazardly on curbs, the occupants probably having been shot dead by soldiers or each other long ago.

"Guess it gives the phrase 'killed over a can of soup' a whole meaning, eh?"

Again, Tyson didn't laugh. He didn't think it likely he'd ever laugh again.

Tyson pulled the Ford-F150 over to the curb. He looked at the two-story blue stucco they had pulled up in front of. The front door had been ripped off its hinges, and two of the front windows had large holes through the glass. Perhaps if the occupants had left in a hurry, they'd left some food behind. Even if they hadn't, there was bound to be something useful. Tyson hung his head in exhaustion. Besides, he had to get Marianne to eat something. If it would improve her condition, even a little...

"You know it won't," whispered the cold, empty voice in his head.

He ignored it. He reached behind his seat and tapped Marianne on the shoulder.

"Honey?" he asked gently, struggling to keep his voice steady.

She didn't move.

"Marianne, baby?" he tried again, prodding her a little harder this time.

From somewhere deep in the ball she'd curled up into, she let out a single low, weak cry of pain, and then was still. Tyson felt as though he were suddenly underwater. Every sound seemed to come from a long way off, and everything around him seemed to be moving very slowly. There was a faint ringing in his ears. He didn't prod her again. Even without the cruel voice telling him, he knew there was no point. In perfect silence, he got out the truck, opened the back door, wrapped his arms around his daughter, and carried her like an infant down the silent, empty street.

CHAPTER 60

Jody slowly opened her eyes to an unfamiliar bedroom. She sat up slowly, scanning her surroundings. She had little memory of the events that had taken place over the last forty-eight hours, since those two strange men had found her in the middle of a worn-tar city street and saved her life. But she was fairly sure she hadn't fallen asleep here. So where was she? A small bedside table, a copy of "Gulliver's Travels" sitting cover up beside the bedside lamp. A pair of massive wooden bookshelves sitting side by side against the opposite wall. A large bay window leading out to a small wooden balcony on her right. A large ornately carved wooden dresser drawer standing sentinel on her left, next to a spacious walk-in closet. The entire room was painted a faint, pleasant yellow, besides the floor, which was draped with thick, fluffy, white carpet. None of this gave her much information. She could hear several faint voices in another part of the house. Jody winced as a searing pain pierced up through both her legs as she tried to sit up. She gingerly removed the bed sheets, revealing the thick, white gauze bandages covering both her legs. She slid herself over to the edge of the bed so that her bandaged legs draped over the side.

Jody smiled wanly.

"Maybe there were still a few good people in this world," she thought.

Maybe just a few good people because that was all it needed, really. It was all she needed to carry out her mission, and whatever would come after it.

"Maybe…the war is not lost," she whispered, feeling a single happy tear slide down her cheek.

She looked up as the voices outside suddenly rose, following a cacophony of confused yelling. Jody slowly lowered her injured legs to the floor, grabbing onto the bookshelf for support as they nearly gave way beneath her. Ignoring the terrible bolts of pain coursing through the lower half of her body like white-hot electrical charges, she stumbled towards the bedroom door and the raucous voices. From the sound of things, someone needed her very badly.

Chapter 61

When Tyson first heard the faint voices, he didn't acknowledge them. They were in his head, of course, just more bodiless entities of his mind's own making designed to punish him for his failure as a parent, as a husband, and as a human being. He looked down at the little girl cradled in his arms, her complexion ashen, her entire body completely limp. She'd taken her final breath a few moments ago. Tyson sighed heavily. She didn't have to feel the pain anymore. She didn't have to feel the hunger anymore. She didn't have to beg her weak, useless father for food or shelter, or water anymore. That brought him a little comfort. Enough to make him keep walking, anyway. He didn't have the strength to bury her and hated himself for admitting it. He looked up, and saw a three-story, red brick house on the corner with a black pickup truck parked in the driveway. It resembled his daughter's childhood home.

He looked down at her lifeless body, wondering what she'd say if she knew what he was thinking right now. Would she be angry? Would she cry? Would she be happy? Would she tell him she loved him? He knew the answer to this last one. Marianne had always loved her father and had never been afraid to show it. No matter how weak he might've been, no matter what struggles he might've gone through, through everything, she'd loved him unconditionally. Marianne and Alison both had. His two girls. Both gone now.

"Yes, that would be alright," he thought. "Go to that house over on the corner. Lay her down in her bed like you would at bedtime every night. Let her have that much. It's the least you can do for her."

He stumbled weakly down the street towards the house that so resembled his own, the voices growing louder with each step. If only they'd leave him alone for a few minutes.

"Can't you just give me a bit of peace?" he thought savagely. "Just so I can put my little girl to sleep one last time?"

But the voices only seemed to grow more insistent as he approached the house. Exhausted nearly to the point of death, Tyson Sanders was concentrating so intensely on simply putting one foot in front of the other that he didn't notice the group of half a dozen people crowded in the living room. Nor did he notice when Grace started tugging on her mother's sleeve and pointing out the front room bay window at the strange man walking up to the house carrying something in his arms. It was only when Jennifer screamed at the sight of poor little Marianne's lifeless body that he looked up to see the door to the house fly open, sending the crowd in the living room spilling out onto the lawn.

Tyson stared as they approached him, their wide-eyed gazes fixed on Marianne's body cradled in his arms. Then a man emerged from the sea of faces. It was Ben

Alrite. He stared solemnly at Tyson for a moment before shifting his gaze to his daughter's lifeless body. He slowly shook his head at the sight.

"Tyson," he started.

"No, no," Tyson sobbed, his stony expression shattering into a million pieces. "You don't...you don't have to be sorry, man," he stammered.

Then Tyson Sanders, who had never cried a single tear in his entire life, cried a biblical flood.

CHAPTER 62

The group silently stood sentinel around the lifeless body of the little girl lying on the sofa. Ben was grateful that Jennifer had shooed Grace out of the room when they'd brought Marianne's body in.

"There's nothing out there," Tyson said hollowly from a rocking chair in the corner, his head in his hands. "It's all gone. The medical center back in New Jersey…it looked like it had been bombed out. There's…there's nothing left."

No one even tried to argue with him. For Ben's part, he was not terribly surprised at this news. They'd been on the road for about a week before they'd arrived at the house, and what they'd seen in that time aligned perfectly with Tyson's description. Abandoned houses, windows dark and doors boarded up. Store fronts so badly damaged they wouldn't have looked out of place in the midst of a civil war. Streets strewn with glass and bullet casings. Abandoned vehicles lining the streets. Downed military helicopters still billowing smoke, the bodies of their crews lying haphazardly inside or several feet away in a few cases. It had only hit home for Ben during the last several days just how alone they were. He had not brought this up to the rest of the group. As far as he was concerned, they were scared enough as it was, although he suspected they were thinking along similar lines.

Mike felt the anger rising in him as he looked down at poor little Marianne. Having an absentee father and a cocaine-addicted mother meant Mike had spent most of his childhood roaming the streets of his city. He'd done a lot of things he cared not to think about back in those days. He'd always wondered if the presence of a loving, caring parent would've changed things. He'd known Tyson for years. Tyson was exactly what all children needed; a strong, loving father who could be both strict and supportive in equal measure. The way he doted on his little girl always made Mike smile. To see that family ripped apart in such terrible fashion, to see Tyson crying his eyes out as his dead child lay a few feet away, to know that there would be no justice for this terrible crime made Mike want to clock somebody hard in the jaw. He forcefully unclenched his hands from the fists they'd inadvertently made, the marks where the nails had dug into his palms visible.

"We should bury her," Ben said quietly. "In the backyard, by the swing set." He turned to Tyson. "She had a swing set at home, right?"

Tyson nodded.

"Yeah," he said. "Yeah, I think she would like that."

He got up from the chair.

"I should do it."

Ben nodded solemnly. Tyson started to leave the room, knowing there was an old shovel in the garage. Everyone looked up as Jody hobbled into the room,

188

leaning heavily against the wall for support. Lorenzo caught her as she nearly fell. Wrapping an arm around her shoulders, he helped her over to the couch where Marianne's body lay.

"Thank you," she gasped, struggling to catch her breath.

Tyson paused with his hand on the doorknob.

"Sleep well?" Serena sniffed, wiping her eyes dry. She glanced uncertainly at her husband, who was eyeing Jody curiously.

"Yeah, it was alright," she said, not wanting to discuss the nightmares that had plagued her. "Appreciate you stitching me up," she said, smiling at Lorenzo.

"No problem," Lorenzo replied, still eyeing Jody curiously. "If you don't mind me asking," Lorenzo said, "what made you get out of bed?"

"I was going to bring you breakfast in bed!" Grace said enthusiastically, smiling at Jody.

Jody smiled wanly at the happy little girl. With her dark hair and sweet demeanor, Grace reminded her of Kaitlyn.

"No, I didn't need anything," Jody said, turning to Marianne's still form, her expression melancholy. "I was called." She ran a hand gently over Marianne's pale face. "This little one needs me."

Her voice was very soft, almost girlish, but there was a deep, rhythmic quality to it that made her sound much more mature. It was the kind of voice a mother would use to soothe a crying child. Tyson had rejoined the group surrounding the sofa. His expression was unreadable.

"She's dead," Tyson said hollowly. "I'm sorry, but it's too late. There's nothing you can do."

Jody didn't seem to hear him. She continued to gently stroke Marianne's face, smiling sadly.

"There's still fire in this one," Jody said, tracing her slowly down Marianne's chest. "I can feel it. Where there is fire, there is always life."

Ben glanced at Tyson, who was beginning to look uncomfortable. Lorenzo stepped forward.

"Jody, look, I'm sorry, but Marianne is gone. We're going to bury her."

Again, Jody didn't appear to have heard. She placed a hand over Marianne's heart and murmured something under her breath. Tyson was beginning to feel slightly annoyed with the strange young woman, but Ben recalled the day they'd found her. She'd lost enough blood to kill another person, especially one of her size. That was what Jason had told him that night.

"Frankly," he'd said. "It was a miracle she was still alive."

And there was something else with her when they'd found her. Ben had felt it as they'd approached. A dark shadow, its presence so malevolent it had made Ben shiver. Ben held out a hand to stop Tyson as he started towards Jody.

"Let her try," Ben whispered, confusing himself as much as Tyson with these words. "It can't hurt."

Tyson, still looking very uncomfortable, slowly stepped back, eyeing Jody suspiciously.

Jody continued murmuring under her breath, running her hand over the small girl's chest, which had begun to grow warm under her touch. She stiffened as a soft, warm breeze brushed against her back. It faded quickly, but she could still feel the heat radiating from somewhere in the far corner of the room. She didn't have to look to know Kaitlyn was there, watching her intently.

"So, you're back huh?" Jody thought bitterly.

She felt Kaitlyn recoil slightly at her harsh tone and found she didn't care.

"Where were you when this little girl was dying?" she thought angrily.

Kaitlyn didn't reply. Jody could feel herself tense. She was getting angrier by the second. All the frustration, all the tears, all the losses that she'd barely been holding back were spilling out of her in a tidal wave that threatened to drown the sane part of her brain.

The heat radiating from Marianne's chest was beginning to fade. Jody was losing her.

"Look," Jody thought. "You can be angry at me, you can punish me all you want, but don't take that out on this poor kid."

Kaitlyn remained silent.

"Marianne doesn't deserve to die, not like this. Please..." she begged.

Kaitlyn said nothing.

"DAMNIT, WHAT DO YOU WANT FROM ME!" Jody screamed aloud, whirling around, and causing the entire group to jump backward, startled.

She was staring hard at the corner where she knew her childhood best friend was hiding, her eyes boring into the spot where the white plaster met the dark oakwood floorboards. She turned back to Marianne.

Terrified of what she was about to find, she pressed a hand over the little girl's heart. There was nothing. The heat was gone.

"She's gone," Jody whispered, her voice shaking.

"What?" Tyson asked, stepping forward.

"SHE'S GONE, GODAMNIT!" Jody screamed in his face. "SHE'S GONE, I CAN'T FUCKING SAVE HER, SHE WON'T FUCKING SAVE HER!" she screamed, pointing at the corner where Kaitlyn was hiding. "She won't..." she sobbed, burying her face in her hands. "She can't..."

"But you can..." Kaitlyn whispered. The voice startled Jody so much she nearly cracked her neck from whipping it around so fast to look at the corner where Kaitlyn remained hidden.

"Jody," Kaitlyn continued, speaking like a mother talking down a toddler throwing a temper tantrum. "This little girl didn't die of any illness. Not really. The day her mother died, that was when she lost the will to go on."

"I can't help her, Kaitlyn," Jody sobbed, collapsing on the sofa next to Marianne's lifeless body and burying her tear-stained face in her hands. "I don't know how."

"Yes, you do," Kaitlyn whispered, her tone remaining soothing but becoming more insistent. "You've been where she's been. You know how it feels."

At these words, Jody stopped crying. Suddenly, she was back in the ER the night after she was attacked, just a poor, broken little kid bawling her eyes out while the doctor who had just told her both her parents were dead hung his head, none of his extensive medical training giving him the slightest idea of how to comfort his patient.

"You know, Jody," Kaitlyn whispered again. "You spent so many years after that lost, angry, alone…"

"Broken," Jody murmured, the group that had gathered around her long forgotten. "I just felt so broken for such a long time, and I just…"

But the rest of her words were lost in a fit of crying. Grace started forward, looking as though she might cry herself, but Ben held up a hand to stop her.

"Not now," he murmured. Grace, who could feel tears welling up in her eyes at the sight of Jody, nevertheless obeyed.

Jody felt a spectral arm wrap around her shaking shoulders.

"No child should have to go through that," Kaitlyn murmured in her ear. "You can't change the past, kid. But what you can do is make sure that this child doesn't have to suffer through what you did. She's lost right now, just like you were. She doesn't know how to go on."

Jody recalled the many fights she'd had with her foster parents during the years before she'd been kicked out at eighteen and shook her head sadly.

"You can give her the spark, Jody. It might be buried deep inside you, but you still have it."

Jody raised her head out of her hands and gazed at the spot where she knew Kaitlyn was sitting, invisible to everyone but her. She could feel her best friend's warm smile.

"It only takes one person, Jody. You can be that for this poor little girl. You can heal her."

Jody felt a wan smile cross her face. "You're right," she whispered. "I can bring her back."

Jody turned back to Marianne as the others watched silently. She began to stroke a hand down the cool skin of the little girl's cheek, murmuring under her breath, stroking the little girl's hair in an almost motherly way. She could feel the heat beginning to rise in Marianne's chest. An invisible force suddenly began tugging at the back of her neck, struggling weakly to drag her forward. Jody's breath caught in her throat. The girl was reaching out to her, struggling to get to her. She needed to help Marianne close the distance. Jody slowly leaned over the little girl, pressing her face so close to Marianne's that their noses touched. The group had crowded back round the sofa, staring at the spectacle in awe. Tyson was watching Jody intently, beads of sweat running down his face.

"I'm right here," Jody whispered, cupping Marianne's face in her hands. "Come back to us."

Jody pressed even closer, so that her nose brushed lightly against Marianne's occipital bone.

"You're strong, kid," she whispered, lightly nuzzling Marianne with her nose. "You can come back from this, I believe in you, we all believe in you!"

The heat radiating from Marianne was so strong Jody could feel it coming out of her chest in waves. Jody reached down and placed a hand over her chest. There was still no heartbeat. The pull was so strong she couldn't have moved away from the little girl even if she'd wanted to. She was so close. But she couldn't quite cross the barrier yet. Then she felt it. A momentary stab of heat pierced her chest. The spark. The same one that had started the fire that had saved her life all those years ago. Jody felt the pull between them grow stronger. Jody felt tears of happiness gush from her eyes. Marianne wanted the spark. She had chosen life.

Jody raised the little girl's face to her own so that their lips touched. She pressed a little deeper, closing the seal between them. She could feel the heat rising in her chest, into her throat, passing through her open mouth. And then it was gone. For a brief instant, Marianne's entire body burned like fire, the sudden explosion of heat causing the entire group surrounding them to jump backward. Jody unglued her mouth from Marianne's, hoping, praying...She heard a collective sharp intake of breath. Jody let out a happy cry, tears flooding her face as Marianne began coughing, gasping for air as if she'd been held underwater for several minutes.

"Jesus..." she heard Ben whisper.

Tyson was crying too. Jason helped Jody off the sofa, allowing Tyson to sweep Marianne up into a bear hug, sobbing her name over and over again. Jason and Ben helped Jody get away from the chaos as the entire group threw themselves onto Tyson and Marianne, many of the women sobbing along with them.

"Daddy," Marianne sobbed into her father's shoulder. "She saved me. The woman I dreamed about."

Jody smiled wanly when she heard this. Jason and Ben helped Jody into the bedroom and laid her down gently on the bed.

"Jody, my god, how did you..." Jason started to say but Ben held up a hand to silence him.

"Let her rest," he said calmly, and Jason nodded.

"Thank you," he said as they turned to leave.

Jody managed a tired smile.

"You saved my life," she said. "I suppose it was only fair that I return the favor."

Ben smiled.

"I appreciate it. We'll leave you be for a while," he said as he shut the door behind him.

Jody lay back on the bed, her eyelids suddenly feeling like lead balloons. She allowed them to slide closed. She smiled at the cacophony of excited voices echoing from the living room.

"Maybe the good guys do finally have a chance," she thought as she drifted off to sleep. "Thanks Kaitlyn."

CHAPTER 63

A s he pulled the Chevrolet the group had piled into away from the driveway, David Veranda glanced back one last time at the spot where they'd buried his wife the previous night. He'd wanted to do it alone, but Roy had insisted on helping, and David, not having the strength to argue, hadn't refused him. They hadn't been able to find her a tombstone. Instead, they'd taken a dozen small rocks from the garden and laid them in a circle around the spot where they'd buried her. David had carved an inscription into a block of wood he'd found in the garage with a paring knife:

"Here lies Anna Veranda, a loving wife and mother."

It was simple, certainly not as good as she deserved, but it was the best he could do. When he'd finished, Roy and David had stood side by side, not admiring their handiwork but rather holding a vigil for Anna. There was nothing to be admired.

"Should I say a few words?" Roy had asked.

David had shaken his head, and that had been the end of the discussion. He hadn't bothered to wake Maria. She'd already been through enough that night. Now, leaving that place behind, David felt as though he were leaving a part of himself behind. And he knew then, even as he pulled the Chevrolet out of the neighborhood, David knew that he would never truly be whole again. He glanced at his daughter, who was sitting beside him in the passenger seat. She was staring out the window at the passing houses, seemingly lost in thought. David knew she was in shock. It had been like this when Lilly had gone away. She'd barely been in the house at all, staying later and later after school to train with the swim team, avoiding meals, mostly ignoring her parents when she was home. This had gone on for several months until one night she'd finally broken down, crying hysterically about how she'd felt lost since Lilly had left, and that she couldn't do this anymore. That had been the start of several years of therapy and antidepressants, but the happy, loving, outgoing little girl David had doted on with such enthusiasm was gone.

It deeply saddened David to see Maria shut down this way. He knew, even without her therapist explaining it to him multiple times, that it wasn't a healthy coping mechanism. It was moments like these when he most needed Anna. She would've known what Maria needed; she could've gotten through to her in a way that David simply couldn't. He would do the best he could, of course, but what happened when your best simply wasn't good enough? For that, he didn't have an answer. They didn't seem to have any particular agreed-upon destination as they sped east along route 70. Roy suggested that they could try Cincinnati, but David figured it wouldn't be any less dangerous or thoroughly looted than any of the other major U.S. cities. Laura suggested the Wayne National Forest, which wasn't far away, but given that no one in the group had much experience with hunting or identifying edible wild berries, they weren't sure what they would do for food once they got there.

So, for the moment, they continued east along route 70 past overturned and defunct cars lining the side of the road, occasionally being forced to maneuver their way around one that had been left in the middle of the road, towards whatever mystery destination awaited them, no one speaking much, except to voice the occasional suggestion for a target destination, which was either immediately shot down or ignored. No one felt much like socializing after the events of the previous night. The scene around them wasn't improving anyone's mood. When they passed by the city of Columbus, it looked like something out of a war movie. Most of the skyscrapers had given way completely, bathing the streets below in a flood of twisted metal and broken glass, and the ones that were still standing had enormous craters in their walls that looked like they had come from grenades, shot out windows, some of which had bodies hanging out of them, and the occasional spark from a severed electrical wire or broken LED light bulb. Some were still smoking in several places.

The streets below were just as bad. From what they could see from the highway, every inch was covered by broken glass, occasionally supplanted by melted, twisted metal or plaster. Entire city blocks were occupied by fallen office buildings that reminded Roy of news footage he'd seen of the falling of the twin towers. Shell casings, used grenades, knives, rifles, and broken bottles were strewn everywhere, along with the bodies of dead soldiers and civilians alike.

"Jesus," Laura whispered as they drove past.

Roy echoed her. David sighed. It hadn't struck him until that moment just how fucked they really were. For all he knew, they might well be the last surviving people on earth. The only one who didn't seem shocked at the sight was Maria. Her only focus was on the eleven-year-old boy sitting a few feet away. Dylan.

"But is it really Dylan?" she thought absurdly. "How...how could a kid...do something like that?"

To Maria, it simply didn't make any sense. She knew Dylan had killed her mother. Radiation sickness hadn't killed her mother, as the others seemed to assume. Although Maria was not an expert, she knew enough to be sure her mother had never entered the final stages of acute radiation syndrome. Her mother had died of asphyxiation by choking on her own vomit. Just before she'd left her mother's side last night, she'd felt something lying in her pocket. It was a bottle of sleeping pills. She'd removed it with trembling fingers and stared at the pills in the bottle for several minutes, not really understanding why she was doing it. And then it hit her. The pills were white, round, about the shape of a penny, just like a sleeping pill would've been. But they were blank.

A memory of talking to Lilly about an experiment she'd done that involved dissolving sleeping pills into a culture of yeast cells when she'd been working in her lab at MIT came rushing back to her.

"How do you keep track of everything in your lab? All those different reagents," Maria had said, smiling.

194

Lilly had laughed.

"Well," she said. "The sleeping pills are pretty easy. I just check the bottle before I dissolve them in solution. They always have labeling of the dosage from the manufacturer."

These pills had no such labeling. They were fake. Maria, overcome with emotion, had thrown the pills back down on the bed and ran out of the room. She lay awake for several hours after that, thinking.

"Do it!" he'd screamed at her as she aimed the gun at her father.

It had been Dylan's voice. Could it be that he'd somehow...she'd dismissed the thought as absurd at first. Dylan was just a kid; how could he have...

"Nobody is safe here anymore..." That's what she'd told her father when she'd woken up.

There had been something else there with her, in her vision. A cold, dark, empty voice that had boomed inside her head like a bass drum. A dark shadow that had chilled her to the bone. Dylan hadn't had a face, his entire visage concealed in shadow. Could it be...Again, she'd dismissed the thought. It was absurd, an eleven-year-old kid killing her mother. The sleeping pills might've been perfectly normal, and her mother had just taken one too many, yes, that had to be it, that made far more sense to her. She'd taken too many pills, vomited, and asphyxiated herself. Just an accident, nothing more. Still, her fear of the little boy, however irrational, remained, and she found herself wishing desperately as they sped down route 33 towards the small town of Lancaster to get herself and what remained of her family as far away from the little boy as possible, unaware that both Laura and Roy, sitting in the backseat next to Dylan, shared similar sentiments.

Maria rested her head against the back of her seat, the sun slipping beneath the tree line as they left highway 33 for the night. A small sign off to their right announced that they were entering the city of Athens, population 23,462.

"Hey David," Roy said sleepily from the backseat. "You sure you want to go into the city at night?"

"Not the city," David replied, as they turned off the exit ramp. "I agree that it's too dangerous, especially at night. I'm hoping we can find an empty cabin over by that lake," he said, pointing to a large, dark body of water a few miles to the east.

Maria closed her eyes. After a long day of non-stop driving, the thought of a warm bed and fresh water sounded heavenly to her.

"Might even be food there," David went on. "It's a pretty remote area, so probably hasn't been looted as heavily as the rest of the city."

"Even if not," Roy replied, "we can get our food from the lake. A day of fishing out there sounds relaxing. Granted, it's been a while since I've actually tried it out."

"Well, Roy," David said, grinning. "Maybe if I teach you how to fish, your wife can get rid of you for the weekend."

They both laughed heartily. Maria smiled, glad that the mood had lightened a little after the entire day had consisted mostly of uncomfortable silences.

"Hell," Laura said, punching Roy lightly on the arm, "maybe if you fall out of the boat, I'll finally get to sleep in on the weekends!"

Everyone, even Maria, laughed at that. In fact, the only person not laughing as the Chevrolet approached the lakefront was Dylan. Dylan had been quiet all day, lost in his thoughts. The sheer number of competing voices in his head was beginning to wear him down. Early that same morning, a new player had entered the arena that had become Dylan's psyche to fight for the controls. Another young man who was a few years older than Dylan. He seemed friendly. He'd even introduced himself to Dylan shortly after he'd arrived. His name was Kaden Versantos.

CHAPTER 64

Roy sat next to David on the wooden dock that stretched out over the water. They'd managed to find a pair of battered metal fishing rods stashed beneath a bunk in the cabin, along with a small bait and tackle box. As it turned out however, they would only need to fish recreationally. The kitchen cabinets had revealed an untapped reservoir of mac and cheese, rice, bread, peanut butter, spaghetti noodles, and a large assortment of MREs. Laura had brought a large metal saucepot down to the lake to collect water, and David had found, to everyone's great relief, several large propane tanks in the maintenance shed, one of which, with some help from Roy, he'd managed to attach to the gas main connected to the stove. The rest of the group was inside, eating mac and cheese they'd boiled for dinner. Roy looked out at the dark, clear surface of the lake.

He hadn't fished since he was a boy and had only done it a couple of times with his father. He'd never really been all that into it. He might well have given up and gone back inside out of boredom if he hadn't had David around to keep him company. Although truth be told, David wasn't all that into it either, and the whole idea had mostly been an excuse to talk to Roy out of earshot of the rest of the group.

"Maria okay?" Roy asked, playing absentmindedly with the white fishing line hanging taut along his rod.

"Honestly," David replied, squinting intently at his bob as it gave an irritable little jerk in the water. "I think she's still pretty shook up. You've never had teenagers, but anything that keeps them quiet for a full twenty-four hours is either a miracle or something that's gone very wrong."

Roy didn't laugh. David couldn't blame him.

"Well, given the state of the world right now, I'd have to guess the latter," Roy replied, starting a little as his own bob vanished beneath the surface.

"You got it?" David asked.

"Yeah, this I remember," Roy replied, pulling the line in a few feet, then releasing a little out. He repeated this motion several times. "Catch and release, my dad always used to say."

David smiled wanly.

"David," Roy asked. "At risk of sounding like a scared kid, do you think we're safe here?"

"Safe as we'd be anywhere else," David replied, frowning slightly as Roy strained to pull his catch in.

"Give it a little slack," he said, "or you'll bust the line."

Roy nodded, and let a little slack out of the line, which immediately relaxed.

197

"There's food here, water, even propane to boil it with. We can probably stay for a while."

Roy nodded. "That's not a bad idea. Like you said, it's not much, but it's better than just about anywhere else."

David nodded.

"Speaking of feeling safe," he said, the memory of his daughter telling him wide-eyed that none of them were safe flashing through his mind, "I'm still trying to wrap my head around the way Maria introduced herself to you."

"Hell of an introduction," Roy said, tugging on the line, which was now no more than thirty feet away from shore. "You ever seen her do anything like that before?"

"Shoot at somebody? Hell no," David said. "She's been in therapy for a few years, ever since her big sister got sent to a mental hospital, but she's never been violent, certainly nothing like what she did to you."

"She was scared of you," Roy said, bringing his catch within twenty feet of the dock. "I saw it in her eyes. She was going to kill you."

"Don't remind me," David said, the memory still very painful for him.

"Don't you touch her!" she'd screamed at him.

But there had been no one in the room with her besides himself and Roy. And yet when she'd woken up, she hadn't seemed angry at all, just...scared. David shook his head. The whole thing didn't make any sense.

"David," Roy said seriously, pulling a rather large small-mouth bass out of the water and setting it on the dock, where it flopped ferociously about, struggling futilely to reach the safety of the water. Roy gave it a small kick with the toe of his boot, sending it careening over the edge of the dock into the dark water and out of sight. "Have you noticed anything strange about Dylan?"

David turned to Roy, his expression quizzical.

"I mean sure," David replied. "Unlike the rest of you, he didn't take well to my great sense of humor."

Roy managed a grin.

"Apart from that, he hasn't said a word all day to anybody, as far as I can tell," David went on. "Probably just in shock, no different than Maria. I mean, we've all been kind of in shock since this whole thing started. Maybe it just hit him harder than the rest of us."

"I wouldn't doubt that," Roy replied, his voice suddenly hollow. "He lost his mom and sister right after all of this started."

David was suddenly silent.

"Soldier got them," Roy went on. "Saw the whole thing. Gunned them down like animals. That's how he ended up with us."

"Jesus," David whispered. "To go through all of that at his age...I can't believe he's coping with it as well as he is."

"Well, that's the thing," Roy said, staring down at the dark, glassy surface of the lake. "I'm not sure it's just coping. He didn't even seem upset right after it happened. He just seemed to shut down."

"Like he was keeping it all inside," David said, thinking of Maria.

Roy nodded.

198

"Thing is," David went on, "something like that happened with Maria. After her sister went away, she didn't talk to us for weeks. She was barely ever at home. This went on for a while, and then she finally broke down to us one night. She couldn't keep it in anymore." He paused. "I don't suppose Dylan has..."

"No," Roy replied quickly. "He hasn't, but that's not what bothers me. David, Laura is scared of him. I can see it in her eyes every time she looks at him. It's the same way that..." he paused, unsure whether he should continue.

"It's the same way she used to look at me every time we talked about her dad."

David remained silent, unsure whether he should probe further, or if he wanted to at all.

"Did he hit her?" David asked finally.

"Yeah," Roy replied. "Something like that. There's something else, too. A few weeks ago, we were staying with an old farmer who lived out in the country. We found Dylan staring out into the cornfield. He told us something like 'He's out there.' And the look on his face...it looked like a rabid dog eyeing a juicy steak, scared Laura half to death."

David said nothing. He'd certainly gotten an unpleasant vibe from the kid, but dismissed it, figuring he was just on edge.

"He might've just been..." David trailed off. Just what exactly? Insane? Out of it? Deteriorating? Even for a kid Dylan's age who'd watched his mother and sister get gunned down right in front of him, that seemed like a stretch.

"It's not just the kid that's bothering me either," Roy said. "Laura's been having nightmares again. Wakes up screaming almost every single night. It hasn't been this bad in years. Those pills she gave Anna...she hadn't used them in years."

"Roy," David said, trying to remain calm, "this situation we're in, it's put a lot of stress on everyone."

"I don't think it's just that," Roy continued. "This didn't start until we'd been with the kid for almost a week. Even on the day of the attacks, she seemed perfectly fine. It was only after we started traveling with the kid. How can you explain that?"

David said nothing. Maria hadn't just been distant. She'd been genuinely afraid of him. And the whole thing with the gun...

"Something's wrong here," Roy said, his voice shaking slightly. "And I think it's bigger than any of us. Even the way this started...I still can't process it. Petrov just deciding to hit the big red button...I mean he was a KGB agent during the cold war, he knew the consequences...something must've set him off. Something powerful."

David shook his head, suddenly wishing that they could stop talking about this. The idea that there was some invisible monster out there manipulating people with the sole purpose of destroying civilization was almost too much for him to bear.

"Has she told you what she sees in her nightmares?" David asked as he reeled in his fishing line, dreading the answer.

"Yeah," Roy replied hollowly. "Always the same. She wakes up in her childhood bedroom. She's twelve years old again. She tries to scream, but her dad clamps a hand over her mouth, the exact same way he did the first time he…" Roy trailed off, but David got the idea.

"There's one more thing," Roy said as David got up to leave. "Her dad's eyes. They're black. Not just the irises. The entire eyeball, even the whites."

David shuddered, the image sending a deep chill up his spine. Roy got up to leave.

"I know I might sound crazy," he said as they walked side by side towards the cabin. "But I think we were put here for a reason. I think whatever this thing is, it's going to come after us, sooner or later. And when it does…we're going to have to fight it."

David nodded, wanting very much to tell Roy that he was crazy, but somehow not quite believing it himself.

CHAPTER 65

Roy carefully opened the bedroom door so as not to disturb Laura, who was lying awake on the twin bed next to the window, staring up at the dark ceiling. Roy sat down on the other side of the bed, looking out the window at the still lake.

"You awake?" he asked.

"Yeah," Laura replied, sitting up. "I've just been thinking about what happened to Anna. Honestly...I feel responsible."

"Hey," Roy whispered, sliding a comforting arm around his wife. "It is not your fault what happened to her. The woman was already sick. For all we know, she could've had..." he trailed off.

"Could've had what?" Laura asked, not meeting his gaze.

"An adverse reaction to the pills," Roy said softly, but knowing deep down that it wasn't true.

Laura noticed.

"You don't really believe that do you?" she asked.

Roy shook his head. There was silence for a moment. Roy was choosing his next words very carefully.

"Do you think Dylan might know what happened?" he asked. In truth, he wanted to ask his wife if she thought Dylan killed Anna but couldn't bring himself to do it.

Laura shook her head.

"Honestly," she said, "I don't know what to believe anymore. I mean, honestly, I've been so on edge lately, it's probably nothing, and he's been through so much, maybe..." she trailed off.

"Maria's afraid of him too," Roy said automatically. He'd pieced it together just then. When she'd said they weren't safe, she'd been talking about Dylan.

Laura looked at him, her expression gaunt.

"Did she tell you why?" Laura asked.

"No, I don't know why," Roy said. "Laura...the night Anna died...I saw something..."

Laura suddenly looked very frightened. Roy saw that her hands were shaking.

"Right after you fainted, Dylan came into the room. I don't think he even noticed either of us. He was staring at Anna's body. He looked...angry. He looked so damned angry when he saw her like that, almost like..."

"Almost like someone else was supposed to die," he almost said, but stopped himself.

"Could he have known something?" Laura asked nervously.

"I mean, he must've," Roy replied, the trembling in his own voice making him even more nervous. "How else would he have shown up right after she died? He showed up well before the others, and he wouldn't've had time to wake up…"

"Stop, stop," Laura stammered, and Roy trailed off. "I don't believe it, it's not possible. It had to be the pills, she just misheard me, and took more than she was supposed to, it was just an accident, just an accident…"

Roy wanted to believe her, he really did. But a feeling of deep uneasiness was slowly spreading through him.

"Those pills," Roy said, struggling to keep his voice steady. "What's the normal dosage?"

"Ten milligrams," Laura said weakly, staring at the floor.

"She would've had to have taken at least a dozen to overdose," Roy said. "How much time passed between when you gave her the pills and finding her body?"

"N-not more than a f-few minutes," Laura stammered, her voice shaking.

Roy was thinking hard.

"It doesn't make any sense," he said finally. "Even if she'd misheard you, there's no way she would've swallowed half the bottle, which is about what it would take for her to overdose. And even in that case, she wouldn't've died so quickly."

"I-I don't know," Laura sobbed, burying her face in her hands. Roy embraced her, holding her tightly against him.

"I just want this to be over, it's all so horrible, I…"

They both jumped as the bedroom door swung open. Dylan was standing in the doorway, his expression as cold as ice, one hand concealing something behind his back.

Laura screamed. Roy moved protectively in front of his wife as Dylan shuffled into the room, giving them both a look that suggested that he thought they were insane. Roy stood up, trembling slightly. He wanted to subdue the poor kid but didn't want to hurt him unless he had no other option. Laura was cowering on the bed, staring at Dylan wide-eyed.

"Dylan don't!" she screamed as she saw him slowly remove the arm behind his back that would surely reveal a knife. Roy raised both arms, bracing himself. Only to feel them flop back to his sides uselessly as Dylan extended the white pill bottle to him.

"Jesus," Roy muttered, wiping the clammy sweat from his forehead, and snatching the bottle from Dylan's outstretched hand. "Scared me there, kid."

Dylan continued to look at Roy as though there was nothing wrong. Somewhere behind him, he could hear Laura taking several deep breaths to calm herself down, but she was still eyeing Dylan fearfully.

Roy eyed the bottle curiously.

"Where'd you find this, buddy?" he asked, careful not to let his voice shake.

"I found it tangled up in Anna's sheets the night she died," Dylan said, and Roy realized with a small start that it had been weeks since he'd heard Dylan's deep, smooth voice. It struck Roy how mature Dylan sounded for a person at the ripe old age of eleven.

"Well, just wanted to give it back to you, I know how important those things are to help you sleep," he said, looking at Laura, who quickly averted her eyes.

"Yeah," she said softly. "Thanks, Dylan." It didn't occur to her to ask how he knew about the pills.

Dylan turned to leave, seemingly unperturbed by their strange behavior.

A thought suddenly occurred to Roy.

"Dylan!" he called. Dylan paused, and Roy saw him tense noticeably.

"The night Anna died, we're still not sure how it happened."

"She died of her illness," Dylan said, a little too quickly. "Obviously, there's no doctors around, so whatever she picked up on the road must've taken her."

Dylan was looking at Roy now, and there was a definite note of fear in his gaze, carefully concealed beneath his hard stare.

"We don't think so," Roy said, taking a step toward Dylan, who shrank away in return. "We think she died of an overdose. There was vomit clogging her airway when she died, and even if she'd just been sick, she could've run to the bathroom and expelled it."

Somewhere in the background, Anna was whispering frantically to Roy, telling him to knock it off, but Roy ignored her.

The kid was backing away from him now. He knew something, Roy was sure of it.

"Any idea what might've happened?"

Roy suddenly froze. Dylan had stopped backing away from him, and something in his posture had changed. He no longer looked afraid. In fact, he looked downright angry. His eyes were blazing, and his jaw jutted out aggressively towards Roy. His entire face was suddenly concealed in a shadow that Roy swore hadn't been there a moment ago. This time it was Roy who took a step backward. Dylan didn't move but continued to glare at Roy. Anna had stopped talking. She looked very frightened. Roy slowly backed up towards the bed and sat down next to his wife. Dylan's eyes did not shift away from Roy.

Roy broke eye contact, unable to meet Dylan's gaze. There was a deep malevolence to it that sent shivers down Roy's spine.

"We're just gonna get some sleep. We can talk more in the morning," Roy said, trying to sound casual as he stripped off his jeans and t-shirt and laid them on the floor next to the bed.

Dylan didn't move.

"Goodnight, Dylan," Laura said, her voice shaking badly as she pulled the covers over both of them. Dylan remained silent for a moment longer, then turned and strode from the room, slamming the door behind him. A second later, Roy heard Laura breathe an enormous sigh of relief.

CHAPTER 66

D ylan stormed into the hallway, muttering angrily under his breath, running his hands over his face in exhaustion every few seconds. He kicked a plastic toy fire engine that had been left in the hallway furiously out of his way, sending it skittering into the kitchen.

"God it never ends," he thought helplessly, running a hand agitatedly through his short dark hair. First one of them would demand something of him, then the other would demand the opposite, then the first would demand something else, back and forth over and over. If he listened to one of them, the other would grow louder, and then when he tried to do what that one wanted to settle it down, the other lost its mind.

"I'm about to lose mine," Dylan thought angrily, throwing himself down into a kitchen chair and staring blankly out the kitchen window at the dewy grass bathed in bright moonlight. He wasn't sure how much longer he could do this.

"Kill her..." the magician whispered, gesturing towards the knife rack sitting on the counter.

Dylan glanced up at it balefully.

"You have no choice," he whispered. "She knows. She knows what you have become. You must stop her before she tells the others."

"But you do have a choice," Kaden whispered, breaking in. "You can tell them what you did to Anna, they won't hurt you, it's not too late for you." The sudden presence of the new voice sparked Dylan's anger. The magician's commands had been terrifying enough alone, but with the both of them constantly fighting for control of his psyche, his brain was constantly in danger of splitting in two.

"Goddamnit," Dylan muttered, grabbing his head in frustration. "CAN'T YOU BOTH JUST SHUT THE FUCK UP!" he screamed aloud.

He eyed the knife rack, the enormous silver butcher's knife gleaming in the moonlight. Maybe he should just kill Laura. That would probably shut Kaden up. It would certainly shut his master up. At least for a little while.

"Dylan." Kaden was back.

"Shut up," Dylan muttered, laying his head down on the wooden dining room table. "Please for the love of god, SHUT UP!"

But Kaden wouldn't shut up.

"Dylan, I need you to see this. The magician is only using you..."

"I DON'T CARE!" Dylan roared, jumping up from the table, his hands balled into tight fists. "I DON'T FUCKING CARE, DON'T YOU GET IT!" he screamed, tears stinging his eyes. "DAD, MOM, MY SISTER, EVERYBODY, THEY'RE GONE, FUCKING GONE, AND THEY'RE NEVER COMING BACK, GET OUT! GET THE FUCK OUT!"

Blinded by rage, Dylan lashed out ferociously, his outstretched fist punching through the aging plaster of the kitchen wall. Dylan, breathing hard, stared at the hole, a grim sense of satisfaction creeping through him.

"It felt good, didn't it?" the magic man whispered. The body of the boy he'd stabbed at the orphanage flashed through his mind.

"Yes, it did feel good," Dylan thought viciously, his gaze turning towards the small knife rack sitting on the counter, the steel blades illuminated in the moonlight filtering through the kitchen window. It had felt incredible. He'd felt so powerful that day while his tormentor's blood had flowed through his fingers. He hadn't stopped laughing even when the police had arrived and hauled him away. Dylan slowly approached the knife rack, never taking his eyes off the large silver butcher's knife. He'd felt so worthless and weak over the last several weeks, unable to control even the voices that tormented him in his own mind.

"Well," Dylan thought coldly, slowly reaching for the gleaming butcher's knife. "That's about to change. I'll shut that little bastard Kaden up. For good." The thought brought a brief predatory grin to Dylan's face, which quickly morphed into a mask of hardened, steely determination as his fingers began to close around the hilt of the blade.

"Dylan?" Roy asked.

Dylan paused, his hand inches from the hilt of the knife.

"Damn," Dylan thought furiously. In his ecstasy, he hadn't noticed Roy's approaching footsteps.

"Dylan," Roy said more firmly, walking into the kitchen. "You need to tell me right now what really happened that night."

Dylan stared at him unblinkingly, forgetting temporarily about the knife. His brain whirled as panic slowly settled over him like a thick fog, a single thought managing to penetrate through the maelstrom:

"He knows. He knows everything."

Dylan felt himself tense, suddenly remembering the knife.

"I could do it," he thought, realizing how tantalizingly close the hilt was, no more than a foot out of reach. "One second, maybe less...I could bury it in his throat before he even knew what hit him..."

Roy took another step towards Dylan, his expression ice cold.

"Tell me," he said firmly, advancing to within a few feet of the boy, the lines in his face pulled taut with anger.

Dylan inched slowly backward towards the counter, his whole body tensing as he prepared to spring. The bastard was so close, he could practically grab the knife and slice his jugular in one swift, brutal motion.

"TELL ME!" Roy shouted furiously, his face so close Dylan could feel his hot breath on his face. Dylan's fingers closed on the handle of the knife, the blade sliding from the rack seamlessly...

"NO!" Dylan paused, the knife hanging poised in the air.

The two men stared at each other, Roy's eyes suddenly widening with fright at the sight of the knife.

Roy felt a cold sweat break out on his forehead. It wasn't just the knife that scared him so badly. There had been a moment, just before Dylan swung on him, when he'd looked into the kid's eyes, and saw...nothing. Just nothing. An inky blackness that could only lead to some deep dark corner of an unspeakable hellscape. As Roy stared, trembling all over, the color slowly returned to Dylan's eyes. The knife fell with a clatter onto the marble countertop, but neither of the men made a grab for it. Dylan finally broke eye contact with Roy, staring down at the floor. It took Roy a moment to register the deep shame in his eyes.

"Kaden," he whispered. "Kaden stopped me."

It had been Kaden's voice he'd heard. And he hadn't been alone either. The realization slowly rolled over Dylan like an ocean wave. The second voice he'd heard had belonged to his father.

Almost immediately, he could feel the rage, the malevolence, the utter cold empty darkness sliding off him, replaced by a deep, profound sense of grief unlike anything he'd ever experienced before.

"Dad," Dylan whispered, his voice trembling. "I'm so sorry, dad."

Roy tensed as Dylan reached for the knife but relaxed again as Dylan set the blade calmly back in the slot. They stared at each other unblinkingly, both men breathing hard.

"What are you?" Roy whispered, his voice trembling.

Dylan shook his head, feeling bitter tears welling up in his eyes. The familiar feeling of his head being cleaved in two was slowly coming back. He rushed past Roy out of the kitchen, averting his tear-filled gaze. Roy stared after him, dumbstruck. Then, trembling all over, he slowly shambled down the hallway to the bedroom, locking the door behind him.

CHAPTER 67

Maria Veranda opened her eyes to bright late afternoon sunshine cascading down through a thin canopy of oak leaves, a thicket of enormous oak trees dominating the scene in front of her. She was standing at the edge of a large clearing in the middle of a forest which, judging by the piles of dead leaves piling up on the forest floor, was in the midst of late autumn. Maria walked into the middle of the clearing, her bare feet crunching dead leaves beneath her. Feeling calmer than she had in weeks, Maria turned her face towards the bright blue sky, enjoying the feeling of the warm sunlight on her face. The distressing memories of the last several weeks had faded into the distance.

The scene in front of her was so peaceful. She walked towards a small creek running through a grove of trees and sat down beside it, dangling her bare feet in the cool, rushing water.

"I never want to leave this place," she thought, gazing around at the scene in front of her.

"I often wished for the same thing, when this was my home," a woman's voice said behind her, causing Maria to jump.

A tall, athletic brunette dressed in jeans shorts and a tank top was walking through the trees towards her. Although she was smiling, there was an unmistakable sadness to it. Maria stood up, gazing at the woman curiously.

"Who are you?" Maria asked.

"My name is Jody," the woman said.

"Will you walk with me, Maria?" she asked.

Maria nodded, not bothering to ask how the woman knew her name. In fact, as they started walking side by side together down a narrow path through the woods, Maria began to suspect that this woman knew a lot more than she could possibly imagine.

"How are you holding up, kid?" Jody asked. "I know you're going through a lot right now."

"I'm absolutely fantastic," Maria said sarcastically. "In the last few weeks, there's been a nuclear holocaust, I've watched my father drown someone with his bare hands, my life has been in danger because of an eleven-year-old kid, and my mother…" Maria trailed off, fighting back tears.

She felt a comforting hand on her shoulder.

"It's alright, kid," Jody whispered. "It's alright. I know it's hard. I've…I've been there before."

Maria looked at her. Jody was staring off into space, seemingly lost in thought.

"My father, he…he tried to kill me."

"Why?" Maria asked nervously.

"It wasn't him," Jody replied. "Not really, anyway. Let me ask you something Maria, why are you afraid of Dylan?"

"I almost killed my dad because of him," Maria replied. "Somehow, he…he made me see my sister. I saw dad…pull a gun on her. I…I don't understand Jody, how is that possible? He's just a kid."

"Yes," Jody replied solemnly. "He's only a kid, but the entity that has a hold of him right now…"

"Entity?" Maria asked, her voice trembling slightly.

"All of these things you're seeing, not just your sister, he wants you to see them," Jody went on. "He is trying to use you, just like he's using Dylan?"

"Why?" Maria asked. "What does he want from us?"

"He is afraid," Jody replied, her expression unreadable. "He is afraid of you. Of all of you. He knows you are stronger than him, but only if you stand together."

Maria gasped as Jody opened her hand, and a small ball of white fire erupted from her palm. It burned merrily against her skin, but it didn't seem to harm her.

"What is that?" Maria asked in awe.

"Something that can save the world," Jody said, "or destroy it."

Jody turned to Maria, the fire dancing on her palm.

"Fire is a delicate thing, Maria. It must be fed, nurtured, protected, just like a small child. And as with any child, it must be used in the right way when the time comes. Because fire is a powerful thing. It can be used for growth and new life, or for destruction. I hope when the time comes," she said, looking directly at Maria, "that you will make the right choice."

Jody slowly pressed her palm against Maria's chest. Maria felt a quick stab of heat as the white flame entered her chest, the deep, soothing warmth spreading slowly throughout her entire body.

Maria closed her eyes, the fire acting as a mild sedative as she slowly drifted into sleep. Jody caught her by the shoulders, holding the smaller woman against her as her body faded into mist.

"Travel east," Jody whispered in her ear, her voice echoing in Maria's head. "Travel east, and you will find the answers that you seek, I promise you."

Maria woke up with a start, drenched in sweat as if she'd just run a marathon. She sat up, glancing at her surroundings. She was in a small living room, lying on a cushiony beige sofa with a threadbare red blanket pulled over her. Morning sunlight was streaming through the oversized bay window to her left. She sat up and began the process of dressing herself. She'd had a very strange dream. She'd been walking in a forest, talking with a woman she didn't recognize. She couldn't remember what they'd been talking about exactly, but she remembered a strange, warm, soothing sensation passing through her entire body just before she'd woken up. As she pulled her t-shirt up over her head, she realized with a small start that the sensation was still there.

She pressed a hand gingerly against her breast, just above her heart. The skin there was unnaturally warm. If she hadn't known better, she would've guessed she had a fever. She suddenly realized that the constant anxiety she'd borne over the last several weeks had vanished too. She felt calmer than she had in years, ever since

Lilly had called her on that fateful morning, sobbing that something terrible had happened to her. She felt...confident. It was not a word she would've used to describe herself at any point since her family's lives had been turned upside down by Michael Pines. She turned at the sound of footsteps shuffling their way down the staircase. A few seconds later, her father appeared. There were visible dark circles beneath both eyelids, and his face, which Maria was so used to seeing well-kempt and shaven, sported the beginnings of a thick, bushy black beard. Still, he managed to smile when he saw her.

"Hey, kid," he said, sliding across the wooden floor in his socks. "You want some breakfast?"

Maria smiled wanly at these words. It was not a phrase she thought she'd hear again for a very long time. He started towards the kitchen.

"Dad," Maria said, giving David pause. "We can't stay here."

David turned to look at her, startled by the intensity of her gaze.

"Why not?" David asked quizzically. "There's food here, plenty of shelter, no one around to bother us. I'd say we got lucky with this place. What good will going back on the road do us?"

"Jody Razitsky," Maria said quickly.

David frowned. He swore he'd heard that name before, but he couldn't quite place it. The fire burned brighter in Maria's chest, so much so that she felt sweat break out under her armpits.

"She needs our help. I think she might..." she trailed off, struggling for the right words.

"Think she might what, kid?" David asked.

"I think she might be able to save the world."

CHAPTER 68

Maria sat behind the wheel of the Chevy, her expression stony as she carefully guided the vehicle onto the shoulder around an overturned semi in the middle of the two-lane highway. She had insisted on driving today, on the pretext that her father needed to rest. He'd wanted to argue but resisted the urge when he thought of what Maria had told him earlier that morning.

"I think she might be able to save the world."

In any case, Maria didn't feel tired in the slightest despite having lain awake most of the night. If anything, she felt extremely energetic, as if she'd forced down several cups of espresso. The strange warmth in her chest had persisted throughout the day and it gave her hope today. Hope that she would find Jody. Hope that no one else would die. Hope that...what remained of her family would survive. The tires skidded momentarily as the Chevy pulled off the shoulder before finding solid asphalt again.

"You're not bad at this for someone your age, you know that?" Roy said from the passenger seat.

Maria merely nodded as she quickly swerved to avoid hitting a pickup truck that had overturned in the middle of the road. When they'd begun the drive, Maria had suggested that Laura stretch out across the third-row seat and take a nap, and that her father sit next to Dylan in the backseat. This had two advantages. For one, her father was the only person among them not afraid of Dylan, so he would be most comfortable sitting next to him. Secondly, with Roy in the passenger seat, he was free to talk to her without the others hearing. After another hour, as the sun gradually rose overhead, Laura was stretched out across the third-row seat, sound asleep. David had fallen asleep as well. Even Dylan seemed to be drifting in and out of consciousness. Maria waited for another thirty minutes to ensure he was fully asleep.

"Roy," Maria said as she guided the Chevy past a large road sign that announced they were a few miles south of the town of Fairplain on route 77. "I need to tell you something. About Dylan."

Roy glanced behind him to ensure the others were asleep.

"Go ahead," he said calmly, staring out the window at the passing farm fields, the occasional cow or chicken pausing its grazing to watch curiously as the Chevy sped past.

Maria was a bit taken aback by how easily he accepted the strange request.

"The day we met, the day I almost shot you...the reason I panicked so much..."

"You were running from your dad," Roy finished. "I never quite understood that, why were you running from your own father?"

Maria remained silent for a moment.

"I saw...I saw my father do something terrible," she said.

Roy was looking at Maria now, his expression unreadable.

"The thing is though, I didn't see it with my own eyes," Maria continued. "Well, I did, but someone showed it to me."

"Who?" Roy asked.

"I...I'm not sure," Maria replied, fighting to keep her voice steady.

But the way she said it, Roy suspected that she knew.

"Was it Dylan?" Roy asked.

Maria started so badly that she yanked the wheel hard to the left, nearly sending the Chevy into the ditch.

"Jesus," she muttered as she brought the car back onto the road. "Sorry, I just..." she shook her head.

"Was it Dylan?" Roy asked again.

Maria nodded. Roy was silent.

"I don't understand," Maria said. "I mean, how is that even possible? How can an eleven-year-old kid show me things that happened in the past? And even if he could, why would he do something like that? It doesn't make any sense."

Roy was thinking hard. His eyes had changed color...there had been nothing behind them.

"Have you ever heard the phrase 'the eyes are the window to the soul'?" Roy asked.

Maria nodded.

"I saw something last night," Roy went on. "I can't explain it."

"Dylan came into our room as we were going to bed," Roy explained. "He gave us the pill bottle Laura gave Anna. He said he found it in Anna's pocket."

"That's odd," Maria said. "How could he have known that's where he would find it?"

Roy shook his head.

"But that wasn't the weirdest part," he continued. "He went into the kitchen. He was muttering to himself, almost like he was angry. I confronted him, and he..."

"He what?" Maria asked, almost dreading the answer.

"He tried to kill me," Roy said softly.

Maria gasped.

"He pulled a knife, was about to swing it, but then...something stopped him."

Maria stared at him, her eyes wide.

"His eyes, just before he stopped...there was nothing there, Maria. Just empty blackness. And then the color came back. Right after he froze mid-swing."

Maria forced herself to look back at the road. She suddenly looked very afraid. Roy cast a worried glance back at Dylan, whose head was lolling forward in his sleep.

"There's something else," Maria said. "I know how my mom died. It was the pills."

"Laura gave Anna the bottle to try and help her sleep," Roy said hollowly.

"Only they weren't the pills she was supposed to take," Maria went on. "Roy, when was the last time Laura took one of those pills."

"It's been years," Roy said. "Not since she was in therapy."

Maria nodded.

"She got lucky. Those pills my mother took, I think they were poisoned."

"How do you know?" Roy asked nervously.

"My sister did an experiment with sleeping pills in a yeast culture in her lab," Maria went on. "Sleeping pills always have labeling from the manufacturer, so you know what the dosage is."

Roy gasped.

"The pills in the bottle," he stammered, the realization slowly hitting him like a freight train striking a disabled SUV. "They were...they were blank. I...I didn't even notice..."

Maria stared blankly ahead, not crying, not screaming. She felt absolutely nothing as the picture formed in her head. Judging by the look on Roy's face as they passed a defunct minivan on the side of the road, he was thinking the same thing.

"But he spared you," Maria whispered. "Why?"

"I...I don't know," Roy stammered as a large red barn flew past them on the left. "None of this makes any sense."

Maria thought back to her conversation with Jody. She had produced fire from thin air and put it inside Maria. Even now she could feel it, singeing her heart with every beat, giving her strength. But if Jody was God...then who was the devil? She had to have a counterpart, right?

"But say that's true," Roy said. "Where would an eleven-year-old kid even get access to a poison powerful enough to kill, let alone one that's perfectly disguised as a sleeping pill which happens to match the one Laura takes?"

"Fire can be used for growth and new life, or it can be used for destruction..." Jody had said.

"An eleven-year-old kid, no matter how angry he might be, couldn't have done these things on his own," Maria said simply. "Roy, I had a dream last night. About a woman. She said we needed to go to Fairfax. That's where I'm taking us right now. Roy, I saw her conjure fire from thin air."

"Are you saying..."

"If there's a god, there must be a devil," Maria said matter of factly. "I think whatever that devil is...he has a hold of Dylan."

"Like he's possessed," Roy asked, casting a nervous glance back at Dylan.

"Something like that," Maria said, although she didn't really believe it.

If this devil, whatever it was, wanted them all dead, he could've possessed Dylan and killed them all in the blink of an eye. And the fact that Dylan hadn't killed Roy...almost as if he was fighting back somehow.

"I think that's why Jody wants us to find her. She can help Dylan."

"Like Jesus casting out demons," Roy whispered. "Maria, if he really killed Anna, why didn't he kill me too? What stopped him?"

Maria shook her head, thinking hard. After a moment, she finally spoke.

"I don't know this for sure, Roy," Maria said. "But I think you might owe Jody your life."

CHAPTER 69

The house had been quiet for most of the day. Apart from the fact that the entire group seemed to have silently agreed to keep noise to a minimum to allow Jody to rest, they were all extremely tired. Jody was still asleep in her room. Jennifer had fallen asleep with Grace on the sofa in the living room. Ben was sitting nearby in the rocking chair, drifting in and out of consciousness. Marianne was asleep in the guest bedroom. Tyson was sitting sentinel at the foot of the bed, still struggling to wrap his head around the events of the last few hours. Less than four hours ago, his little girl had taken her final breath. And yet here she was, not only alive, but seemingly perfectly healthy. Her complexion had returned to its usual light brown, her ribs were no longer visible beneath her shirt. Even the few cuts and scrapes lingering from the accident seemed to have faded. There was a soft knock on the bedroom door. Feeling himself tense, Tyson went to open the door. Lorenzo was standing there with his wife, Serena.

"Mind if we come in?" Serena asked kindly.

"Sure," Tyson replied, opening the door fully.

"We won't disturb her," Lorenzo said as they moved into the room. "How's she doing?"

Tyson grinned and rubbed a hand on his forehead.

"I can't explain it," he said. "I mean it's amazing. She was dead. I heard her take her final breath four hours ago. How can she be alive?"

"Not even just alive," Lorenzo said, peering intently at Marianne's face. "She appears to be perfectly healthy. She died of radiation sickness, right?"

"Yeah," Tyson said. "She looked like she was on death's door for the last week. That woman, Jody..."

"She's no doctor," Lorenzo said quickly. "Or at least if she is, she doesn't practice any kind of medicine I've ever come into contact with."

"She might not have been dead," Serena said, gently pressing her fingers against Marianne's neck to feel for a pulse. "She could've been in a state of catalepsy. Her pulse would've become so shallow you wouldn't've been able to feel for it, and her breathing would've been so shallow you wouldn't've noticed it if you were in shock. But even so, to suddenly be in perfect health..." She turned to Lorenzo. "It's a miracle, to say the least."

Lorenzo nodded. Tyson did too, although in his heart, he knew Serena was wrong. In his heart he knew Marianne had been dead, and Jody had, by some act of God, brought her back to life.

"Fire..." he thought. "She said anything with fire in it has life."

He started to say something but paused abruptly at the sound of an approaching car from outside. The three of them tensed noticeably. The type of people who would come to call, especially at this hour of the day, didn't tend to be friendly.

"Lorenzo, are you armed?" Tyson asked as they left the bedroom, drawing his own Sig Sauer P226.

"I am," Lorenzo replied, drawing a Glock 17 from his waistband. "Ben has his Beretta. Let's hope we don't need them."

Tyson nodded, knowing the last thing he wanted to do after his own daughter had been brought back from the dead was take another person's life. Jennifer, Grace, clutching at her skirt, Ben, Jason, Mike, and Serena, all met them in the living room, both Mike and Jason sporting guns of their own.

"What's going on?" Jennifer asked, holding Grace tightly to her.

"We have visitors," Mike said, his expression grim.

"Jen, take Grace into the guest bedroom and lock the door," Ben said quickly, approaching the front door, Beretta raised.

Jennifer wordlessly scooped up Grace and hurried down the hallway towards the back of the house. Lorenzo could see the large Chevy Silverado pulled up to the curb in front of the house, its occupants having already disembarked. As Ben approached the front door, he felt Mike's hand on his shoulder.

"Let me go first," Mike said. "If they start shooting, I'd rather be the one to go. You've got a family you still need to take care of."

Ben smiled.

"Appreciate it, old friend." Mike brushed past Ben to stand next to the front door. He placed his hand on the doorknob and nodded to Ben, Lorenzo, Mike, and Jason, all of whom had their weapons at the ready. Jason nodded at Mike.

"On my count," Mike whispered. "3...2...1..."

214

CHAPTER 70

When they'd first surveyed the house from the street, they'd believed it was abandoned. It certainly looked the part. The windows were dark, several of them had been broken. The driveway was empty. It was eerily silent, no different from the rest of the neighborhood. It was only when they were about halfway up the front lawn from the front door that this notion was proven false. The front door exploded open with a bang, sending a half a dozen men hurtling toward them, their faces taut with rage, guns drawn. Roy, suddenly panicked, went for his own gun, and David did the same. Laura let out a little scream and dived behind Roy, pulling Maria and Dylan with her.

"Who are you?" demanded a tall, strongly built African American man toting a hunting rifle, his dark eyes blazing.

"My name is Roy Forsin," Roy said, struggling to keep his voice steady. "I'm not here to hurt you. Now how about we all put our weapons down so we can talk like adults?"

Mike looked at Ben, who was staring hard at Roy. Tyson peered around Roy at the woman and two children concealed behind him, and Lorenzo saw his expression soften considerably.

"Ben," Jason said. "I don't think they want to hurt us."

"Damn right," Tyson added, gesturing towards Dylan. "They've got kids. No reason to get heated."

Mike silently agreed. If they were going to start shooting, they would've done it already.

"Ok," Ben said, slowly lowering his gun.

The rest of them followed suit.

"Sorry about that," Ben said apologetically, shaking Roy's hand. "But with the world we're living in today, you never know."

"No problem," Roy said. "Last time I approached a stranger, I almost got shot, so, I get it."

The girl laughed. Mike gestured to her.

"She yours?" he asked Roy.

"No, she's mine," David said, holstering his gun and shaking Mike's hand. "David Veranda."

"Mike Swezenko," Mike replied, returning the handshake.

Ben turned back to the house, where Jennifer and Serena were peering anxiously through the windows.

"It's okay!" Ben called out. "Tell everyone to come outside, we have guests!"

He saw both women breathe a deep sigh of relief, and knew they understood. For the first time in weeks, Ben Alrite felt the stress of perpetually being caught in imminent danger slide off him. He smiled and shook Laura's hand. It was a good feeling.

CHAPTER 71

few hours later, everyone was sitting around the enormous dining room table, talking and laughing over dinner. Roy and David had lugged an enormous box of mac and cheese they'd brought with them from the cabin by the lake, and Laura had made an enormous pot of macaroni for all of them to share. Ben smiled as he shoveled another spoonful into his mouth, savoring the flavor.

"Almost like the good old days," he thought. The only person missing from the dinner table was Jody, who was still asleep in her room. Ben had thought it was best to let her sleep. One person he certainly couldn't miss though was Marianne. She was as full of life as Ben had ever seen her, whispering in Grace's ear constantly, both girls giggling madly each time, laughing wildly at every joke the adults told even when she clearly didn't understand half of them, shoveling in fourth and fifth helpings of mac and cheese. It was amazing. If he hadn't known, Ben would've never guessed that only twenty-four hours ago she'd been on death's door.

Even Dylan seemed to be having fun. David was asking Serena if she happened to have a bottle of wine stashed somewhere in the basement for special occasions, sending her into a joyous fit of laughter. It was the happiest any of them had felt in what felt like a lifetime. In fact, the only person who didn't seem happy was Maria. She poked at her food, her expression glum, seemingly uninterested in conversation. Laura, who was sitting next to her, asked her jokingly if, in the event they did find a bottle of wine, if she could be Maria's date for valentine's day. Maria shook her head sadly and returned to staring at her food.

"Hey," Laura asked, suddenly feeling self-conscious.

Maria didn't look up.

"I'm sorry," she went on. "If there's anything you need..."

Maria stood up wordlessly, wiping her eyes with her sleeve, and left the table.

"Hey, everything alright?" Roy asked.

"Yeah, it's okay," Laura said quickly. "Maria's upset. I think I was a bit insensitive."

"She'll come around," Roy reassured her. "The kid lost her mom. That's hard on anybody. All you can do is be there for her, and when she's ready, she'll come out."

Laura smiled, grateful for the millionth time for having such a wonderful partner.

CHAPTER 72

Maria stormed down the hall, tears flooding her eyes. All of them, even her own father...how could they act like everything was normal? They didn't seem sad at all. On the contrary, they seemed to have forgotten about Anna completely. The familiar feeling of cold isolation began to creep into her heart. It was a feeling she'd experienced so many times before. Ever since Lilly had gone away. But this was different. Her mother had always been there to comfort her, to dry her tears at times like this. But now Anna was gone. Maria was all alone. She burst through the door to the guest bedroom without thinking where she was going and threw herself down into the rocking chair, sobbing into her hands.

"It just isn't fair..." she whispered. "It just isn't fucking fair..."

She was crying so hard she didn't hear the bedroom door open, or Jody's heavy, dragging footsteps over the carpet. Maria stiffened as Jody slid her arms around her shoulders.

"It's alright, child," Jody whispered, stroking Maria's hair.

"No," Maria whispered. "No, it isn't. It won't ever be alright again."

Jody pulled her closer, holding Maria tightly against her. The way a mother would hold her own child.

"I want my mother..." Maria whispered. "I want my mother..."

"Shh..." Jody whispered. Maria felt her feet leave the floor as Jody picked her up and carried her over to the guest bed. Maria's sobs quieted as Jody pulled the covers up over her.

It was a feeling she hadn't experienced since she was a very small child.

"Sleep, child," Jody whispered, stroking her. "I'll be here when you wake up."

She started toward the bedroom door.

"It's you, isn't it?" Maria whispered.

Jody turned, a small, wan smile crossing her face.

"You're the woman I saw in my dream, aren't you? You brought us here?"

"I didn't bring you anywhere, kid," Jody said softly. "I merely extended my hand to you. I saw that you needed me. You chose to take it. Let us hope that others will follow you."

Maria drifted off into a deep, dreamless sleep as Jody closed the bedroom door behind her, comforted by the familiar, warm glow of the fire in her heart.

CHAPTER 73

Leo Rinolski stumbled drunkenly down the side of the highway, each step threatening to send him plunging over the guardrail and into the freezing river below. His dark eyes swept the scene in front of him, which resembled something out of a post-apocalyptic fiction novel: cars piled up on both shoulders, many of them overturned, some of their owners' corpses slowly withering away under the gaze of the bright autumn sun. A few of them were still smoking slightly. Spent shell casings were scattered across the highway by the thousands. Leo saw the corpse of a middle-aged man who looked to be in his sixties sitting behind the wheel of a rusted-out Volkswagen beetle. His head was resting against the seat back. A colt revolver lay in his lap. Dried blood covered his chest and neck.

"At least the old bag had the sense to do it himself and get it over with," Leo thought dully as he shuffled past. "Which is probably more than I can say for most of these people."

As if on cue, he walked past a young woman in a tank top and jean shorts. Her dark hair pulled back into a tight bun, lying in the grass just off the side of the road. Her eyes were wide open with fright, a pair of bullet wounds covered with dried blood visible on her abdomen. Leo smirked.

"Got another one for you momma," he hollered. He broke down in a fit of laughter and nearly tumbled off the road into the tall grass bordering it.

He took a moment to steady himself, eyeing the edge of the road where the shoulder dropped off warily. He continued towards a small farm in the distance. The experience was rather odd for Leo. He wasn't sure what was so important about this farm, apart from the fact that his mother had ordered him to go there. But there was a plan. His mother, as tough and unfeeling as she could be, was always prepared.

"Good work," he muttered as he stumbled off the shoulder and into the grass, heading in the direction his mother had indicated for him the previous night.

"We're doing good work today, momma."

He could almost sense her smiling down on him, and wondered if soon, she might finally forgive him for his past misdeeds. There would be no more beatings then, no more yelling, no more fights, just mother and son, like Leo had always wanted it to be ever since dear old dad had passed away. The thought was enough to cause a broad grin to break across Leo's sunken, dirt-streaked face.

"I love you, momma," he whispered, raising his face up to the pale blue afternoon sky. For a brief moment, he almost imagined he could see her up there, watching over him.

"I'll make you proud, I swear I will."

As he approached the dirt road leading up to the house a few minutes later, he could hear faint voices from somewhere in the house. Men's voices, roughened by years of cigarette and alcohol abuse. Leo smiled. His mother hadn't left him alone after all.

As Leo wandered up the dirt path to the small farmhouse, he wasn't at all surprised to see the torn screen door open, revealing a tall, muscularly built middle-aged man in a lead-gray muscle shirt and grease-stained athletic shorts, his long grizzled gray hair pulled back into a ponytail. A black tattoo of a skull with a knife in its teeth was visible on his left forearm. A cigarette dangled loosely from the corner of his mouth. As the man approached him, Leo saw that there was nothing behind the man's cold, dark brown eyes, only an inky black emptiness. Leo smiled and shook the man's hand.

"Believers," he thought. "Thanks momma."

"You Leo?" the man asked.

"I am," Leo replied cheerfully. "Who do I have the pleasure of speaking with?"

"Axel Rodriguez," the man said gruffly, taking a long draught on his cigarette.

"How many in your party?" Leo asked.

"Three including me," Axel said. "These are my guys, Jack and Mason," he said, gesturing behind him at the ripped screen door, where two more strongly built men, both of them slightly younger than Axel, were emerging.

Leo nodded at them as they approached.

"We were soldiers," Axel said. "National guard. We were all in the same regiment stationed in Chicago when the world went to shit. We stayed for a bit but got out when people started getting sick from the radiation." Axel paused, his eyes downcast. "Unfortunately, we weren't quite fast enough." He glanced back at Mason, who let out a loud, harsh coughing fit.

It was only then that Leo noticed that he could see the man's ribs poking through his ragged t-shirt.

"Poor guy has been vomiting non-stop for weeks," Axel went on. "Can't keep anything down. I don't know what to do for him."

Leo walked over to Mason and put a comforting hand on his shoulder. Mason had heavy dark circles beneath both eyelids, and he was slumped over slightly, as though he lacked the strength to stand up straight.

"Don't worry, son," Leo said. "Where we're going, there's someone who can help."

Mason sat up a little straighter.

"A doctor?" he asked wearily.

Leo nodded.

"Yeah, something like that. From what I've heard, she brings the dead back to life."

CHAPTER 74

Jody sat in the rocking chair from her bedroom, which Ben had brought out onto the porch earlier in the day so she could get some fresh air, staring out at the light scattering of stars that had become visible in the early evening sky. She sighed and closed her eyes. For as young as Jody was, she often felt much older, as though the wear and tear from three previous lifetimes was still affecting her.

"God places the heaviest burdens on those who can bear them," she whispered.

She had certainly borne hers, and quite well in her opinion. In spite of everything she had suffered in her twenty-three years of life, she was here, lying in a rocking chair in a house somewhere in Virginia with a large group of strangers talking over dinner somewhere in the background. She was relatively at peace, apart from a dull ache in her legs, both of which remained heavily bandaged.

The pain had improved greatly over the last few days, however, and she'd even managed to get out of bed and walk out to the porch without having to lean on someone. This had been a great relief for her. Her physical independence would soon become a necessity. A storm was coming, and with it would come a great test of her willpower.

"You have a very important quality that is shared by few people. Strength of character. You have an unshakable belief that the world is naturally good."

Jody sat up a little straighter, her eyes sweeping the lawn, sure she had heard Kaitlyn's soothing voice. Not seeing her, she leaned back in the chair, feeling slightly disappointed that her best friend had chosen not to reveal herself.

"Do they believe it though?" Jody thought, thinking of the many adults who were passing around a bottle of wine they'd found stashed in the basement around the dinner table. More importantly, could she believe it?

"I believe it," Kaitlyn whispered. Jody closed her eyes, imagining her friend's bright smile.

"I know," Jody whispered, feeling slightly calmer. "Thanks for always being there, even when I don't deserve it."

Jody looked up as the screen door swung open, and Maria stepped out into the cool night air sporting light gray shorts and a black tank top, her curly dark hair swaying in the light breeze.

"Back on your feet?" she asked, smiling.

Jody smiled back.

"Working on it," she said. "Not hungry?"

Maria shook her head.

"I ate a little. I made a point of leaving the table before dad could get too much wine in him."

They both laughed.

"You want to sit down?" Jody asked.

Maria nodded and sat down next to Jody, wrapping an arm comfortingly around her shoulders. After a moment, Jody reciprocated.

"It's nice to see something normal for once," Maria said, gesturing to the star-filled night sky.

"I agree," Jody replied. "It's the little things that keep us sane in times like these."

Maria smiled and leaned her head against Jody's shoulder.

"I appreciate what you did for me the other night," she said. "I've just been going through some shit lately. My mom, she was…she was always my rock whenever dad wasn't around. You know what I mean?"

Jody nodded.

"My dad was the same way with me," Jody said. "I was always close with him when I was little."

"What happened?" Maria asked.

"He passed away," Jody replied a little too quickly.

Maria nodded, not wanting to pry further. She figured if Jody was keeping something from her, she had a very good reason. Jody hugged Maria closer to her.

"I'll always be here for you kid. I want you to know that."

There was a moment of silence.

"Hell," she continued, "pretty soon, I'll need you to know that."

"What do you mean?" Maria asked.

Jody sighed, debating how much to tell the young woman.

"There's a storm coming, kid," she said finally. "Pretty soon, we'll all have to make the choice whether to place the needs of others above our own."

Jody sighed, casting a glance back towards the house.

"I pray they make the right choice."

Maria nodded.

"You said in my dream, that you hope I make the right choice when the time comes." She looked up at Jody. "Do you think I will?"

Jody was silent for a moment, choosing her words carefully.

"Honestly kid," Jody replied finally, "I can't see the future. But if I was going to bet on anyone, I would bet on you."

They both looked up as the screen door opened, and Dylan emerged. Jody felt Maria tense beside her.

"Hello, Dylan," Jody said kindly, concealing her own nervousness.

The moment Dylan had stepped out on the porch, Jody had felt the temperature drop by at least ten degrees. It was the same feeling she'd had back in Philadelphia when the Puppeteer had cornered her. Dylan stood beside the rocking chair avoiding eye contact with Jody.

"Ben wanted to know if you were hungry and if you wanted any noodles."

Jody was a bit taken aback. There was no hint of fear or anger in that voice. He sounded just like any normal child his age. Jody had met many people who had succumbed to their frustrations and started down dark paths over the years. A small number of them had been Dylan's age or younger. While the adults usually could conceal it, there was always a very subtle change in the children's voices.

Ordinary people never noticed it, but Jody never missed the barely concealed rage, pain, and fear that combined to make the volatile knife's edge that the Puppeteer unleashed for his own amusement.

But Dylan didn't have it. Jody shook her head.

"I'm okay, thanks for asking though."

Dylan nodded and turned to Maria, who was looking very pointedly away from Dylan.

"She ate already," Jody said quickly before he could open his mouth.

Dylan paused for a moment, looking like he wanted to say something else, then merely nodded, and started back towards the house. Jody heard Maria breathe a deep sigh of relief.

"Jody," Dylan said suddenly.

He was standing in front of the screen door. His entire body had gone rigid, and there was a definite note of fear in his voice.

"I like you, Jody," he continued. "We both do. That's why Kaden wanted me to warn you…"

He paused, his mouth opening and closing soundlessly like a fish gulping on air. He glanced over his shoulder, his eyes wide with fright, as though he were afraid someone might be listening.

"Be wary of the man with the skull tattoo."

He said this so quickly Jody almost didn't understand what he'd said. Before she could say another word, Dylan hurried back into the house, the screen door slamming shut behind him.

CHAPTER 75

A xel Rodriguez walked silently up the dark street, the pistol concealed beneath his waistband. His expression was stony. To a passerby, if there had been any, he would've come across as just another ordinary citizen taking a walk alone after dinner. But deep within him, Axel could feel the burning rage he'd long harbored rapidly bubbling to the surface like magma rising within a soon to be erupting caldera. Axel had grown up in his own dark place. He'd been born to a heroin addicted mother living in a tent on the streets of Los Angeles. Unloved, badly bruised, and deeply malnourished, he'd been on death's door before an LAPD detective had found him lying in the street and taken him to social services. His mother had never come for him. It could be that she'd finally overdosed, or maybe she'd just never cared. He'd spent most of his childhood in various foster homes, a lonely, scared, angry kid living without a single friend or person who gave a shit whether he lived or died.

Most of the fathers had beaten him. One or two had sexually abused him. But all of them put on brave faces whenever the social workers came knocking. At least for a while. They all slipped at some point. He always had some hope whenever this happened. Maybe the next home would be better. But it never was, of course. He'd run away when he was fifteen, bouncing in and out of juvenile hall, peddling drugs and robbing people on the street to survive. Throughout those years, his feelings towards his mother had slowly turned from distress at her absence to pure, unbridled rage. Every problem he had, every time he got busted, every beating he received from the big kids in juvie, every drug deal gone wrong, all of it was her fault. He'd joined the army when he was eighteen, after completing a court-ordered rehabilitation program.

There had been a sense of order. He'd had friends. He'd been clean. Even his anger towards his mother had died a little. Until the attacks. One by one, he'd watched his comrades either get shot dead in the street or die of radiation poisoning. He'd escaped the city, along with two others, once it became clear no one was coming to restore order, but the old hatred had come back. It was his mother's fault. It always was, somehow. But Leo was going to help him remedy that, finally. All the wrongs of the past would be righted tonight. Axel smiled grimly as the house came into view. He felt the weight of the gun on his hip. He felt his hands curl into fists. There she was. Sitting in the rocking chair looking up at the stars, the same enormous beer belly and fat on her arms and legs, the poorly drawn tattoos scrawled on her arms, the dark orange turban tied around her head to hide the hair that had fallen out over the years, it was all there.

She was leaning back casually, smoking a cigarette, gazing lazily up at the star-filled night sky, probably too doped up to even notice him coming. But he was coming alright, oh yes, Axel Rodriguez was about to deliver some justice to the one person who had wronged him more than any other, to the person who was responsible for the destructive and meaningless path his life had taken. His hand shifted to the holster concealed against his hip, his knuckles white on the grip of the revolver. He exhaled slowly as he approached the house.

"Hey mama!" he called, grinning savagely as he withdrew the gun from its concealment. "It's been a long, long time!"

CHAPTER 76

Jody felt the hairs on the back of her neck stand up when she saw the strange man walking down the street. Even from this distance, she could see the tattoo on the man's left forearm. A human skull with a knife held in its teeth.

"Be wary of the man with the skull tattoo…"

Had he been warning her? He'd looked terrified when he was speaking, almost as if…

"Like he was afraid someone might find out," Jody whispered.

Jody stood up from the chair, her bandaged legs groaning in protest. Maria had noticed the stranger too. She glanced at Jody nervously. The stranger was walking up the driveway now. He was removing something from his waistband. Maria screamed as the revolver gleamed menacingly in the moonlight.

"Maria, get inside the house," Jody ordered, not taking her eyes off the approaching assailant.

Maria didn't move.

"Go!" Jody demanded.

He was within one hundred feet now.

"Get the men, tell them to bring their guns, go now!"

That snapped her out of it. Maria bolted into the house, the screen door slamming behind her.

Jody turned back to face the strange man, who had closed the distance to seventy-five feet, the gun poised in his right hand.

"Who are you?" Jody demanded, stepping down from the porch and onto the asphalt sidewalk.

"Fifty feet…" she thought, her lower lip quivering slightly.

"Never thought you'd see me again, did you?" the stranger shouted, his knuckles white from gripping the gun so tightly. "Probably thought I died out in the street where you left me, that right?" he screamed, spit flying from his mouth with every word.

He was close enough that Jody could see his eyes now. There was nothing behind them, only empty darkness.

"This man is angry enough to want to kill me, and yet I've never even…"

Jody gasped as the picture slowly pieced together in her mind.

"Memories…" she whispered. "That's how he controls them. He uses their worst memories against them. He doesn't see me at all, only what the Puppeteer wants him to see."

The man was within thirty feet now, screaming incomprehensibly, his face bright red.

"Please listen to me," Jody said placatingly, raising her hands in a gesture of supplication. "I know you're angry. I know you're scared. But I'm not the person who hurt you."

The man continued to move forward, oblivious to Jody's words.

"If you put the gun down," she continued, "I can help you. You don't have to do this."

But either the man wasn't listening to her or didn't care. He smashed the butt of the gun hard into her temple, sending her sprawling. Bright lights danced in front of Jody's eyes. The world swam in and out of focus as the man loomed over her, breathing hard. From somewhere far off, she could hear yelling voices.

"Too late..." she thought as the man raised his gun. "I'm sorry, Maria," she whispered.

"Finally," the man growled. "After all these years. Just so you know, I'm going to enjoy this."

Jody reached out a trembling hand as the gun pressed against her temple. The man began to squeeze the trigger.

And then he froze as his mother's hand made contact with his chest, directly over his heart. A soothing warmth spread through him like a warm bath. He relaxed his finger on the trigger. He could've almost fallen asleep. And then he heard it. The voice.

"Axel. That's your name, isn't it?"

It was not his mother's voice. The woman was much too young, her voice far too smooth and gentle. The gun fell with a clatter onto the pavement. He didn't try to pick it up.

"Axel, when you look at me, what is it you see?"

The warm, soothing voice seemed to be coming from inside his head.

"I see my mother," he replied, shocked by how calm he sounded. "The woman who ruined my life."

"What happened?" the woman asked.

Axel closed his eyes.

For an instant, Jody's vision faded to black. She heard a soft rush of wind. And then she saw it. A dingy, dirty street in the middle of an enormous metropolitan landscape. Hundreds of tents packed so tightly it was difficult to see the pavement. Hypodermic needles, broken bottles, spent beer cans, cigarette butts, homemade joints, and small piles of human feces were scattered about haphazardly. Cigarette and pot smoke wafted through the air in all directions. A few of the occupants were stumbling around dazedly under the hot summer sun. An old man with a messy white beard downed half a bottle of Jack Daniels and threw it absentmindedly into the gutter, where it shattered into a thousand gleaming pieces.

Jody turned as the flap of a bright red, one man tent opened a few feet away, A toddler wearing a diaper so full it sagged down to his knees stepped out, his bare feet crunching on loose gravel as he wandered absentmindedly into the street. Jody sighed heavily.

"So, this is how it started then?" she asked.

227

Axel didn't reply. He didn't need to. The toddler wandered past a small blue tent at the edge of the encampment which was surrounded by dozens of spent hypodermic needles. Jody felt herself tense as the toddler stopped by the side of the tent, eyeing one of the needles curiously.

"Don't…" she whispered. "Please, don't do it."

But she could only watch helplessly as the toddler that would grow up to become Axel Rodriguez wandered over to the tent and picked up one of the needles, eyeing it closely. Jody felt tears come to her eyes.

"No, don't, DON'T!" she screamed.

She saw the poor child's expression go slack as the plunger pierced its palm, drawing blood. The needle fell silently onto the pavement. The child swayed once, then collapsed onto its back, its eyes closed. Jody screamed, tears flooding her eyes.

"HELP HIM!" she screamed into the sea of tents rippling in the slight breeze. "GODDAMNIT SOMEONE HELP HIM!"

But she might as well have been talking to the wall for all the good it did. Jody collapsed on her knees beside the child, whose breathing had become very rapid and shallow.

"Someone come," Jody whispered. "Please God, someone come."

"It might've been better for me if no one had," said a voice.

Jody looked up. A full-grown Axel Rodriguez stood above her, staring disheartened at the toddler lying unconscious in the street.

"The torture would've been over for me then," he continued.

Axel let out a heavy sigh.

"As it was, I would be forced to endure forty additional years of torment."

Jody looked up at the sound of running footsteps. A tall, muscular male uniformed officer was sprinting towards them, his partner on his heels.

"Dispatch, we have a child lying in the middle of the street," he said into his radio, kneeling beside the baby. He gasped as he saw the mark on its palm. "Looks like it was pierced with a hypodermic needle, most likely overdosed on heroin or something similar. We need an ambulance now."

Jody looked back at Axel as the two officers began working on the child. His expression was stony.

"It didn't get any better after this," Axel said coldly. "Abusive foster homes, bouncing in and out of juvenile hall, living on the street. I never really felt at home anywhere. All because of her."

He pointed to the red tent where his mother was undoubtedly lying unconscious, either sleeping off a high or a hangover.

"Axel, listen to me," Jody said. "I'm sorry for what you went through as a child, no one should have to go through any of that." She sighed heavily. "Truth is, I can't change the past. I can't erase the pain you must feel. But you can't let it consume you. You can't let it control you. Because then they win. All the people who hurt you, all the people who abandoned you, they win if you let them."

Axel was looking at her now, and he saw the pleading in her eyes.

"You're stronger than them, Axel, you survived everything they put you through. They don't have control over you unless you give it to them. He doesn't have control over you unless you give it to him."

Axel felt his jaw drop. It suddenly all made sense now.

"My mother died years ago, didn't she?" Axel asked calmly.

Jody nodded, not bothering to wonder how she knew this.

"And the person I saw in the chair, the person I tried to kill, that was you, wasn't it?"

Jody nodded again.

"Then who…" he didn't finish the sentence.

The scene around them slowly faded to black. Then they were back in the driveway of the house in Virginia, Jody sprawled on the pavement, Axel towering above her, his gun lying uselessly on the ground beside him. David, Lorenzo, Jason, David, Roy, and Mike had gathered on the porch behind them, guns drawn.

"Leo…" he whispered. "Leo Rinolski." Jody gasped when she heard his name. The scene at the hospital flashed through her mind.

The feeling of the scalpel piercing her breastbone, driven forward by brute, superhuman strength. The feeling of floating away into mist as her soul abandoned her body.

"Leo…" she whispered. "Is it really him?"

Axel nodded slowly.

"His eyes," Axel whispered, suddenly sounding panicked.

"Jody, you have to get out of here, he's…"

Jody heard the crack of a single rifle shot echo from the trees. Axel Rodriguez stuttered wordlessly for a few seconds, then collapsed to the ground, blood spreading from the spot where the bullet had pierced through the back of his skull. Jody's terrified scream was drowned out as gunfire erupted all around her.

CHAPTER 77

B en Alrite, whose attention had been entirely focused on the strange man, saw the muzzle flash out of the corner of his eye through the trees. He reached instantly for his holster, but it was too late. With a weak cry, the man keeled over dead, the bullet wound clearly visible at the base of his skull. The invisible assailant's second shot missed Jody by inches, striking one of the old porch steps and splintering the whitewashed wood. An explosion erupted to his right as Tyson fired the hunting rifle at the source of the shot. Within seconds, all five men had their weapons raised, and all hell broke loose. Automatic rifle fire erupted from the trees as three men emerged into the moonlight, the shots striking the wooden beams of the porch and slamming into the wall behind them. Ben ducked behind a large wooden support column as a bullet whizzed past his ear and connected with the wooden storm door behind him.

"Jesus," Mike shouted over the cacophony of gunfire. "They've got assault rifles!"

"Even with the six of us, we're outgunned!" Roy shouted as a bullet missed him by inches, shattering the porch window just above his head. Ben returned several shots of his own, nearly connecting with a tall, dark-haired man toting an M16.

"Forget the others, take her!" one of the men shouted.

Ben chanced a glance through one of the thin slats between the wooden support beams. Jody was cowering behind the dead man's body, completely pinned down as the three men advanced on her.

"We have to protect Jody!" Ben shouted back, ducking as a bullet splintered the wooden beam to his left.

"On my count, everyone lay down cover fire!"

"Are you crazy!?" Lorenzo demanded. "We'll be cut to pieces!"

"Go now!" Ben shouted, ignoring Lorenzo. He jumped to his feet in one swift motion, firing as fast as the semi-automatic weapon would allow, and to his great relief, the others followed suit.

One of Ben's shots caught the dark-haired man in the shoulder. He cried out in pain and went down, dropping the rifle at his feet. Two bullets connected with the man in the middle, piercing his left shoulder and abdomen. To Ben's shock however, he continued firing his weapon, seeming not to notice.

"Jody, run!" Ben shouted as another bullet struck the man on the right in the chest, sending him sprawling.

David ducked as a spray of bullets launched over his head.

Jody, seeming to understand, jumped to her feet and sprinted towards the safety of the porch. The one remaining shooter, who had been concentrating his fire on David and Lorenzo, immediately aimed his weapon at the back of Jody's head and fired.

"NO!" Ben screamed, firing off two rounds.

It happened in slow motion. The first bullet whizzed past Jody's ear, striking the support beam inches from Ben's left leg. The second bullet raked her hairline as she ran, shattering the window behind Ben. Ben's shots caught the attacker in the chest, staggering him. His weapon clattered to the ground. Jody launched herself over the porch steps, diving behind the roof beam where Ben had taken cover.

"You hit?" Ben asked.

"No," Jody said, her eyes wide. "Ben, I need to tell you something."

But whatever Jody said next, Ben never heard. The shooter, now sporting four fresh bullet wounds across his chest and abdomen, had retrieved his weapon, and launched a spray of bullets in Ben and Jody's direction.

Ben ducked, shoving Jody down forcefully as the bullets whizzed over their heads where they'd been a split second before.

"What the hell!" Roy demanded. "You just hit him twice Ben, how's he still shooting!?"

Ben barely heard him.

"The man's eyes," he whispered to Jody. "They're not..."

"Not human." Jody finished the sentence for him as another dozen rounds smashed into the support beam behind them.

"Ben, we need to get out of here now!" David shouted over the roar of gunfire. Lorenzo fired two more rounds, both of which hit the monster in the neck. Blood gushed from the wounds, but the monster, seemingly unfazed, retaliated immediately, one of his shots catching Lorenzo in the shoulder.

"You good?" Ben shouted.

"I'm fine!" Lorenzo called back, grimacing in pain. "Only grazed me. But I'm all out of ammo."

"Me too!" David called.

"Everyone back in the house!" Jody shouted. "Ben, you cover them!"

Ben nodded. Ben jumped up, firing several more rounds into the monster, bullets striking the woodwork all around him. Without question, the others followed Jody through the screen door into the house, slamming the door behind them. Ben fired his last round, which punched clean through the monster's skull. Knowing he had only seconds, Ben sprinted for the door as the monster stumbled, the shot dazing it momentarily. He slammed the bullet-riddled storm door behind him a split second before the shots resumed from behind him.

CHAPTER 78

Leo Rinolski breathed in deeply, feeling his muscles relax as the skin and sinew surrounding his wounds stitched itself back together and the pain gradually subsided. He absentmindedly flicked a speck of blood from the neckline of his t-shirt. He glanced back at the driveway where the bodies of his fallen comrades lay still. He bent down next to Mason and peeled back his left eyelid. They had returned to their normal color, and he could make out a network of blood vessels and faintly, the optic nerve behind the eye. Leo smiled. He was gone. He wouldn't have to suffer anymore.

"Don't worry kid," Leo murmured, "mama will take good care of you."

Laying the dead man's head gently back on the ground, Leo stood up and walked quickly over to where he had dropped his M16 in the grass. He picked it up hurriedly and started towards the house.

"GODAMNIT LEO, KILL THE BITCH!" his mother roared suddenly, and Leo winced as an invisible hand struck him hard across the face.

Leo groaned, rubbing the spot where his mother had slapped him.

"C'mon mama, I'm trying," Leo whined, hurrying in the direction of the house.

"Get a move on," his mother spat, tapping her foot impatiently. "Don't you go disappointing me again, or I'll have you thrown out for good this time."

Leo shuddered at these words as he pushed open the storm door.

"I'll get it done, mama, I will, I promise," Leo muttered as he entered the front hallway, running a hand agitatedly through his short dark hair.

He moved quickly through the door at the end of the hallway. He swept the small living room with his rifle, his eyes scanning for movement. He was unsurprised to see none. Of course they wouldn't have lingered. Not if they valued their lives. He nevertheless strode over to the sofa and threw back the blankets just to be safe. It was empty. He crouched down to check the space under the sofa. Nothing there either. Leo strode into the kitchen. The kitchen chairs were pulled out, several dishes of food still spread out across the counter.

Leo smiled. He had to give Jody credit. For as weak as she was, she had done one thing impressively well. Standing here in the brightly lit kitchen, several gas camping lamps blazing in the corners, Leo could almost feel like he was back in his old family home again. Like everything was normal again. Leo turned and started towards the dining room, satisfied that the kitchen was empty. Never thinking to check the cabinet beneath the sink as he passed by, where, just a few inches from him, Mike had a hand clamped tightly over Marianne's mouth as the legs of the monster passed by.

Mike felt the weight of the gun against his hip as he watched the legs of Leo Rinolski pass slowly by their hiding place.

"Two rounds left..." he thought.

He was in a minor state of shock. He'd just watched an attacker get shot four times and keep coming like nothing had happened. Would two more rounds, assuming he had time to get both shots off, really make any difference? Mike, who had not seen Ben put a bullet through the man's skull, thought he knew the answer. He did not believe in God. He did not believe in miracles. He was a die-hard atheist who only believed in the things he could see with his own two eyes, which in his mind, worked pretty damn well, and, based on what he'd just seen, their attacker was on something. Whether it was crack, PCP, or some other shit didn't matter.

What mattered was that he had rationalized the problem, and the solution was simple: put a bullet in the man's brain, and it didn't matter what kind of shit he had in his system, a shot to the back of the head would undoubtedly stop him. He heard Marianne whimper and clamped his hand tighter over her mouth. The gun felt as though it weighed a thousand pounds in its holster. Even with the element of surprise, he still didn't like his odds. He released Marianne.

"Mike," she whispered.

"Shhh!" Mike hissed, placing a finger to his lips.

Marianne nodded.

"Marianne," he whispered. "I need you to do something. In a few seconds, I'm going to jump out at the bad man. When I do, I need you to run away as fast as you can, do you understand me?"

Marianne nodded, but Mike could see she was trembling.

"Hey," Mike said, lightly squeezing her shoulders. "I need you to be brave for me, okay? Can you do that?"

Marianne hesitated for a moment, then nodded.

"Okay," Mike said, bracing his shoulder against the cabinet door. "3...2...1..."

Chapter 79

It all happened in a flash. Leo heard the cabinet door burst open behind him. He spun around, coming face to face with the barrel of Mike's pistol. The gunshot echoed in the small space. Leo stumbled backward, blood pouring from the open wound. Through his blurred vision, he could see Marianne sprinting away in the background, and he felt a sudden surge of anger. Another gunshot, causing Leo to scream in pain. He felt as though his head had been cleaved in two. But very quickly, the rush of anger he felt at the sight of the escaping little girl overtook the unbearable pain, returning strength to his limbs. As Mike swung the butt of the empty pistol towards him, Leo grabbed his outstretched arm with both hands.

"You won't stop me, old man," Leo growled.

Mike's face went white. The man's cold, poisonous voice…the inhuman strength of his grip that made Mike's entire arm scream in protest…

"Jesus," Mike thought. "The bullet wounds. They…they disappeared. There's…there's no blood."

He barely had time to register this thought before he felt his feet sweep off the ground and into the air. He crashed to the floor hard enough to knock the wind out of him. Leo let out a low, guttural growl and aimed the rifle at Mike's head.

"NO!" screamed his mother.

Leo paused, momentarily stunned.

"FORGET HIM, GET THE GIRL!"

Mike was staring blankly up at Leo, his expression somewhere between terror and confusion. He felt a heavy object slam into the side of his head. He collapsed flat on the floor, the world around him slowly going dark. Leo stood up, breathing hard. He would've dearly liked to kill the old bastard, but his mother had spoken. He turned and walked back into the living room, his eyes scanning the room for signs of the little girl.

CHAPTER 80

Marianne ran for her life, neither knowing nor caring what was happening between Mike and Leo. The only things that existed in the world for her were the pounding of her bare feet against the wooden floor as her leg muscles propelled her forward, the sweat trickling down her face, and the brutal, pervasive fear that blinded her to every rational thought short of survival. The living room flew by her as she sprinted past. She didn't even register the fact that Jody, who was hiding in a small cupboard beneath the staircase, peeked out of her hiding place as Marianne flew past her, bounding up the stairs three at a time. She collapsed to her knees on the landing, struggling to catch her breath.

"Move!" her brain screamed.

She struggled to her feet on wobbly legs and threw herself into one of the small bedrooms, locking the door behind her.

Wondering vaguely how much good it would do her, her eyes darted around the room, searching desperately for anything she could use as a weapon. The tops of the dressers were completely devoid of anything she might be looking for. She threw open dresser drawers, tearing through piles of clothes, desperate for anything she could use to defend herself. She couldn't hear any footsteps outside the room, but she could sense him getting closer with each passing second. She threw aside a pair of gray jogger's shorts. Revealing a large brass letter opener stashed at the bottom of the drawer. She grabbed it by the hilt and dashed over to the walk-in closet, shutting the door behind her. Struggling to catch her breath, she pressed herself against the back wall behind shirts and dress pants still swinging listlessly on their hangers, the letter opener raised in her right hand.

Waiting. Waiting for the monster to open the closet door. Marianne whimpered in fear. Jody, debating whether or not to go after Marianne, quickly snapped the door of the cabinet shut as the monster entered the living room, his dark eyes sweeping for signs of the little girl and landing on the enormous staircase. Of course, the little brat would try to hide upstairs. He'd seen Jody looking in that direction when he'd entered the room. He started towards the cabinet where she was hiding, then felt the rage burn hot in his chest again as he approached Jody's hiding place.

"Deal with the others later," his mother commanded. "Get the girl, I need the girl."

Leo nodded and started up the staircase, neither he nor the Puppeteer realizing what the decision would cost both of them.

Leo calmly approached the bedroom door, guided by his intuition.

"Hiding under the bed," he thought. "It's what a child would do during a game of hide and seek. That's all this is really. A great big game of hide and seek, the only difference being you die if you lose."

Smiling bemusedly at the thought, he went to open the door, only to find that it wouldn't budge. Leo stepped back a few feet, aimed the rifle at the door handle, and fired. The bullet ricocheted off the brass handle and lodged itself in the wall above his head. Confident that the lock was broken, Leo tried the door handle again. The door swung open easily this time. Immediately upon entering the room, Leo knew he'd found his target. Drawers pulled open haphazardly, their contents scattered everywhere. Marianne clapped a hand to her mouth to stop herself from crying out as Leo bent and stuck his head beneath the queen-sized bed.

Her trembling knuckles were white on the letter opener. As Leo stood up, his back towards her, Marianne inched towards the closet door, the letter opener raised.

"I could do it right now," she thought, shocked at her own cold-heartedness. "I could rush him right now while he has his back to me and bury this blade in his neck before he even knew what was happening."

She raised the letter opener above her head, her fingers inches from the closet door, her entire body preparing to spring. Then she froze. The figure standing in the middle of the room turned, her lovely chocolate brown eyes that so resembled Marianne's own looking directly at her. Her dark hair fluttered behind her in spite of the lack of a breeze. She smiled lovingly at Marianne. Marianne gasped as she approached the woman.

"M-mama?" she stammered, tears filling her eyes.

The woman smiled knowingly at Marianne. There was a trace of sadness to it that Marianne didn't quite understand.

"Oh mama," Marianne sobbed, flinging herself into her mother's arms.

Alison held her close, stroking her gently.

"Mama, I'm so scared," Marianne whispered. "I miss you so much, I just wish you were here."

Alison said nothing. Marianne looked up into the face of her mother.

"Why are you so sad mama?" she asked.

Alison continued to smile sadly, saying nothing.

"Don't you love me mama?" she asked, her voice rising slightly.

"Oh, I love you very much, dear," Leo replied in his own voice, smiling.

Marianne gasped as the illusion faded. Revealing the monster standing in front of her. Marianne screamed as Leo lifted her under the arms and pinned her down on the bed. She thrashed and screamed, struggling desperately to get out from underneath him. Leo, holding Marianne down with one arm, tossed the rifle aside, and, with a wicked grin, produced the razor-sharp brass letter opener she had tossed aside.

"You got away from me once," Leo whispered in her ear. "I won't be making that mistake again, I promise," he whispered, raising the letter opener above his head, the blade gleaming brightly in the moonlight streaming in through the bedroom window.

Marianne let out a final helpless scream and squeezed her eyes shut, preparing for death. Not realizing that Jody had heard her screams from downstairs. Not realizing that she and Leo, both held under the spell of the moment, didn't hear the rapid footsteps pounding up the staircase. As Leo raised the letter opener, his expression filled with savage triumph, the bedroom door exploded open in a ball of fire, the flames singeing Marianne's hair as it slammed into Leo with the force of a semi striking a disabled Volkswagen beetle.

Leo flew off the bed and into the air, the fire powering him through the bedroom window, the windowpane shattering into the thousand glimmering pieces. Leo screamed as the fire entered his body, scorching his organs, his bones melting, the oils on his skin igniting, consuming him inside a giant fireball. Then he fell out of sight. Marianne turned her eyes wide with fright. Jody stood in the doorway, her hands balled into fists, every line in her face etched with white-hot fury.

"You don't touch my girl," she whispered.

Marianne gasped as Jody stormed over to the window where Leo had fallen.

"Jody, your eyes," Marianne whispered.

Jody froze.

"There's…there's nothing behind them," Marianne sobbed. "Only the darkness."

In slow motion, Jody sank to her knees, transfixed by the jagged hole in the window where Leo had smashed through. Jody hung her head, feeling tears brimming in her eyes. Maria burst into the room, followed by Tyson, who wrapped a sobbing Marianne in a bear hug. The others trickled in behind them as Maria slowly approached Jody, her fingers trembling as she touched Jody's shaking shoulders.

"I'm sorry," Jody whispered, her voice breaking into a hundred pieces. Maria quickly embraced Jody as she began to cry freely, her tears quickly staining Maria's shirt.

"What have I done?" Jody bawled. "GOD WHAT HAVE I DONE?" Maria quietly motioned to Ben, who signaled for the others to leave the room. After a moment, Jody and Maria were left alone.

"You had no choice," Maria whispered.

Jody shook her head violently.

"There's always a choice, kid. There is always a choice. You can't let it control you. You can't let it win, no matter what, you understand me?"

Maria pulled Jody closer, now crying just as hard as the woman who felt more like a parent to her than anyone else in the entire world.

CHAPTER 81

"Y ou alright, kid?" Jody asked, turning over the spit carefully so as not to burn herself.

It was dusk, the stars in the night sky beginning to show their bright faces. They'd constructed the spit earlier in the afternoon. It consisted of a thin tree branch hung between two small boulders that were placed on either side of the small campfire. Strung on the tree branch was a fat, brown rabbit that David had managed to catch earlier in the day, the fire sizzling with every drop of fat that fell into it. Their current residence was a small field in the George Washington National Forest in southwestern Virginia. After the events that had taken place a few days ago, the group had unanimously agreed that they would be safer staying well away from the cities. They had crossed the entire state the next day and ended up here. While they had originally only intended to stay the night, no one had really felt like moving on, especially with the stream flowing nearby with clean freshwater, and enough edible berries nearby to keep them fed for at least a few days.

As an added bonus, David, Lorenzo, and Jason had been able to work out between the three of them how to build a very effective makeshift snare, which was responsible for the meal now sizzling over the fire in front of them, as well as several other small game that had fed the rest of the group, most of whom were now asleep in their tents. Jody had been offered food earlier, but had resisted, wanting the chance to talk to Maria, who had remained isolated in her tent for most of the day, but had finally been coaxed out around an hour ago when she could no longer ignore the aching hunger gnawing at her gut. David, who had gone to bed about ten minutes ago, had set the rabbit up on the fire for the two of them, and had shown Jody how to rotate it so the rabbit would be cooked all over.

Maria nodded in reply.

"I'm alright," she said hollowly, although she didn't feel alright in the slightest.

Jody nodded, feeling it wasn't worth pushing the issue.

"Good time to get your casts off, huh?"

Jody nodded, smiling. Apart from the fact that they would be very impractical in their current environment, Jody's legs had healed enough over the last several days that she no longer had any trouble walking on her own and each step was no longer accompanied with stabbing pain. With some help from Jason, she'd removed them less than twenty-four hours ago, revealing the heavy scar tissue that now ran up and down her legs. Jody didn't mind. They all had their scars, it just so happened that hers were the most visible.

"What happened the other night, do you regret it?" Maria asked.

Jody was silent for a moment before replying.

"Yeah," Jody said. "No one deserves that fate, not even him."

"Would you do it again?" Maria asked.

Jody nodded.

"To protect you and Marianne, yes. Even if it means I have to live with it for the rest of my life, I'd do it again."

"Thank you," Maria said, turning to look at Jody.

Jody stared into the flames, avoiding the younger woman's eyes.

"Jody," Maria said, her voice trembling. "I need to ask you something."

Jody didn't react. She was sure she knew what was coming.

"Did Dylan kill my mother?"

At first, Jody didn't reply. She knew the truth. But what would be the repercussions of telling it? Was it better to protect the poor girl, who has already lost so much?

"Could use your help with this one," Jody thought.

No response. She hadn't really expected one. Kaitlyn had stayed away for the last several days. Perhaps she was angry with Jody, although Jody didn't think that was quite it. Maybe this was Kaitlyn's way of telling her to figure it out for herself.

"Jody," Maria said firmly. "I need to know. Did he kill her?"

Jody rested her hand on her forehead and sighed heavily.

"No," Jody replied. "The thing that killed your mother, that wasn't Dylan not really."

Maria stared into the flames, her expression unreadable.

"So, you admit it then. He did kill her."

It wasn't a question. Jody sighed.

"Maria..."

"He had a choice," Maria said sharply, anger creeping into her voice. "We all have a choice. That's what you told me the night you killed Leo."

"Maria..."

"He attacked us," Maria shouted, jumping up. "You said you had no excuse to kill Leo, even after he tried to kill Marianne!"

Angry tears were flooding her eyes.

"My mother was innocent, she was my rock, and Dylan took that from me! How can you sit there and defend him!"

Jody was staring into the flames, her expression haunted.

"Maria, listen to me..."

"Fuck that!" Maria screamed, tears splashing down her face. "I've been listening my whole damn life! I listened when they told me that bastard Michael Pines was innocent, I listened when they told me my sister was crazy, I listened when the psycho who murdered my mother tried to tell me to kill my own father! I'm done sitting back and fucking listening!"

Without another word, she turned on her heel and stormed off. Jody breathed a heavy sigh and rested her chin on her hands, her eyes brimming with tears as Maria disappeared into the woods.

"Please," she whispered. "Don't let her destroy everything tonight. If you're out there, you can be angry with me all you want, but please don't take it out on this poor girl."

Silently, Jody stood up. She glanced in the direction where Maria had gone. She'd vanished into the dark trees beside the clearing. Silently praying for her safety, Jody walked to her tent, filled with worry. Never seeing Dylan step silently out of the shadows next to the woods, Ben's gleaming steel cigarette lighter clutched in his hand.

CHAPTER 82

For Dylan Teryon, the last few days had been nothing short of hell. It was as if he'd graduated from a mild case of dissociative identity disorder to full-blown schizophrenia. Having the magician and Kaden fighting for control of his psyche had been migraine-inducing by itself. However, a third voice had joined the arena since the night he'd almost killed Roy: his own. He'd alternated constantly between brutally berating himself for his failure and panicking about how close he'd come to doing the unthinkable. The dull ache that had formed in his temples had evolved into a large steel hammer repeatedly bashing against the inside of his skull. It was a wonder he hadn't developed a concussion. The worst part was that he had no choice but to deal with it on his own. If he tried to tell Jody, she'd press him for more information until she worked out that he'd killed Anna, and then what?

Dylan shuddered at the thought of what she might do to him if she found out. Kaden had spent most of the day insisting otherwise, but Dylan found it impossible to believe that Jody, or anyone else for that matter, could possibly forgive him. He'd briefly thought of Roy, but the memory of that night flashed through his mind, and he'd immediately scrapped the idea of going to him. And Laura? Laura was terrified of him. She'd be more likely to pull a knife on him than to listen. Dylan sighed heavily. It seemed the magician had gotten what he wanted. Dylan was all alone. His anxieties had been of no help. Laura being frightened of him was one thing. But it wasn't just her. Maria knew what he'd done, he could sense it. The magician had, of course, screamed this fact in his ear countless times, but he would've known anyway.

He was fairly sure Jody knew as well. In fact, everyone in the group seemed to be a little wary of him, if only a little. He'd thought of running, but where would he go? There was no one left alive out there, the magician had made sure of that. Suicide? That would only ensure he was delivered to the magician faster, and somehow, he didn't think he'd be welcomed with open arms. That left one final option. Dylan stepped out of the shadows and crossed the field, heading straight for the bright green, two-man tent where Jody was sleeping. He flicked open the cigarette lighter, enjoying the warmth of the bright blue flame on his hand. Dylan sighed. He didn't want to do this. But as the magician had told him many times, and as he was beginning to realize himself, he no longer had a choice.

CHAPTER 83

Maria Veranda collapsed against a large oak tree, bitter tears spilling down her face. She was so tired. She was so goddamn tired of all of it. All this death, all this suffering, all this loss, and for what? There was nothing left to fight for, no one left to stay strong for. Despondency was creeping into Maria. She felt as though a part of her had vanished. There was a large gaping hole in her chest, the motivation to go on having departed.

"Jody," she whispered, her voice breaking. "I trusted you. Goddamnit, I needed you!"

It was irrational. Maria knew it was irrational. But she thought it, nonetheless. Jody had let her mother die. The thought brought another barrage of angry tears spilling down Maria's face. She buried her face in her hands and sobbed.

"Jody let my mother die," she thought. "She let her fucking die so that I would come to her, so that I would go on this fucking useless suicide mission."

Maria laid her head against her knees, her arms encircled protectively around her legs. She didn't want to move. She wanted to lay here and cry her eyes out until she died from dehydration, anything to shut the cruel goddamned world out. Whatever was waiting for her on the other side, it couldn't have been any worse than this terrible, cold emptiness.

"Maybe you'd even see Lilly…"

Maria sat up, her eyes suddenly wide with fright. She scanned the shadowy trees surrounding her. She was all alone.

"No, I'm not," she thought suddenly.

Maria shivered. The voice hadn't come from inside her own head. Someone else had spoken.

"Not someone," Maria thought nervously. "Something."

The thought was enough to make her shudder. Maria stood up on shaky legs, staring hard at something standing against a tree in the shadows about one hundred feet away. She could faintly see the outline of a long black cape dangling around its ankles. A tall black top hat stood atop its head. Its face was concealed in shadow.

"Who's there?" Maria called out anxiously.

The stranger didn't move. Maria shuddered. Even though she couldn't see the stranger's face, she could feel its eyes on her.

She could feel a deep chill seeping into her bones. Those eyes were so cold, so empty…she felt that if she gazed into them, she would fall through that dark hole into the infinite void beyond. Then she heard it again. The voice.

"Maria…" it whispered.

She stood rooted to the spot, her brain working furiously to identify the speaker.

"Maria...I'm sorry I've been away for so long. Would you like to come out and play?"

Maria moaned in terror. The voice. It belonged to her sister Lilly.

"C'mon Maria," Lilly said, no longer whispering. "Come out and play!"

Without warning, Maria felt her legs begin to move irresistibly forward, propelling towards the voice. Lilly stepped out of the shadows, her long red hair fluttering in the breeze. She was wearing a light blue sundress and her favorite pink crocs. She smiled at Maria.

"Do you remember when we used to play in the river as kids?" she asked.

Maria grinned broadly. Of course she remembered. They'd spent entire weekends out at the campground when they were kids. Those were Maria's favorite childhood memories. When the two of them had been together.

"We can be like that again," Lilly said, reaching her arms out to hug Maria. "Come here, little sis, let's be a family again."

Maria started forward, reaching out her arms to embrace her big sister.

"Get the hell away from her."

Maria froze. The voice, probably a teenage boy's, was nevertheless powerful. Lilly slowly lowered her arms, looking confused at Maria's sudden hesitance.

"Don't you want to come play with me, little sis?" she asked. Her voice was kindly enough, but the timbre was different. It sounded darker, colder, almost like a very calm person barely managing to conceal their rage.

"Get the hell away from her," the voice repeated, stronger this time.

"Do not interfere, foolish boy!" came a sharp hiss.

Lilly closed her eyes, her hands balling into fists.

"You will not stop me!" the second voice hissed again.

"I told you," came the boy's voice, "TO GET THE HELL OUT OF HERE!"

Maria screamed as a blinding flash of light erupted in front of her, the heat singing her hair as a brilliant, bright blue fireball crashed into Lilly, sending her flying backward into a large oak tree. A loud crack erupted as Lilly's skull smacked headlong into the tree. She crumpled at the base of the tree and lay still. A small trickle of dark red blood oozed down her forehead.

"Lilly!" Maria cried out.

She heard a deafening scream of rage.

"Run!" the boy shouted.

Maria didn't hesitate. She turned and ran into the dark trees, cutting her exposed arms and legs on unseen brambles and tree limbs, trying not to think about what was happening to Lilly.

"It's not her..." she thought as she jumped over a large gray rock. "He makes you see what he wants you to see."

Nevertheless, she felt tears begin to run down her cheeks as she tore out of the woods and into the campsite.

"I'm sorry, Lilly," she whispered as she ran towards Jody's tent, her mind spinning.

She'd seen him. The monster.

"Jody!" Maria cried as she approached the bright green two-man tent. "Jody, I..." she froze in front of the tent flap.

Dylan Teryon was standing next to the side of the tent, the steel cigarette lighter raised above his head, the bright blue flame hovering inches from the canvas.

CHAPTER 84

"I don't have a choice," Dylan muttered under his breath, raising the flame to meet the canvas. "I have to do this."

"But you do have a choice, kid." It was Kaden again.

Dylan lowered the lighter and was immediately irritated with himself.

"No, I don't," he insisted, raising the lighter again. "These people took everything from me, why should I have any sympathy for them?"

"Did they?" Kaden asked calmly.

Dylan hesitated, the lighter hanging suspended in midair inches from the canvas. Dylan shook his head, trying to chase the thought away, but it persisted. The lighter trembled in his hand.

"Why is Anna Veranda dead?" Kaden asked.

His voice had the air of a schoolteacher trying to convince a first grader that two plus two does indeed equal four.

"I killed her," Dylan muttered bitterly, his voice shaking slightly. "She wasn't supposed to die. The pills I gave her…they were meant for Laura."

"Why Laura?" Kaden asked.

Dylan could feel the heat rising in his face.

"Just do it!" his brain screamed. He raised the lighter again.

"Why Laura?" He hesitated. It wasn't Kaden speaking this time. It was his own voice. He thought of his mother and sister.

"They left them there," he said hollowly. "They left them there to die."

"But they saved you." It was Kaden speaking again. "They saved your life."

Dylan heard a small click as the lighter snapped shut. His hands balled into fists, bitter tears forming in his eyes.

"They killed Annette! They killed mama!"

"No, they didn't," Kaden said.

And then he was back in the alley, watching his mother and sister run for their lives as the soldier chased them, rifle poised.

"The soldier…" Dylan whispered as the rifle shots echoed off the alley walls, sending his mother and sister falling to the pavement. "His eyes…"

Kaden said nothing. He didn't need to. Then the scene faded, and he was back beside Jody's tent, his entire body trembling, tears spilling down his face.

"He killed them…" Dylan whispered. "He killed them…to get to me…"

"What are you doing?" Dylan jumped at the sound of the voice directly beside him.

Maria was standing by the tent flap, looking slightly startled. He could see from the redness in her eyes that she'd been crying. He quickly stashed the cigarette lighter out of sight, but he knew he was too late. Judging by the rapidly darkening expression she wore, there was no way she hadn't seen it.

"What are you doing?" Maria demanded.

She no longer appeared nervous. On the contrary, her tear-streaked face was turning red with anger. Dylan didn't answer. He suddenly noticed the weight of the coin in his pants pocket. Only it no longer felt like a coin. It had elongated and he could feel a sharp edge rubbing against his leg. Dylan gasped audibly. The magician had given him a knife. As if on cue, the magician's sharp hiss of a voice echoed in his head.

"Kill her."

Dylan shook his head.

"No."

Maria took a small step backward, suddenly very nervous. Dylan was staring at her so intensely she could feel his eyes burning holes in her skull. His hands were trembling with anger. He was slowly reaching for something concealed in his pants pocket, setting off alarm bells in her brain.

"Run," she thought desperately. "Run now!"

But her legs suddenly felt as though they'd been stuck in cement blocks.

"Kill her!" the magician screamed again, so loudly that the words echoed off the inside of Dylan's skull. He could feel his hand enter his pants pocket, reaching for the knife.

Maria took a shaky step backward away from him. In turn, he took a step towards her, his expression murderous, his eyes darkening with each passing second.

"No," Dylan thought as his fingers closed around the knife, preparing to spring. "I won't do it, you hear me, I WON'T!" He froze. He felt his grip on the knife release.

Maria gasped. His eyes...they were lightening, the black irises slowly fading to their normal dark brown. The magician remained silent, apparently too stunned to speak. Maria stared at Dylan, her eyes wide with terror.

"I..." Dylan stuttered, struggling to speak. "I...I was just taking a walk. To clear my head, you know?" He was shocked at the evenness in his voice, as if the previous few minutes had never happened.

Maria slowly nodded. Dylan turned and hurried toward his tent, eager to get away before Maria could ask him any more questions. Maria never took her eyes off Dylan as he walked away, the anger slowly rising within her. Her hands were balled into trembling fists. The image of the bright blue flame hovering inches from the side of the tent flashed through her mind.

"He was going to kill her," she thought. "He was going to kill Jody."

A new sensation joined the rage slowly building to a crescendo in her chest. A searing, acidic heat she might've mistaken for acid indigestion in another life. Her old life. The life that had been stripped away for good when Dylan had killed her mother. She felt the white-hot flames migrate through her arms, congealing in her hands.

"Fire can be used for growth and life..."

She slowly raised her right hand so that her palm pointed directly at the back of Dylan's head. The fire swelled, growing so blisteringly hot she nearly cried out in pain.

"…Or destruction…"

Maria froze, the small orange flame that had formed in the palm of her hand snuffed out instantly. The memory of that night flashed through her mind.

"When the time comes, I hope you make the right choice."

The scene shifted. She was standing beside the house in Fairfax on that fateful night. Leo's broken body smoldered in front of her, the ashes drifting lazily into the sky and gradually fading into nothing. She could hear Jody's mournful sobs drifting through the shattered bedroom window.

"When the time comes," Jody's voice whispered in her ear, "I hope you make the right choice."

Maria lowered her hand, the heat slowly fading away into nothing.

"I did what you asked," Maria whispered, her voice trembling. "You told me he can be saved, and I believe you." Maria sighed heavily, sitting down beside the tent flap. "I just hope you don't make me regret it."

A few minutes later, Maria crawled into the tent. As she was crawling into her sleeping bag, she saw Jody smile in her sleep.

"Don't worry, kid," Jody whispered. "You'll understand soon, I promise."

Maria smiled.

"I know," she whispered.

"I love you, Jody."

"I love you too, Maria," Jody whispered back.

Chapter 85

Kaden Versantos awoke with a start as the pickup truck bounced its way over a small pothole in the middle of the road.

"Where we at?" he mumbled, rubbing his head where it had smacked against the headrest.

His father, who was struggling to stay awake himself after having driven most of the night, mumbled something about route 64. Kaden yawned and sank back against the seat, watching the distant horizon where a faint orange glow was peeking out from behind the tree line. It was probably about six o'clock in the morning. He glanced at his father. There were heavy dark circles beneath his eyelids. He was bent slightly over the steering wheel as if he no longer had the strength to sit up properly. They had spent the last several days driving almost non-stop, taking a few hours here and there to rest and refuel. Although Kaden's father insisted they were looking for a safe place to take shelter, Kaden was fairly sure his real objective was to get as far away from the lake where Kaden had had his last vision as possible.

Kaden couldn't blame him. He wouldn't have drowned, he'd been under for far longer without it happening, but his father didn't know that. As far as he was probably concerned, he'd almost lost his only son again. Kaden hadn't tried to explain his ability to his father. Apart from the fact that he almost certainly wouldn't understand, it would probably only scare him worse. Hell, if Kaden were honest with himself, the whole thing, despite having lived with it his entire life, still scared him sometimes.

"We should probably stop soon," Kaden mumbled sleepily as the sun gradually inched its way above the tree line in the distance.

Kaden's father nodded, not really listening as they passed a small, derelict gas station on the side of the road dubbed by a large red and white sign as "Harry's Fill-Up Station." Kaden sighed. Apart from the fact that they both needed a few days' rest, the sight of the gas station reminded Kaden of the gas gauge which was now reading less than a quarter tank.

Kaden's father slowed the truck down as they approached a three-car pileup in the middle of the road. The pile of twisted metal crossed the entire roadway, which had no shoulder. Kaden felt a slight bump as his father carefully brought the truck down into the grass at the side of the road.

"Dad," Kaden said as they pulled back onto the road. "About what happened the other night. I'm sorry. I didn't mean to scare you."

His father didn't reply. In truth, Martin Versantos had done his best to forget about the events at the lake, but it had been hanging stubbornly at the back of his mind like an irritating mosquito that stayed just out of his reach. He knew his son wasn't normal, of course. He'd known that since the day a clinical psychologist had told them Kaden was mute when he'd been four years old. He'd never made a big deal about having a developmentally disabled child.

He'd learned ASL in the span of a couple months following the meeting, he'd set up pictographic charts at home to help Kaden communicate until he was old enough to learn to sign himself. He loved Kaden, and he would do anything for him, that had always been his response when other parents asked him if any of this bothered him. That was until a few months ago, when Kaden had suddenly started talking. Kaden's psychologist, who had seemed confused herself, simply told him that unusual cases happened sometimes, and there wasn't always a good explanation. He might have considered it a miracle, if it hadn't been accompanied by a near-drowning and the end of the world. Couple that with the incident at the lake, and one could see why Martin Versantos had reason to be on edge.

The stress had acted as a very powerful stimulant for him ever since that night. He had taken no more than a few hours to rest in the last several days, his relentless determination to get his son away from the terrible place where his life had nearly ended for the second time in a few short months pushing him to drive east almost non-stop. Although after his latest near fourteen-hour shift at the wheel, the effect of the stimulant was beginning to wear off. Martin rubbed his eyes in exhaustion as they passed by an overturned Honda Civic on the side of the road. It was going to be another long day.

CHAPTER 86

David Veranda woke up to the sound of a car engine coming from outside. Startled, he threw the sleeping bag off of him, reaching for his gun which he'd stashed beneath his pillow before he'd gone to sleep.

"Soldiers…" he thought, holstering the weapon. "Bastards can't even give us one day of peace."

He reached over to shake Maria awake. Only to find that her sleeping bag was empty.

"Shit," David muttered as he stepped out into the faint morning sunlight, the dew-soaked grass brushing against his bare legs. "Must've gotten up early."

His eyes swept the camp. No sign of movement from any of the other tents. As far as he could tell, he was the only one awake.

"Maria!" David called as he walked past a navy blue two-man tent where Roy and Laura were sleeping. "Hopefully, she'll have gone into the woods," David thought nervously as he walked through the field in the direction of the rumbling car engine. "She'll be safe there at least if this gets ugly."

The thought caused his forehead to break out in a nervous sweat. It was a miracle none of them had died when the bastards had come knocking back in Fairfax. David thought it unlikely that they would be so lucky this time. From behind him, he could hear rustling sounds from inside several of the tents. Not pausing to wait for the others, David tentatively approached a large beige pickup truck that had just pulled up into the clearing in front of him. He unholstered the gun as a large, strongly built middle-aged man with a spectacular bushy flaming red moustache to match his close-cropped hair wearing a dark gray muscle shirt and faded blue jeans stepped out of the truck, toting a Winchester pump shotgun. Both men raised their guns in unison. David felt himself begin to sweat nervously. This man did not look like the type to take prisoners.

"Who are you?" David demanded.

"I might ask you the same!" Martin Versantos shouted back.

Martin's commanding voice, combined with his impressive physique, gave him a very powerful appearance that would intimidate most men. Of course, David, having spent his entire career first in the military and then in law enforcement, was not most men. David heard several pairs of running footsteps behind him.

"David, what's going on here?" Roy exclaimed, sounding very frightened.

"We have a visitor," David said, tightening his grip on the gun. "And he doesn't look very friendly."

David saw a muscle twitch in Martin's jaw.

"Okay, everybody, let's calm down," Jason said, inserting himself between the two men but not quite bold enough to stand in front of the weapon barrels.

"I don't know," Martin said ferociously. "I'm not really in a place to calm down when a stranger walks up to me and sticks a gun in my face."

Martin, who had spent the last several hours on the verge of collapse, suddenly felt completely recharged, anger propelling him forward. His ability to think rationally had been all but exhausted, allowing the volatile cocktail of stress and fear that had been swelling in him over the last several days to take over.

"Neither am I," David replied angrily, his knuckles white on the gun.

"If we could just put our guns down," Jason continued, "and talk about this like reasonable adults, I think that would be better for everyone."

David glanced at the truck, and suddenly noticed a small boy sitting in the passenger seat. The realization slowly formed in David's mind.

"He's not being aggressive at all," David thought. "He's being protective. Good lord, he's got a kid."

"I'm willing to talk," David said, bringing the gun down. "Be a lot easier if you put that thing down."

Martin kept the shotgun raised.

"Speak for yourself," he said. "Clearly I made a mistake stopping here, I'll be leaving now if you don't mind."

Both men turned as the door to the pickup truck opened and a small boy stepped out onto the grass. He was staring intently at his father, seemingly not even noticing the others gathered around him.

"Kaden, get back in the truck," his father ordered as he inched towards the driver side door. "We're leaving."

Martin, a few paces from the door, suddenly paused. Something in his face changed. David shot a quizzical look at Jason, who shrugged.

"Lower your weapon."

It was his son's voice Martin was hearing, but it didn't come from his son's mouth. It seemed to be coming from the inside of his own head.

"Lower your weapon," the voice repeated.

Martin turned to look at his son. He had not moved from his spot beside the passenger door. His eyes were closed, and his face was screwed up in concentration. Martin could feel himself lowering the shotgun to his side. His face had gone slack.

"Jesus," Martin thought. "He's not talking at all. He's a voice in my head. Jesus Mary and Joseph, he's a goddamn telepath!"

"Dad, this man is not a threat to you. I want you to talk to him. It's important that we stay with these people. I can't explain everything right now, but you have to trust me."

Kaden opened his eyes. He nodded to his father, who was staring at him open-mouthed. David, now thoroughly confused, lowered his own weapon. Martin cautiously approached him, still looking suspicious but no longer as angry or scared as he had before. David holstered his weapon and extended his hand out to Martin. Martin, after a moment's hesitation, accepted it. Out of the corner of his eyes, David saw Kaden grin and wondered vaguely if he'd done something to calm his father down.

251

"Wouldn't be the weirdest thing I've seen happen the last few months, not even remotely," David thought as he shook Martin's hand.

"Martin," Martin said. "Good to meet you."

"David," David replied. "It's a pleasure."

"Do you have others with you?"

David glanced around. It looked like only Roy and Jason had joined them.

"Yeah, we've got a few more." David replied, starting back towards camp.

The others followed.

"Sorry to almost shoot you," Martin said apologetically to David. David saw Roy smile at this. David grinned.

"No worries brother, it happens."

Everyone laughed except for Martin.

"What?" Martin said, grinning. "What's so funny?"

David threw an arm around his shoulders, laughing bemusedly.

"That my friend," he said, "is a story for another time."

CHAPTER 87

Kaden began to feel slightly nervous as they approached the small circle of tents pitched a few hundred yards from the dense tree line. He'd communed with the little boy again last night after a laundry list of failed attempts the last few weeks. He'd broken through at the perfect time. The poor boy had been a moment away from destroying the last hope they had. Dylan, his name was. Kaden sighed as several women poked their heads out of the tents to see what was going on. Dylan had been through so much, far more than any person, let alone someone his age, should be forced to endure in one lifetime. But the thing that had nearly destroyed him was the murder of his mother and sister. He'd seen the memory, replayed it dozens of times. It was him. The bastard had used one of the mercenaries to kill them. Dylan, of course, had been his ultimate target. But Dylan had seen through the lies, at least for a moment, Kaden was sure of that much.

Whether he'd become fully unplugged from the magician's influence was entirely another matter. As Kaden had learned many times over, the magician had a way with people, especially those who had experienced as much trauma as Dylan had. And if they met now, and he hadn't been unplugged... Kaden shuddered, refusing to dwell on the terrible thought. He needed to see for himself, that was all there was to it. There was something else too. Kaden had felt the magician's presence here, while he was communing with Dylan. If the situation hadn't been so urgent, he would've run immediately. At first, he thought the magician was searching the mist for him, and there was a moment when he was sure he would finally be caught. But the magician's attention had been diverted away from him. He'd been focused on someone else. But with his own attention focused on Dylan, he hadn't been able to see the face of the magician's target. He was fairly sure she was a few years older than him, female, dark hair...but that was all. She could've been a hundred miles away from here, for all he knew.

"Dad!" Kaden turned as a girl with long dark hair came flying out a bright green two-man tent and flung her arms around David. "Jesus, you scared me! What happened?"

As David began to console the girl who Kaden assumed was his daughter, Kaden suddenly gasped.

"Maria..." he whispered.

It was her. The magician had been after her.

"Sorry what?" she said, looking at him curiously.

"I...I need to speak with you," Kaden stammered as the others gathered around the fire pit and took turns trying to start the fire. "Preferably alone."

David immediately moved protectively to her side.

"Whatever you need to say, son, you can say to both of us. Go ahead."

Kaden, feeling slightly annoyed, nevertheless continued.

"Last night, did you see something in the woods?"

He knew the answer immediately when he saw the haunted look in her eyes. David was looking at her curiously.

"You did, didn't you?" Kaden asked.

Maria nodded slowly.

"How...how did you know?" she asked nervously.

"That's not important," he said quickly, ignoring a warning look from her father. "The only important thing is what you saw out there."

Maria shook her head, looking slightly scared. Kaden nodded, understanding.

"She doesn't want to scare her father," he thought. He pondered this for a moment. "Can you give me your hand?" he asked.

Maria gave him a quizzical look.

"I know this is a lot to ask, considering you just met me, but can you trust me?"

He reached out his right hand to Maria.

"Just place your hand over mine and close your eyes."

Maria was about to refuse when it suddenly occurred to her that he knew about what happened in the woods. Suppose she wasn't the only firebrand besides Jody? Suppose this boy was one too? It certainly would make sense. He was remarkably mature for someone who couldn't have been older than fifteen or sixteen years old, and Maria had the strange feeling that despite having only known him for a few minutes, he knew a lot more about her than she realized.

With some trepidation, she extended her hand to Kaden, who placed it between both of his own. He closed his eyes, his expression serene. Maria closed her eyes while her father watched nervously. She had no idea what this strange boy was about to do, but she felt an inexplicable sense of trust towards him. It was the same feeling she'd had when she'd first met Jody in her dream. If she'd learned anything from the older woman, it was that this unorthodox intuition was usually correct. She closed her eyes as the world around her began to fade, first to gray, then to black. A strong rushing wind ruffled her hair as it passed. Maria opened her eyes. She was standing in a small meadow, the sun hanging high above her in the sky. It was around mid-day. It was pleasantly warm, and she could feel a slight breeze.

A few feet away, a small stream chuckled lazily along. Something about this place was vaguely familiar.

"Do you remember this place?"

Maria turned. Kaden was standing a few feet away, staring out at the slowly moving stream.

"Yes, I do, a little," Maria replied, standing next to him.

"You came here during your childhood. With Lilly. You would play in the stream for hours."

Maria nodded. She remembered now. It had been a tradition in her family when she was little. They would drive up to this place every weekend and rent a small cabin a few miles from the water. Her most fond childhood memories had happened here with her family. The time she'd held her breath for nearly a minute and a half after Lilly bet her she could hold hers longer when she was six. The time her father had tried to make flapjacks on the propane stove and nearly burned the entire cabin to the ground. The many hours she and Lilly had spent racing each other from one side of the stream to the other.

"Maria, would you join me?" Kaden asked, bending down and removing his shoes and socks. "The water is rather nice today."

Maria nodded and removed her own shoes as Kaden waded a few feet out into the water so that it barely came up to his ankles. A moment later, Maria joined him, enjoying the sensation of the cool water rushing between her bare toes.

"I'm sorry about your mother," Kaden said.

"How did you know?" Maria asked, not at all taken aback.

"This place," Kaden said. "I don't fully understand it, but I brought you here to get a look inside your head."

"Is that what you do then? Get inside people's heads?" Maria asked, remembering the voice that had spoken to her on that night in the woods.

Kaden nodded.

"More or less," he said. "I can commune with people, as I've done with you, but I can also see their memories. The latter, however, is a bit more difficult. It requires a very serene environment so there is less interference. As you can imagine, that is quite difficult to come by, especially in these times."

"Yeah," Maria agreed. "I imagine that a nuclear holocaust makes it pretty difficult to have some peace and quiet."

Kaden didn't smile. Maria couldn't blame him. She hadn't really meant for it to be funny.

"The point is," Kaden went on, "in this place, I can see bits and pieces of your memories. How did your mother die?"

"Dylan killed her," Maria said icily, her expression suddenly gaunt.

Kaden nodded. "He is troubled. I have communed with him and have seen the trauma in his past. He is very vulnerable to manipulation, as I'm sure you have seen."

"So that's why he killed my mother?" Maria asked bitterly. "He was manipulated?"

"His perception was twisted," Kaden replied with the air of a father trying to calm an upset toddler. "The magician, I'm not exactly sure how, but he uses people's worst memories to make them do terrible things."

"He shows them things that aren't real," Maria said, suddenly remembering the day she'd nearly killed her father.

Kaden nodded.

"He shows them things that make them angry, or scared," Maria went on. "Things that force them to act. I almost killed my father once, because of the things he made me see."

Kaden was silent, pondering what Maria had just said.

"You stopped him from killing Jody last night, didn't you?" Maria asked.

Kaden nodded.

"I spent weeks trying to commune with him, but he always shut me out. I finally broke through last night." Kaden paused, choosing his next words carefully. "But I didn't stop him. He stopped himself. I didn't physically restrain him from burning that tent. I showed him the truth." He looked at Maria very seriously. "That's all you can do for people who have suffered like him. You have to take all that anger they feel and redirect it somewhere where they can use it. Somewhere where it won't destroy them or the people around them."

Maria nodded.

"So, the magician just winds them up, and directs them at whatever he wants them to destroy?"

Kaden nodded.

"Just like a puppet master," he said. "He just pulls on the strings and his marionettes dance."

"Do you think he can be fixed?" Maria asked, dreading the answer.

Kaden considered for a moment, then shook his head.

"I don't know," he said. "I don't know if he can really be saved. People like Dylan are very volatile, they can be fine one moment, then something sets them off, and...well, you've seen it for yourself."

Maria nodded.

"Last night," Maria said, "I saw something. Something in his eyes. The darkness, it..."

"Faded," Kaden finished. "Yes, I felt it too. He became unplugged. He broke free if only for a moment." He sighed. "But like I said, people like Dylan are volatile. The magician preys on people who are volatile, exploits them for his own destructive ends. I will do whatever I can to save him, but in the end, it's going to be up to him to save himself."

"Do you think he can do it?" Maria asked.

Again, Kaden shook his head.

"I don't know. He's a strong kid, but the magician is strong too. But one thing is for sure. We need to keep an eye on him. As long as he is fighting this battle, he poses a threat to all of us."

Maria nodded.

"I will," she promised. "I won't let him hurt anyone else."

Kaden smiled.

"You're strong, kid. We might be in for a fight, but as long as we have you, I think we have a chance."

Maria smiled back.

The scene around her slowly faded until she was back at the campsite, her hand still clasped in both of Kaden's. Kaden opened his eyes. David hadn't moved from Maria's side.

"What happened?" he asked Maria.

Kaden turned to David and smiled.

"Mr. Veranda, your little girl has become a very strong and capable woman. You can trust her."

Maria turned to her father.

"Dad, I know we've been through a lot the last few years. I know we've lost a lot that we care about. I know it looks bad right now. But for the first time in a long time, I think we have a chance to make it out of this okay."

She turned to Kaden, smiling.

"There's a small stream not far from here. Want to go swimming?"

Kaden nodded, grinning. They started away from the campsite, chattering away as casually as a high school couple. David smiled. A few weeks ago, the idea that they might all come out of this okay would've sounded crazy to him. Now, seeing his daughter's beaming face shining in the bright morning sunlight, he really started to believe it.

CHAPTER 88

Kaden shuffled restlessly in his sleeping bag. He couldn't sleep. He'd been staring up at the pair of crossed poles for what felt like several hours. He rolled over to see if his father was having similar problems, then remembered that he was out on watch with David. After what had happened that morning, David had insisted on a two-man night watch. No one had argued against it. His father had left with David at dusk and hadn't said when he would be back. Kaden sighed and rubbed his eyes. Not his father would be able to do much as far as helping him sleep, but it would've been comforting to know he was nearby, nonetheless. Kaden's brain had been swirling with the day's events for the last several hours. It had proceeded more or less normally after the excitement of the morning. He'd swam in the river with Maria for a couple of hours. A little girl named Grace, who he'd later learn was Ben's daughter, had come to join them after a while.

Kaden had spent the remainder of the day getting to know the rest of the group members, although he'd only been half paying attention during their conversations. He'd been focusing most of his attention on Dylan, who'd retreated into his tent shortly after Kaden had arrived at camp and hadn't re-emerged for the rest of the day. Kaden had purposefully walked past the tent where he was taking refuge several times, trying to reach out to him, but hadn't gotten any response. It appeared that Dylan was blocking him out again. This made Kaden nervous for two reasons. First, it was impossible to tell whether Dylan had truly become unplugged. Second, it made it impossible to continue making progress with him. A horrible thought had been lurking at the back of Kaden's mind all day. Suppose the magician had gotten to Dylan.

Suppose he were working on him right now while Kaden couldn't interfere. He'd brushed it off at first, trying to tell himself Dylan would never turn to the magician again, not after last night. But the more he thought about it, the less sure he became. Kaden had never encountered a person with more past trauma than Dylan. The magician could've tapped any number of wells filled with traumatic memories to sway the volatile balance of power in his favor. And right now, Kaden could do nothing to stop him.

Kaden shook his head. He couldn't do this on his own. He needed to speak with Jody. Of everyone in camp, he had spoken to Jody the least, but she had made the strongest impression on him. He could immediately tell she was a firebrand, and a much more powerful one than Maria or himself. He was shocked when she described to him how Ben and Mike had found her. It struck him how no one besides the two of them seemed to realize just how close they'd come to losing the best, and possibly the only hope they had of winning this war. Kaden sighed. Maybe Dylan couldn't be saved, but at least she would have a better idea than he would.

"Besides," he thought as he threw the sleeping bag off him and opened the tent flap, "it would be nice to not have to sleep alone."

He stepped out into the cool night air, the moon shining high overhead. In the distance, he saw David and his father walking along a small ridge, David's pistol at his side, his father toting his shotgun. David said something to his father which caused him to let out a big, booming laugh that echoed all the way back to the campsite. Kaden smiled.

"Glad to see they're getting along," he thought as he crossed to the blue, two-man tent where Jody was asleep.

Kaden hesitated, not sure how to wake Jody without disturbing Maria, then remembered that Maria was sleeping in her father's tent. He opened the flap noiselessly and crawled inside, zipping it up behind him. To his surprise, Jody was lying awake, staring up at the ceiling of the tent. She sat up when Kaden entered the tent.

"You up?" Kaden asked, sitting down beside her.

"Am now," Jody replied grinning. "Nah, don't worry kid, you didn't wake me. I've just been thinking a lot lately. Makes it hard to sleep."

Kaden nodded.

"Yeah, I get it," he said. "Crazy day today, huh?"

"Yeah," Jody agreed. "You want to talk about it?"

Kaden nodded.

"David and my dad," he said.

"They were ready to kill each other just this morning. Now they look like they've been friends forever. Kinda crazy, huh?"

Jody grinned.

"Well Kaden, you'd be surprised how well men get along after sharing a few cigarettes."

They both laughed. Ben had passed a pack of Marlboros around with his father and David after dinner. It was a bit odd to see his father smoking, but if it helped the men get along, Kaden was all for it.

"I'm happy to see them getting along," Jody said. "We all need to stand together. The sooner we learn to join hands, the better."

Kaden nodded.

"So, he is coming then?" Kaden asked.

"He's already here," Jody replied. "He's going to throw every obstacle in our path that he can. He's afraid."

Kaden gave her a quizzical look.

"He's been hunting me for years," Kaden replied. "Whenever I enter the mist, I can feel him there, searching for me. He's not afraid of me."

"Not you," Jody said. "All of us. He's afraid of us being together. I knew that when he ran away from Ben and Mike the day they saved my life. That's why he tries to isolate us and pick us off one by one."

"Like he's doing to Dylan," Kaden said.

Jody shook her head.

"He's isolated Dylan for sure, but he's an instrument to the Puppeteer. A useful tool to carry out his dirty work," she spat disgustedly. "To do that to a child...I hope I can make the bastard suffer for it."

"Do you think he can be saved? Dylan, I mean."

Jody paused, considering the question carefully.

"Honestly," she said, "Dylan Teryon is the strongest person I've ever met. Trauma does one of two things to us, Kaden. It either destroys us or strengthens us. In Dylan's case, he's become stronger than anyone his age should need to be. He has a good chance."

"He's fighting it," Kaden said. "I felt it the other night, when I was communing with him."

He said nothing about what Dylan had been doing when he'd communed with him, although he wondered if Jody might know anyway.

"There was a moment, when..."

He paused, choosing his words carefully.

"He broke out of it. He became unplugged."

"Fully unplugged?" Jody asked, sounding a little startled.

Kaden nodded.

"He was in total control," Kaden said. "I've never seen anything like it."

"Me neither," Jody said.

Jody had worked with many of the Puppeteer's victims over the years, both those that were in the process of converting and those that had been fully converted, many when she was very young before she'd become fully aware of the extent of her powers. When someone was still converting, she'd had a few cases where they were given the right help and were able to come out of it, but they were rare. Often, the right help either wasn't available, or no one cared enough to provide it.

While it was not impossible for a full convert to become unplugged, it was incredibly rare, and she'd only seen it happen a handful of times. Even in those cases, it had taken years, and a remarkable level of unwavering support had to be provided. But for a full convert like Dylan to do it on his own...it was incredible.

"Can you tell if he's still unplugged?" Kaden asked.

Jody shook her head sadly.

"He's been blocking me, so I can't see inside his head."

"He's been doing the same to me," Kaden said. "It worries me. I'm afraid the magician will approach him when we're not there to help."

Jody sighed.

"There's only so much we can do, kid. In the end, it's going to come down to him. He has to decide to save himself."

Kaden nodded. Jody yawned.

"I should at least try to get some sleep," she said, laying back down in the sleeping bag, her head resting on a small throw pillow she'd taken from the house in Fairfax.

Kaden started to get up, then remembered why he'd come there in the first place.

"Mind if I stay?" he asked. "It gets a bit lonely when dad's out on patrol."

Jody smiled and nodded. Kaden lay down on top of the sleeping bag next to Jody, not bothering to remove his clothes.

"You miss your mom, don't you kid?" Jody whispered.

"Yeah," Kaden said, a trace of melancholy in his voice. "Every day."

"Well," Jody said, "I'm not your mom, but I'll still take care of you the best I can."

She wrapped her arms around Kaden, who snuggled close to her chest. They fell asleep that way a few minutes later. When Martin Versantos came back from patrol an hour later, he found the tent empty. He spotted Kaden's shoes sitting outside Jody's tent. He found them sleeping together, Jody cradling his son like a small child in her arms. He smiled, glad to see that his boy had a mother again.

CHAPTER 89

About twenty miles away, Rick Goldson was hunched over a small campfire in the middle of the rapidly darkening woods, staring intently at the flames. "Careful doing that," Kane said as he returned with a thick tree branch that he set beside the fire. "You'll go blind if you stare into flames like that for too long."

Rick ignored him. Ordinarily, he might have found it funny, but he was in no mood to appreciate his comrade's sense of humor at the moment.

"You seen Cetan?" Kane asked, squatting down beside Rick.

Rick shook his head. Cetan had ordered them to build a fire and walked off into the woods a couple of hours ago. Neither of them had seen him since. Both men had become very wary of Cetan ever since the night at the farm a few weeks ago. Although neither of them had said it out loud out of fear of being heard, both men wanted desperately to leave the group. Their lives were in danger as long as they were around Cetan.

On the night at the farm, Rick had gone so far as to stash the keys for the van beneath the driver's seat and was moments away from leaving when Jacob had beaten him to it. After the way the escape attempt had ended for Jacob, Rick had dropped the idea. This man, Cetan, if he was a man at all, had been granted extraordinary power by some sort of deity, an evil deity at that. Both Rick and Kane could feel it every time he came near them. There was another presence there with Cetan, shadowing him. It scared the living hell out of both men, both of whom had gone into survival mode after Cetan had killed Jacob the same night he'd killed that poor little girl.

In their minds, if they just did whatever Cetan asked of them, and did it well, and they could accomplish whatever task he'd set out to do, they had a chance to walk away from this with their lives. The idea of killing Cetan had occurred to Rick. If Cetan were a normal human being, he probably would've done it already. But that was the problem. Cetan was no ordinary man, and Rick had the nasty feeling that even if he managed to put a bullet in Cetan's head, Cetan would wrench the rifle out of his grasp and shoot him dead without missing a beat. Whatever higher power was lending Cetan power would never allow him to be stopped by a mere bullet.

"Think he's coming back?" Kane asked, sounding almost hopeful.

"Oh, he'll come back," Rick said flatly.

"What do you think he's doing out there?" Kane asked.

Rick shrugged. The truth was, he didn't have the slightest clue what Cetan was doing right now, and he wasn't especially interested in finding out.

"How you holding up?" Rick asked.

"Fine," Kane said. "I mean, it's too bad about Jacob, but it's his fault really. He abandoned the mission. He betrayed us."

Kane sounded as though he didn't really believe what he was saying. Rick nodded, not wanting to argue. Both men were thinking the same thing: it could've easily been them rather than Jacob. For Rick, it nearly had been.

"What do you suppose Cetan did to him?" Kane asked with a hint of trepidation, as though it was a question he wasn't really supposed to be asking.

"Killed him," Rick said flatly. "Shot him dead, that's what he told us."

"Well, okay, that's a bit obvious," Kane said, and Rick felt a twinge of annoyance. He didn't like where this was going.

"What I mean is, what did he do other than kill him?"

Rick shook his head.

"C'mon," Kane whispered conspiratorially. "You know Cetan isn't a normal human. Hell, he's probably not human at all. What do you suppose..."

"Shut up," Rick muttered, and Kane fell silent.

The sounding of footsteps crunching over twigs and dead leaves was rapidly approaching from behind them. Both men looked up as Cetan entered the clearing, his expression cold. Both men shuddered as his eyes swept over them suspiciously.

He said nothing as he approached them. The sudden silence was unnerving.

"So, what's the plan?" Rick asked finally, struggling to keep his voice steady. Cetan wordlessly waved his hand. Kane jumped as the fire was instantly extinguished, faster than if he'd poured a bucket of cold water on it. Rick stared at Cetan nervously. A muscle was twitching in his jaw.

"Shit," Rick thought. "He heard us. And now he's probably gonna kill us."

Rick felt the weight of the pistol on his hip. Even if it wouldn't work, he had to at least try. He slowly reached for his holster, his hand trembling violently as it closed around the grip of the gun. Kane closed his eyes, preparing for death.

Cetan hung over them like an enormous blackbird, his visage skeletal. Rick tensed, his gun arm preparing to spring.

"Get in the van," Cetan said sharply, sweeping past them in the direction of the vehicle.

Rick released his grip on the gun, exchanging a quizzical look with Kane.

"Get in the van," Cetan repeated, a hint of anger creeping into his voice.

Rick and Kane got up and hurried after Cetan.

"Boss," Kane called. "Where are we..."

"Blacksburg," Cetan called carelessly over his shoulder. "Our quarry will be there within hours."

Rick flinched as Cetan's expression broke into a predatory grin.

"We're going to throw them a little housewarming party."

CHAPTER 90

Dylan Teryon stared out the window of Martin Versantos' pickup truck as they trundled steadily west along route 64, David's Chevrolet speeding along just a few feet in front of them. He barely noticed any of the passing scenery. As had been the case almost continuously for the last several months, he was lost in thought. For the second time in as many days, he'd disobeyed a command from the magician. He'd refused to kill Jody and Maria, just like he'd refused to kill Roy. He still couldn't understand why he'd done it. He'd spun it over and over again in his mind, trying to work it out like a complicated jigsaw puzzle, but the answer had remained out of his reach. It simply didn't make any sense. When he'd killed Anna, there had been no question of disobeying. Hell, he'd been furious when he'd realized the wrong woman was dead.

"Is that really why you were angry?" said a voice in his head.

Dylan nearly jumped. Kaden was looking directly at him, his expression unreadable. Dylan stared at him, his lower lip quivering.

"Telepathy?" he thought.

"Yeah," came the reply a second later.

"I understand that it's a bit awkward with us sitting right next to each other, but I don't want the others to hear us."

Dylan nodded.

"So, getting back to my question, why were you angry after Anna died?"

"I wasn't supposed to..." Dylan paused.

He saw a faint grin cross Kaden's lips as the truth slowly came to him.

"I didn't want to kill her at all," Dylan said slowly. "I wasn't angry at myself for not killing Laura, I was angry because I killed Anna. She was..." he stuttered for a moment. "She was a good woman. A good mother. She didn't deserve to die."

Now Kaden was definitely smiling.

"I didn't kill Jody," Dylan went on, "I couldn't. I just couldn't, no matter how much he screamed at me, no matter what he showed me, it was...it was wrong. I knew it was wrong."

"You've been through a lot, kid," Kaden said. "I know that, Jody knows that, and I'm sorry." He paused, choosing his next words carefully. "But being angry and taking it out on people doesn't help you. You've got to rise above it, you've got to look beyond all the bad stuff and see the bigger picture."

Dylan remained silent.

"I can help you with that. Jody can too, but in the end, it's up to you. You can do this."

"I am," Dylan said. "I will."

Kaden nodded, grinning broadly.

"I know you will, kid."

Dylan felt a small smile cross his face for what felt like the first time in years.

"Thank you," Dylan said gratefully.

Kaden nodded.

Dylan went back to staring out the window at the passing towns and road signs as they turned onto the exit ramp for route 77. And then Dylan saw him. He was sitting cross-legged on top of a sign pointing out nearby gas stations and lounging options, his black top hat sitting slightly askew on top of his head. He waved a gloved hand at Dylan as they passed, grinning wickedly with his pointed teeth. Dylan, realizing with a jolt that he felt no fear, held the monster's gaze, staring him down defiantly. The monster's smile slowly faded. The muscles in his face pulled taught with anger, giving him an almost skull-like appearance. Dylan held his gaze, refusing to back down.

"You can see him, can't you?" came Kaden's voice from somewhere far off.

Dylan nodded as they passed, and the monster faded into the distance.

"Remember, whatever he shows you," Kaden said, "he wants you to see it. None of it is real."

"Kaden," Dylan asked. "Why does he show me these things? What does he want?"

"He uses trauma to twist people's perception," Kaden said. "He'll take all the pain you feel from your worst memories and redirect it at someone he wants you to harm."

Dylan thought for a moment before nodding to show he understood. It suddenly made perfect sense to him. He returned to staring out the window as they maneuvered their way around a four-car pileup on the entrance ramp for route 77, no longer scared at the prospect of seeing the magician everywhere he went. No, in that moment, the thought of that monster popping up again filled him with a burning, righteous anger.

CHAPTER 91

Cetan brought the van to a stop on the curb, his expression stony. He eyed the rifle he'd lain on the passenger seat. He smiled coldly. It would be put to good use soon. One of his master's prized recruits had stepped out of line and needed to be dealt with. Cetan slung the rifle over his shoulder and stepped out of the van, joining his two comrades, their own rifles at the ready. Cetan eyed them both suspiciously, but neither of them showed any signs of thinking twice. They were ready, Cetan could feel it in his bones.

"Kill anything that moves," he said flatly before turning on his heel and starting down the street.

Rick and Kane hurried to keep up with him. Rick exchanged a look with Kane. Both of them were thinking the same thing: I don't want to be here tonight. Despite Cetan's certainty that both men were fully plugged in, if anything, they had become more unplugged in the last several hours.

"Kill anything that moves," could include women or children. The thought scared both of them very badly. It wasn't right, and they both knew it. But fear of Cetan kept them hurrying down the street after him, towards the doomed house second from the end of the street. The thought of shooting Cetan in the back of the head and running crossed Rick's mind, but he resisted the temptation. The bullet wouldn't stop him, Rick was well aware of that by now. Kane was trembling, but not from the cold despite being clad in athletic shorts and a tank top. Cetan however, remained blissfully unaware of what was happening in the minds of his comrades as he marched up the driveway to the house, his focus solely devoted to the task ahead. He looked up as the door opened and Roy Forsin emerged, pistol at the ready.

His eyes widened in surprise when he saw Cetan.

"Hey there, old friend," Cetan called, grinning.

Roy slammed the door shut as Cetan fired off three rounds which smashed into the heavy wooden storm door. Laura screamed as the front windows shattered on either side of them, the bullets ricocheting off the walls behind them. Roy grabbed Laura and pulled her into the other room as more shots zoomed through the broken windows. Mike fired back, managing to get off a couple of shots before another barrage flew through the window in his direction.

"Serena!" Lorenzo shouted, firing off several rounds of his own. "Get the kids out of here!"

Serena, along with Jennifer, grabbed Grace and Marianne's hands and pulled them out of the room, Dylan on their heels.

Cetan felt a muscle twitch in his jaw. The little bastard was trying to escape. He could feel the anger building in his chest as he stormed up to the front door. He threw the door open, casually pinning down two shooters on his left as they attempted to halt his progress, never taking his eyes off his target who was fleeing down the back hallway with two of the women and their children.

"I'll teach you to defy your master," Cetan thought furiously. A stray bullet cut across his shoulder, spraying blood down his shirt and onto the floor. Cetan barely noticed. He fired off a barrage in the direction where the shot had come from, nearly connecting with Tyson, who ducked behind a large bookshelf just in time. His quarry ran after the women out the back door. Cetan followed, ignoring another bullet which sliced into his left calf, every fiber in his being concentrated on the little boy now flying out the door after his companions.

CHAPTER 92

D ylan Teryon raced after Grace and Marianne, his eyes wide with fright. Every few seconds, he shot a terrified look over his shoulder. He hadn't believed his eyes when he'd first seen him. It was the soldier who'd killed his mother and sister. The magician's loyal servant, here to kill him for defying his master. It only occurred to him as he sprinted across the back lawn towards the garage how stupid he'd been. The idea of exhibiting righteous anger towards an entity that had the power to snuff out his existence with a wave of his hand seemed completely ridiculous now. Was he really naïve enough to think that Kaden and Jody could protect him? He had seen his master's power, had felt it for himself. Even Jody was nothing compared to him. He could sweep her aside as easily as a ball of lint.

The back door exploded open behind him, Cetan rushing after them, his dark, predatory eyes locked on his target. Dylan, driven by fear, pumped his legs even faster, rocketing over the ground. But he wasn't fast enough. He heard a high-pitched cry of pain, and suddenly, Marianne was no longer running beside him. Dylan turned. Marianne was lying on the ground, clutching her ankle, her face screwed up in pain. Cetan loomed over her, the rifle aimed at the little girl's head. He smiled wolfishly.

"Yet another who won't get away," he whispered, his finger squeezing on the trigger.

"NO!" Dylan, sprinting back towards them, grabbed for the rifle as Cetan fired, the barrel swinging wide of its target, the bullet bouncing harmlessly into the grass.

Cetan furiously threw Dylan off, turning the rifle back on Marianne, who was cowering on the ground. Dylan threw herself on top of Marianne, shielding her. Cetan's eyes narrowed. He began to squeeze the trigger. Dylan closed his eyes, preparing for death.

"Why did you do it?"

Cetan paused, temporarily stunned. It took Dylan a moment to realize he'd spoken.

"Why did you do it?" he repeated.

Something in Cetan's stone-cold face shifted.

"Why did you kill my mom and sister?"

Cetan's expression continued to shift, like someone had pulled the wrong brick out of a Jenga tower and the whole thing was crumbling. He looked almost…vulnerable. Cetan stuttered, completely forgetting about the existence of the rifle.

"Anger," Dylan continued. "Fear. They're probably the two most powerful forces in the human psyche. And I think you have plenty of both."

Cetan stared at the little boy, dumbstruck.

"I can see your trauma," Dylan said. "It's right there in your eyes. I don't know what you went through back then, but I'm sorry. For all of it."

Cetan felt himself lowering the rifle. It was now pointing at the ground. Somewhere in the back of his mind, he heard his master screaming incoherently, but Cetan's attention was too fixated on Dylan to take notice.

"I went through hell when I was a kid, just like you," Dylan continued. "I was angry too, for a long time. I did things that I hate myself for now. I hurt people that I care about. I think we blame ourselves. It's a way of rationalizing all of it. If we think we had control back then, it feels less hopeless, like we can just do better next time. The truth is a lot of that stuff is out of our control. It isn't fair. None of it is. But you've gotta find it in yourself to let go, to forgive yourself, even to forgive them. Because if you don't, you let it control you. You let him control you. That's what he does. He takes the worst experiences of your life and redirects all that pain and suffering at someone who isn't responsible for any of it. You've gotta find it in yourself to move on and live the best life you can. That's the only way you'll ever be happy."

Jennifer, Grace, and Serena were staring at the pair of them from across the lawn, dumbstruck.

Cetan felt his grip loosen on the rifle. It clattered to the ground. Marianne scrambled away, running to Jennifer, who caught her and held her tightly. Dylan reached his hand out to Cetan, a small smile crossing his face.

"It's hard, at first," Dylan said. "It will always be lurking in the back of your mind, even years from now. It never fully disappears. All you can do is keep going forward. It will get better, I promise." Dylan saw a wan smile slowly cross Cetan's lips. For a brief moment, Dylan saw the ghost of a much younger, happier man in that face. A man full of life. A man who had strong character.

Cetan slowly reached a trembling hand out to Dylan. Dylan's eyes suddenly went wide as the soldier appeared at the back door, rifle poised. Marianne screamed and covered her ears as the shots rang out. Cetan went rigid, three circular blood stains slowly spreading across his chest. He swayed once, then collapsed, stone cold dead.

Dylan stared numbly at the man's body, tears forming in his eyes. He looked up as the soldier approached, toting the rifle, but there was no venom in his expression. On the contrary, he looked almost sorrowful. He shook his head as he approached.

"I'm sorry," Rick said, extending a hand to Dylan.

Dylan took it, allowing Rick to pull him to his feet.

"I'm sorry for all of this," he called to the women, who had shrunk away against the garage wall. "Your people are okay, no one got hurt. He…he was behind all of this," Rick said bitterly, pointing at Cetan. "I wanted to leave, I really did, I was just…scared." He shook his head miserably.

Dylan turned as the back door opened again. Several men emerged, including Ben, Mike, Lorenzo, Tyson, Jason, Roy, Jody, Kaden, and another man toting a rifle who Dylan recognized as the third shooter.

269

"We didn't mean any of this," Rick said, turning to the group at the back door. "But there was something in this man. Something that wasn't…human. I suggest you all leave this place soon, because I have a feeling he'll be back."

It happened in a flash. One second, Rick was standing in the midst of the group, staring disgustedly at Cetan's lifeless body. The next second, he was ten feet in the air as if he'd been hoisted by an invisible rope, hands clutching uselessly at his throat, the rifle lying forgotten on the ground. Dylan screamed and ran to Jody, who caught him in a hug, staring open mouth at the spectacle in the sky. Rick struggled against his invisible bonds, his face turning purple, his hands grappling uselessly at his throat.

"I'LL TEACH YOU TO DISOBEY ME!" a deep, cold voice screamed into the night air.

Rick's head was suddenly ripped backward one hundred eighty degrees, the bones in his neck snapping sickeningly. Kaden screamed and covered his eyes as the man's eyeballs exploded like grapes, thick dark blood gushing onto the lawn below in a river of deep vermillion.

"YOU'RE NEXT BOY, YOU HEAR ME!" the voice screamed, rounding on Dylan. "YOU THINK YOU CAN OVERCOME ME, I'LL SHOW YOU THE MEANING OF FEAR BOY! I'LL SHOW ALL OF YOU! I'VE BEEN PLAYING GAMES WITH YOU SO FAR, NO LONGER! I'LL HAVE YOU BEGGING FOR DEATH ONCE I'M FINISHED WITH YOU!"

Rick's body hit the ground with a sickening crack. Serena screamed. Dylan fell to his knees, staring up at the place where the magician hung in midair, invisible.

"I'm not afraid of you," he whispered, his voice breaking. "I'M NOT FUCKING AFRAID OF YOU, YOU HEAR ME?!" Dylan felt a sudden chill as the magician landed right next to him.

"You will be, son," the magician whispered in his ear. And then he was gone.

Dylan heard a scream from somewhere far off. The world faded to gray around Dylan as he lost consciousness, slipping into the blissful darkness.

CHAPTER 93

Kane Lewellyn's knuckles were white on the steering wheel as the van sped west on route 81 at seventy-five miles per hour. He looked like a complete wreck. His face was paper white, the skin pulled taut over the bones, giving him a skeletal appearance. His eyes, lined with deep purple shadows, were wide with fright and badly bloodshot. He was emaciated from not eating for the last several days, his throat so parched he could barely speak aloud. He was badly in need of a shave, judging by the dark stubble erupting from his cheeks and chin. Every few seconds, he glanced fearfully in the rear view mirror as if expecting to see another car coming up on him, the Puppeteer grinning behind the wheel. Kane shuddered at the thought. His eyes flickered to the gas gauge. It read slightly less than a quarter of a tank. The thought of stopping, even for a few minutes, to try and siphon gas from a car on the side of the road was unthinkable for Kane. He could not stop, not now, and probably not ever.

If he got desperate, he could ditch the van and continue on foot, although the idea did not exactly thrill him. He shot another fearful glance behind him, half expecting to see the Puppeteer sitting in the back seat, knife in hand. The sight of the empty seat gave him no relief. He thought of Jacob. He'd only been twenty years old, barely an adult yet. They'd spent three years serving in the same platoon in the Marine corps. Jacob had joined their unit when he was only seventeen years old after running away from an abusive foster home, lying to the local recruiter about his age so that he could enlist. Kane shook his head sadly. Jacob had been fond of joking about this, saying that the marine corps didn't care how old you were as long as you were capable of being effective cannon fodder. They'd laughed together about it back in the day, speculating how long it had taken the recruiter to decide to ignore Jacob's age and allow him to enlist after he found out. Kane had estimated about five minutes. Jacob, laughing, had said it was probably closer to three.

"Marines," Kane thought numbly. "Stands for 'Muscles are required, intelligence not essential.'" Their platoon used to laugh about that one too over throwaway card games. Kane sighed heavily as he turned the van onto the exit ramp for route 26. Thinking about it now, however, he didn't think it was funny at all.

Kane continued south on route 26, the gas gauge gradually dipping lower with each passing mile. A small yellow light that indicated low fuel appeared on the dashboard as he passed by a sign that announced an exit for the city of Asheville. Kane felt the migraine he'd been developing over the last several hours tightening beneath his eyeballs. He tried desperately to remember how to hotwire a car the way Rick had shown him several years ago.

271

"Rick..." The terrible image of Rick being yanked into the air, choking to death on an invisible rope flashed through his mind, rewinding over and over again until Kane nearly cried out in terror. What would the Puppeteer do to him when he caught up with him? Would he simply slit his throat? Would he torture him first?

Kane shook his head violently, forcing himself to focus on the road ahead. He couldn't afford to think like that right now, not if he wanted any chance of survival. He shot another nervous glance over his shoulder. The road behind him remained empty, save for a few wrecked cars lining the shoulder. A few minutes later, the snow began to fall, lightly at first. Kane switched the windshield wipers on, squinting hard out the window as his visibility was gradually reduced until he couldn't see more than a few feet in front of him through the driving snowfall, which was now coming down in droves. He felt himself growing increasingly nervous as the snow began to obscure the roadway in front of him until the lines were no longer visible, and he was perpetually in danger of drifting off onto the narrow dirt shoulder. Kane reduced his speed to around thirty, nervously tapping the dashboard as the needle on the gas gauge hovered around empty. If he broke down here, now, in the middle of what had gradually developed into a full-blown snowstorm, with nothing for miles around...Kane shuddered. It was the loneliest feeling in the world.

Kane shivered. According to the temperature gauge, it had dropped to single digits in the last hour. The number of potentially available replacement vehicles lining the roadside, either to hotwire or siphon fuel from, was dwindling. He did not like the prospect of continuing on foot, considering he was hardly dressed for the sudden weather in only sweatpants, a t-shirt, and light rain jacket, nor was waiting for the weather to clear an option. He could feel the dark shadow of the Puppeteer lurking somewhere in the back of his mind, searching for him. Kane trembled, but not from the cold. He was close. Too close. And if he were caught...Kane shuddered. He preferred not to think about it. The dark shape appeared out of nowhere in the middle of the road. Kane screamed, jerking the wheel to the left, missing the man by inches.

At the same moment, the van skidded over a patch of black ice, sending it completely out of control. Kane fought desperately to bring the van back onto the road as it spun out onto the shoulder. He felt himself lift out of the seat and into the air as the van slid over a small embankment. Kane's head smacked against the roof of the van, his vision narrowing down to a tiny pinprick as he nearly lost consciousness. The van rolled over and tumbled end over end until it came to rest at the bottom on its side, a small wispy trail of white smoke pouring out of the engine.

Kane groaned weakly, rubbing his head where it had struck the roof. His trembling fingers came away drenched in his own blood. His face stung where shards of flying glass had pierced it. His chest burned each time he drew breath, likely from broken ribs. He was lying on his side on the snow-covered ground, not having bothered to secure his seat belt. Kane pulled himself gingerly into a sitting position, his broken ribs protesting from the effort. Very slowly, he tried to stand, only to fall back almost immediately as his wobbly legs wouldn't support him.

Kane sat still for a moment, struggling to catch his breath. Outside, the wind howled mournfully, the snow blowing in on him through the broken passenger's side window.

"Kane..." Kane went rigid at the sound of the icy, hissing voice. It was him. "Kane..." His heart began to race. The voice sounded so close. He needed to run now. Kane reached up for the broken passenger's side window, his fingers scrabbling uselessly at the edges. "I don't want to die, not like this," Kane whispered, struggling to raise himself to his feet, only to fall again. "Kane..." the voice was getting closer.

"Not like this, NOT LIKE THIS!" he screamed aloud, forcing himself to his feet, managing to grab the window frame as his legs gave out beneath him again. Kane roared in pain as shards of broken glass lining the edge of the window sliced through his fingers. His broken ribs screamed in protest as he forced himself upward through the broken window, dark red blood running freely from both of his hands, dripping down onto him and staining the snow beneath him. His face was bright red, every muscle in his arms burning with lactic acid as he fought to push himself upward. Finally, when he was more than halfway through, he tilted forward, allowing his lower body to come through at an angle, his muscles gasping in relief as the tension eased. He slid over the edge of the van's side, doing a midair somersault before landing hard on his back in the snow, knocking the wind out of him.

"Kane..." the voice hissed again.

"Jesus, he's right on top of me," Kane thought, panicked. He forced himself to his feet, leaning on the van for support, his wobbling legs struggling to support him. "I am not gonna die here," Kane whispered. "I AM NOT GONNA FUCKING DIE HERE!" he screamed, forcing his shaking legs to carry him forward through the heavy snow. He stumbled towards the tree line, half blinded by the driving snow, his face numb from the cold. He could feel the dark shadow of the Puppeteer chasing after him, gaining on him. He forced himself to run, ignoring his screaming muscles and the inferno building to a crescendo in his chest with each step. He floundered into the dark trees, his vision narrowing as dehydration threatened to send him into unconsciousness. "I am not gonna die," he whispered, forcing himself to go on. Thankfully, the snow was much lighter here due to the tree cover.

"Kane..." the voice whispered in his ear. Kane screamed in terror, forcing himself to run faster, unseen branches whipping at his frozen face and arms as he sprinted through the darkness. Despite the freezing conditions, Kane's entire body was drenched with sweat. The burning sensation in his chest made him feel as though he had ingested battery acid. He threw a terrified glance over his shoulder and saw the dark shadow standing at the edge of the tree line. Although his face was almost completely concealed in shadow, Kane could still make out the rapacious leer punctuated by a band of white, abnormally sharp canine teeth.

"You won't take me you fucker!" Kane shouted, forcing himself to run faster. He nearly tripped and fell over a small tree stump half buried in the snow. After several minutes, he collapsed against a fallen birch tree, unable to run anymore, gasping for breath. His brain screamed at him to run, but he could no longer feel the shadow close to him. The numbing effect of the adrenaline quickly wore off, allowing the pain in his ribs and hands to return in full force. He gazed at his hands, which were covered in cuts and dried blood.

He collapsed to his knees, the dehydration and exhaustion finally overwhelming him. He plunged his aching hands in the snow, the intense cold acting as a mild sedative for the pain. The Puppeteer watched him from a distance, grinning coldly. He could take him now, of course, and given how poorly things had been going lately, it certainly would've been the prudent option. But he often made the mistake of valuing pleasure over prudence, and tonight, he simply couldn't help himself from savoring the man's fear for a little bit longer before taking him. Particularly with a defiant servant like Kane who he was determined to punish, the Puppeteer enjoyed letting him believe he might have a chance of survival, at least for a few hours, before stripping that notion brutally away. The Puppeteer's grin widened. He supposed it couldn't hurt to have a little fun with Kane before taking him.

Kane, still struggling to catch his breath, glanced around nervously, sure he would see the Puppeteer lurking in the trees. What he saw instead made his heart skip a beat. Standing just a few hundred feet away in a clearing, was a small wooden cabin that was probably frequented by hunters during the spring and fall. Struggling to his feet, Kane stumbled drunkenly towards it, wondering vaguely through the haze of pain how he hadn't noticed it before. It was almost as though it had appeared out of thin air when he wasn't looking. A few minutes later, Kane stumbled through the front door of the cabin, amazed to find it unlocked. In the darkness, he could make out a kitchenette with a small dinner table, a leather recliner sitting in front of an ancient looking box television set, what looked like a bathroom set off in the corner, and a single person mattress set atop a steel spring bed frame situated next to a wooden chest of drawers opposite the bathroom.

He stripped off his soaked tennis shoes and socks and threw them into a corner. Kane, somewhat disbelieving of his luck, wandered into the bathroom, and to his astonishment, found a perfectly maintained large marble bathtub waiting for him. Kane stripped off his soaking wet clothes without any hesitation and started the hot water, never taking into consideration how odd it was that the water even worked, let alone that it remained heated despite the lack of a functioning electrical grid. Kane submerged his broken and battered body into the scalding bath water, the heat soothing the pain in his ribs. He closed his eyes, allowing himself to drift off. Never noticing the dark shadow lurking by the door, no longer smiling, his eyes blazing with hatred.

Kane snapped awake suddenly. His eyes darted fearfully around the strange room. It took him a few seconds to remember where he was. He stepped out of the bath, the water, which was freezing cold by now, dripping off his naked body. He dressed himself, pleased to find that his soaking wet clothes had dried considerably during the time he'd spent in the bathtub. The pain in his now shriveled hands had also eased significantly. The bath water had cleaned the cuts and the size of them had been noticeably reduced even in just the last few hours. Kane glanced around nervously as he stepped out of the bathroom, trying to remember what had woken him up. No answer came to him as he wearily approached the small mattress stashed in the corner, figuring he could use some sleep.

"Kane, honey, is that you?" came a woman's high-pitched voice from somewhere behind him. Kane's face went stark white. He whirled around, gooseflesh erupting on both his arms at the sight of her. She was standing in the middle of the room in a ghostly white nightgown, her dark hair pinned up in a high bun. She was smiling at him in a way that an outsider might mistake for welcoming, but Kane knew better. It was the look his mother wore whenever he'd committed some infraction. And committing any infraction, no matter how small, in the Lewellyn household meant punishment. Kane stood rigid as she approached him, the smile looking more and more like it had been drawn on the face of Bianca Lewellyn by a cartoon artist who had only the vaguest idea of what a smile should look like.

"Kane," Bianca said with that strange cold cheeriness. "You left your dishes in the sink this morning, honey." She was no longer smiling. "What do I always tell you?"

"P-put them in the d-dishwasher," Kane stuttered.

"That's right," she said, her face twisting into an ugly sort of leer. "You know I don't like having to pick up after you," she continued. Kane stammered, struggling to reply.

"I...I..." The hand swung out in a flash, slapping Kane across the face hard enough to send him sprawling to the floor.

Kane stared wide-eyed as his mother loomed over him, her expression twisting more and more with rage as each passing second went by.

"I don't like picking up after you, Kane," she whispered in a deadly voice, advancing on him. Kane scrambled away on all fours, whimpering pitifully. "I DON'T LIKE PICKING UP YOUR MESS!" Bianca screamed. Her foot swung out hard, smashing into Kane's ribs. He howled as his chest exploded with pain. "YOU MADE A MESS!" she screamed, her foot striking him in the head this time. Tiny bright lights danced in front of Kane's eyes. "YOU MADE A MESS, YOU MADE A GODDAMN FUCKING MESS!" she raged, her foot lashing out wildly, connecting with Kane's face, his legs, his ribs. A hard kick struck him in the ear, causing a faint ringing to erupt inside his head. Kane crawled desperately for the open bathroom door, half blinded with pain. "YOU LITTLE SHIT YOU MADE A FUCKING MESS!" Biance screamed, grabbing for Kane's ankles as he made it to the bathroom door. Kane cried out as she pulled with all her might to drag him back into the room. He held onto the door frame for dear life, his lactic-acid drenched muscles struggling to keep up with their adrenaline-charged counterparts. Bianca screamed in rage as Kane broke free, jumping to his feet and slamming the bathroom door in her face as she threw herself against it. Kane braced his shoulder against the door as she threw herself against it again and again, screaming incoherently. Tears streamed down his face.

"Stop," he whispered. "Please, just stop, I'm sorry!" he cried. Finally, she gave up and stormed off, muttering under her breath. Kane collapsed with his back against the bathroom door, sobbing uncontrollably into his hands. He heard a cold, deep, echoing laughter in his ear and turned away, refusing to look his master in the face.

Kane lay on his side on the cold tile bathroom floor, shivering violently, massaging his gooseflesh-covered arms. Although he couldn't see it, he could feel the dark shadow hovering somewhere nearby, savoring his fear, which had risen to paralyzing levels. Somewhere outside the bathroom door, he could hear his mother's footsteps lightly scraping against the bare wooden floor, pacing back and forth, waiting for him to emerge, her face screwed up in petulant frustration. He heard the soft slap of a leather belt against her palm. He moaned, bitter tears forming in his eyes. He still bore faint scars on his back and shoulders from where the clasp of the belt had struck him. Outside the window, the wind howled wildly, the snow coming down in thick, crooked sheets. Kane rolled over onto his back in the darkness, moaning softly like an abandoned child. He was a full-grown adult in a terrified nine-year old's body, the dark haunting memories of his childhood having just as much power over his adult self as the real thing had over him as a child. He no longer felt any pain. All he felt now was a deep, cold sense of emptiness.

"There's nothing left..." he whispered, his voice trembling. "There's nothing..." Everything was gone. Rick and Jacob, his brothers in arms. The good people back in Blacksburg, surely murdered by his master by now. Even Cetan. It sounded strange to say, even to Kane himself. But through everything, one moment stuck out to him. Cetan's eyes had changed. At the end. When he was reaching for that little boy's hand, they were no longer black and soulless.

"He broke free..." Kane whispered with a hint of admiration. "He broke free of all the fucked-up shit that must've brought him to that point, and realized what the right path was." He almost smiled at the thought. "But he never got the chance to do right..." Kane thought, hanging his head in defeat. "Because Rick shot him. He was so scared, he couldn't see that anything had changed. I guess that's how it is for people like us. Even when you try to change, all anyone ever sees is the damage you've already caused." Tears began to brim in Kane's eyes. "I'm sorry, brother," he whispered. "I'm sorry I couldn't get you out of whatever dark hole he was keeping you locked in. We follow a code to never leave a man behind. I broke that code when I left you behind and tried to run. I guess I understand how Jacob felt." He smiled wanly. "I guess he figured it out a while ago, didn't he? That's why the Puppeteer made you kill him, right? He broke free, just like you did." Kane shook his head. "But even then, he couldn't get away. There's only one way to break this cycle, isn't there?"

Kane reached out and slid the door to the bathroom cabinet beneath the sink open. Lying on the floor of the cabinet was a length of rope. He eyed the shower head hanging above the tub. Figuring it would probably be high enough, he removed the length of rope from the cabinet and walked over to the bathtub, all the fear and pain of the past few hours fading with every step. He tightly knotted one end of the rope onto the steel bar connecting the shower head into the wall and fumbled with the other end for a few minutes until he had managed to make a noose. He stepped onto the side of the tub, slipping the rope around his neck. He closed his eyes and sighed heavily.

"Hang in there a little longer, Jacob," Kane whispered. "I'll be there real soon." And then he stepped off the small platform, allowing the noose to tighten around his throat. He choked and gagged, thrashing around incoherently while the noose did its work, his complexion darkening from red to blue to deep purple, and finally black. Shortly after, Kane Lewellyn hung still, finally free of his pain forever.

CHAPTER 94

Dylan groaned and pushed himself to his feet, the room around him concealed in shadows. The floor beneath him was draped in a thick, white shag carpet. To his left, he could vaguely make out a large, plush purple sofa with small square throw pillows piled on either end. To his right, a handsome, brick fireplace lay black and empty. Faint moonlight was filtering through an oversized window on the opposite wall, allowing Dylan a limited ability to make out his surroundings. He walked in a circle around the sofa, taking in the shadows surrounding him. This place…felt familiar somehow. He was fairly confident he hadn't fallen asleep here, so that meant someone had brought him here.

"Weird," Dylan thought. "You'd think if someone would go through all that effort to bring me here, they'd at least stick around to greet me."

He crossed over to the door and found that the handle wouldn't budge. He felt a twinge of apprehension. He crossed back to the window and peered out of the glass. It was a twenty-foot drop on the low side. He sighed and threw himself down on the sofa, staring pensively into the blackened logs lying uselessly in the brick fireplace. Someone had gone to considerable effort to bring him here, and then made sure he couldn't leave. He felt the small twinge of nervousness swell a little. Something was wrong here.

"You will be afraid of me, son." The magician's cold, hissing voice echoed in his ear.

A cold sweat broke out on Dylan's forehead.

He suddenly wanted very badly to leave this room this very second, to run as far as he could as fast as he could and never look back. His eyes moved to the small, metal fire poker resting on the hearth. Dylan eyed it curiously. He glanced back at the locked door.

"Seems like a stupid idea," Dylan thought. "Busting the lock with that thing? No way. And trying to break the door down…" Dylan shook his head. It sounded ridiculous even without him saying it aloud. But the more he thought about it, the less options he realized he had. He could feel his anxiety worsening with each passing second. He needed to get out of this room now.

Dylan stood up, reaching out for the poker when the door burst open behind him, causing him to jump in surprise. He whirled around and came face to face with Marianne. The little girl's eyes were frantic as she sprinted past him.

"Marianne, what…" he didn't manage to get another word out before she threw herself into a small broom closet in the corner next to the bay window, slamming the slatted wooden door behind her.

Dylan stared perplexedly at the closet door for a full minute before he shook his head, unable to make sense of it. He started to make his way towards the slatted wooden closet door, determined to comfort the scared little girl.

"She's frightened of you."

Dylan whirled around. Standing a few feet away, his haggard face illuminated in the faint moonlight, was Kaden. He sported heavy dark circles beneath both eyelids, and the skin on his face was pulled taut over the bones, giving him a skeletal appearance. Kaden slowly approached him, his expression filled with trepidation.

"Why is she scared of me, Kaden?" Dylan asked imploringly. And then a horrible thought occurred to him. "Does she know?" he asked. "Does she know what I did to Anna?"

Kaden shook his head.

"Then why?" he asked again.

Kaden sighed heavily.

"Dylan, you are the greatest threat the Puppeteer has ever faced. Because you have strength of character. You're not easily manipulated. That's not so common for someone your age."

"We're most malleable when we're young, so because you developed that strength at such an early age, it will be incredibly strong by the time you're grown up. The magician thought he could use you, but he's realizing he was wrong. What he wants now more than anything is to get you out of the way, along with me and Jody."

"I already told him," Dylan said firmly, "I'm not gonna hurt anyone for him anymore."

Kaden sighed again.

"I know you won't, Dylan. But he will. A body is only a vessel, Dylan. It's the soul inside that powers it. If you corrupt the soul, whoever that person was before ceases to exist."

Dylan's eyes widened as he slowly understood.

"I'm sorry," Kaden said, his eyes downcast. "I'm so sorry, Dylan."

Dylan's blood turned to ice as the temperature in the room plunged. Within seconds, his breath turned to mist in front of him. A cold sweat broke out all over his body as the dark presence swept into the room. Dylan shivered, but not from the sudden cold. He was here. Right here in the room with him and Kaden. Kaden's eyes widened in fear. He was trembling all over.

"Dylan…" came the cold, bodiless, hissing voice of the magician. "Dylan…you've been a bad boy. And do you know what happens to bad boys, Dylan?"

Dylan cried out in pain as an invisible object smashed into the back of his shins, sending him tumbling hard onto his knees.

"Bad boys get punished, Dylan…" the magician hissed, his voice tightening with anger.

A heavy object crashed into the back of Dylan's skull. Lights danced in front of his eyes.

He bowed, resting his aching head on his knees.

"That's better," the magician hissed, grinning wickedly. He bent down so that his face was inches from Dylan's. "Now," the magician said icily. "You listen to me very carefully. There will be no further insubordination. There will be no further disrespect. You will obey my every command without question." His grin grew wider. "Or the next punishment you receive will be much less pleasant."

Dylan raised his eyes, glaring defiantly at the magician, whose smile instantly faded.

"I'm not afraid of you," Dylan whispered.

The magician's eyes grew wide.

"What did you say?" he whispered in a deadly voice.

"I'M NOT FUCKING AFRAID OF YOU!" Dylan screamed.

In an instant, Dylan was hauled ten feet into the air as if by an invisible rope. His arms were pulled apart painfully as if he were being stretched, his feet pulled downward as if by one-hundred-pound weights. Dylan cried out in pain as his head was yanked roughly backward so that he was staring straight up at the ceiling, his neck screaming in protest. The magician stared up him, laughing coldly.

"If you are not afraid of me, then you are naïve. I will correct that very quickly."

The magician snapped his fingers. Dylan gasped as his father, mother, and sister swam into view. Only it wasn't quite them. Their limbs were...stiffer somehow, the angles in their faces sharper. It took Dylan a moment to realize he was staring at a trio of wooden dummies. But it was them. He could feel it deep in his heart. The magician had somehow placed their souls into these once lifeless puppets. The puppets stood poised on a brightly lit stage that overlooked a darkened auditorium. As Dylan stared in horror, they began to tap dance around the stage, their wooden feet clomping heavily against the stage floor.

"I can destroy everything you love with a simple wave of my hand," the magician whispered in his ear.

The entire stage suddenly went up in flames. The puppets stopped dancing, screaming in agony as their bodies melted.

Dylan screamed with them, screaming the names of the people he loved more than any in the world as they burned to death before him. Then they were gone. Dylan crumpled into a heap, landing painfully on his right shoulder. Dylan hung his head, his eyes filled with tears. He felt the magician's gloved hand grasp his chin hard and force it upward to stare into his own face.

"Do we have an understanding?" the magician said, leering down at him.

Dylan was about to open his mouth to reply but then paused suddenly.

"It's not real." Kaden's voice echoed in his head.

Dylan suddenly realized that Kaden was no longer standing in the room with him.

"It's not real," Kaden repeated.

"It's not real," Dylan thought. "It's not fucking real, just like everything else he shows me."

The magician, grinning wolfishly, extended his hand. The silver blade of the steak knife gleamed in the moonlight.

"Now do as I tell you," the magician hissed in Dylan's ear, nodding towards the corner where Marianne was hiding. "Bring me the body of that little girl."

Dylan, his hand trembling, reached for the knife. The magician's grin widened.

"Good," he whispered. "Seems you've learned."

Dylan stood up, the knife clenched in his trembling hand. "No," he whispered, dropping the knife to the floor.

"I won't."

The magician's grin faded as Dylan turned to face him.

"Fuck you," Dylan whispered, his voice quivering.

The magician stared at him for a moment, his expression unreadable. Finally, he sighed heavily, shaking his head.

"Fine. So be it," he said in a voice that was dead calm. The magician turned on the spot, his black cloak billowing behind him, and then he vanished with a small pop.

For a split second, Dylan felt a small explosion of joy erupt in his chest.

"I did it," he whispered. "I..." Dylan screamed at the top of his lungs, falling to his knees, writhing on the ground in pain as his entire body caught fire, the pain so intense he felt as though his bones were melting and his skin was being scraped off in layers.

His scream joined Marianne's, who was wailing in terror at the sight of him. Kaden, unheard by either of them, screamed in terror as the dream faded around him. Dylan twisted and writhed, his high-pitched screams echoing off the walls, the pain so unbearable he was sure it would kill him soon, he could not live like this for another second, he must die, it was over, over, over...And then it stopped. Marianne stared, her eyes wide with terror as Dylan slowly stood up, the knife clenched in his hand. He turned to face her, his entire body quivering with rage, his soulless black eyes locked onto hers. She screamed as he let out a feral roar and charged, the force of the stab piercing her breastbone, the blade slicing her aorta in two. Dylan stared mercilessly down at Marianne's lifeless body as her lifeblood slowly flowed out of her, not a hint of emotion in his gaze.

CHAPTER 95

Kaden woke up screaming, his entire body bathed in cold sweat. He sat up in bed and rubbed a hand over his pounding forehead. It took several deep breaths to calm himself down. His wide eyes darted around every dark corner of the small bedroom, half expecting to see the outline of a small boy concealed in the shadows, holding a knife blade illuminated in the moonlight. The image made Kaden shiver.

"He's here though," Kaden thought nervously. "He's somewhere in this house right now. The magician got him." Kaden had seen it in Dylan's eyes. They had darkened to a pair of soulless, coal-black orbs. He felt a single tear streak down his face.

"He healed. He overcame all the shit he went through, and he's not even in control of himself anymore." Kaden froze. Somewhere outside the bedroom door, he heard the soft creak of a loose floorboard. As he listened, the feet shuffled past the bedroom door and down the hallway.

Towards the other bedrooms.

"Jody…" he whispered. "He's going to kill Jody." Kaden ran for the bedroom door, throwing it open in time to see Dylan wander up to the bedroom door at the end of the hallway, the blade in his left hand illuminated by the moonlight.

Dylan turned as Kaden froze outside the bedroom door, his expression cold, his eyes absorbing every speck of moonlight that fell upon them.

"Dylan," Kaden whispered, his voice trembling. "If you can hear me, please, don't do this."

Dylan took a step towards him, brandishing the knife, his lips pulled back into a snarl. Kaden slowly began to back up, bracing himself to turn and run. Suddenly, Dylan froze. The bedroom door behind him opened, and Marianne stumbled into the dark hallway in her nightgown, rubbing her eyes sleepily.

"Daddy?" she mumbled, yawning. "I had a bad dream, I…" she trailed off at the sight of Dylan, who was eyeing her like a rabid dog eyeing a fat rabbit.

"You escaped me once," Dylan whispered savagely, slowly advancing on her. "And it will be the last time."

Marianne screamed and bolted out of the way just as Dylan swung the knife, the blade missing her by inches.

"Shit…" Kaden whispered and chased down the hall after them.

CHAPTER 96

Marianne sprinted down the dark hallway, guided only by the faint moonlight filtering in through the windows, her heart pounding with the effort. Somewhere behind her, she could hear the monster's footsteps racing after her, its breathing heavy in her ear.

"That's not Dylan," she thought as she flew around a corner into the dining room, nearly tripping over a fallen wooden chair lying in her path. "The monster's taken him."

Dylan grunted in pain as his shins smashed into the unseen chair, sending him sprawling to the kitchen floor in a heap. Not bothering to look back, Marianne darted through the kitchen doorway into another dark hallway. She could hear voices and doors opening in other parts of the house.

"Please," she gasped. "Please, somebody stop him." Her heart felt as though it was about to explode out of her chest. She couldn't run anymore. She ran around another corner, and slammed hard into Jody, sending them both tumbling to the floor in a heap.

"Jody, Jody!" Marianne stammered, struggling to get to her feet. "He's here, he's after me! He's..." The rest of her sentence was lost in a fit of hysterical sobbing.

Jody, scrambling to her feet, picked up the little girl and held her close to her chest.

"Who's after you, honey?" Jody whispered.

"The monster," Marianne cried. "He got Dylan."

"What do you mean he got Dylan?" Jody asked, looking at her sharply. But all at once a feeling of deep uneasiness crept into Jody's chest at the terrified look on Marianne's face.

"He...he tried to kill me," Marianne whispered, her lower lip trembling. "Dylan tried to kill me. But it wasn't him, it was..."

Jody didn't hear the rest of her sentence. She was already flying down the hallway where Marianne had just come from, her eyes wide with terror.

The idea of a direct possession was a possible scenario that had been lurking in the back of her mind ever since she'd learned from Kaden that Dylan had become unplugged, but it still came as a complete shock to her system. She burst into the dining room to find pandemonium. Dylan was screaming like a banshee, wrestling with Ben and Tyson, who had pinned his arms behind his back and were trying to wrestle him to the ground. Roy and Laura were staring at the scene, wide-eyed with fright.

"What's...what's wrong with him?" Laura stammered.

Jody shook her head, moving towards the scuffle, where Tyson had managed to get Dylan in a headlock with his powerful arms. Dylan thrashed aggressively like a cornered animal, trying to sink his teeth into Tyson's forearm.

"Dylan," Jody whispered, bending down so that they were eye to eye. "It's me. Do you remember?"

Dylan showed no indication that he had heard her. He continued to gnash his teeth aggressively, glaring at her with an expression of utmost hatred.

"Laura, do you see his eyes?" Jody asked, straightening up.

Laura nodded, a small sob escaping her. Kaden burst into the room, his eyes widening when he saw the scene in front of him.

"Jesus..." he whispered.

"Kaden," Jody said, turning to him. "You're sure he was fully unplugged."

Kaden nodded.

"I've never seen anything like it. He was a full convert and he completely regained control on his own. It was a miracle. Until tonight."

"What happened tonight?" Jody asked.

Everyone's eyes were on Kaden now. He shook his head sadly.

"The magician came to him in a dream. He tried to scare him into obedience. It almost worked too. When Dylan refused, he...he..." Kaden stammered, struggling to utter the terrible words aloud.

"He took control," Jody whispered, looking back at Dylan, who had not let up in his struggle. "He's directly possessed." Jody shook her head, a tear forming in her eye. "I'm sorry, Dylan," she thought. "I'm sorry I let you down."

Tyson groaned, struggling to hold onto Dylan.

"Need some help here," he grunted. "Jody, can you do anything to reverse it?"

Jody shook her head.

Tyson cursed loudly as Dylan finally drove his teeth into the meat on his forearm, blood oozing from between his teeth.

"Damnit, get him off me!" Tyson screamed, struggling to pull his arm out of Dylan's grip.

Mike hurried over and grabbed Dylan around the neck, forcing him away from Tyson who scrambled away, blood soaking his arm. Jason and Lorenzo stepped forward, each man pinning down one of Dylan's wildly thrashing legs while Mike held him in a bearhug.

"DO YOU REALLY THINK YOU CAN STOP ME!?" Dylan screamed in an unnaturally deep voice. "I AM THE ALL-SEEING EYE, I MADE ALL OF YOU, I CAN ERASE YOU WITH A WAVE OF MY HAND!"

"There has to be something we can do for him," Tyson said, holding on to Marianne while she sobbed her heart out on his shoulder.

"Well, whatever you're going to do, do it fast!" Mike exclaimed, straining to hold Dylan, who was thrashing even harder, his eyes burning with hatred as he glared around the room at all of them.

"Jody," Laura choked out.

Everyone turned to look at her. Her eyes were red from crying.

"Let...let me try..." she whispered.

Jody watched nervously as Laura approached Dylan, who was struggling desperately against Mike's hold.

"Dylan," Laura whispered, bending down so that they were eye to eye. "I know you miss your mom, and I know you miss your sister. I...I'm not your mom. I don't know you the way she did, and I acknowledge that. But I've spent the last several months looking after you, and I can tell you with some certainty what kind of person you are."

Dylan continued to struggle, but his attention had shifted fully on to Laura.

"When I first met you, you were falling apart at the seams. You went down a bad path. I was scared of you for a long time." Laura let out a sob. She laid a hand on Dylan's cheek, whose struggles seemed to be weakening. "I was afraid. I didn't know what you were going through. I wasn't there for you like I should've been. I'm sorry." Laura hung her head. A dry sob escaped her. "But I've watched you grow since then. I've watched you become a man. You have overcome more than most people three times your age can imagine. You are a good person. I..." She choked on the words. She laid her forehead gently against Dylan's. "I love you, Dylan. I love you like I loved..." Laura choked on the words, "I love you like I loved my daughter before she left us. We all do."

Maria, whose face was also streaked with tears, stepped forward.

"Dylan, I was afraid of you for a long time," she said. "I was so angry. I hated you for what you did to my mother. But that's..." she stammered. "That isn't who you really are, I saw that on that night in the woods. You wouldn't hurt me or Jody, no matter how scared or angry you were. You've been through so much, but in the end, you didn't let it control you. You overcame it, and that's what's important. I..." she struggled for the words. "I...I love you, Dylan," she sobbed.

"KILL THEM, KILL THEM, KILL THEM!" the magician roared in Dylan's ears.

But Dylan barely heard him, the rage seeping out of him as if someone had removed the drain plug from a full bathtub. And then his eyes suddenly widened with shock at the sound of another voice.

"I love you Dylan," his father said. "And nothing you say or do will ever change that."

"You can beat him!" Annette cried out. "Fight Dylan, fight back!"

Jody gasped. Dylan's eyes were lightening, slowly turning back to their normal dark brown. He was barely struggling anymore.

"NO, NO!" screamed the deep voice of the magician again. "THEY HATE YOU, THEY DESPISE YOU, THEY WANT YOU DEAD, KILL THEM!"

Dylan began to thrash and scream with renewed vigor, his eyes darkening to black.

"Dylan," Kaden said, stepping forward. "I know you. I know who you really are. I watched him torture you, I watched him show you your family burning to death. But you didn't give in. You fought him, you wouldn't hurt that poor little girl no matter what he did to you. I love you," he said firmly, "and you deserve to have a life, a real life far away from all this. Come back to us, let us be a family again."

For the second time, Dylan's struggles grew weaker.

"NO, NO, HE'S LYING, THEY'RE ALL LYING, KILL THEM!"

But the words seemed to have less of an effect this time.

"D-Dylan," Marianne stammered, leaving her father's side and approaching the struggling little boy.

Jody felt herself tense as Marianne sat down next to him and laid a hand on his shoulder.

"I know you didn't mean to hurt me," she said, her enormous brown eyes locked on his. "The monster wanted to hurt me, he took you away. I want you back. You were always nice to me before he came. I'm..." Marianne stammered for a moment.

Dylan had stopped struggling entirely.

His black eyes were locked on Marianne's, but the color hadn't changed yet.

"I'm not afraid of you," she said finally. "If you can hear me, come back to us. I..." she let out a dry sob. "I miss you. We all miss you. We're not afraid of you. We love you." Her expression hardened suddenly. "So, you can't be afraid of him. For us. Don't be afraid of the monster, Dylan."

All at once, Dylan jumped to his feet. Tyson made a move forward, but Dylan's attention was no longer focused on Marianne. He stumbled drunkenly across the room, groaning in pain, grabbing the sides of his head with both hands.

"Dylan!" Marianne cried out. "Don't be afraid of him! Fight! Fight him!"

They all stared, aghast, as Dylan slammed his head ferociously against the dining room table, his own screams mixed with the magician's, both entities struggling desperately for control.

"NO, NO, NO, NO!!!" the Puppeteer screamed in agony.

"Fight, fight, FIGHT!" Marianne screamed.

Dylan, roaring in pain, thrust out his hand, and Marianne flew backward as if launched by an invisible slingshot, smacking her head against the back of the sofa. The world spun in front of her, then slowly faded away as she lost consciousness.

"Fight him, Dylan!" Maria shouted. "Come back to us!"

Dylan let out a snarl and charged her, hands reaching for her throat.

Mike jumped between the two of them, the bigger man shoving Dylan backward hard. Enraged, Dylan raised a hand above his head, dragging Mike into the air as if hoisted by an invisible noose, hands clutching at his throat, his face turning purple as he suffocated.

"NO!" Ben shouted, tackling Dylan around the middle. Ben was wrestling with Dylan, who was screaming like a banshee, tearing at his hair as his head split in two, his body unable to hold both entities occupying it.

"Ben, bring him here!" Jody shouted, running toward the pair of them as Dylan dug his nails into the side of Ben's face.

Ben howled in pain as Jody grabbed Dylan roughly by the shoulders and yanked him to his feet. Dylan drew his arm back, preparing to swing. Jody closed her eyes.

"GET OUT OF HIM!" she screamed, the fire swelling up in her chest. LET HIM GO, LEAVE HIM ALONE!"

Dylan froze in mid swing, the searing heat penetrating into his limbs.

"Fight him son!" his father's voice erupted in his head again. "Fight back!"

The Puppeteer let out a deranged scream of terrible agony. Dylan let out a scream of his own and swung, hitting Jody across the face hard enough to send her sprawling to the floor. Dylan advanced on her, raising his arm to strike her again.

"Dylan..." Dylan froze. It was his mother's voice. "I'm so sorry, son," she sobbed. "I love you so much, and I was too selfish to show it. But I'm here for you now. We're here for you. All of us."

The entire room went eerily silent as everyone stared at Dylan with anticipation.

"You can beat him, Dylan!" Annette echoed. "Fight him!"

"GET THE HELL AWAY FROM OUR SON!" his mother and father roared in unison. Dylan's face suddenly went oddly slack, his mouth hanging open slightly, his now brown eyes glazed over.

"Leave them alone you son of a bitch," he muttered.

The Puppeteer let out a final scream of rage. A black, wispy cloud exploded out of Dylan's chest with a sound like a gunshot, throwing him back so violently into the air, he overshot the sofa and smashed clean through the window on the opposite wall, the glass shattering around him with a terrific crunch. For a split second, he hung in midair, his expression blissful.

"Thank you," Jody heard him whisper before gravity took over, sending him plunging out of sight.

CHAPTER 97

Everyone stared in open mouthed shock at the spot where Dylan had vanished. Serena was the first to break the silence.

"Do you think he..." she stammered, her voice trembling.

"There's a chance," Lorenzo said hollowly. "It was only about a two-story drop."

Jody shook her head.

"He's gone," she whispered, struggling not to cry. "His final revenge. He won't have left him alive."

Laura broke down crying at these words. Maria hung her head, tears glistening in her eyes. Without another word, Jody turned on her heel and stormed into the nearest bedroom, slamming the door behind her. She collapsed onto the bed, sobbing hysterically into her hands. It was not the knowledge that Dylan was dead that upset her so much. Knowing what would soon happen to him was far worse.

"He's in the theater," Jody whispered, her entire body trembling. "That poor boy is trapped in his realm, and I can't save him, I FUCKING FAILED HIM!" she screamed, jumping to her feet, her eyes locked on the dark ceiling above her.

"WHY DID HE HAVE TO DIE!" she screamed. "WHAT DID HE DO TO DESERVE THIS?" She collapsed back onto the bed, burying her face in her hands.

Dylan was the only one. He was the only one she'd ever seen become fully unplugged on his own after converting. How could he die after overcoming such a thing? It wasn't just unfair. It was unnatural.

"Death is the natural end of life." The smooth, gentle voice echoed through the room as if it had been spoken through a megaphone. Jody looked up. Kaitlyn was standing in the corner of the room, her gentle smile visible even in the deep shadows of the room.

"No," Jody choked out. "No, there's nothing natural about someone dying after overcoming so much."

"He is dead," Kaitlyn said matter of factly, striding over to the bed and sitting down next to Jody. "But he is not lost."

Jody looked at her, nonplused.

"He is in the magician's realm. I cannot enter..."

"Not alone," Kaitlyn interrupted.

"But you are not alone anymore, surely you must realize that by now."

Jody didn't reply. Kaitlyn smiled and shook her head.

"This last part, you can't do it by yourself. It requires a bond between all of you. If you can achieve that, you might be able to save the boy."

Jody hung her head, her eyes brimming with tears.

"How, how can..."

Kaitlyn fixed her with a very serious stare.

"You've avoided it your entire life," she said matter of factly. "Hell, I can't say I blame you, given what you went through in that place." She sighed, shaking her head. "Once again, I am forced to ask too much of you."

Jody turned to look at Kaitlyn, slowly beginning to understand.

"The house, it's still there, isn't it?"

Kaitlyn nodded slowly.

"Jody," she said calmly.

"I know," Jody said, her expression suddenly resolute. "This needs to end. I..." She shook her head. "I need to end this."

A few minutes later, Jody left the bedroom for the dining room, where the entire group continued to hold their silent vigil for Dylan. Maria and Kaden looked up as Jody entered the room.

"You okay?" Maria asked.

Jody nodded.

"Everyone, I need you to listen to me," she said.

Every head in the room turned to look at her. Many of the eyes that greeted her were red from crying.

"What happened tonight...I can't watch it happen again. I can't lose any of you the way I lost Dylan tonight." She bit her lip to keep it from trembling. "We need to end this."

"What do you suggest?" Tyson said bluntly, his enormous hands on Marianne's shoulders.

Marianne was looking up at Jody with an expression somewhere between curiosity and wonder. Jody turned to look at Tyson.

"We need to go to the place where this all started." She took a deep, rattling breath. "We need to go to my childhood home in Mauvilla."

CHAPTER 98

ylan Teryon woke up in the dark on what felt like a roughly hewn wooden floor. He pushed himself to his feet, glancing around at his surroundings. From what little he could see, he appeared to be on stage in front of a large auditorium. He looked quizzically up at the dark ceiling and saw the reason for the lack of light: every single one of the LED bulbs lining the ceiling appeared to have shattered, the glass shards littering the seats below. Dylan didn't have to ask where he was. He walked to the edge of the stage, peering intently at the dark auditorium in front of him, trying to locate his adversary. He could sense the same dark presence nearby that he'd felt back in the house in Blacksburg, staying just out of sight, sizing him up hungrily.

"I know you're there," Dylan muttered. "You might as well show yourself."

There wasn't a trace of fear in his voice. He would not show weakness to the monster that had taken everything from him.

"Come on!" Dylan demanded, anger rising in his tone. "Show yourself!"

For a brief moment, the space was dead silent.

"As you wish," an ice-cold voice whispered in his ear.

An invisible hand closed around Dylan's throat, lifting him into the air. Dylan sputtered, struggling to breath against the sudden intense pressure placed on his windpipe. There was a small popping noise, and then the magician appeared, his dark eyes locked on Dylan's, his lower lip curling into a vicious sneer.

"You've been a thorn in my side for quite some time," the magician whispered. "I admit, I don't fully understand whatever power it is that you possess, but rest assured, I will snuff it out as easily as I snuffed out your little sister."

Dylan grunted angrily, struggling against the magician's grip.

"Go ahead then," Dylan whispered, staring the magician down defiantly. "Kill me."

The magician's sneer grew wider.

"Oh, I'm not going to kill you," he whispered. "You deserve much worse than that."

The Puppeteer angrily threw Dylan to the floor. He landed painfully on his knees. Dylan bowed his head, gritting his teeth to keep from crying out. The Puppeteer paced back and forth in front of the small boy, his eyes blazing with scorching hatred.

"You know, it's funny," he said through clenched teeth. "For a long time, Jody was my biggest problem. Most people are weak, malleable, easy to sway. She was not. I spent many years chasing after her, but she resisted my every advance." The Puppeteer shuddered angrily, wringing his gloved hands.

A hand suddenly lashed out and smacked Dylan across the face, hard enough to draw blood.

"But you," he seethed. "You evoke a different breed of anger in me." He stopped directly in front of the cowering little boy, his hands shaking violently with rage.

"Not only did you fail in your mission to kill Laura Forsin, not only did you defy me again, and again, and again, but through your actions, you have single-handedly TURNED A SIMPLE CLEAN UP JOB INTO A FUCKING ATROCIOUS MESS!!" he raged. His foot swung out hard, connecting with Dylan's ribs with a resounding crunch.

Dylan doubled over in pain, gasping for breath, his face bright red.

"No," the Puppeteer said coldly, resuming his pacing. "You, my friend, are special for all the wrong reasons. You have managed to spin dust from gold." His arm swung out, hitting Dylan in the stomach, knocking the wind out of him.

Dylan's eyes were watering with pain.

"Little boys need to learn to behave themselves," the Puppeteer said quietly, shaking his head in disappointment. "You've been a very bad boy these last few weeks, Dylan. You must be disciplined appropriately. It is what any good parent, any good master must do."

Dylan stared up at the Puppeteer, trembling as he ran his black-gloved hand over his pointed chin, pondering.

"I could simply erase you from existence," he said casually, evoking a violent shudder from Dylan. The Puppeteer grinned wickedly at the sight. "That would be the prudent thing to do. And prudence is an important quality I have been lacking these last several months."

He looked sharply down at Dylan, who squeezed his eyes shut, preparing for the torture to begin.

"But..." he said, turning away, "you could still be useful to me." He paused, his chin resting on his hand. "There is a battle coming soon, Dylan."

"I'll never join you," Dylan muttered angrily.

The Puppeteer, facing away from Dylan, was silent for a moment.

"I think you misunderstand," he said matter of factly. "Allow me to demonstrate."

Dylan cried out in shock as he was hoisted into the air as if by a number of invisible strings, his limbs flying out of his control in all directions.

His stomach shot up into his throat as the strings dropped him twenty feet to the stage floor, holding him up so that his ankles barely brushed against the floor.

"Dance!" the Puppeteer commanded, waving his hands like an orchestra conductor.

Dylan felt his legs begin to shuffle back and forth against his will, pulled by the invisible strings, moving in a fast tap dance across the stage floor, his arms bobbing and weaving randomly at the will of the strings. The Puppeteer waved his hand, and Dylan dropped to the floor, gasping for air. The Puppeteer bent down, forcefully lifting Dylan's chin so that their eyes met.

"Now you see the idea, son?" he asked, grinning.

Dylan held his gaze, saying nothing, trying to appear defiant despite the terror wracking his whole body. The Puppeteer's grin faded after a moment. He threw Dylan roughly aside and stormed to the edge of the stage.

"I always enjoy this part," he whispered. He closed his dark eyes, concentrating hard.

Dylan felt a wave of terror roll over him as the magician's face began to change, the mouth lengthening and thinning, the eyeballs flattening and folding back into their sockets, the nose disappearing into the skull, his complexion slowly darkening until it faded to black. Now the whole face was folding inward so that it appeared concave, the skull itself now folding backward until Dylan was staring at an empty, dark hole that seemed to have no bottom, the darkness of that abyss absolute and unyielding.

Dylan stared at the terrifying spectacle, his entire body quivering with fear. Then he saw something in the abyss. A small spark of flame that existed only for a brief instant before vanishing. Dylan suddenly screamed, writhing on the floor in unbearable agony as his blood turned to liquid fire in an instant, searing him from the inside out as if he'd just been tossed into an enormous barbeque pit. A terrible melting sensation reached his bones, his organs liquifying from the insane heat. The pain was impossible to explain with words, he couldn't bear it another second, surely it would kill him, his body surely wouldn't survive more than a few seconds of this. His bones now felt as though they were lengthening, the fire hardening them into plates of steel.

Except his skin was hardening too, as though he'd suddenly grown scales all over his body. He cried in pain as his lips twisted into a perfect square, hardening into solid bricks. The Puppeteer stood silently, not moving, not blinking, unmoved by the spectacle. Finally, Dylan couldn't take it anymore. His eyes rolled up into the back of his head and he collapsed to the stage floor. The Puppeteer sighed as he approached the wooden puppet, shaking his head in disappointment. It wasn't the outcome he wanted, not by a long stretch. But for as much suffering as Dylan Teryon had caused him, he could still be useful. The Puppeteer waved his hand absentmindedly, launching the puppet into the air where it joined its fellows floating lazily along the dark ceiling. He followed its progress for a moment, before turning on his heel and storming back behind the dark purple curtain separating the auditorium from the backstage area, already running through the preparations he would soon need to make in his head. It was time for the grand finale.

CHAPTER 99

"Laura, can I ask you something?" Roy said.

They were lying in bed next to each other, staring up at the dark ceiling. They had spent the entire day driving across Virginia and Tennessee and had stopped at an abandoned hotel in Knoxville for the night. Laura snuggled close to her husband, not answering right away.

"I'm only asking," he continued, "because, after what happened the other day..." he trailed off.

There was silence for a moment.

"Should we stay? With these people? With Jody?"

Laura was silent for a moment

"Yes," Laura said finally. She turned to look at Roy, whose gaze was clouded with worry. "She's the best hope any of us have. I mean, she saved Marianne's life. The rest of us thought she was already gone, remember?"

Roy nodded.

"And somehow, I think she's the reason we're together like this in the first place," Laura went on.

"I mean think about it. The night after her mom died, Maria drove us straight to Fairfax. No directions, didn't even know where she was going, she just...did it."

"Yeah, I remember," he replied. "I am not worried that she doesn't know what she's doing. Hell, I think she knows more than any of us can possibly imagine from what I've seen. But after what happened to Dylan, I just..." he paused, unsure whether he should continue. "Laura, there's something you need to know. The night Anna died, Dylan he...he attacked me."

Laura's eyes widened.

"He attacked you?" she gasped. "Roy, what..."

"Well, he didn't actually attack me. He almost did though." Roy shook his head. "I can't really explain it. There was a moment when he pulled a knife, but then he just...stopped..."

Laura's eyes were suddenly as wide as headlamps.

"What do you mean he stopped?" she asked nervously.

"I mean..." Roy paused, struggling for the right words. "He was about to swing on me, and then he just froze..." He turned to look at Laura, his expression very serious. "Laura, there was something else. I saw something in his eyes. Something changed..."

"Were his eyes black?" Laura asked, suddenly remembering her dream from the same night. "Like soulless dark holes?"

Now it was Roy's turn to look shocked. He slowly nodded.

"How did you..."

"I had a nightmare," she went on. "The same night, it was like the nightmares I used to have about my dad, only his eyes were like you described. Black empty holes."

"They were," Roy said. "For a moment. But then they changed."

Laura gave him an inquiring look. "Like they turned back to their original color."

"Jesus Roy," Laura muttered, shaking her head.

"I'm sorry," he said apologetically. "I should've told you, I just didn't want to frighten you anymore, not with what we were already going through."

"Do you think Jody stopped him?" Laura asked.

Roy stared at her with astonishment.

"What do you mean?"

"I mean, do you think she stopped him somehow?" Laura asked again. "Look at what happened with Marianne, Jody brought her back to life Roy, she's not just a strong leader Roy, she's…different somehow."

Roy nodded. It was certainly an odd way of saying someone possessed supernatural abilities, but he probably wouldn't have put it any differently.

"Maybe," he said. "It certainly makes sense with the timing. If she was trying to help him, she would've wanted him to be in the same place with her as quickly as possible."

He paused again.

"But that's what I'm worried about too," he continued. "She was trying to help him. I still don't really understand what happened that night, but he tried to kill Marianne. He would've killed all of us if he'd gotten the chance."

"But he fought," Laura insisted. "He fought back against whatever had a hold of him and…" she trailed off.

"He got thrown out a window," Roy finished hollowly. He sat at the edge of the bed, resting his forehead on his knees. "You said Dylan overcame a lot when you were talking to him," Roy said.

Laura nodded.

"I talked with Maria a few days ago. It seems like whatever monster had a hold of him, it was using his trauma to control him." He looked at her, his expression very worried now. "Laura, you've been through so much." He laid his hands on her shoulders. "I can't lose you the way we lost Dylan. And I'm afraid that because of your trauma, he'll try to use you against me."

Laura held her husband's gaze, her eyes filled with a deep tenderness.

"Dylan fought," she whispered. "After losing everything, he fought back for a group of strangers he barely knew. He had nothing. I have you." She rested her head against his shoulder.

Roy held her tightly, stroking her curly blond hair.

"You are my life," she whispered. "I'm not going anywhere. Not as long as you're around. Whatever trauma that poor kid had in his past, he overcame it. You were there for me when I was at my most fragile, and I am so much stronger today because of it."

Their eyes met.

"No matter what he shows me to try to turn me against you, it will never happen. When I'm with you, I can overcome anything."

"I know," Roy whispered, kissing her forehead. "I love you."

"I love you too," Laura whispered, her hand moving to his groin. Roy started to say something else, but his words were lost in a kiss. His hands found her bottom as he lifted up her nightgown. She raised her arms to allow him to undress her.

"Come here," she whispered, allowing him to enter her as she laid back on the mattress, moaning with pleasure as his groin moved seamlessly against hers. She giggled as he buried his face against her neck, shoving him away playfully. Roy gasped, the muscles in his groin spasming as he climaxed. Laura cried out in ecstasy as the hot fluid shot inside her, triggering an immediate orgasm of her own.

"Wow," Roy gasped, sliding off her. "When's the last time we did it like that?"

Laura giggled.

"The last time we did it like that, you could perform!"

Roy laughed, kissing her on the cheek. Laura snuggled close to him, resting her head against his chest.

"Roy?" Laura whispered.

"Yeah?" She nuzzled him gently.

"Thanks for everything, babe."

CHAPTER 100

R oy sat up in bed, rubbing the sleep from his eyes.

"Nightmares and sex," he thought absurdly, "two free over the counter medications for psychological problems, guess big pharma hasn't totally cornered the market yet."

The idea of big pharma, considering the situation they were in right now, was so absurd he nearly burst out laughing, but restrained himself so as not to disturb his wife. He glanced over at Laura, who appeared to be sleeping peacefully, and smiled.

"Glad to see I'm the one with the bad dreams tonight," he thought, swinging himself out of bed and walking over to the window which overlooked the deserted highway save for the dozen or so defunct cars lining both shoulders.

Outside, the snow, which had started as a light snowfall at dusk, had quickly developed into a raging flurry.

"Going back out there tomorrow," he thought. "It sounds crazy to say, but we're following a lady who can conjure fire out of thin air through a snowstorm to a backwoods community in southern Alabama to try and save the world." He smiled. It sounded like the plot for a bad horror movie.

"Only difference is we're not just staring at a screen screaming at the jump scares and laughing at the dumb decisions the characters make," he thought. "We're running for our lives and there's some asshole out there trying to kill us all." Roy sighed heavily and ran a hand through his short brown hair.

"How can we win?" Roy thought hopelessly. "Hell, how can we even fight against an enemy that can do that to somebody? What do we do if it happens to Maria, or Kaden, or Ben? Hell, what if it happens to me?" he glanced over at Laura, who was still fast asleep, and shuddered.

He didn't want to believe he could hurt Laura. But after seeing what the monster had turned Dylan into, he no longer thought it was impossible. He stared out at the dark highway far below, trying to think of what trauma he had that the monster would try to use against him. He came up empty at first. Then, just as he was about to give up searching, a memory surged forward.

"Myrtle..." he thought, tears coming to his eyes at the thought of his lost daughter. "Annette was with Myrtle that day. That soldier, he...he must've gotten her." Roy hung his head, the tears spilling freely now. He'd half forgotten about Myrtle in all the chaos of the last several months. Now the grief he'd been holding back came out in full force.

"Myrtle," he whispered, wiping his eyes. "Myrtle, I'm so sorry honey. If I could see you again, just hold you one more time, I'd..." He shook his head sadly.

"Daddy, I'm right here," came a high-pitched little girl's voice from directly behind him.

Roy jumped about three feet in the air and whirled around, startled. Sitting cross-legged on the edge of the bed in a yellow sundress her mother had given her for her seventh birthday, grinning broadly at him with her slightly crooked teeth, sat Myrtle Forsin. Roy stared at her, open mouthed, the air suddenly gone from his lungs.

"Hi Daddy," she said cheerfully, jumping down off the bed and hugging him. Feeling numb, Roy wrapped his arms around his daughter.

"She's real," he thought. "Jesus, she's real."

"Daddy, why are you crying?" she asked curiously as he released her.

Roy wiped the tears from his eyes.

"Nothing honey, daddy's okay," he said quickly. He hung his head. "Honey, I'm so sorry," he said.

"It's okay daddy," Myrtle said happily, bouncing on the balls of her feet with excitement.

"I came to see you. I miss you daddy," she said, her smile fading slightly. "I miss mommy too." She looked wistfully over at Laura, who was still asleep. "I want to play with you in the backyard again like we used to when I was little. I want you and mommy to push me on the swing again. I..." she stuttered, her lower lip quivering. "I want to go home."

Roy pulled her into his arms as the tears began to spill down her face.

"I WANT TO GO HOME!" she bawled. "I WANT TO GO HOME, I WANT TO GO HOME!"

"I know baby, I know," Roy whispered, stroking her.

Never seeing the gleaming blade of the knife rise above her head.

CHAPTER 101

Roy's scream of pain jolted Laura awake. She shot up in bed, her eyes darting around the room for the source of the disturbance. Coming to rest on the scene at the foot of the bed. Roy's stark white face was twisted with agony, his eyes wide with shock, the knife buried up to the hilt in his collarbone, dark red blood soaking his shirt. Standing over her husband, her expression a mask of twisted hatred, was a little girl with curly blond hair wearing a bright yellow sundress…Myrtle. Laura blinked uncomprehendingly. It was impossible. Myrtle wrenched the knife out of Roy's shoulder, sending a spray of blood across the floor. Roy, his eyes wide with shock, his mouth opening and closing wordlessly, fell silently to the floor, twitching. Laura erupted with a blood curdling scream as Myrtle rounded on her, the blood-stained knife raised above her head.

Myrtle's expression broke into a murderous grin as she surveyed Laura, who was shaking and crying uncontrollably.

"Myrtle…" Laura stammered over and over again, convinced she was seeing a ghost, or a demon, sent by God to punish her for abandoning their daughter.

"Hi mommy," Myrtle said coldly as she climbed up on the bed and started to crawl towards Laura, brandishing the knife, the blood-stained blade gleaming in the moonlight.

Laura screamed and drew her knees up protectively against her chest, pressing her back against the headboard. Myrtle's grin widened as she approached her cowering mother.

"Don't worry mommy," Myrtle whispered, raising the knife above her head. "We'll all be together again soon, I promise."

Laura screamed and curled herself into a ball against the headboard. She squeezed her eyes shut, preparing for death. Myrtle loomed over her, the knife poised above her head, her bright almond eyes gleaming with triumph. Then she froze.

"Get out!" a voice in her head screamed. It took her a full minute to recognize it. Her master was calling her. For a moment she stood frozen, utterly perplexed.

"Get out!" the voice screamed again. And then she understood. The firebrand had been awoken by the commotion. She was in immediate danger.

Laura opened her eyes in time to see Myrtle's body disappear into mist, the knife landing soundlessly on the mattress in front of her.

298

CHAPTER 102

Jody's eyes snapped open at the sound of the scream. She threw herself out of bed immediately, running for the door.

"It's happening," she thought in a panic as she threw herself out into the hallway, sprinting in the direction where the screams were coming from. "Jesus, it's really happening. He knows we're coming and now he's doing everything he can to stop us."

Terrified at the prospect of what she was about to find, Jody threw open the door to room 402 to find Laura lying on the floor in a puddle of blood, sobbing over the lifeless body of her husband. The room spun in front of Jody, and she swayed dangerously, nearly losing consciousness. She stumbled and nearly fell as Ben and Tyson rushed past her to Laura's side.

"Get his shirt off," Tyson said from somewhere far off. "He's lost a lot of blood. We have to stop the bleeding now."

"Roy, wake up, please, wake up," Laura sobbed as Ben positioned Roy's arms above his head to allow him to remove Roy's blood-stained t-shirt.

Tyson quickly removed his own shirt and held it tightly against Roy's collarbone.

"Help me apply pressure," Tyson snapped.

Ben quickly moved to his side and pressed down against the makeshift bandage.

"C'mon buddy, breathe," Ben muttered as Lorenzo and Jason burst into the room.

"Jason, get the toilet paper out of the bathroom," Lorenzo ordered, kneeling beside Roy.

Jason disappeared into the bathroom and came out a moment later with a roll of toilet paper. Jody stumbled into the room on trembling legs as the four men began pressing toilet paper over the wound, which was almost immediately soaked with blood.

"What happened?" Lorenzo demanded.

Laura, who was curled up into a ball in the corner, didn't reply. Jody collapsed onto the bed into a sitting position, her expression gaunt.

"He did this," Jody said hollowly.

Lorenzo shot her a nervous glance as he was applying more toilet paper to the blood-soaked mass they'd already accumulated.

"He knows we're coming. He's…he's going to do everything he can to try and stop us."

"Ok, I think we've got the bleeding under control, start CPR," Lorenzo said, hurrying towards the door. "I saw an AED in the lobby earlier, let's see if we can still bring our boy back."

The three remaining men sat silently around Roy, anxiously awaiting Lorenzo's return while Ben kept pressure on the makeshift bandage and Jason performed chest compressions.

"Laura," Jody whispered, her voice shaking. "Laura, I'm so sorry."

Laura shook her head, crying silently into her hands.

"I trusted you," Laura whispered. "I trusted you, even after what happened to Dylan, and now he's dead because of you."

"Laura..." Tyson started to say.

"He's gone," Laura whispered, glaring at Jody, her eyes stinging with tears. "He was my everything, and I lost him because of you." She stood up and stormed out of the room, slamming the door behind her.

Jody shook her head sadly, laying her forehead in her hands in defeat.

"This is what he wants, isn't it?" Tyson said hollowly. "We can't beat him unless we all face him together. That's why he tried to take Marianne from me, and that's why he took Roy. He wants us divided."

Jody nodded slowly.

"Jody," Ben said hollowly, staring down at Roy's lifeless body. "When you said he's going to do everything he can to try and stop us, this is just the beginning isn't it?"

Jody nodded, at the same time hating herself for doing so.

"How many?" Ben asked, his voice trembling. "How many of us have to die to stop him?"

Jody didn't reply. They all looked up as Lorenzo burst into the room, the AED clutched in his hand.

"I'll get the pads," Lorenzo said as he kneeled beside Jason. Jason nodded without pausing compressions. Lorenzo pressed a button and the machine whirred to life.

"Apply AED pads on patient's chest," said a robotic voice.

Lorenzo quickly removed the pads from their plastic cases and plugged the cord into an outlet on the machine.

"Applying AED pads," he said.

Jason immediately ceased compressions, allowing Lorenzo to attach the adhesive side of the AED pads to Roy's bare chest. The tension in the room was palpable as the robotic voice began to speak.

"Do not touch the patient, analyzing heart rhythm. Shock advised."

Without waiting for the instruction, Jason slammed down the shock button on the machine. Roy's torso gave a small jump as the shock was administered. Jason pressed his right middle and index finger into the soft flesh of Roy's throat, his face shining with anticipation.

"No pulse, go again," he ordered, ignoring the instructions the robotic voice was now issuing.

Lorenzo immediately hammered the shock button again. Roy's torso gave another jump. Jason rechecked for a pulse and shook his head.

"Nothing, give him another one."

Lorenzo hit the shock button again, and without waiting for Jason, checked for a pulse. After a few seconds, he shook his head dejectedly. Jody hung her head, the tears beginning to well up in her eyes.

"He...he was already dead," Jody sobbed.

All four men turned to look at her.

"He was dead before you came in the room. I...I felt his spirit leave his body right when I opened the door."

The room fell completely silent.

"But thank you," she said. "Thank you for trying."

Jason, his expression pale, sat down on the edge of the bed. Tyson, his face twisting with anger, punched the wall hard enough to drive his hand clean through the aging plaster. Lorenzo shook his head and left the room, muttering to himself. Ben, who looked shaken up himself, sat down on the bed next to Jody, staring at the floor.

"You okay?" Ben asked, his voice hollow.

Jody shook her head.

"I'm not sure I'll ever be okay, not now, or ever again," she said distantly.

Ben said nothing.

"Ben," Jody said, turning to look at him. "I don't want to see anyone else die. I know you don't either." She sighed heavily. "But no matter how many people we lose, no matter how hard he drives to divide us, we have to keep going. It's the only way we can end this. It's the only way that everything we've lost, everything we've overcome, everything we've fought for means something."

Ben said nothing.

"I'm sorry," Jody said. "I know this isn't fair to ask. Of any of you. None of you deserve what's happening right now. Anna, Dylan, Roy, they didn't deserve what happened to them. But we can't stop. Because if we stop, he wins. If we give up, they all died in vain."

Ben turned to look at Jody, his expression unreadable.

"I know," he said flatly. He stood up and left the room.

Tyson, still fuming, got up and followed him, slamming the door behind him. A moment later, Jason silently got up and followed them, leaving Jody all alone. She looked over at Roy's dead body, and she felt tears well up in her eyes.

"I'm sorry," she whispered. "I'm so sorry Roy." She rested her forehead in her hands, her whole body quivering.

"I couldn't protect him," she sobbed. "Hell, I don't know if I can protect any of them. The only way we win this battle is together. But they're losing their faith in me, and honestly, I can't blame them. But if I'm not the leader they think I am, if I can't rally them behind me when we go into this battle..." She shook her head, tears running down her face. "I know I've made mistakes. I know I've let you down. But please, give them the strength to keep going. Just for a little while longer." She paused, choking back a sob. "These people are strong, stronger than I could ever hope to be. They are the last bit of candlelight we have in this broken world. Please, give them your strength, and maybe, just maybe, they'll have a chance at saving it."

301

CHAPTER 103

Michael Swezenko sat stony faced in the driver's seat as he guided the Ford F150 down the two-lane highway south alongside the scrub brush dotted mountain face they had been following for the last fifteen miles or so. Tyson sat in the passenger's seat beside him, staring pensively out at the passing mountainside. Marianne was taking a nap in the backseat, her head lying in Laura's lap, who was staring unseeingly out the front windshield, absentmindedly stroking Marianne's hair. Laura wondered vaguely if this is what it felt like to die. She had become completely numb to the world around her, deaf to the conversations between Mike and Tyson happening only feet away, the scenery outside the window passing by meaninglessly. If the monster who'd killed her husband appeared to her now, grinning wickedly, black gloved hand outstretched, she would've taken it without a second thought.

"Mike, can I ask you something?" Tyson asked, not shifting his gaze from the window.

"Sure," Mike said.

"Do you trust them?"

Mike didn't reply.

"Ben and Jody, I mean."

Mike said nothing. Ben had given them a small speech when they'd gathered in the lobby that morning about the need to move forward and finish the journey. Jody, who had appreciated this very much, had watched their reactions carefully, worried by what she saw. Many of them had looked uncomfortable. A few had been whispering to each other urgently. Even Jennifer, clutching her daughter's hand, didn't look especially happy. She could see their resolve weakening. Ben hadn't said anything to her, but she could tell he'd noticed it too. He'd walked off slightly dejected as they'd left the lobby for the vehicles, his brow furrowed with worry.

Mike finally shook his head.

"Honestly," he said, "I don't know. I really don't know."

Tyson said nothing.

"Look," Mike went on, "I'd love to be able to say that I trusted them. Ben was like a brother to me before the world went to shit. I followed him for a long time, but after what's happened the last couple of days..." He shook his head as he moved the Ford slightly left of the centerline to avoid a semi overturned on the shoulder. "I just don't know anymore. I don't feel safe with these people. Not after what happened to Dylan and Roy. I don't know what that Jody girl has gotten herself into, but whatever it is, it seems to have put a target on our backs."

"So, you don't believe any of that supernatural shit?" Tyson asked.

Mike shook his head, steering the Ford around a Volkswagen beetle and an Elantra that had crashed head on in the middle of the highway.

"Honestly, I'm not sure what I believe anymore. I've never been much for superstition. After what happened with Marianne, I guess I had to believe it, at least a little."

"She was dead," Tyson said contemplatively, glancing in the rearview mirror at her sleeping form. He was pleased to see that Laura had fallen asleep with her head on Marianne's shoulder. After the events of the previous night, Tyson knew they both needed it. "I know it sounds crazy," Tyson went on. "But I could feel it. She was gone. And Jody brought her back."

"So that means you're on board with all this?" Mike asked.

Tyson was silent for a moment.

"I was," he said. "I mean, Jody saved Marianne. You don't forget something like that. It was only after Dylan died that I started to have...second thoughts." He paused. "I mean...she's a good person, Mike. I know that much. I just think she might be in over her head."

Mike nodded. Tyson turned to look at Mike, his expression very serious.

"All I can say is, if you're going to ask people to follow you into hell, you'd better have a plan to climb out."

CHAPTER 104

Jody slowly opened the door of the bedroom to find Laura lying on top of the sheets, fully clothed, staring emptily at the blank TV screen on the opposite wall.

"Knock knock," Jody said, trying to sound friendly.

Laura didn't look up.

"I didn't see you at dinner," Jody said, gingerly shutting the door behind her. "You okay?" She sat down on the edge of the bed, realizing almost immediately what a stupid question it was.

After a moment, Laura slowly shook her head, refusing to meet Jody's eyes. Jody nodded.

"Fair," Jody said, dropping her fake cheeriness.

There was silence for a moment.

"Laura," Jody said, her tone suddenly very serious. "For what it's worth, I'm sorry about what happened to Roy. I made a promise to protect all of you when you came on this journey with me." She sighed heavily. "And I have failed in that."

Laura said nothing. She was staring down at her hands folded in her lap, both of which were trembling slightly, refusing to look Jody in the eye. Jody sighed and shook her head, resting her forehead in her hands. She suddenly felt a deep sense of helplessness, like a child that is struggling to articulate to a concerned parent the reason for their frustration.

"He was my everything," Laura whispered, her voice shaking. "He saved my life. I.." she stammered, the words catching in her throat. "I was in such a dark hole when I met him. I was drinking myself to sleep every night. All I wanted to do was shut the world out for good. I was just so damn tired of the nightmares, of the constant anxiety, of carrying around a hundred-pound weight in my chest every day, of knowing that not one person in this world gave a shit about me!" She broke down crying, sobbing her heart out as she curled up into a ball against the headboard. "I was gonna do it," she wailed. "The day I met him, I was going to go home and end it. I was in that bar to have one final martini when he came in and started talking to me."

Jody remained silent, not knowing what to say.

"I am alive today because of him. How can I possibly go on without him?" she sobbed.

"Because he would want you to," Jody said calmly.

Laura finally looked up at Jody, her face streaked with tears.

"He would want you to go on. He would want us all to go on together." Jody sighed heavily. "Laura, I know I'm asking too much of you, and I'm sorry. But we have to do this together. All of us. It's the only way we can beat him." Jody paused, debating her next words carefully. "It's the only way his death means something." Jody shook her head sadly. "Laura, I'm hurting too. We all are. And I can't..." she paused, choking on her words. "I can't let them have died in vain. Roy or Dylan. You might hate that kid, and I couldn't blame you if you did. But he fought harder than any of us could possibly imagine. He was fighting to turn his life around. And he was...he was winning that fight. That's why he died."

There was silence for a moment.

"I never hated him," Laura said finally. "I was scared of him, for a while, because somehow, I knew he wasn't himself. He wasn't in control, was he?"

Jody shook her head.

"When I told him that night that I loved him, I meant it. That kid lost everything. I felt responsible for him. I know I wasn't his mom, I could never be his mom, but I cared about him like I was." Laura squeezed her eyes shut, tears leaking out between the lids. "He deserved that much at least."

Jody remained silent.

"But you're right," Laura said after a moment, wiping her eyes. "We have to go on, don't we? For them. It's the only thing I can give them now." She was silent for a moment. "Roy gave me everything, Jody. The least I can give him back is my life."

Jody felt a tear slide down her cheek at these words. She embraced Laura, hugging the older woman tightly to her. After a moment, Laura returned her embrace.

"I'm not going to let that happen," Jody whispered, her voice trembling but somehow firm. "You are not going to die on me, you hear me, kid?"

Laura squeezed Jody tighter.

"I know you won't," she whispered. "You're going to win this war, Jody. And we're all going to be standing behind you. I promise you that."

At these words, Jody began to cry.

CHAPTER 105

D avid slumped over the steering wheel as he pulled the Chevy into the driveway of the abandoned house, completely exhausted. The drive would've only taken about four hours under normal circumstances, but the highway they'd been driving on had been strewn with abandoned vehicles that they'd been forced to constantly maneuver around on the shoulders or even in the grass just off the shoulder a handful of times, and they'd been forced to double back on several occasions when they'd encountered blockages they'd been unable to bypass. In the end, the four-hour drive had taken most of the day, and the sun was setting as Tyson's Ford F150 pulled up behind them in the driveway.

"You okay dad?" Maria asked, walking over to him as he stepped out of the Chevrolet, rubbing his aching temples.

"Yeah, I'm alright, kid," he replied, trying his best to smile but only managing a sort of half-hearted grimace.

The wind whipped at their faces as they walked into the house, the snow blowing past them in great big fluffy white drifts. It had snowed again today during the drive, so that the entire world was blanketed white by dusk.

The snow had come as a slight shock to David, who until yesterday had completely forgotten that it was late November. Late last September, around the time when the whole thing had started, felt like an eternity ago. Maria, who had also been a bit startled to realize it was already late November, nevertheless welcomed the arrival of the snow. It was the one thing in the world that felt normal to her right now. It brought her a modicum of comfort to know that even if everything else in the entire world had fallen apart, at least the snow still fell in winter and melted in the spring.

"You miss her, don't you?" Maria asked.

David looked at her, slightly taken aback.

"How'd you know?" he asked.

"Not sure," Maria said as they walked through the front door into the house. "Guess Jody is rubbing off on me."

David smiled.

"Well, if there was anyone I'd want to rub off on my kid, especially at a time like this, it'd be her."

"Well, just don't expect me to start conjuring fire out of thin air," Maria teased, causing them both to laugh.

"But seriously, dad," she said, "you're thinking about her, aren't you?"

David nodded, setting himself heavily down on the living room sofa and running a hand across his forehead. Maria sat down beside him, looking at him a little anxiously.

"Both of them, actually," David said after a moment. "Lilly and your mom."

Maria nodded.

"I think about them a lot too."

David wrapped an arm around her shoulders, his expression softening.

"I'm sorry, kid," he said. "I know I haven't been there for you like I should be lately. I mean, after your mom died, I guess I tried to shut that part of me down."

Maria sighed, laying her head on her father's shoulder.

"I get it," she said. "It's too painful, so you just try to block it out. I think we've all been doing that a lot lately."

David sighed and shook his head sadly.

"It's not healthy," David said. "I know it's not. I guess I just...I don't want to forget them. Even if we win this war, I'm always going to feel like there's a piece of me missing."

Maria nodded.

"I know how it feels," she said. "When mom died, I just kind of...broke. I couldn't feel a thing. I didn't want to die, not exactly, I just...didn't care if I did or not. Does that make sense?"

David nodded.

Maria looked around at the sea of faces now in the house, some sitting, some talking, a few checking the cupboards and other small spaces for any food the homeowners might have left behind.

"They all feel it, I think. On some level. Maybe not in the same way we do, but they understand what they lost. And they're angry. I can feel it. Something changed after Roy died. If the monster was trying to scare us away by killing him, I think he underestimated us."

"Do you think we can beat him?" David asked seriously. Their eyes met, David looking worried, Maria determined. After a moment, Maria nodded.

"If we stand behind Jody, and we channel all that pain into creating something better, we can do it."

"Do you think we can rebuild the world one day?" David asked. "From all of this chaos and destruction?"

Maria nodded.

"Do you remember what Jody said right after Tyson came back?" she asked.

David shook his head.

"Where there's fire, there's life," Maria said. "Dad, there's fire here. Can you feel it?"

David nodded. He had definitely felt a shift in the group over the course of the day. They no longer seemed afraid. They seemed angry, determined to crush their enemy.

"If they can channel that fire into something good, I think this world has a chance," Maria said. "It might take decades, even centuries, but we can rebuild this world. Fire is the source of all life. We just have to shine the firelight in the darkest corners, one at a time."

David smiled and hugged Maria.

307

"Your mother would be proud of you, if she were here," he whispered. "So would Lilly."

"I know, dad," Maria said, returning the hug. "But you're here right now, and you're proud of me. That means everything."

CHAPTER 106

David was sitting on the porch, staring out at the empty street, toting an M16 they'd pulled off a dead soldier lying in the middle of the street earlier in the day, along with a few extra ammo clips he'd clipped to the waistband of his jeans. He could hear the sounds of the group talking and eating dinner from inside. He had declined to join them. He didn't feel much like eating.

"Not hungry?"

David turned as the screen door swung open and Martin stepped out, toting his Winchester shotgun. David shook his head.

"Me either," Martin said, sitting down next to David and removing a pack of Marlboros from his breast pocket. "Figured I might as well be useful and join you on watch. You smoke?"

David shook his head.

"I used to, but I stopped when my first was born."

"Same here," Martin said, removing a stainless-steel lighter from his pants pocket and lighting the end of the small brown pipe. "Didn't do it for over a decade. Only started again a few months ago, right after this all started."

"Well, I'll give you credit there," David said. "You were rehabilitated for eleven goddamn years, took the end of the world to get you to relapse."

Martin grinned and took a long draught on the cigarette.

"Well, you haven't relapsed yet," Martin said. "What's keeping you in the game?"

David shook his head.

"I'm not completely sure, honestly. I guess I still have some hope that there's an endgame to all of this, that we might still have a chance to come out of it okay." He thought of Anna. "Or come out of it, at least."

"I feel you," Martin said sadly. "My wife died a few months ago. Radiation sickness."

"I'm sorry to hear that," David said, shaking his head. "Pretty amazing how good we are at killing each other, isn't it?"

"Well, amazing isn't the word I'd use," Martin replied. "Disgusting is more like it."

"Fair enough," David said.

There was silence for a moment.

"Who did you lose?" Martin asked finally. David hesitated, debating how much to share.

"My wife, Anna," he said finally. "She was sick too. It didn't kill her though. That kid Dylan, you remember him?"

Martin nodded.

"The possessed one, right?"

David nodded.

"Laura takes sleeping pills. She gave Anna a couple to help her sleep one night. Turns out the kid had switched them with poison pills."

"Jesus," Martin muttered, shaking his head. "I'm sorry man."

David solemnly shook his head. Neither of them seemed to know what to say.

In the distance, the orange setting sun slipped behind the tree line, plunging them into darkness. Martin tossed his spent cigarette onto the ground and quickly stamped it out with the toe of his hiking boot. The sudden darkness unnerved David a little.

"Do you think there's others out there?" David asked, carefully concealing his nervousness.

Martin nodded.

"Must be," he said. "We can't be the only ones left, right? I mean, I won't lie, it kind of feels that way right now, but I don't think we can possibly be the only ones left. Someone else has to have survived, right?"

"I suppose so," David replied, tightening his grip on the rifle. He hesitated for a moment before voicing his next question. "Do you think they'll come after us?"

Martin gave him a quizzical look.

"What do you mean?"

"I mean, like when Leo showed up in Fairfax and turned the house into a shooting gallery."

Martin said nothing.

"If Leo was somehow in league with that monster, there must be others, right? And we haven't seen any of them for a while, so they're probably overdue for a visit, right?"

"What makes you think they'll come tonight?" Martin asked.

"If it's true what Jody's been saying, and by now, I'm inclined to believe it is, the monster isn't going to stop until he's killed every single one of us. Something's bound to happen."

"All I know," Martin said, "is that if anybody shows up here tonight..." he pantomimed firing the Winchester, "they're dead. That's why we're here right?"

David nodded and sat back down. Martin joined him, the crumpled remains of the cigarette smoking beside him.

"Guess you shoot first, ask questions later, huh?"

Martin looked taken aback.

"You were a marine right?" Martin asked.

David nodded.

"Three tours, all during the Iraq war."

Martin shook his head.

"Sorry, I guess I'm a little shocked to see a guy who served in a forward area so shocked at the idea of shooting first and asking questions later."

"I'm not really shocked by it," David replied with a hint of indignation. "I've been out of the military for a long time. Law enforcement only uses deadly force as a last resort. Guess I've gotten used to that."

"Well, I guess it's not a bad way of thinking," Martin said sheepishly. "My wife always used to nag me for keeping a gun on the nightstand in our bedroom. Said it made her nervous, but I never gave in."

David grinned.

"This might be hard to believe, but she was looking out for you. Hardest thing for a soldier is to leave the war behind. I know the feeling. When I first met my wife, I always tried to convince her to go on a date with me to the gun range. She finally gave in after about a year."

"What was the verdict?" Martin asked, his face breaking into a grin.

"Said she preferred getting nailed. Never brought it up again."

They both burst out laughing at once.

"Sounds like a good woman," Martin said once he'd managed to contain his laughter.

"Yeah," David said wistfully. "Best woman in the whole damn world."

There was silence for a moment.

"Your boy okay?" David asked.

Martin nodded as he lit another cigarette.

"He was shook up at first. I mean, who wouldn't be? But Kaden's always been...different..."

"Different how?" David asked, watching a fat brown squirrel dart behind a large oak tree.

"More mature. I always have the weird sense that he knows a lot more than he lets on. It's easy to forget he's a kid sometimes. Even when his mom died, he hardly cried at all. Seemed to just take it like a fact of life."

"I think a lot of parents feel that way," David replied, kicking a stray bit of cigarette ash off his shoe. "I know I have."

"No, this goes way beyond just understanding that hearing your parents fight every night after you go to bed probably means they're divorcing." He paused, a memory floating up from the dark recesses of his brain. "David," Martin said slowly, "remind me, what was your wife's name?"

"Anna," David replied, fixing him with a quizzical look.

Martin's eye slowly widened as the shock rolled over in a tidal wave.

"The Puppeteer used Dylan to kill Anna..."

"What, what's wrong?" David asked, seeing the shock on Martin's face.

"He knew..." Martin whispered. "He tried to warn me that night, and I..."

Suddenly, everything made sense. Kaden's strange behavior over the last several months. The constant nightmares and inability to sleep. The incident the night Anna had died (and Martin would've bet his life it happened on the same night). Even his near drowning in the bathtub before all of this started made sense now.

Martin slowly lowered himself down onto the porch, his face a mask of deep contemplation. He'd known. Somehow, Kaden had known.

"He tried to warn me," Martin said to David, who by now looked completely stunned. "He tried to warn me the night Anna died, he tried to help her, and he nearly drowned doing it."

David sat down next to Martin, both men sitting in stunned silence.

"If that's true," David said slowly, "then your boy really is something else."

Martin absentmindedly tossed his cigarette on the ground, stamping it out with the toe of his boot.

"I should probably go watch out back," he said, standing up to leave. "Yell if you need anything."

Martin walked into the house, allowing the screen door to slam behind him, leaving David sitting alone on the darkened porch with his thoughts.

David snapped awake as the back of his head struck something hard. He groaned and rubbed the injured spot.

"Damn, must've dozed off," he thought. "Just have to make sure I say, 'In Jesus' name, amen,' as I raise my head when the CO comes around." He smiled at the thought.

It was something their platoon used to joke about back in his military days whenever he'd be placed on guard duty with one of his buddies. He scanned the surrounding darkness, suddenly wishing he had a flashlight. The thought of something sneaking up on him in the dark unnerved him a little.

"Besides," he thought, "it is a bit lonely out here."

He thought briefly about calling Martin back but decided against it. It was better to have one of them on each side of the house so that no one could sneak up on them.

Although David didn't like to think about it, after the events of the last few nights, he thought it likely that something would probably happen again tonight. He sighed and closed his eyes. It really was lonely out here, and it went beyond Martin's absence. He suddenly realized just how lonely he'd been ever since...ever since Anna died. He sat down on the porch and hung his head. When Lilly had been taken away from him, it had been the worst day of his entire life. To see the little girl he loved so much destroyed by a sick, narcissistic asshole like Michael Pines, to see the law fail to get her justice, to see her having a complete nervous breakdown when she realized how badly her life had been screwed up...it had almost killed him.

Anna had saved him. Hell, Anna had saved all of them. She'd held the family together through a time when it could've easily fallen apart. She'd been his rock in the midst of a raging, stormy sea brought on by constant legal battles, Maria's increasing absence from the house, a PR nightmare, and nearly losing his job over the whole mess. And now she was gone at a time when he needed her probably more than he ever had before. David grinned sardonically.

"Suppose that's why you took her from me, right?" he thought savagely. "Because you knew it would destroy me, or at least weaken me for when we finally meet face to face. Well let me set you straight. I don't cry for her anymore. Every time I think of her, I can feel the fire flaring inside of me. I am not afraid of you. I will stand by these people when we go to battle, and we will burn your house to the ground."

Cold, deep laughter echoed through the chilly night air at these words, causing David to sweep the yard with the barrel of the rifle, every muscle prepared to shoot. A bead of sweat trickled down his forehead.

"Good luck," a hissing voice whispered in his ear, followed by more laughter.

David fired off several shots in rapid succession, the bullets flying off harmlessly into the darkness. David swore loudly, realizing he had missed his intended target. He swept the barrel of the rifle from side to side, straining to see through the darkness. The Puppeteer watched him from the shadow of the large oak tree a few hundred yards away, grinning wickedly. This was going to be fun.

"Where are you?" David whispered, taking a few steps out into the yard, aiming the barrel of the rifle at anything that moved. "C'mon out, you bastard," David growled. "Show yourself!"

"If you insist," the Puppeteer whispered, his grin widening.

"Daddy..." a girl's voice whispered from somewhere behind him. David whirled around, his grip on the rifle tensing.

"Who's there?" he demanded, although a horrible feeling had already begun to form in the pit of his stomach.

"It's me daddy," the voice said. It took him a second to recognize her voice because it sounded so young.

She couldn't've been any older than eight or nine. The rifle clattered to the ground.

"Lilly?" he whispered, his lower lip quivering.

And then he saw her. She was standing in the front doorway, wearing her favorite sky-blue sundress from when she was little, her long dark red hair rippling in the light breeze. Her enormous bright green eyes were sparkling with happiness. David fell to his knees, his mouth opening and closing soundlessly.

"Daddy, it's me!" she squealed with delight. "Stop being silly, come play with me!" She turned and ran into the house, the screen door slamming behind her.

David remained still for a moment longer, too shocked to move. Finally, he struggled weakly to his feet and followed his oldest daughter into the house, completely speechless. Never seeing Martin hustling around the side of the house, rifle raised.

"David!" he shouted.

"What happened, I heard gunshots, what's going..." he trailed off at the sight of David, who was stumbling up the porch into the house, his face paper white, his mouth hanging open in shock. His eyes were glazed over, and he didn't appear to have heard a word Martin had said.

"David!" Martin shouted.

David ignored him. A moment later, the screen door slammed shut, leaving Martin standing alone in the darkness, completely in shock, his mind racing. Slowly, the truth dawned on him like a hideous beast emerging from a dense fog. It suddenly struck him that the wind had inexplicably grown icy cold, the deep cold settling into his bones like a dense frost. The darkness seemed to press in on him, as if hundreds of small animals with razor sharp teeth were eyeing him hungrily from the shadows.

And then Martin saw him. The shotgun fell from his hands and clattered to the ground. He made no attempt to pick it up. He was standing in front of the large oak tree a few hundred feet away, dressed head to toe in black, a tall black top hat sitting atop his head, a long black cape billowing around in the wind behind him. He grinned at Martin with a mouth full of unnaturally sharp canine teeth. He raised a black gloved finger to his thin lips.

"Shh..." he whispered, nodding his head in the direction of the front door.

Martin gasped.

"Shit," he whispered, sprinting for the house. "Shit, shit, shit, SHIT!"

"Lilly, honey, where are you going?" David called.

Lilly giggled and sprinted towards the wooden staircase.

"Come get me daddy!" she called.

David followed her, grinning ear to ear. It was a game they often played before bedtime. Lilly jumped up and grabbed the banister. She contorted herself so that she was hanging upside down.

"Careful honey," David said, smiling indulgently.

"I'm not gonna fall, daddy," Lilly smirked, rolling her eyes. "I do this all the time."

She pulled herself upright and swung her legs over the banister, grinning down at David.

"Come and get me!" she giggled, sprinting up the stairs.

David started after her, but then paused suddenly.

"David!" a man's voice shouted from somewhere far off. David shook himself. He had to be imagining it.

"David!" It sounded so familiar. But David found, to his slight surprise, that he simply didn't care.

His daughter was calling for him again. A smile slowly spread across his face.

"Coming honey!" he called, chasing up the stairs after her.

"David!" Martin shouted again.

This time, he was ignored completely. Martin shook his head, running up the stairs after David. He caught him at the landing.

"David!" Martin shouted directly in his ear, grabbing him by the shoulder.

David shook him off so violently he stumbled and had to grab the banister to avoid falling down the staircase. Martin stared at him, flabbergasted. He hadn't even turned around to look at him.

"Okay, honey, where'd you go?" David called, grinning.

Martin stared after him as he walked down the hallway, his anxiety worsening. Whatever the monster was doing to David, Martin had no doubt as to what the intended end result was.

Martin's mind whirled as he sprinted after David, struggling for a solution short of shooting the man in the leg, which he wouldn't do unless he had no other option.

"Dad!" came a voice from the bottom of the stairs.

Martin turned to see his son, who had been patrolling downstairs while Jody slept, standing at the bottom of the staircase, his expression clouded with worry.

"Dad, what's going on?"

Kaden made his way up the stairs as Martin stuttered, struggling to explain the situation.

"Is he here?" Kaden asked as he reached the landing, suddenly looking very afraid.

Slowly, Martin nodded.

"Yes son, he's here," Martin replied. "And he's taken one of our own."

David wandered down the hallway after Lilly. Giggling madly, she threw open the door to the bedroom at the end of the hallway and disappeared inside, slamming the door behind her. David hurried after her. Something strange was happening to him. With every step he took he seemed to be growing weaker, as if the energy were slowly being stripped from his body, so that the walk to the door seemed to be a thousand miles instead of a few short feet. He stumbled and nearly fell in front of the door, grabbing onto the wall for support.

"Honey are you in there?" he called, his voice barely above a whisper. The words felt like shards of glass in his throat.

No answer. He heard it again. That same cold, deep laugh he'd heard in the yard. It seemed to be all around him, as if he were a dying gladiator in an arena being laughed at by thousands of spectators.

"He's mocking me," David thought weakly. "He knows I'm weak. He knows I have no fight left." He sighed heavily. "He's taunting me with her. She's not even real." The realization hit him like a tornado striking a two-story house head-on. "She's not even real..." he thought.

He knew it was true. Hell, he'd known from the minute he first saw her. And yet he'd followed her anyway. Just hearing her voice again...it made him want to cry. Just seeing her laughing, smiling again, it made him feel whole. He hung his head, slamming his fist against the wall in frustration. All he wanted was to pick her up and hold her in his arms.

"She's not real..." he whispered.

She would fade into mist the second he touched her. There was only one way he could ever hold his little girl again. He shook his head, bitter tears spilling down his face. He couldn't do this anymore. He sighed. God he was so weak. He couldn't even say the fucking word.

"I'm sorry, Maria," he whispered. "But I can't anymore. I just can't."

"David..." He looked up, startled.

The door to the bedroom was slightly ajar. His hand trembled as he reached for it, pushing it all the way open. Lilly was standing in the middle of the room, smiling wanly at him. David gasped audibly when he saw the woman standing behind her, her hands resting on Lilly's shoulders. She was wearing a thin purple nightgown that highlighted her exceptional figure. Her curly blonde hair was pinned into a bun at the base of her neck. He stumbled in the doorway and fell to his knees. His mouth opened and closed soundlessly as he stared up into the woman's beautiful face.

"Daddy, I found mommy!" Lilly said happily, jumping up and throwing her arms around the woman's neck.

Anna Veranda smiled and embraced her daughter, rocking her back and forth in her arms like a baby.

"Stop it, mommy, I'm too old for that!" Lilly laughed.

David stared soundlessly at the pair of them, struggling for words.

"Anna…" David whispered, struggling to his feet on rubbery legs. "Anna…"

Anna set Lilly down and turned to David, her expression full of melancholy. David reached out for her, for a second terrified that she would vanish at his touch. But then Anna embraced him, and the fear vanished instantly, his entire body filling with blissful happiness at her touch.

"Anna…" he whispered, tears stinging his eyes. "Oh Anna, I'm so sorry honey."

He felt Lilly hug him somewhere around his middle.

"We miss you, daddy," she sobbed. "Me and mommy miss you so much."

"I know baby, I know," David choked out, refusing to let go of Anna. "I love you both so much. I want us to be a family again."

"We can be, daddy," Lilly whispered, releasing him.

David released Anna and looked down at her, slightly confused.

"We can be a family again, daddy," she said, her lower lip quivering slightly.

He gave Anna a quizzical look. She smiled, stroking her hands gently down the back of his neck.

"I want to be with you again. I want us all to be a family again."

"Daddy, we want that too," Lilly said. She sounded older suddenly, more mature. Her voice had deepened considerably. She sounded like she was around sixteen or seventeen years old, although her outward appearance hadn't changed at all.

"I want to be with you again," she sobbed, tears filling her eyes.

"Honey," David whispered, hugging her tightly. "I want to be with you too, I want that more than anything…"

"Then come with me!" she sobbed, tugging on his hand. "Come with me and mommy!"

It was only then that David noticed that the window was open, the curtains fluttering in the breeze. He turned back to look at Lilly, startled. She wasn't there. Neither was Anna. He turned back to the open window. It beckoned invitingly. He sank to his knees, tears of bitter frustration filling his eyes.

"I want to be with you again…" he whispered. "I want us to be a family again…I can't live without you…"

He shivered, and not from the cold wind blowing through the open window.

"I can't live without you…"

He closed his eyes. A faint ringing had developed in his ears. He looked up at the open window.

"I can't live without you…"

A deep sense of unreality washed over him. He felt himself slowly rise to his feet. He watched himself walk over to the windowsill and lean against. He watched David Veranda stare down at the twenty-foot drop, snow blanketing the ground below. He saw David Veranda hang his head in defeat, knowing he was going to jump.

"Don't…" he whispered.

David ignored him. He swung one leg over the windowsill.

"DON'T!"

316

Only it wasn't him screaming this time. He turned. Maria was standing in the doorway, her face filled with panic, angry tears spilling down her cheeks.

"DAD!" she cried, running into the room, followed by Jody, Kaden, Martin, and several others.

He swung his other leg over the windowsill, preparing to fall.

"Dad, please don't!" Maria cried out. "Don't do this!"

David shook his head. He could feel tears beginning to form in his eyes.

"I'm sorry," he whispered. "Maria, you shouldn't be here. You shouldn't have to see this."

"Dad, I'm not going to leave you," Maria sobbed. "I will never leave you. You can't leave me like this. I will never forgive you if you do."

"David," Jody said firmly, stepping in front of Maria. "What did he show you?"

David sighed heavily, edging out a little further on the windowsill. He could feel the icy breeze on his face. It felt strangely pleasant. Kaden stepped forward.

"David, whatever he showed you, it doesn't matter. None of it is real. He only shows you what he wants you to see!"

David shook his head.

"It doesn't matter," he said weakly, edging a little further out into the open air. "I knew they weren't real as soon as I saw them, and the truth is, I didn't give a shit." He shook his head sadly. "You don't get it. Any of you. We're marching to our deaths. All of us. We can't beat him."

"David, listen to me," Jody said, a definite note of panic in her voice.

David shook his head.

"We can't beat him," David whispered. "We just can't. I don't have any fight left in me. I can't do this anymore." He edged himself out a little further. He could feel himself starting to slip. He closed his eyes, embracing the cool night air.

"I'm coming," he whispered.

"DAD!" Maria screamed, tears spilling down her face. "DAD, DON'T DO THIS, COME BACK WITH US, PLEASE!"

David turned to face his youngest daughter one last time. He smiled. It was the saddest smile Maria had ever seen.

"I'm sorry, kid," he whispered. "But I'm going home."

He closed his eyes, inhaled deeply, and let go. Maria wailed, diving for his hand as he fell from the windowsill and out of sight, her outstretched fingers closing around empty air. Her vision blurred with tears, she glimpsed her father's lifeless body lying on the pavement below before the world faded away and she slipped back into the darkness.

317

CHAPTER 107

Maria opened her eyes. She was lying on the ground in a small clearing, surrounded by a thicket of enormous oak trees. She sat up, brushing a few oak leaves off her sweatshirt. Bright sunlight was streaming down on her from the canopy. Birds were calling cheerily back and forth high above her head. It might've even been pleasant under normal circumstances. But as Maria stood up and looked around at the scene before her, all she saw was ugliness. There was nothing beautiful about the scene. It was like looking at a family photo album the day after your parents passed away. All this place did was remind her of what she had lost. She angrily kicked a pile of dead leaves out of her way as she stormed into the trees, barely seeing what was in front of her, not knowing, not caring. Suddenly, she didn't want to be here at all. She just wanted to shut the world out for good. She never wanted to look at the terrible inescapable ugliness of the world ever again.

She began to run, unseen tree limbs whipping at her arms and legs as she ran blindly through the trees. Tears began to spill down her face as she ran. She nearly collided with a large oak tree, cracking her funny bone hard against the thick tree trunk. Crying out in pain, she stumbled and fell on her knees in the shade of another large oak tree.

"Why?" she sobbed, crying uncontrollably. "Why did you do this?" She lifted her tear-stained eyes to the bright blue sky as if expecting an answer.

Nothing. The forest had gone strangely quiet. She slammed her hand down angrily in the dirt.

"WHY?" she screamed, angry tears spilling down her face. "WHY DID YOU TAKE HIM FROM ME? WHY DID HE HAVE TO DIE? FIRST YOU TOOK LILLY, THEN MOM, NOW DAD! YOU'VE DESTROYED EVERYTHING I LOVE! I AM ALL ALONE IN THIS FUCKED UP WORLD BECAUSE OF YOU!" She buried her face in her hands, sobbing uncontrollably. "I can't," she whispered. "I am all alone. I…I can't do this alone. I'm sorry."

"But you aren't alone," came a woman's voice.

Maria looked up. Even through her tears, she couldn't mistake the figure walking towards her through the trees.

"What are you doing here?" Maria whispered, a trace of anger in her voice.

Jody shook her head sadly as she approached Maria.

"Because you need me," she said. "Maria, I'm sorry…"

"No," Maria said firmly, abruptly cutting Jody off. "I don't need you now. I needed you the night mom died."

"Maria…"

"She's dead, Jody," Maria spat angrily. "Dad killed himself to be with her. I am all alone." She buried her face in her hands, angrily tears spilling down her face. "Why am I here?"

"Maria…"

"WHY AM I HERE?" she screamed at Jody, her expression shattering into a thousand pieces.

Jody sat down next to Maria, her expression unreadable.

"I'm sorry, Maria," Jody said solemnly. "I'm sorry so much burden fell on you. But I promise you, there is an endgame to this."

"I'm not playing any goddamn endgame," Maria said savagely. "Fuck your god, fuck his plan, fuck these people, and fuck life! I am done being a piece in whatever twisted chess game your god is playing! He has done more than enough, and I am going to spend the rest of my life nursing the scars he has inflicted on me that will never heal!"

Jody was silent for a moment.

"Why me?" Maria asked. "Why did he take everything from me?"

Jody said nothing.

"You don't know, do you?" Maria asked, glaring at Jody. "You don't have a goddamn clue…"

"He's afraid," Jody said.

"Of what?" Maria asked.

"Of you. He knows what's inside of you. He is doing everything he can to destroy you."

"Well, frankly," Maria said, "it's working. I don't have any fight left in me anymore."

"You're wrong," Jody said. "When life tries to tear you down, you can do one of two things. You can either let it beat you up, or you can fight back."

Maria stared silently down at her hands.

"You've been fighting for a long time, kid. Do you remember what you did after your sister was attacked?"

"I went radio silent," Maria said. "I didn't talk to anybody, not even my own family. I would stay for hours after swim club practice, swimming laps. I would spend hours jogging, playing tennis, anything physical that would get me out of the house. I was just so damn angry, all I wanted to do was keep running and never stop. I guess I thought if I did that, I wouldn't ever have to face the mess that my life was becoming."

"You fell down," Jody said. "You didn't want to get back up."

"I didn't want to face the world," Maria said hollowly. "I just wanted them all to fuck off. It's taken me years to get past that." Maria turned to Jody, her expression somber. "I'm not sure if I ever did get past it at all. Maybe that's just another lie I keep telling myself."

Jody sighed, sliding a comforting arm around Maria, who accepted it gratefully.

"You've got to find it in yourself to get up again, kid," Jody said. "You've got to find it in yourself to keep fighting."

"We all do," Maria said. "We've all lost a lot."

Jody nodded.

"The Puppeteer thinks he can tear us down," Maria continued. "That's why he's doing this. But he's wrong. We all have a fire inside of us. That's why we were chosen for this. All the pain, all the suffering, all the loss, it's only making the fire burn hotter." Maria turned to Jody. "We can stop him. I know we can."

Jody nodded, a wan smile crossing her face. Maria sighed heavily.

"I have to go back, don't I?"

"It's your choice," Jody replied matter of factly.

"No, I have to," Maria said. "We have to stand together, all of us." She shook her head. "I can't run away anymore. Not like I did back then. I have to finish this fight." Maria stood up and started to walk away.

Jody abruptly grabbed her arm.

"Maria, wait. I just want you to remember..." Jody averted her gaze, eyes downcast.

"What?" Maria persisted. The forest was beginning to fade around her. For a brief moment, she felt Jody embrace her.

"I love you," Jody murmured.

At these words, tears brimmed in Maria's eyes.

"I love you so much, kid. No matter what happens, no matter how angry you are with me, no matter how many times you fall, that will never change."

Maria threw her arms around Jody, tears blurring her vision as the scene around her faded.

"I love you too," Maria whispered. "Thank you for everything."

And then she was gone.

CHAPTER 108

M aria squeezed her eyes shut against her growing headache as she pulled the Chevrolet up beside the lakefront, which was already beginning to freeze over despite the surprising warmth of the day. The headache had been steadily developing throughout the entire day, until now, when she felt as though someone had placed a nail gun to her temple and fired off several rounds in rapid succession.

"Guess that's what I get for volunteering to drive towards the sun all day," Maria muttered as she killed the ignition and her passengers disembarked. Still, it was better than dwelling the terrible events of the previous night the entire day, which she would've done otherwise. She stumbled out of the driver's side door, rubbing her aching head.

"You alright?" Roy asked, sounding concerned.

"Yeah, I'm fine," Maria muttered, waving him off. "I just need to lie down for a few minutes."

The sun was rapidly setting behind the treetops as they pitched their tents in the clearing between the lakefront and the forest behind them. Thankfully, it had been warmer that day, so most of the snow had already melted by the time they arrived. However, the temperature began to drop rapidly as the sun dipped behind the trees.

"Let's hurry this up!" Tyson shouted over the howling of the wind as he drove another stake into the hard frozen ground. "We need to get these up before we all freeze to death!"

"I agree!" Mike shouted back. "Last time my balls were this cold, I was still living with my ex-wife!"

"Why'd we come out here anyway?" Roy demanded, shoving a tent pole roughly into a pouch on the flat canvas in front of him. "Wouldn't it have made more sense to stay in the city?"

No one answered him. They were all thinking the same thing: of course it would've made more sense to stay in a city, in an abandoned house, where there would've been shelter from the cold. But after the events of the previous night, they'd all silently agreed that they couldn't stand the thought of staying in another abandoned house, even if it was over a hundred miles away from the house where David Veranda had committed suicide. It was too painful for all of them, especially for Maria. As Maria sat down by the trunk of a dead oak tree, staring out at the frozen water on the lake, she realized that she really couldn't care less about the cold. The five of them huddled around the small fire in the darkness, shivering in the freezing cold. It had taken them over an hour to get even the miniscule fire that now lay before them started with the high winds and the melting snow making it impossible to find dry wood. The rest of the group had retreated into their sleeping bags long ago. No one seemed to care about dinner. Mike had floated the idea of trying to spear a rabbit but dropped it when he realized no one was interested. None of them were especially hungry after the events of the previous evening. It suddenly occurred to Maria that she hadn't eaten anything for the last twenty-four hours. She found that she didn't care in the slightest. Jody was staring into the smoldering embers, her expression mournful. Her head had felt like it weighed a thousand pounds all day. She wasn't exactly sure what contributed more to that weight, dwelling on what had happened to David or on what was coming next. Because she had no doubt, there was a storm coming. She looked around sadly at the people sitting beside her. They had no way of knowing it yet, but compared to what they were about to face, they hadn't even faced the headwinds of the storm yet. Any of them. She shook her head sadly. She was leading them directly into the abyss, and this fact made her feel terrible every waking second she was forced to bear it.

"So, Jody," Ben said, "what's the plan?" His tone of voice was friendly enough, but there was an edge to it that suggested he would fly into a rage if he did not receive the correct answer.

Jody looked at him, recoiling very slightly at the intensity of his gaze.

"There's a house," she said. "About a hundred miles south of here. In a small town called Mauvilla. It's unincorporated, hell, you can't even find it on a map. It's…" She paused, struggling for the words. "It's the house where I grew up. It's where this all started."

"Okay," Tyson said, rubbing his gooseflesh-covered arms. "And say we survive long enough to make it there. What then?"

Jody didn't answer. Tyson looked at her and saw that her eyes were closed. He thought of his little girl sleeping a few feet away and felt a muscle clench in his jaw.

"Jody…" he demanded.

"Immergo…" she whispered, and Tyson abruptly fell silent.

"Immergo…"

The word had been floating around aimlessly in her brain for the last several months, coming in and out of focus like a broken radio transmission, but it wasn't until now that she was finally able to place it. Mike jumped to his feet, his face red with anger.

"You mind explaining what the fuck…"

"Wait!" Ben said sharply, cutting Mike off.

"Immergo…I've heard that word before. In fact…" he froze, the memory slowly reaching the surface of his mind.

Jody was looking at him curiously.

"The vision I had that night. It was a foretelling, wasn't it?"

She slowly nodded. Tyson was looking back and forth between both of them, his expression somewhere between confusion and frustration.

"Someone want to tell me…"

"A few months back," Ben interrupted, "I heard that word. And there's something else." He paused, struggling for the right words. "I saw something. A dark body of water. There was no bottom. And I was drowning."

Everyone was staring at Ben now.

"I still don't understand it completely. All I know is, if we want to stop this, we have to journey into the darkness. We have to go into the abyss, where he is."

Jody glanced out at the lake, which churned lazily in the high wind, thin chunks of ice floating about on the dark surface.

"Journey into the darkness..." Jody thought, the picture slowly coming together in her mind.

She turned to Ben. "I think I understand," she said slowly. "I think I know what we have to do."

Ben glanced out at the dark lake, then back at Jody, seemingly confused.

"Would one of you please explain what's going on?"Tyson demanded.

"You all should get some rest," Jody said, standing up. "I need some time to think. I will address the entire group in the morning."

"Okay," Mike said exasperatedly, standing up and rubbing his eyes. "I'm going to bed."

"Ditto,"Tyson said, looking irritated as he stalked off to his tent.

Ben sighed heavily and stood up.

"All I can say is, I hope you know what you're doing," he said, and then he left for his own tent, leaving Jody and Maria alone by the fire.

Maria sighed and ran a hand through her curly dark hair, which was mottled with snowflakes. Jody laid a hand on her shoulder. "I know you're going through hell," she said.

"We all are," Maria replied, a little too quickly. "We all agreed to follow you. We knew it would be dangerous. We did it anyway. Because we believed in you."

"The feeling is mutual," Jody said, a sad smile crossing her face. "I believe in you, kid.You're ready."

Maria smiled. "Thank you," she whispered.

Jody looked down into the dying embers.

"Maria, this next part..." she paused, and Maria was alarmed to see tears forming in her eyes. "This next part is going to be hard. But know that I will still help guide you. I will be your strength through everything."

"You're my strength," Maria said. "You always will be, no matter what."

Jody smiled, but there was a deep sadness to it that made Maria a little uncomfortable.

"You don't need me anymore, kid," Jody said. "You're strong enough on your own." She got up from the dying fire and started to walk away towards the trees.

"Wait, where are you going?" Maria called.

Jody turned and looked at her, the same deep sadness etched in her smile.

"To think," she said. "I'll see you in the morning, kid."

Without another word, she turned and walked away into the darkness. Maria stared after her for a moment, feeling slightly puzzled. Finally, she got up and started towards her tent, wondering for a brief moment if she should've gone after Jody.

CHAPTER 109

Jody wandered through the dark trees as the snow began to fall around her, her eyes downcast, her gait slow and slightly off balance. She was distracted. That wasn't good, and she knew it. She needed to have her wits about her for this moment above any other that had happened in her entire life, but the terrible guilt of what she was doing made it impossible. She didn't want to leave them. Hell, she had no right to leave them on their own, especially at a time like this, when they were about to journey into the darkness. She kept trying to convince herself that she had gotten Maria ready for this fight as best she could, but despite her outward confidence in the young woman, it still didn't feel right. Staying was not an option of course, she knew that perfectly well, she had to at least protect them as best she could, but if they couldn't finish the fight without her...she shuddered.

Everything they'd fought and died for would be in vain. In her opinion, it was a fate worse than death. Their blood was on her hands. She'd led them all to their deaths. She shivered as a cold blast of wind struck her through the trees. She'd spent days silently praying that no one else had to die on her watch, but she was a realist. Being stabbed to death by her own father had a way of permanently stunting her optimism. And honestly, if she began to think pessimistically at a time like this, she would either flee back to the camp in terror and probably get every single one of her people killed in the process or collapse dead from exhaustion right then and there. Realistically, this battle was going to lead to more deaths, there was no denying it. So, she'd stopped praying for the death to end and instead begged that if they had to die that they at least win this fight, at least they stop that son of a bitch before he wiped them out completely.

Jody stumbled along through the blowing snow, absentmindedly kicking small drifts out of her way as she went. She was protecting them. By isolating herself, she was ensuring he would focus all his attention on her and not on them. But it was more than that. Like she'd said, she was a realist. Jody sighed heavily and brushed a few stray snowflakes from her hair. The fire was dying in the group. She had felt it happening for the last several weeks, but it hadn't begun to really scare her until after David had died. She'd overheard a conversation between Lorenzo and his wife Serena back in Blacksburg debating whether to leave the group the same night that Dylan had been killed. They'd decided to leave, a few minutes before the attack had happened. And it hadn't been the only such conversation to take place over the last few weeks. Jody sighed heavily.

Although it was an awful thought, and she hated herself for it, it was almost a good thing that Dylan had been killed. She felt a tear slide down her cheek as the thought crossed her mind. It had kept them going. As much as she hated herself for thinking so, it had kept them going. It had kept them fighting. They'd been angry. At least for a while. But David's death had been different. He hadn't been murdered like Dylan or Roy. He'd chosen to take his own life. They had all seen it.

"We can't beat him..." David's voice echoed through her mind.

His death hadn't ignited her people. It had scared the shit out of them. Now more than ever, they were thinking of running away. They were all thinking about David's declaration that they couldn't win. And they believed it. Jody could sense it. In their minds, they were all walking to their deaths. She shivered, but not from the cold in spite of the freezing wind howling through the trees in her wake. She wrapped her arms protectively around herself. Not that it did much good.

"Although," she thought bitterly, "I'm not really trying to protect myself from the cold, am I?"

"Yeah, that's right," Jody whispered, her trembling lips stuttering over the words. "I know you're here. I know why you're here. Why don't you just stop hiding in the dark and show yourself so we can get this shitshow on the road?" She glanced around through the dark trees, half expecting him to appear.

He didn't, of course. He was taunting her. It was part of his game. He savored the fear of his victims. And that's what she was right now. His victim. The thought made her shudder. She jumped at the sound of the booming voice echoing all around her through the darkness.

"Oh, Jody," the Puppeteer's cold voice boomed as if he were speaking through a megaphone. "I've been waiting a long time for this."

"Yeah?" Jody replied bitterly. "Ever since you went after my dad, I suppose. That right?"

The Puppeteer laughed, his cold cruel voice ringing in her ears.

"You see Jody, that's your problem. You've never seen me for what I really am. You talk about your father as if I forced him to attack you."

Jody could feel her hands balling into fists, her nails digging deeply into her palms.

"The truth is Jody," he went on, "I don't force my disciples to do anything. All I do is expose their true nature for what it is."

"Disciples?" Jody spat. "Is that what you call them, you sick bastard? Is that why you go after kids, because they worship you so devoutly?"

"Your father attacked you of his own free will," the Puppeteer replied, a hint of malice in his voice. "Dylan killed Anna of his own free will..."

"Don't you talk about her!" Jody screamed, cutting him off. "You killed Anna, not Dylan!"

"I am a neutral being," the Puppeteer said calmly. "I do not expose anything that was not already present to begin with. I do nothing more or less than encourage people to reveal their true selves."

"You're a liar," Jody growled. "Vessels are born empty, they are filled with either light or darkness by whatever influences are present in their life. When people are born in situations where no one will show them the light, they turn to the darkness for comfort. They come to you, and you take their suffering and use it to turn them into monsters!"

"Human beings are monsters!" the Puppeteer boomed, a hint of anger in his voice. "I am not a monster! You talk about me as if I manipulate these people! Manipulation is a concept invented by your people to excuse evil behavior! You use words like influence, manipulation, circumstances to shift the blame for people's actions on to an invisible scapegoat which so happens to be me! I am neutral, as is your god! People are their own worst enemies. They wear their hearts on their sleeves and wallow in dark memories. Do that for long enough, they become consumed by these memories, and they forget the original source of their pain. Unable to recall the source of their pain, they blame it on the world, and they lash out at anyone who comes close."

Jody stared defiantly into the darkness, her whole body trembling, completely speechless.

"Which is why your father lashed out at you. I don't suppose you know why, do you?"

Jody didn't reply.

"His father sold him," the Puppeteer whispered in her ear. "He spent most of his childhood on street corners, handing junkies their fixes. He tried to steal the money a couple of times, ended up in the hospital on both occasions. It was explained away of course. His father died when he was seventeen. Heroin overdose. He spent the next twenty years harboring his anger, hating the world. And that night, when he attacked you, was merely his anger finally coming out."

"You were there," Jody whispered, her voice trembling. "I could feel your presence for weeks. I didn't realize it at the time, but you were pushing him towards murder, tormenting him with suppressed memories of childhood suffering."

"As I said," boomed the Puppeteer, "I don't push people to do anything. I was merely watching, wondering if he would actually commit the deed. And I was right. Your father is an evil son of a bitch, just like the rest of them."

There was silence for a moment.

"Why do you think I'm here?" the Puppeteer asked. "I am on a mission to exterminate the last survivors of a species that has destroyed itself. To cleanse the universe of the putrid sick waste that is the human race. Is that so wrong?"

"You're here for your own amusement," Jody spat angrily. "And you caused all of this."

The Puppeteer, concealed a few feet away in the shadows, grinned and shook his head, chuckling under his breath. Jody looked up as he stepped out of the shadows and into the faint moonlight filtering through the canopy, smiling predatorily at Jody with his abnormally sharp canine teeth.

"Jody, Jody, Jody," the Puppeteer said patronizingly, shaking his head. "Your people launched the warheads that caused all of this destruction, whether on orders, or indirectly through their orders. The human race caused their own extinction."

Jody didn't back down. She stood firm, staring the Puppeteer down defiantly as he slowly approached.

"You seem to be under the impression that you are abandoning your people," he said matter of factly.

"Well, allow me to correct that notion. Your people abandoned the light you hold so dear a very long time ago. They abandoned your god and set themselves on a dark and destructive path through their own obsessive self-indulgence. This candle flame you treasure so much went out a long time ago." The Puppeteer marched up to her so that there was no more than a single foot separating them. "It's true what you told Maria," he said. "Fire can lead to growth and life." He shook his head. "But unfortunately, there is no fire left in this world. Your people smothered it for their own personal gain. And now as you can see," he said, gesturing into the empty dark night, "the destructive and selfish path they have taken has finally destroyed them."

Jody continued to glare defiantly into the Puppeteer's lifeless eyes, but she could feel her entire body trembling violently with the effort of keeping herself standing upright.

"Human nature," he said matter of factly. "That's what killed you that night. Not me. I merely watched as your father stabbed you over and over again like a piece of meat until you finally lay still."

The scene from that night flashed through her mind. Seeing her father through the thin slat in the closet door, the bloody meat cleaver clutched in his hand. Her scream as he charged. The door swinging open. The fiery explosions of pain as the knife was driven into her again and again and again. Finally, the strange, listless emptiness as her spirit departed her body for good. As she slowly rose into the air, she saw her father standing over her, smiling with triumph. She saw his eyes. Light hazel. Human eyes. Without even realizing it, Jody had sunk to her knees in the snow, her expression despondent.

"You were right," she whispered. "You were right all along. He attacked me of his own free will." She looked up into his face.

His grin widened, his soulless eyes dancing with a strange light. She could feel bitter tears forming in her eyes.

"We are evil," she whispered. "We're sick and twisted sons of bitches, and we destroyed our own species because of greed." She hung her head, tears spilling down her face and into the snow. "I'm tired," she whispered, shaking her head in defeat. "I tried to save them, but they were so ungrateful. They tried to leave me. The only thing that kept them around was telling them that they'd die anyway. The truth is they don't give a shit about one another."

"They don't give a shit about me. They only want to save their own skin. Hell, they'll probably wake up tomorrow and see that I'm gone, shrug, and go their separate ways. I suppose you'll pick them off one by one on your own time, right?"

The Puppeteer didn't need to answer. His grin was all the response Jody needed.

"Good," Jody said exasperatedly. "Because I'm done being a pawn in this game. I've had enough of trying to help people who neither want it nor deserve it. You can kill them all if you want to, because I don't care." She looked up into the Puppeteer's face, her face bright red and streaked with tears. "Go ahead," she whispered, her voice trembling. "Take me. Do it. I have nothing to live for anymore."

The Puppeteer's grin faded.

"As you wish," he whispered. He closed his eyes, clasping his hands together just above his navel. He began to chant a soft ritual under his breath.

His face began to change. The eyes collapsed flat against the skull and vanished, the eye sockets pushing out to fill the gap. The forehead and cheeks lengthened and stretched to create a perfectly flat surface. The ears shriveled up, the tissue disappearing into the ear canals, which were quickly filled seamlessly with cartilage and bone. The chin shrunk and folded in line with the cheeks to create a smooth surface. The nose receded as if the bone were retreating into a hole in the skull. The lips shriveled up and retreated into the mouth, which was filled with more tissue, until Jody was staring at a perfectly smooth oval of a head resting beneath the Puppeteer's tall black top hat.

Then the skull itself began to retreat, caving in on itself to form a shallow bowl at first, then retreating deeper and deeper until Jody was staring at a bottomless pit, the utter darkness where the face had once been leading into the infinite abyss beyond. The place where the Puppeteer dwelled. The place her people would soon find themselves. Jody felt herself falling forward. She saw the dark hole that was the Puppeteer's face rising up to meet her. She reached out her arms, smiling even through her tears, embracing the darkness as it rose up to swallow her whole.

"Thank you," she whispered as the world around her faded to black. "Thank you."

And then everything was gone.

CHAPTER 110

Maria lay awake most of the night. The hour or so of sleep she managed to steal was haunted by disturbing dreams of her drowning in a dark underground lake. She woke up drenched in an icy sweat after each iteration. She was trembling in her sleeping bag by the time the sun began to rise over the treetops, and not entirely from the cold night air that easily penetrated the thin canvas either. It would've been a relief getting out of bed for Maria that morning, if she weren't terrified of what she was about to find outside. The camp was completely silent as she strolled past the small semicircle of tents. Her shoes crunched over the frost hardened oak leaves littering the snow-covered ground. The snow, which came up around her ankles, quickly soaked through her shoes and socks. Maria found that she didn't care in the slightest as she nervously approached the edge of the forest.

A terrible feeling of dread weighed her down as if her blood had turned to lead. She wanted to run as fast as she could in the opposite direction. But she couldn't. She had to see for herself what had happened. As she walked into the trees, she glanced back over her shoulder. To her surprise, she saw the others following behind her. Ben and Mike led the group. The others, Grace, Tyson, Marianne, Laura, Jason, and Lorenzo, Jennifer, and Serena followed at their heels. It made her feel a tiny bit better to know they had her back.

"I love you..." Jody's voice whispered in her ear as she struggled on through the deep snow.

"I love you too," Maria whispered, her voice shaking a little from the cold.

The sun had risen into full view now, the sunlight filtering through the trees dimly lighting the path in front of them. Maria didn't need any directions, nor did any of the others. Maria followed the faint sound of Jody's voice whispering to her through the trees. The others followed Maria, none of them needing to ask what this was about. They had all noticed by now, even the children, that Jody was not among their number. That was all the answer they needed.

Maria stumbled and fell to her knees in the deep snow, all the strength gone from her body. Her vision narrowed to a pinprick and for a second, she was sure she was going to faint. Ben and Mike hurried to her side when she fell.

"You alright?" Ben asked, kneeling down beside her.

Maria shook her head.

"Look up," she whispered. "All of you, look up."

They all looked up at the tree in front of them in unison. Ben heard a collective gasp from behind him. Jennifer screamed. The lifeless body of Jody Razitsky hung from a rope about twenty feet off the ground, the noose still tied firmly around her neck, her complexion coal black from asphyxiation. A small wooden sign, affixed to the rope, hung just above Jody's head. Engraved in the wood was a single word: "Traitor." Serena, who had begun to cry, flung her arms around Jennifer, both women sobbing uncontrollably onto each other's shoulders.

Marianne threw herself into her father's arms, tears forming in her ears.

"Why'd she do it?" Marianne whispered. "Daddy, why'd she do it?"

"I don't know, baby," Tyson whispered, struggling not to cry himself. "I don't know."

Ben was shaking his head sadly.

"No, no, no," he kept muttering under his breath, as if trying to convince himself the scene in front of him wasn't real.

Mike was staring open mouthed at the body swaying back and forth in the breeze, completely speechless.

"You don't need me anymore, kid…you're strong enough on your own…" The words sounded absurd to Maria now.

Of course she needed Jody. She couldn't do this alone. The idea of facing him, of walking into the abyss on her own without Jody, sounded insane even in her own head.

"How could she leave me?" Maria whispered, her voice shaking. "How could she do that?"

Ben continued to shake his head wordlessly, unable to think of anything to say.

"Traitor…it's almost an accurate moniker," Maria thought bitterly. "She betrayed us. She left us after we followed her all the way here, after we sacrificed everything for her…"

"I love you…" The words echoed in her brain again.

Maria shook her head, tears of frustration forming in her eyes. It didn't make any sense.

"It doesn't make sense," Maria choked out. "Why would she do it? She led us all the way here just to commit suicide?"

Ben continued to shake his head wordlessly. Mike had stormed off into the trees, unable to bear the sight of Jody's body for another second. Maria raised her eyes to the noose holding Jody's neck. Something suddenly felt very wrong, even discounting the fact that Jody had apparently hung herself twenty feet off the ground when plenty of much lower and more accessible limbs, even on this particular tree, existed. And then there was the sign.

"Traitor…"

"According to who…"

The thought startled even Maria.

"According to who…"

He had made it, of course. The Puppeteer. If he was trying to stop them, he wouldn't've missed the opportunity to erode their will to fight to the maximum extent possible.

But if he was here, suppose he had…Maria gasped audibly. Ben gave her a questioning look. Maria held up a hand to silence him as he opened his mouth to speak, staring intently up at the rope holding Jody. She closed her eyes, concentrating all her energy on a single spot on the rope. She could feel the heat rising inside of her, filling her chest like a helium balloon. She directed the heat outward, the invisible warm air current shooting high into the air to meet its target. Ben felt the warm breeze rush past him as it exited Maria's body. He looked up and saw bright orange flames gnawing hungrily at the thick woven threads of the rope holding Jody, which was already starting to fray. A few seconds later, the rope severed entirely, sending Jody plummeting. She landed hard on the snow-covered ground, her body half buried in the thick white powder. Maria sprinted over to her and began uncovering her lifeless body from the snow. Ben kneeled down beside her and began throwing snow aside until they had completely uncovered her. The rest of the group approached nervously behind Maria and Ben. A moment later, Mike joined them, his face still slightly red with anger.

Maria, grasping the sides of Jody's head with both hands, raised Jody's face to meet her own. They were so close that their foreheads touched.

"Jody, I'm here. It's Maria," Maria whispered. "Can you hear me?"

No response.

"Jody," Maria whispered, "I need to know what happened here. Can you tell us who did this to you?"

At first, Maria heard nothing. She hung her head, frustrated with herself, when Jody's voice whispered in her ear.

"Doesn't matter…"

The voice startled Maria so badly she nearly jumped back in fright. It echoed through the trees around them as if Jody were speaking through a megaphone.

"You…you have to go on."

"Jody," Maria whispered miserably. "You sound so weak…"

"Stop worrying about me, damnit," the voice argued back.

"I am worried about you," Maria whispered, tears forming in her eyes. "Jody, I can't lose you, you're all I have now…"

"No," the voice whispered. "No, I'm not. Look around."

Maria obeyed. The faces surrounding her looked empty and broken but simply seeing them there made her feel a little better. They had stayed, they had pushed on, they had made every terrible sacrifice and done so willingly…Maria smiled.

"I'm not alone," she whispered. "Not when I have all of you."

Marianne, peering out a gap in her father's arms, smiled wanly at Maria. Somehow, Maria could tell that Jody was smiling.

"Listen to me, kid," Jody whispered. "You have to stop this. You have to go on."

Maria nodded, suddenly filled with determination.

"I know," she said. "Oh Jody, I'm so sorry…"

"Don't be sorry," Jody whispered, and it suddenly dawned on Maria that only she could hear Jody speak now. "I'll always be with you, kid, no matter what. You are the child I never had."

Maria began to sob at these words, her face flooding with uncontrollable tears.

"Even after I'm gone, you'll continue this fight. Be the candle flame for these people. Make sure the world never follows this destructive path again."

"I will," Maria choked out. "I will, always. Jody…" Maria kissed her forehead. "I love you."

"I love you too, kid." And then she was silent. Maria, wiping her eyes, gently lay Jody down in the snow. She reached out with a trembling hand and slid Jody's eyelids closed.

"She could almost be sleeping," Maria thought as she stood up. She surveyed Jody's body with a mixture of deep sorrow and admiration. Without another word, she turned on her heel and stormed back towards the camp site, her expression a mask of steely determination.

The others remained behind for a moment, holding a silent vigil for their lost leader. Mike and Tyson hoisted Jody's body onto their shoulders. Then they turned and silently followed Maria, carrying Jody between them, the others following in their wake.

CHAPTER 111

The black Chevrolet traveled silently down the lonely stretch of narrow road, Martin's red pickup in tow. It was around dusk, and the light was rapidly fading around them. The gnarled, twisted dead trees surrounding them seemed to press in on them as the fiery orange sun slipped beneath the horizon, and darkness fell. The snow had begun to fall lightly earlier in the day, and now, as darkness began to fall, it was blowing down on them sideways in droves, adding to the overall tension of the occupants of the small, two-car caravan. Lorenzo sat in the driver's seat of the Chevrolet, squinting hard to see the road through the growing darkness and blowing snow outside the windshield. Kaden was lying asleep in the back seat between Serena and Laura, his head lying in Serena's lap. Serena held him close to her, gently stroking his hair.

Maria, who had been staring silently out the passenger's side window for most of the day, had noticed something odd over the last few hours: the farther they traveled south, the fewer abandoned vehicles they saw by the roadside and clogging the roadway. It had started when they'd left Birmingham, and they had gradually thinned out more and more until the roadway they were traveling on now, which was completely devoid of any vehicles. A rational person might've chalked this up to the fact that they were now in the deep south, and traveling on mostly back roads where fewer people would likely have fled following the attacks. But nothing they'd experienced in the last few months had been rational in the slightest.

The closer they got to Mauvilla, the worse the leaden pit of uneasiness that had formed in Maria's stomach became. He knew they were coming. She could feel it. And he had no intention of stopping them anymore. That's why they saw fewer and fewer vehicles the closer they came to the house. He was clearing the path for them. He wanted them to come. Somehow, this terrified her more than anything else. The weather even seemed to be cooperating. As she watched, the snowfall became lighter and Lorenzo, with assistance from the headlights, was able to resume his normal speed. Maria, watching through the window, silently pleaded for the snow to pick up again. For her, the house in Mauvilla loomed in front of her like a hungry monster lurking in the shadows, waiting for her to get close enough to spring. He was waiting there, ready...

"How are you holding up, kid?"

The question from Lorenzo startled her so badly she nearly jumped up in fright.

"You okay?" he asked, sounding like a concerned parent.

Maria shook her head sadly and went back to staring out the window. Lorenzo sighed and turned back to the road.

There was silence for a few minutes.

"I know how it feels," Lorenzo said finally. "I know it might not seem like it right now. I've worked in medicine for half my life. I've had kids die in my arms while their parents watch. I've had doctors tell me there's nothing more we can do. I've had to explain to patients that they have less than a month to live."

Maria said nothing.

"Until a few months ago, I thought the world was just a fucked-up place where fucked up things happen, and it wasn't anybody's fault."

Maria remained silent.

"But that's not true, is it? If it's true what Jody said, and there's a monster out there causing all of this destruction, then maybe I can tell the families of those victims that God didn't take their baby to punish them. He did for his own amusement. I suppose there's an irony in that, isn't there?"

"Wouldn't make them feel any better though," Maria said without looking away from the window. "I think it would just scare them."

Lorenzo nodded slowly.

"I mean, what good is it knowing the person's motive for killing your child?" Maria went on. "It doesn't bring anyone back... it doesn't give you any closure. All it does is burn into your brain that people are fucking pieces of shit."

Lorenzo was silent for a moment.

"Do you believe that?" he asked. "That people are inherently evil?"

Maria was silent for a moment.

"Honestly," Maria said, "I'm not sure what I believe anymore. I've lost everyone I've ever loved in the last several months. I watched an eleven-year-old kid get thrown out a window because he refused to kill me. I watched my dad commit suicide because he couldn't stand the thought of living in this fucked up world anymore. I watched the people in power destroy civilization over a proximity war!" Maria sighed heavily. "I never wanted to believe people are evil," she whispered, her voice trembling. "But honestly, after everything I've watched them do to each other, I honestly don't see how I can't. Can you blame me?"

Lorenzo shook his head.

"Honestly, I guess I can't," he replied. "Not after what happened to your dad."

Maria shook her head, resting her face in her hands. Her entire body was shaking visibly.

Lorenzo remained silent as they pulled onto an exit ramp heading off to their right.

"I was gonna leave," he said.

Now Maria looked up at him, her expression completely taken aback.

"Me and Serena. The night after Roy was killed. I was angry. Serena was crying the whole time. We had a huge fight about it but in the end we both agreed. We were going to go through with it."

"Why didn't you?" Maria asked.

"Because I couldn't live with myself," Lorenzo replied. "I couldn't stand the idea of walking away after what happened to Roy, and Alison, and Marianne..." He paused briefly. "She was dead, Maria. Jody brought her back."

Maria stared at Lorenzo, looking startled.

"You don't know that..."

"Yes, I do," Lorenzo said firmly. "And you do too. She was gone. Jody brought her back to life. If there was ever a person I'd follow into hell, it was her. She trusted you, Maria. She trusted you to see this through."

Maria shook her head sadly.

"I'm sorry," she said. "I really am, but I don't know if I can..."

"Bullshit," Lorenzo said sharply, cutting her off.

Maria looked startled.

"Look kid," he went on. "I don't if I believe that there's a monster out there that manipulates people into doing bad things, and I don't know if you do either. But right now, belief is the last thing that matters. The only way we win this war is if we fight together, that's what you said. And you were right."

Maria was silent for a moment.

"You're wrong about one thing," Maria said. "Belief is the only thing that matters right now, and honestly, I'm losing faith that we can win this war. I can't lead you into this fight not knowing if any of us will come out the other side. I've cost you too much already. I'm sorry."

They sat in silence for several moments while the Chevrolet moved smoothly along the two-lane road surrounded by twisted, dead husks of oak trees, the brick red pickup in tow. A bright gibbous moon had risen overhead.

"Your dad," Lorenzo said. "I spoke to him earlier in the day the same night he died. He was perfectly fine. No sign of depression, let alone suicidal ideation. Something happened."

Maria said nothing, privately wishing Lorenzo would drop the subject.

"Do you remember what Jody said right before he jumped?"

Maria shook her head, refusing to meet Lorenzo's eyes.

"She asked him what the monster showed him. The monster did this, Maria."

"Don't you think I know that?" Maria burst out, tears suddenly erupting from her eyes. "Don't you think I know the bastard killed my dad, and Roy, and my mom, and Tyson's wife, and the other billions of people who died in those attacks! Don't you think I fucking know that!"

She buried her face in her hands, sobbing uncontrollably. Lorenzo shook his head sadly.

"All those deaths," he said dejectedly. "What do they mean?"

Maria looked up at him, her face streaked with tears.

"They mean our lives never belonged to us. They always belonged to him. He is the end all be all, Maria. We all live or die based on his whims. He wanted Roy to die to scare us, so he did." Lorenzo sighed. "He wanted your dad to die to break us, so he did."

"The all-seeing eye," Maria whispered, wiping her eyes. She sighed heavily. "Lorenzo," she said nervously. "He knows we're coming. He wants us to come. He's...he's ready for battle."

Lorenzo sighed and ran a hand through his thick graying hair.

"He'd better be ready," Lorenzo said stolidly, turning to Maria, "because in all my life, I've never been on any team that I'd rather go into battle with than the one I'm on right now." A small smile crossed his lips.

After a moment, Maria smiled too, but there was a weariness to it that made Lorenzo wonder, if only for a second, if they really stood a chance.

CHAPTER 112

They drove in silence for a long time after that. Laura had woken up, but she didn't seem to be any more inclined to talk than Lorenzo or Maria was. She stared pensively out the window at the steadily falling snow and the forest of bare, dead oak trees dwarfing the roadway on either side, but Maria could see the pain in her eyes. She had no doubt who Laura was thinking about. Maria knew how she felt. In the short time she'd known Roy, she'd been attracted to his maturity, strength, and force of character. He was a good man, and a good husband. What happened to him hadn't merely been wrong, it had been unnatural. It reminded her of a Shakespeare play she'd read for history class where the king's horses ran wild and resorted to cannibalism after their master was murdered, as if the natural order of the world itself had been disturbed by Roy's passing.

A road sign announced they were approaching General WK Wilson Jr. Bridge. Maria stared out at the dark water beneath the bridge, feeling a tiny bit dizzy at the sight of the long drop into the water. The black surface of the river, which was only partially frozen despite the snow the last several days, flowed aggressively south, breaking apart thin sheets of ice in its wake. Maria closed her eyes. It was strangely calming to listen to the sound of the ice being broken apart by the flowing river. She could've almost fallen asleep, the scene around her was so peaceful…and suddenly, she was no longer sitting in the passenger seat beside Roy. The ground was gone, the black waves cresting up over her head, threatening to drown her with each passing. She screamed for help, but the water stretched endlessly in all directions. She was all alone.

She fought to keep her head above water as the crest of a wave passed over her. Startled, Maria swallowed a mouthful of lake water, the sudden intake blocking her nose and mouth, suffocating her. Maria fought her way to the surface, gagging and choking. She could feel the strength leaving her limbs, the weight of her clothes dragging her under the surface. Her movements grew weaker. She closed her eyes as darkness surrounded her, embracing her fate. It was so soothing to be free of the heavy burden she'd been carrying around for the last several weeks.

"Maria…" the cold voice hissed.

It was him. A scream erupted from her throat as the abyss rose up to meet her from the lake bottom, swallowing her whole, her screams muffled by the suffocating darkness…

Maria's eyes shot open. Her entire body was soaked with cold sweat. Her eyes darted around in fear, sure she would see him looming over her, hungrily watching as he prepared to devour her…Then she saw the thin line of trees surrounding them on either side, the bright moon hanging overhead, the bridge already fading into the distance.

337

"I'm back in the car," she whispered, the breath she'd been holding erupting in a long rush. "Jesus, I'm back in the car, it was just a dream."

But it hadn't been a dream. Maria had experienced lucid dreams a handful of times in her life, and none of them had been as real as what she'd just experienced. She'd been physically in that place in a way no dream could possibly replicate. It had been real.

"You okay?" came Jason's voice from beside her.

Maria turned. His brow was furrowed with worry.

"You were talking in your sleep. You sounded scared."

Maria shook her head.

"I'm okay," she said, a little too quickly. "Bad dream."

Jason nodded, not wanting to push the subject any further. They drove in silence through the dark woods for another couple of minutes. Maria saw a sign announcing they were approaching the city of Creola, and realized they were getting very close. Jody had mentioned having a childhood friend from Creola, and that they'd gone to school together.

"Maria," came a sleepy voice from the backseat.

Maria glanced in the rearview mirror. Kaden was sitting up, rubbing the sleep from his eyes.

"We need to think about what we're going to do when we reach the house."

"That's not a bad idea," Jason added. "What's the plan?"

Maria thought for a moment, choosing her words carefully.

"I think I know what we have to do," she said. "But I need a night to think it over. When we get to the house, you should all get some rest. I'll talk to you in the morning."

Jason, who didn't look especially satisfied with this answer, nevertheless nodded and turned back to the road. Maria returned her gaze to the passenger side window, her expression one of deep contemplation. A picture was beginning to form in her mind, although she was already dreading what she would see when it was completed. About ten minutes later, Jason slowed the Chevrolet down as they approached the two-story oak wood cabin propped up in the middle of a thin grove of trees. Maria felt a leaden ball of anxiety form in her stomach as they approached the house.

"Ladies and gentlemen," she whispered under her breath. "Welcome to the final act of the greatest show on Earth."

CHAPTER 113

Maria didn't sleep that night. She paced restlessly back and forth across the house, listening intently outside every occupied bedroom door she passed for any signs of danger. In spite of the fact that she'd hadn't slept for longer than a few minutes in the last twenty-four hours, Maria felt more awake than she had at any point in the last several months, as if she'd been injected with a full hypodermic needle of adrenaline. Between the pounding of her heart, the blood rushing to her head, and the strange feeling she possessed the strength to lift the entire house above her head if she wanted to, she certainly was feeling its effects. A grim determination had settled over Maria. If he came back tonight, if he made one last ditch effort to stop them from carrying out the ritual, she would be ready for him.

While she was pacing through the house, the thought of the ritual clouded her mind. The picture was becoming clearer by the minute... and the clearer it became to her, the more scared she had become. It sounded completely insane, but then again, with some of the things she'd seen over the last several months, it was hardly the craziest thing she'd experienced even during that short time.

"Immergo..." Maria whispered. Just the sound of the word was enough to make her shudder violently. "I don't know," she thought. "I don't know if I can ask them in good conscience to make such a sacrifice."

But finally, the picture was becoming crystal clear for her. Maria sighed heavily as she walked up the stairs to the second-floor landing. They'd already sacrificed too much. If they turned back now, when they were already so close, it would all be for nothing. And that was worse than the alternative.

She couldn't let them down. Not after they'd trusted her. Not after they'd already followed her all this way.

"And the children?" she asked aloud, her voice rising slightly.

It was a question she'd been dreading asking. The answer came almost instantly.

"You can give them the choice," Jody's voice whispered in her ear. "But their parents, knowing what will happen to them if they stay behind, will want to be with them until the end."

Maria sighed and nodded.

"I know," she whispered, pausing outside of the bedroom door where Tyson and Marianne were sleeping to listen.

Nothing. It was dead quiet in the room. In fact, the whole house seemed to be strangely silent. Maria smiled wanly.

"I promise, I'll see this through till the end. Thank you for everything, Jody."

Somewhere far off, she could almost sense her mother, father, and big sister watching, smiling sadly down at her.

CHAPTER 114

Ben walked into the living room early the next morning, rubbing the sleep from his eyes, to find Maria sitting in a stuffed armchair in front of the fireplace, her expression unreadable.

"Hey," Ben said, sitting down in the matching armchair next to Maria.

Maria didn't look up.

"Good idea starting the fire," Ben said, glancing out the living room window, where the light snowfall from the previous night had developed into a full-blown whiteout.

They could hear the high winds howling in the rafters of the old house. It hadn't occurred to Ben until now that the house, in spite of being abandoned for the better part of a decade and a half, was in remarkably good shape, displaying no signs of rotting in the wooden floorboards or walls. The roof was in near perfect shape, sporting no leaks, and every window in the house was intact. It was also extremely clean inside. The bathroom looked as though it had been cleaned top to bottom just days ago. The books and kitchenware were tucked away neatly in the cabinets.

There was a considerable amount of bottled water and canned food stored away in the cabinets. He hadn't even noticed any dust bunnies lurking in the corners. It was almost as if someone had been expecting them to show up. The thought made his arms break out in gooseflesh.

"You know," Ben said, turning to Maria, "I wonder who's been keeping this house in shape ever since it was abandoned. What do you think?"

Maria shook her head, not turning her gaze away from the rippling flames in the fireplace.

"I don't think anyone's been in this house in a long time," Maria said matter of factly. "But you're right, someone has been maintaining it." She glanced around the living room, her gaze coming to rest on a dark corner sporting an old dusty reading lamp.

"Can you feel it?" she asked.

"Feel what?" Ben asked, although he noticed the temperature in the room had fallen considerably despite the warmth from the fire.

"Him," Maria said. "He's been here. Hell, he's probably here watching us right now. Guess he thought he'd clean the place up for us before we jump into the abyss," she finished bitterly.

There was silence for a moment.

"Is that what we're doing then?" Ben asked nervously. "Jumping into the abyss?"

Maria hesitated for a moment before nodding, unable to look Ben in the eye as she did so.

CHAPTER 115

O ver the next few minutes, the others began to wake up and file into the living room, gathering around the fireplace, many of them clothed in long, thick sweaters, reaching their hands out to warm them by the fire. It occurred to Maria that they hadn't been carrying the clothes they were wearing the day before.

"Guess he left us clothes too," Maria thought bitterly. "Really put together a goddamned welcoming committee, didn't you?"

It was possible those clothes had been sitting in the drawers for fifteen years or longer, but Maria didn't care. They wouldn't have been there if he hadn't made it so. Just to show he still had control of the situation, just to show that their lives weren't, nor had they ever been, their own. It was so ridiculous that it almost made Maria laugh out loud.

"Okay Maria," Ben said, his chin resting on his hands, "we've trusted you, we've followed you to this place, we've done everything you've asked. We've held up our end of the deal. Now it's time for you to hold up yours. What do we need to do to end this?"

Maria didn't answer for a moment, dreading what she was about to say.

"First," she said, "when the snow lets up, we need to bury Jody. Properly. We owe her that much."

Tyson nodded, thinking about the young woman's lifeless body still lying in the trunk of David's Chevrolet.

"Okay," he said. "I promise we'll bury her. But what then?"

Maria hesitated again. She suddenly desperately wanted to be anywhere else but that room, standing in front of these good people anxiously awaiting her great words of wisdom that would save them from their inevitable deaths. Words she didn't have. She felt a deep sense of helplessness, like a toddler who had lost their mother at the zoo. She wanted to vanish on the spot. Maria took a deep breath and sighed heavily.

"The ritual," she said hollowly, her eyes downcast. "We have to go through the ritual of Immergo. All of us. Together."

They all stared silently at Maria, none of them daring to speak. Maria sighed heavily again, hating herself both for what she had already said, and for what she was about to say.

"There's a creek about a mile from here," she said. "We'll hike there at sunset."

"Won't it be frozen?" Lorenzo interjected.

Maria shook her head.

"I can melt the ice," she said matter of factly.

"You want us to bathe in a frozen river?" Mike asked, looking confused. Maria shook her head.

"No, not bathe," she said, her voice shaking. "Drown. Together."

The room went completely silent. Several mouths fell open in shock. From somewhere behind her, Maria heard Jennifer choke back a sob.

"Jesus," Ben whispered, standing up and hurrying over to his distraught wife. "Jesus..."

Several of the men were glowering at her. Maria would've given anything to vanish on the spot.

"All this time, I trusted you," Tyson spat angrily, clutching Marianne's hand tightly. "All this time, I thought you had a plan." He started for the front door, pulling Marianne along with him. "I'm leaving," he said bluntly, "and anyone who values their lives will join me."

Lorenzo started after him, his wife Serena in tow. Jennifer followed them, carrying her daughter Grace in her arms. Ben glanced from his wife and daughter to Maria and back again, seemingly unsure what he should do.

"Wait!" Jason shouted, causing everyone to pause. "You're leaving? After everything we've been through?"

"Easy for you to say," Tyson said, his face red with anger. "You haven't lost your wife because of these people!" he shouted, shoving his index finger at Maria. "You haven't almost lost your little girl to these people!"

He set Marianne down and approached Jason, looking like he was about to swing at him. Jason didn't flinch, his expression stony.

"If you don't value your life, that's your business, but I have a child to think about," Tyson spat. "Goodbye." He turned on his heel and stormed towards the front door.

"Your wife," Ben said, getting to his feet. "Her name was Alison, right?"

Tyson paused with his hand on the doorknob. "How did she die?" Tyson was silent for a moment.

"Car accident," he said matter of factly.

"Car accident?" Ben repeated, sounding somewhat disbelieving. Tyson shook his head.

"Military attacked us," he said. "Apache helicopter fired on us, forced us off the road. The car rolled and she...she got her arm pinned beneath it. We...we had to leave her behind."

Marianne was staring at her father, her great brown eyes watering with tears. It was the first time she'd heard him speak about her mother's death.

"And you think Maria and Jody were responsible for that attack?" Ben asked.

Tyson shook his head.

"It doesn't matter," he said. "I made a mistake getting mixed up in all this." He turned to Maria, who was looking at him anxiously. "I'm sorry, kid," he said. "I really am. I know you're not responsible for Alison's death, and I'm grateful for what Jody did for Marianne. But I can't follow you down this road anymore. I still have my family to think about." He took Marianne's hand and started towards the door.

Marianne yanked her hand out of his grip.

"Marianne…" he said.

"Daddy, listen to me," she said, so firmly that Tyson looked completely taken aback.

"Jody saved my life. She brought me back to you."

"I know honey," Tyson said placatingly. "I know she did, but…"

"I'm sorry about mom," Marianne went on. "I miss her too. But we can't walk out on her now, not after everything she's done for us."

Tyson seemed to be at a loss for words.

"Daddy, do you know why Jody committed suicide?"

Tyson opened his mouth to reply, then closed it again.

"She did it to protect us," she went on. "She did it so we could get here. She sacrificed herself to save us, so that no one else had to die. How is it fair for us to leave her now?" She turned to the others, who recoiled at her withering gaze. "How could any of you leave her?" she demanded, her voice rising steadily. "She saved all of us, she died trying to protect us, and now you're going to walk out on her when she needs us the most? Don't you even want to save her?"

No one said a word. They were all staring at Marianne as if she had sprouted a second head. Marianne turned to her father, her expression grim.

"Daddy, the only way we'll ever see mommy again is if we stay and fight. I think we…" She paused, struggling for the words. "Daddy, I think if we confront him, we can get mommy back. If we fight, I think we can save her. Don't you want that?"

Tyson, his expression softening, wrapped Marianne into a tight hug.

"Of course I do, baby," he whispered. "Of course I want mommy back. But I don't know if…" He trailed off.

Maria got to her feet.

"She's right," Maria said firmly, holding her head high for the first time in what felt like years. "We can save her. We can save all of them, if we stand together. We are the candle flame for this world. Where there is fire, there is life."

Everyone looked at Maria, their expressions masked with grim determination.

"Where there is fire, there is life," they all chanted in unison.

Maria smiled. Behind her, the fire crackled in the brick fireplace, casting strange shadows on all of their faces. It seemed to burn brighter at the sound of their voices.

"Finally," Maria whispered. "The fire has been ignited. Thanks Jody."

CHAPTER 116

"Y ou okay, kid?" Ben asked.

They were standing in a semicircle in the snow-covered front yard. The blizzard had let up earlier in the day and now, as the sun was beginning its descent towards the horizon in the distance, only the occasional light dusting of snow fell from the rapidly darkening sky. The open grave that Mike and Tyson had dug earlier in the day with a pair of shovels they'd unearthed in the storeroom loomed in front of them. From somewhere behind them, Jason and Mike were busy removing Jody's body from the trunk of the Chevrolet. Maria shook her head, tears coming to her eyes.

"I loved her," Maria whispered. "I really did. Ever since mom died, I just..." she trailed off.

"I've been there before," Ben said. "Or at least, I almost was. I thought I'd lost my brother right after this whole thing started."

He shot a glance back at Mike, who, with help from Jason, had managed to extract Jody's body from the trunk of the Chevrolet and was now slowly approaching the open grave, his head hung.

"He got shot trying to protect an old man that was killed by one of the soldiers blocking the street." Ben sighed. "I thought he was gone." He looked at Maria, whose tear-stained eyes were downcast. "It might not seem like much, kid, but even when people are gone, we don't have to lose them. Remember what she stood for, what she fought for, what she lived for, and she'll always be a part of you."

Maria nodded, wiping her eyes. She didn't look up at Ben, but he thought he saw a sad smile cross her lips out of the corner of his eye. Maria looked up as Mike and Jason approached, carrying Jody's body between them. Maria realized that for once, she was grateful for the cold. The body had been preserved remarkably well. Maria could almost see the ghost of a smile crossing Jody's beautiful face. The sight of it made her want to cry.

The crowd standing around the grave parted, allowing Mike and Jason to pass through with the body. Their expressions were cold and grim, matching Maria's mood perfectly. As much as she hated herself for admitting it, she couldn't afford to shed any tears for Jody. Not when she knew what was coming next. Judging by the looks on the faces around her, the rest of the group felt the same way. In the distance, the sun was already beginning to set beneath the horizon. Strange shadows were cast on the ground around them in the growing darkness as Jason and Mike kneeled down beside the open grave. Together, they gently lowered Jody's lifeless body into the open grave. From somewhere behind her, Maria could hear several of the women crying. Ben was staring into the open grave, his expression mask-like. Maria wanted to cry, she wanted to run away and hide, but she couldn't. Not when there was still work to be done.

She walked wordlessly over to the open grave, picked up one of the two shovels lying beside the grave. Ben walked up beside her.

"Maria, you don't have to do this…"

"Yes, I do," Maria said sharply without looking up, burying the shovel blade in the large pile of dirt standing at the edge of the hole and tossing it on top of the body.

Ben sighed and bent down to pick up the other shovel. The rest of the group stood around them, watching silently as the pair of them slowly reburied the lifeless body of Jody Razitsky, the woman who had saved their lives, the woman who had sacrificed herself to protect them, the woman who would not be there with them as they traveled into the abyss. They tried not to think about this as they watched Ben and Maria work. They were all dreading the task that they knew was soon coming. About an hour later, Maria finally stood up, wiping sweat from her brow. Ben threw his shovel aside, surveying their handiwork.

"It's done," he said.

"No," Maria said. "It's not done just yet." She walked to the edge of the tree line and returned holding a flat rock. She got on her knees beside the grave and pawed out a small clump of dirt with her hands. She placed the rock in the hole and smoothed the dirt out around it.

The group watched in awe as Maria closed her eyes, her right hand outstretched. They collectively gasped as a small blue flash of fire erupted from the rock.

"Look at it," Serena whispered.

The rock, which was still smoking slightly, was now engraved with what looked like a large bird with magnificent plumage erupting from its wings and tail.

"It's a phoenix," Ben whispered.

Maria nodded.

"It's beautiful," Serena said softly.

"It's the least she deserved," Maria said, turning back towards the house.

"We should leave soon," she said, approaching the front door. "The sun's already setting."

She saw several people exchange nervous looks. Ben's expression, however, was almost serene.

"Well," he said, "I guess if we're gonna die, we might as well enjoy ourselves a little, right?" He removed his cigarette lighter, along with a pack of Marlboros, from his breast pocket, both of which he began to pass around. "Been saving these for a special occasion," he said. "Guess this is as good a time as any."

"I thought you'd given up smoking years ago," Jennifer said, declining the offer from Mike as he held out the pack to her, a cigarette clutched firmly between his teeth. She sighed.

"But I suppose if the world is ending anyway, what harm can it do?" She took the pack and the lighter from Serena and lit up, choking a little as the smoke hit her lungs. "Wow," she gasped. "Been a long time since I've had a good nicotine high!"

Ben laughed. Tyson lit his own cigarette and held out the pack to Maria. Maria shook her head.

"I...I just need to be alone for a little while," she muttered. She went back into the cabin, slamming the door behind her.

Tyson stared after Maria, feeling slightly guilty as he realized for the first time just how much burden she'd carried for their sake.

CHAPTER 117

They hiked in silence through the falling snow towards the creek, the shadows seeming to press in on them as darkness fell around them, adding to the eerie atmosphere. Ben walked wordlessly along, his expression set in stone, his daughter clinging to his left hand, his wife to his right. At first, he had considered leaving Grace behind. But then he knew that Maria was right: leaving her behind would only be buying her a little more time, but it wouldn't save her. Grace, however, didn't seem to be afraid of what was coming in the slightest. In fact, her demeanor suggested that she was full of grim determination to carry out the task that lay before them. Marianne seemed to have similar feelings. In truth, they were both thinking about what had happened to Dylan.

He'd been a nice boy, and they had played together many times. Both girls had experienced the same recurring nightmare of Dylan falling out a window to his death over and over again in an endless loop, and it seemed to have steeled their resolve. Ben smiled. She was so strong. Just like her mother. Tyson was clutching Marianne's hand tightly as they walked side by side.

"Marianne," he said, struggling to keep his voice steady. "You don't have to do this."

Marianne shook her head.

"No, daddy, I do," she said firmly. She looked up at her father, her expression filled with determination. "I have to do this. For Dylan. For mom. If there's any chance of saving them, I have to at least try."

Tyson, staring into his daughter's strong, determined face, was reminded strongly of his own mother the day she'd sat him down and told him that he was strong, that he was smart, that if he fought hard, he could get off the mean streets he'd grown up on one day. Tyson pulled Marianne into a tight hug.

"I love you, kid," he whispered.

"I love you too, daddy. We're going to be okay. I know we will," Marianne whispered back.

Maria felt the group collectively tense as they slowly approached the creek, which had completely frozen over. Maria stepped up to the edge of the frozen surface, peering intently at the thick sheet of ice blanketing the creek. The others filed in behind her, staring at the frozen river with apprehensive looks.

"Jody used to come here when she was little," Maria said. "She would play in the creek with her parents for whole days during the summer. She told me that, a few days before she died."

The group remained silent, none of them knowing what to say.

"I guess I know why now," she said, bending down to remove her shoes and socks. She shivered as the freezing cold exploded like fire in her bare feet, quickly racing up her legs and into her abdomen, chilling her down to the bone. She gritted her teeth and undressed herself, throwing her clothes aside one by one until she was standing fully naked at the edge of the frozen river, shivering in the freezing cold.

Everyone was looking at her nervously. She shot a glance behind her. Her grim expression told them everything they needed to know. Within minutes, the entire group was standing naked in the winter cold, everyone shivering violently, their clothes tossed in haphazard piles beside them. Maria closed her eyes, raising her hand to the frozen river before her. Within seconds, the ice began to melt, a gap opening up in the thick ice sheet, growing wider by the second until it was nearly ten feet wide. Maria opened her eyes, sternly surveying her handiwork.

"Maria," Ben asked, "are you sure you want to go through with this?"

Maria ignored him. She stepped up to the edge of the riverfront, her toes resting in the freezing river water.

She looked back at the group, her expression stony.

"Look," she said. "I'm going through with this. Whether you want to follow me or not is up to you. If you want to back out now, that's your choice."

For a moment, no one moved. Then finally, Ben stepped forward. He sat down beside Maria, putting his lower legs into the water up to his knees. He shuddered violently as the cold shocked his system. Slowly, the others followed him, sitting down beside the two of them at the edge of the water. They stared silently out at the dark, freezing water that lay before them, many of them silently praying for deliverance from their maker.

CHAPTER 118

Maria sucked in a deep breath. She was mostly numb by now. Soon, she wouldn't be able to make the jump on her own. It was time.

"Join hands," she said firmly.

Everyone obeyed her without question. She sighed heavily.

"We fight this fight together," Maria said, her lips trembling from the cold. "We fight for everything we have lost. We make this jump together, to show our solidarity in saving this world from an evil that has done everything in its power to destroy us." She looked to her left, and then to her right.

Every face staring back at her was filled with determination. They were ready. Maria closed her eyes. She slid into the water, the cold exploding like a small bomb in her chest.

A second later, the others followed, several of them letting out strangled cries as they entered the freezing water. As they fell with her, plunging to the dark bottom, Maria realized she no longer felt cold. A gentle warmth was slowly spreading throughout her entire body, soothing her. The world faded to gray as she hit the bottom of the creek. The others landed around her. From somewhere far off, she heard their terrified screams. But somehow she knew they felt no pain. A few had their eyes closed, their limbs floating uselessly beside them. Maria let out a distressed cry as she felt Laura's soul leave her body, floating upward towards the surface and out of sight. The world began to darken around Maria. There wasn't much time. She tightened her grip on the hands of the people on either side of her. From the little sight she had left, she saw Ben close the circle by grasping Tyson's hand on his left.

At the same moment, Tyson's soul escaped his body, vanishing into the darkness. Maria cried out in anguish, silently begging for the torture to end. One by one, they began to die, their souls spiraling upward and out of sight. Maria could feel herself growing weak, the pleasant warmth lulling her into sleep. It was almost over. She could see Marianne floating a few feet away, still clutching her father's hand. Her head was lulling against her chest, her eyes closed, her legs floating about aimlessly. To a casual observer, she would've been unmistakably dead. But she was alive. Just barely. With her last bit of remaining strength, Maria glided over to her and wrapped her arms around the little girl, holding Marianne tightly against her chest.

"Hang in there," Maria sobbed. "Hang in there just a little longer love, it's okay, it's almost over."

"Thank you," a little voice whispered in her ear. "I'm okay. It doesn't hurt anymore."

Maria sobbed harder.

"Shh, shh…" Marianne whispered. "It's okay, it's okay. You're going to be with your sister soon. And I'm going to be with my mom. We're all going home, aren't we?"

"Yeah," Maria whispered. "I guess we are."

Marianne went limp in her arms, and Maria felt life fading from her.

"Hey," Maria whispered, "I just want you to know, I love you kid," she whispered, kissing Marianne on the forehead. "I love you."

Marianne remained silent. Her skin was as cold as ice. Maria began to cry as she felt the little girl's spirit leave her body. Then the world faded to black around her, and everything was gone.

CHAPTER 119

The puppet hung limply just a few inches above the wooden stage floor, its head hung so low its chin rested against its chest. Its deep, warm brown eyes which were filled with a strange lifelessness were closed. Its arms were held slightly north of shoulder height as if they were held up by invisible strings. Its polished mahogany limbs glowed softly under the bright shimmering of the stage lights. It was clad in a light gray hoodie and black sweatpants. It turned slowly in a semicircle back and forth in front of the dark auditorium, as if the puppet master holding its strings was distracted and not bothering to monitor its movements. It didn't react as the bright lights all around the auditorium ignited one by one, bathing the dark theater in a warm yellow, fluorescent glow. The enormous crowd of floating puppets hovering back and forth dreamily across the dark ceiling of the auditorium froze at the advent of the bright lights.

"Ladies and gentlemen!" boomed a deep voice from high above the stage. "Come one and all, witness the final act of the great firebrand!"

The puppets began to obediently float down from the ceiling, coming to rest in the velvet backed rows of seats, every face pointed upward towards the stage. If the puppet had looked up, it would've recognized many of the faces staring back at it. Dylan Teryon was sitting between his mother and sister in the second row, his brown eyes wide with interest, his wooden facial features otherwise expressionless. Roy Forsin was sitting in the middle of the fifth row, his deep blue eyes fixed on the puppet hovering on stage. Myrtle was sitting on his lap, her face completely expressionless.

"Welcome everyone!" boomed the voice from above the stage, quickly drowned out by a storm of cheers from the crowd.

The puppet on stage began to twitch uncomfortably.

"Now, as a warmup to our final act, allow me to demonstrate her fealty! You might have once cowered before Jody Razitsky! You might have feared the flames she can conjure from her hands!" The voice suddenly became much lower, almost conspiratorial. "But I can assure you…she poses no threat to us anymore. Allow me to demonstrate."

The puppet began to move back and forth across the stage, its legs performing a blurringly fast tap dance. Jeering laughter erupted from the crowd as they watched. The puppet's lips began to quiver, its eyes squeezed shut with humiliation. If it could've, it would've cried a flood.

"HOW DO YOU LIKE THAT?" the puppeteer screamed down at Jody. "YOU LIKE THAT YOU LITTLE BITCH?"

The laughter from the crowd swelled into a cacophony that echoed off the walls of the theater until it deafened Jody completely. Unable to control her limbs, she squeezed her eyes shut tighter to try and block them out. Even with the hundreds of voices blending together, she could still make out individuals. Even those she hadn't met, she somehow recognized. David, Roy, Dylan, Jacob, Rick, Cetan, Leo, Anna, Josephine, Annette, Kaden's mother…every single one of them had died because of her. Most of them had died for her, and yet here she was, being dragged around like a ragdoll on a stage by the bastard she'd gotten them all killed trying to stop. She wanted with all her heart to die, to vanish, to be doused with gasoline and set on fire, anything for the humiliation to stop.

"YOU AFRAID NOW?" the puppeteer screamed at her, his cold, cruel voice filling her ears in spite of the roaring laughter of the crowd. "YOU AFRAID OF ME NOW, YOU LITTLE BRAT!" He yanked hard on the string controlling her head, forcing her neck painfully backward.

Jody, with no tears to cry, sobbed silently to herself, her entire body shaking uncontrollably as the puppeteer dragged her around the stage with increasing violence. The tap dance had been abandoned. The puppeteer was allowing his full wrath to wash over her now, all semblance of control abandoned. She let out a silent scream of pain as she was dragged ten feet into the air by her ankles.

"NOW YOU GET IT? STILL THINK I'M THE VULNERABLE ONE? STILL THINK I'M THE ONE WHO'S AFRAID OF YOU?" he screamed at her.

Jody screamed soundlessly as she suddenly dropped like a stone, falling ten feet before slamming head-first into the wooden floor. She collapsed in a heap on the ground, her head exploding with blinding pain. She blacked out for a full ten seconds before a narrow slit of her vision returned.

"BUT THAT'S NOT ALL!" the Puppeteer boomed. "TONIGHT, WE HAVE THE PLEASURE OF WELCOMING SOME VERY SPECIAL GUESTS! COMING TO YOU LIVE FROM MAUVILLA, ALABAMA, THEY'RE HERE FOR A SHOW! AND BY GOD WE'RE GOING TO GIVE THEM ONE, RIGHT FOLKS!"

The crowd screamed their approval, the roaring applause outstripping even the Puppeteer's booming laughter. For the first time, Jody slowly raised her head, unable to believe what she was hearing.

"They're coming…" she whispered under her breath, a small bubble of warmth forming in her chest. "Jesus, they're coming for me…"

"DYLAN TERYON! PLEASE COME TO THE STAGE TO GREET OUR GUESTS!"

The puppet that had once been Dylan Teryon wordlessly obeyed, gliding silently above the rows of seats and onto the wooden stage.

"DYLAN WILL BE PERFORMING INTRODUCTIONS TONIGHT!" the Puppeteer boomed. "NOW DYLAN! MAKE SURE OUR GUESTS RECEIVE A WELCOME THAT THEY WILL NEVER FORGET!"

The Puppet nodded, his wooden lips forming a cold, heartless grin.

"Oh, don't worry," Dylan whispered, his grin widening. Jody's eyes widened as Dylan pulled the gleaming butcher knife out from behind his back.

"They won't get away from me this time."

"Jesus," Jody thought, squeezing her eyes shut. "I can't keep watching them die, not for me, not anymore." The warmth began to spread out of Jody's chest, reaching into her arms, her neck, her toes, intensifying with every passing second until her whole body felt as though it was bathed in searing flames. Dylan walked stiffly into the middle of the stage to roaring applause from the audience. He raised the butcher knife above his head triumphantly.

"TODAY!" he screamed. "TODAY ALL OF THIS ENDS! TODAY THE FINAL ACT COMMENCES! TODAY, HUMANITY TAKES ITS FINAL BREATH!"

The crowd roared with approval. Dylan grinned at something up above the stage, where a giant wooden cross piece hung suspended in midair. The Puppeteer grinned back at him. He breathed a heavy sigh of relief. It had certainly taken longer than he would have liked, but it seemed the whole ordeal was finally coming to an end. Jody gasped suddenly. Another presence had just crossed the barrier onto their plane of existence. As it moved closer, Jody felt a sudden rush of hot wind like a summer breeze.

"LADIES AND GENTLEMEN!" the Puppeteer boomed. "IT SEEMS OUR SPECIAL GUESTS ARE APPROACHING!" The crowd roared with excitement at these words. "LET'S GIVE THEM A PERFORMANCE FOR THE AGES!"

The crowd screamed their enthusiasm. Jody could feel them getting closer with every passing second, their heat surrounding her like a warm blanket. She closed her eyes, soothed by the sounds of their approaching voices.

"Yes," she whispered, a small smile crossing her face. "Yes, the final act will be starting soon, ladies and gentlemen. Except there's been a few minor changes to the script." She grinned broadly. It was the same grin she'd worn every Sunday morning as a kid when she and her parents would walk down to the creek for a day of swimming. "We're bringing down the entire house crashing down tonight."

CHAPTER 120

Ben Alrite woke up on a cold stone floor in the pitch dark. He groaned weakly and forced himself into a sitting position. His muscles were extremely sore from lactic acid buildup and seemed incapable of supporting him. He squinted into the darkness, straining to make out his surroundings. He could vaguely make out a number of motionless shapes lying on either side of him in the darkness. He shivered. The air in this place, wherever it was, was strangely cold.

"No," Ben thought suddenly. "It's more than that. It's...empty somehow...as if the lack of warmth doesn't merely extend to the temperature." He suddenly felt extremely uncomfortable and quickly became aware that an icy sweat had broken out over his entire body. His eyes darted around nervously, straining to see through the darkness. There was something very wrong here.

Although he couldn't see any eyes glaring back at him from the deep shadows, he knew they weren't alone. He climbed shakily to his feet.

"We have to get out of here," he thought, panicked. "We have to get out right now." He started in the direction of the dark shape closest to him, which was beginning to move. Ben heard a low moan escape it and immediately realized who it was. "Maria," Ben whispered urgently, bending down and shaking her by the shoulders. "Maria, are you okay?"

Maria groaned and sat up, rubbing her aching head.

"Ben is that you?" she whispered.

"Yeah," he said, kneeling down beside her.

"The others," she said frantically, glancing around. "Are they okay?"

"They are," Ben said quickly, rubbing his head. "Probably all gonna experience a hell of a hangover, but I guess drowning in a frozen river will do that."

Maria cracked a smile.

Ben smiled.

"They'll be okay, kid. They're too tough to be brought down by something so minor."

Maria's smile grew wider. She almost managed to laugh. Ben's smile suddenly faded.

"Is he here?" he asked, suddenly sounding very serious.

Maria didn't answer.

"The magician, I mean," Ben said, glancing around nervously.

"Yeah," came another voice from a few feet away, causing them both to look up.

Kaden was watching the pair of them, sitting with his arms clasped around his knees.

"He's here," Kaden said matter of factly. An uncomfortable silence followed this statement.

"You know, it's funny," Kaden said, getting to his feet and striding towards them. He didn't bother to conceal the biting sarcasm in his tone. "I spent so many years sneaking through the shadows, staying on the move, hiding from this bastard. I was so fucking terrified I thought I would have a heart attack every time I came to this place looking for answers."

He indicated his head towards a small faceless shadow that was lying motionless on the floor a few feet away.

"I watched that poor little girl get stabbed to death right in front of me. It was the scariest moment of my entire goddamn life." Kaden shook his head miserably. "After that night, I swore to myself I would never come back to this place again." He sighed heavily. "And yet, here I am."

Maria sighed.

"Kaden, I'm sorry..."

"But that's okay," Kaden said, suddenly sounding stronger. He held his head up confidently. "I spent most of my life living in fear. I spent years running away, stepping from shadow to shadow, trying to remain invisible, hoping to God the monsters of this world would never see me, that they would just leave me alone." He rested a hand on Maria's shoulder, his expression a mask of determination. "But that ends today. I know it might have taken me a long time, but I'm ready now. I'm ready to end this fight today." Kaden smiled. "And to be frank, I'm getting really sick and fucking tired of running away from my problems."

Maria smiled and hugged him.

"We're going to end this today, kid. I promise you that. You don't have to be afraid anymore."

Ben, watching the exchange, suddenly became aware of the weight of the cigarette lighter in his pocket. He slowly removed it, staring at it pensively. Even in the pitch dark, the silver sheen glowed brightly. Something was unnatural about it, however. The light had a strangely ethereal quality to it, as if it were the product of some invisible spirit. Ben flicked open the top of the cigarette lighter and lit the bright blue fire, creating a small ring of light around the three of them. They huddled together close to the flame, savoring its warmth in the midst of the cold dark empty sea they had plunged themselves into. A moment later, Marianne's face appeared in the light. Her dark brown eyes were wide with fright.

"Maria," she whispered. "Where are we?"

Maria didn't answer at first, not wanting to scare the little girl any further.

"He's here, isn't he?" Marianne asked nervously. "I can feel him. It's so cold here, it's like he's sucked all the warmth out of this place."

Maria pulled Marianne into a tight hug.

"I know this place is scary," Maria whispered. "But I'm not going to let anyone hurt you, I promise."

"Marianne?" came a small, scared voice from the far corner. All of them jumped.

"Is it really you?" the voice asked nervously as its owner slowly approached.

Marianne, who was shaking with fright, jumped backward like a scared rabbit. Maria moved protectively in front of her, her expression mask-like. Ben, a deep unsettling feeling of dread forming in the pit of his stomach, suddenly found himself wishing that he had his gun.

"Marianne?" the voice asked again. "Who's that with you?"

Kaden, who looked nervous himself, could see the outline of the small boy's face reflected in the light cast by the flame. He had no doubt who it was. He should've been smiling, he should've been overjoyed to see his friend alive, but seeing him here, like this…he just felt…scared…

"Something's wrong here," he whispered, his voice shaking. "We need to get out of here, now."

"Guys!" the voice exclaimed, suddenly sounding excited. "I can't believe you're here, did you come here to save me?"

The face finally entered fully into the firelight, so that they could all see it clearly.

"Dylan?" Marianne said nervously. "You're alive?"

"Marianne," Dylan said, reaching for her. Ben quickly got between them.

"Ben…" Dylan whispered.

"What are you doing here?" Ben demanded, his expression cold. He didn't like this one bit. He concurred with Kaden; something was terribly wrong here.

"Hiding," Dylan whispered, his eyes wide with fear. "He's here. He's here right now, watching us," Dylan whispered frantically, his voice rising with every word.

"He's hunting us right now, please, just get me out here!" he begged, tears streaming down his face.

Ben stared down at him, his expression unreadable. The terrible image of Dylan standing over Marianne, his teeth bared, the gleaming knife blade poised above his head, flashed through his mind. Dylan reached out for Ben to embrace him. Ben, panicking, shoved him away, hard enough to send him sprawling to the floor. Dylan stared up at Ben, his terrified eyes brimming with tears.

"Please," Dylan whispered. "I can hear him coming, please, just get me out of here."

"He's right," Kaden said. "We need to get out of here now."

Ben started to turn away.

"Wait," Marianne said, turning to Dylan. "We can't just leave him here."

Ben shook his head.

"He's not coming with us," Ben said. He turned to Marianne. "I'm not going to let him near you."

"Ben," Maria insisted. "He's scared. Look at him."

Ben glanced at Dylan. Dylan was staring at them apprehensively, his eyes darting nervously from face to face.

"He's just a kid," Maria continued.

"Did you forget about the time he almost killed all of us?" Ben demanded angrily.

"No, of course I haven't," Maria shot back. "He made a mistake."

"It was a hell of a lot more than a mistake!" Ben shouted. "He was in league with that monster!"

"He changed his mind!" Maria shouted.

"I don't care!" Ben screamed. "Doesn't it bother you at all that the second we showed up in this thing's house, he appeared out of thin air? Doesn't that worry you at all?"

"Ben!" Marianne shouted, causing all of them to look at her. "He died fighting back against that monster! How can you even think of leaving him here?"

Ben said nothing. He suddenly felt horrible. Marianne was right. The kid had died trying to protect them.

Trying to ignore his steadily building feeling of dread, he turned back to Dylan.

"Dylan, I..." He froze.

Dylan was gone. They all stared at the spot where he'd vanished, the growing panic slowly becoming visible on their faces.

"Shit..." Ben muttered.

"IT'S FUNNY ISN'T IT?" boomed Dylan's voice from all directions, as if it were amplified through a surround sound stereo system.

Marianne screamed.

"IT AMUSES ME HOW EASY IT IS TO MANIPULATE YOUR WEAK MINDS! ALL I HAD TO DO WAS SHED A FEW TEARS AND YOU WERE GOING TO TAKE ME WITH YOU JUST LIKE THAT! I SWEAR SOMETIMES, YOU MUST BE DOING IT ON PURPOSE! NO ONE COULD REALLY BE SO GULLIBLE, RIGHT?" Dylan let out a booming laugh that echoed off the high stone walls. "YOU HUMANS NEVER CEASE TO AMAZE ME, YOU KNOW THAT? THE FACT THAT SUCH A SPINELESS, WEAK-MINDED SPECIES CAN SURVIVE IS SIMPLY FASCINATING! WATCHING YOU DESTROY CIVILIZATION THROUGH YOUR NARCISSISM AND SINGLE-MINDED GREED WAS VERY ENTERTAINING!

Dylan let out another booming laugh.

"BUT UNFORTUNATELY FOR YOU, THE NOVELTY OF YOUR NARCISSISM AND IDIOCY IS WEARING OFF! MY MASTER HAS GROWN TIRED OF YOU! AND HE FIGURED WHAT BETTER WAY TO END THIS BATTLE THAN TO DEMONSTRATE YOUR FEEBLENESS FOR ALL YOUR FRIENDS AND FAMILY TO SEE!"

They all jumped as the dark velvet curtain that had separated them from the stage shot upward and out of sight, the sudden bright strobe lights of the theater nearly blinding them. In the split second before Ben threw his hands up over his face to shield his eyes, he saw endless rows of velvet backed purple seats stretching back into the darkened auditorium seemingly without end. And suddenly, the booming, shrieking laughter returned, ringing in their ears. Only it wasn't just Dylan laughing this time. There were hundreds of voices all laughing in unison.

And somehow, even through the screaming cacophony, they could recognize individual voices. "David... Roy... Dylan... Jacob... Rick... Cetan... Leo... Anna...Josephine...Annette...Kaden's mother..." All of them were sitting out in the audience right now, watching them, laughing at them as they cowered on stage.

Ben was vaguely aware that the others had woken up and were now gathered around them, cowering in the sudden bright glow of the stage lights.

"LADIES AND GENTLEMEN!" screamed a deep, booming voice directly over their heads.

"It's him," Maria whispered, her voice shaking with fright. "Jesus Christ, it's really him."

"TONIGHT, WE WITNESS THE END OF A GLORIOUS ERA! TONIGHT, WE WITNESS THE LAST MOMENTS OF A GREAT, CAPTIVATING SPECIES! TONIGHT, WE WILL WATCH AS THE FIRE IS SNUFFED OUT ONCE AND FOR ALL!"

Ben barely had a second to register the audience's roaring laughter before he was thrown into the air as if by an invisible slingshot. Screams erupted from below as he hung suspended ten feet in the air, clutching desperately at his throat as his airway was cut off by an invisible rope. Ben felt his stomach lurch as he was swung upside down, nails marks becoming visible on his neck as he clawed desperately at the invisible noose choking him, his face turning bright red from the lack of oxygen.

Out of the corner of his eye, he saw the others floating on either side of him. Marianne's face turned a sickly shade of green as she began to spin head over heels in midair. Tyson's face was turning an ugly shade of maroon as he was choking on his own invisible rope, his arms and legs held out at his sides as if he'd been strapped to a knife throwing board at a circus. Maria shrieked in agony as she was hoisted into the air by her hair, her dark brown curls sticking straight up in a tight bundle as if a giant invisible hand was pulling them steadily upward. Ben's vision began to darken, his complexion nearly black from asphyxiation. His head slumped against his chest, the will to fight quickly leaving him.

"Jody…" he whispered. "Jody, I'm sorry…" A split second before he lost consciousness, the rope released him, sending him plummeting fifteen feet to the stage below.

Ben landed hard on his left shoulder. A dull snap resounded from his wrist as he landed. A white-hot explosion of agony raced up his arm. Ben let out a weak cry of pain. One by one, the others landed around him with a series of heavy thuds. Cries of pain erupted all around him. Ben lay motionless on the stage floor, the pain in his wrist nearly blinding him. At that moment, he happened to glance out at the dark auditorium, into the sea of jeering, laughing faces. There was no humanity in any of those wooden expressions. To Ben, they didn't look much like humans at all. Then, through the white haze of pain, he saw her. Ben's mouth fell open in shock. She was sitting in the third row from the stage, her long dark hair tied back in a sensible ponytail. Her dark brown eyes were locked on Ben's. Her posture, in contrast to those around her, was rigid with attention. She wasn't laughing. She wasn't even smiling, her mouth set in a thin, hard line, her expression masklike.

"Jody," Ben whispered.

"You like that folks?" the Puppeteer boomed, striding out onto the stage, his long black cloak billowing out behind him.

The crowd roared their approval, screaming and stamping their feet raucously.

"Well, I don't think they've had quite enough yet, do you?" he asked, glancing bemusedly at Ben and the others as they struggled dazedly to their feet. "You want to see some more?"

The crowd howled their approval, every face in the crowd clamoring for more of the torture. Except for one. Jody was staring hard at Ben. Their eyes met. Ben started when he saw the fire blazing in Jody's eyes. Her face was suddenly a mask of determination. She closed her eyes.

"Ben…"

Ben jumped as Jody's voice echoed in his head.

"If you can hear me, if you can fight, if you have even the strength to stand, do it now."

Ben suddenly realized he was not the only one who could hear her. All around him, the others were getting to their feet, glancing around as if looking for the source of the voice.

"Stand together one last time."

They had all seen Jody now, and every one of them was looking directly at her. The Puppeteer seemed not to notice as he continued to egg on the crowd.

"I love you all so much," Jody continued. "I have watched you grow so much from the time when we first met. I have watched you support each other through unimaginable pain and suffering. I have watched you overcome so many trials together."

They were no longer looking at Jody. Now, every face on the stage was looking at each other, their expressions unreadable.

"You may not understand the human condition. I don't pretend to either. We commit terrible, unforgivable crimes every day, and we commit them of our own free will."

Ben hung his head, feeling slightly ashamed. He could see by their expressions that the others felt the same way.

"But that doesn't make us weak!" Jody shouted, causing them all to jump.

Ben had become strangely deaf to the Puppeteer's booming voice and the crowd's laughter. For him, the only sound in the entire world that existed was Jody's voice. With every word she spoke, Ben could feel the strength gradually returning to his limbs. A heat was slowly rising in his chest, spreading into his face and outward to his limbs, as if he'd swallowed boiling water from a hot spring.

"We make mistakes. I of all people know that. We put ourselves in dark places. But it's what comes after that matters. It's what we choose to do with all that pain and suffering that matters. It's how we fight back, it's how we claw our way out of those dark holes that shows who we really are!"

Out of the corner of his eye, Ben saw Jody smile.

"And I've never met a group of people who's fought their way out of more dark places than all of you."

Ben wrapped his arms around the shoulders of Jason and Serena, who were standing beside him. They did the same, until all of them were standing in a huddle at the edge of the stage, their heads pressed together.

"That's why you chose us, isn't it?" Ben whispered. "Because you knew we'd all fought our way out of our own dark places. Because we fought back."

"I didn't choose you," Jody said. "You came to me because you refused to give up. You refused to believe the lies, and that is more inspiring than anything I have ever seen in twenty-three years in this cruel world." She smiled. "I believe in all of you. You are my candle flame. My firelight."

It was Ben's turn to smile. He looked up at the taut, nervous faces surrounding him. They all nodded in unison. Ben smiled.

"Let's end this," he said.

CHAPTER 121

Ben whirled around as a scream erupted from behind him. As if ensnared by an invisible rope, Marianne was dragged away from the group. Tyson let out a yell and grabbed for her hand, his fingers closing on empty air. Marianne screamed as she was dragged across the stage until she was standing directly in front of the Puppeteer, hovering inches off the ground, her arms and legs held straight out as if by invisible ropes, her chin forcibly tilted upward so that she was staring straight up into the blinding stage lights. The Puppeteer, his expression masklike, grasped her chin with his black gloved hand, tears streaking down Marianne's face as he leaned towards her.

"Well, hello love," he whispered. "You've been quite elusive, haven't you? Shall I?"

He raised his arms high above his head, causing Marianne to shoot several feet in the air. Her fingers clawed uselessly at her neck as she choked on an invisible noose, her face slowly turning red from asphyxiation.

"AND NOW," boomed the Puppeteer, "THIS LITTLE ONE IS FINALLY MINE!"

The crowd roared in approval. The Puppeteer howled with derisive laughter. Never seeing Tyson storming towards him until it was too late.

"Get away from my daughter, you son of a bitch!" Tyson roared, his fist swinging out hard, connecting with the Puppeteer's jaw.

The Puppeteer stumbled backward in surprise, sprawling to the floor. Marianne screamed as she fell, her father managing to catch her just before she hit the floor. The Puppeteer rose to his feet, his expression blazing with hatred. He raised his hand to Tyson as he held his daughter close, his eyes blazing with hatred as he prepared to strike them down.

"NO!" Ben screamed, body slamming the Puppeteer to the ground at the last second, the spell shooting off uselessly into the darkness.

"Get him!" Mike roared, throwing himself onto the Puppeteer, punching him over and over again with all his might.

The Puppeteer screamed in rage. Mike flew backward ten feet and hit the wall of the auditorium, a small trickle of blood left behind on the wall as he slid to the floor, unconscious.

Ben let out an almighty roar and threw himself onto the Puppeteer. Before he could even draw his arm back, the Puppeteer threw him off with superhuman strength, sending him flying back several feet before he crashed hard into the wooden stage floor. Jason charged, brandishing his fists. Suddenly, his feet flew off the ground as if he'd tripped. He did a bizarre sort of pirouette in midair before crashing to the floor beside Ben. The Puppeteer turned just as Lorenzo pulled back his fist to strike and flipped him over his shoulder like a judo expert, sending him crashing flat on his back.

"IS THAT ALL YOU'VE GOT?" the Puppeteer jeered, causing the audience to howl with derisive laughter. "IS THAT REALLY YOUR GRAND PLAN TO DEFEAT ME?" he screamed, catching Tyson by the throat as he charged again, lifting him directly above his head before slamming him brutally to the ground.

He let out another derisive, booming laugh.

"THIS IS THE NIGHT WHEN THE FIRELIGHT FINALLY DIES!"

His expression twisting grotesquely with rage, he advanced on Marianne, who shuffled away on all fours, whimpering in terror as the monster advanced on her, his human face melting like candle wax. Revealing the abyss hiding behind it, the black, empty void stretching infinitely deep. Marianne screamed as the Puppeteer leaned his face down towards hers.

"Finally," he whispered savagely. "I've got you right where I want you."

The abyss tilted up to meet her, Marianne letting out a final weak cry as the darkness swallowed her whole.

Ben charged as the Puppeteer advanced on Marianne, not knowing what he was going to do and not caring, just knowing that he had to protect the scared little girl from the monster now looming over her, preparing to strike. As he ran, he suddenly became vaguely aware of the weight of the cigarette lighter still in his pocket. Without thinking, he withdrew the cigarette lighter from his pocket.

"Where there is fire, there is life..."

Igniting the cigarette lighter, he launched it at the Puppeteer like an MLB pitcher. It struck him in the back of the head, temporarily stunning him. The lighter dropped to the wooden stage floor. For a split second, the wood caught fire, the flames spreading rapidly. Then, just as quickly, they were snuffed out as if someone had thrown cold water over them.

The Puppeteer whirled around, sending Ben flying through the air helplessly before he crashed into the opposite wall, nearly losing consciousness as he slid down the wall to land next to Mike, who was still unconscious. The Puppeteer, temporarily forgetting about Marianne, picked up the silver cigarette lighter, staring at it bemusedly.

"DID YOU JUST TRY TO KILL ME?" the Puppeteer screamed, all hint of amusement gone from his voice. "DID YOU JUST TRY TO SET MY HOUSE ON FIRE?" he roared.

Although his human face had disappeared, Ben had no doubt it would've borne a very ugly look indeed. Forgetting about Marianne entirely, he advanced on Jennifer and Grace, who were cowering at the edge of the stage.

"YOUR FIRE IS USELESS HERE!" the Puppeteer shrieked. "IT CANNOT PROTECT YOU!" He bore down on Jennifer and Grace, who was cowering in her mother's arms. The Puppeteer turned to face Ben, his face masked by the inky black darkness. "NOW YOU WILL WATCH AS I TAKE YOUR WIFE AND DAUGHTER FROM YOU FOREVER!"

Jennifer screamed in terror, clutching her little girl tightly to her chest as the darkness reached upward to meet them, preparing to swallow them whole. Jody, still watching from within the midst of the crowd, sighed heavily and closed her eyes, understanding what had to be done.

Ben closed his eyes, the screams and laughter of the crowd vanishing in an instant, as if someone had slipped a pair of heavy earmuffs over his ears.

"I don't know if you can hear me, kid," Jody said, feeling the heat rapidly rising through her tough, wooden body. "But you are the light of this world. You are the firelight. It's inside of all of us, hoping that one day, we'll be strong enough to accept it."

Ben squeezed his eyes shut, concentrating. He could feel the heat rising in his chest. Jody felt a single tear slide down her cheek as the flames erupted from her torso, spreading rapidly to her limbs until her entire body was engulfed in an inferno.

"You can do this..."

The warmth spread through his entire body, the fire that was consuming Jody at the same moment coursing through him. He raised a trembling hand as the Puppeteer bore down on his wife and little girl, preparing to swallow them forever. Now the warmth was congealing, racing up through his torso and down his arm into his extended hand, which was now so hot it could've melted wax.

"You can do this..."

The darkness tilted up to meet Jennifer, a second away from taking her.

"Do it now!" Ben roared. His hand exploded, the white-hot ball of flame charging across the stage at blinding speed, blasting the Puppeteer ten feet across the stage.

He landed with a heavy thud on the opposite side of the stage from Ben and lay motionless. Jody, her wooden body blackened and crumbling into ash, let out a final weak cry of pain an instant before the world disappeared, her life finally extinguished for good.

"Ben, oh Ben!" Jennifer sobbed, her eyes flooding with tears as Ben sprinted across the stage towards her and Grace, sweeping them both into his arms. "Oh my god..." Jennifer sobbed. "I thought...I thought..."

"It's okay," Ben whispered, holding them both against him more tightly than he ever had in his life. "It's okay, you're safe."

"No," Mike said firmly, getting to his feet, his eyes trained on the unconscious figure lying on the other side of the stage.

"No, we're not yet."

The others had gotten to their feet too and were slowly approaching the Puppeteer. The crowd in the auditorium had vanished. Ben had a strange feeling they'd never really existed in the first place.

"Jennifer," he said, releasing her. "There's one more thing we have to do. We have to make sure this ends."

Jennifer smiled and kissed him firmly on the mouth.

"Show me the way, love," she whispered. "I'd follow you anywhere."

CHAPTER 122

The Puppeteer lay motionless on the stage as Ben and the others approached from all sides, every face twisted with dislike. He raised his head slightly as they formed a circle around him, his eyes darting back and forth nervously between the many faces now surrounding him.

"My eyes," he thought, suddenly very frightened.

His human face had returned. The abyss was gone. He closed his eyes, struggling to concentrate in spite of the swirling buzz of fear that was rapidly encroaching on his brain. It wouldn't come.

"No," he thought, panic beginning to set in. "No, no, NO!" his brain screamed. He squeezed his eyes shut, straining with the effort, but it wouldn't come. "You can't," he spat defiantly. "You can't defeat me! I am the all-seeing eye! I created this puny egg of a universe! I created you!"

He struggled to his feet, glaring at the angry faces surrounding him. He advanced on Mike, who quickly shoved him back into the middle of the circle, every line of his face etched with hatred. The Puppeteer bared his teeth.

"You want your pathetic world back? Fine! I can bring it back for you in an instant if you let me go!" He charged at Tyson, who shoved him back hard enough to send him sprawling to the floor. The Puppeteer scrambled to his feet, looking increasingly panicked. "I can give you power, wealth, women, eternal glory, anything you desire!" he shouted. "I can make you Gods of the earth if you wish!"

No one moved a muscle.

"Anything!" he screamed, his voice rising. "I can give you anything you want! I can...I can bring your loved ones back to you! Their souls still exist in the abyss! I can retrieve them in an instant if you'll let me go!"

Laura felt her throat seize up at these words. The monster's hands had fidgeted nervously as soon as the words had left his mouth. He was lying. Laura felt the strength leave her limbs. She sank to her knees, the world around her lost in a blur of tears. She'd had a terrible feeling, even at the moment of his passing, that Roy was gone. But hearing it for certain now...the feeling was indescribable. She wanted to disappear. She wanted the monster to take her, to throw her into the abyss. Even the infinite darkness had to be better than this unbearable, cold emptiness. She didn't want to live anymore. Not without Roy.

"Laura!" Tyson exclaimed as she sank to her knees, hanging her head as she sobbed uncontrollably. Tyson placed his hands on her shoulders, bending down so that his face was directly in line with hers. "Laura," he said. "Laura, listen to me. We have to close the circle."

Laura shook her head, whimpering.

"We have to end this," he continued. "We can't do this without you."

"I can't," she whispered, her voice shaking. "I...I can't do this without him."

Tyson looked around uncertainly at the others, unsure of what to do.

"Please," Laura whispered. "Please, just leave me here. I can't do this anymore."

Tyson stood up and looked at Maria questioningly, as if hoping she'd have an answer.

"There's nothing left for me back there," Laura said weakly. "My family is gone. At least if I move on, I can put all the pain I've suffered in this life behind me."

She walked resignedly into the center of the circle and sat down beside the Puppeteer. She hung her head, tears spilling down her face.

"Do it," she whispered, her voice trembling. "Please, just do it."

A dozen anxious faces stared at Maria, each desperately hoping for an answer. Maria sighed and shook her head sadly.

"Are you sure this is what you want?" Maria asked.

Laura nodded, more tears flooding the floor beneath her. Maria moved to her spot between Jason and Serena. She closed her eyes and sighed heavily again.

"Close the circle," she said. It took every bit of self-control she had not to break down crying.

Several people gasped.

"Maria..." Serena started.

Maria held up a hand to silence her, the tears beginning to stream down her face.

"We have to close the circle," she sobbed. "This has to end." She looked at Laura, her eyes filled with tears.

"Laura, I'm so sorry," she whispered.

Laura shook her head, more tears spilling down her face.

"It's okay," she said, the ghost of a smile crossing her face. "It's okay. I've been suffering for a long time, tied down to this mortal coil. I'm...I'm free now."

Maria bent down and hugged her tightly, more tears spilling from her eyes.

"I love you, Laura," she whispered.

"I love you too, kid," Laura whispered back. "Thank you. For everything."

A small smile crossed Laura's face. It was the most beautiful thing Maria had ever seen. Maria, wiping her eyes, stood up and rejoined the circle, linking hands with Jason and Serena on either side of her. The circle had been closed. Maria closed her eyes. Wordlessly, the others copied her. Maria felt the heat begin to rise inside of her, spreading through her torso, her neck, her limbs. She could feel it on either side of her, rising in the others.

"Wait!" the Puppeteer screamed.

Laura remained silent.

"Wait, please, don't do this!" the Puppeteer begged desperately.

The heat continued to grow until it reached a fevered pitch, as though the entire room were bathed in flames.

"No, wait, stop!" the Puppeteer screamed as the flames erupted around him, rapidly spreading over the wooden floor, bathing the auditorium in a hot orange light. The Puppeteer charged desperately at Ben, only to be thrown back as a burst of fire erupted from his body. The Puppeteer screamed in agony as his cloak caught fire. The fire hungrily raced up his body, bathing him in bright orange fire. The Puppeteer howled and writhed in pain as his entire body was bathed in flames. He tore at his face with his claw-like hands as the flesh melted like hot candle wax. His top hat toppled off his head and tumbled into the raging fire. The Puppeteer let out one final shriek of agony before his body dissipated completely, his black cloak tumbling to the floor, consumed almost instantly by the roaring fire. And now the theater itself began to crumble around them.

The wallpaper blackened and peeled away from the wall as the fire raced up towards the ceiling. The seats in the auditorium, the velvet having already melted away, blackened to charcoal under the raging firestorm, which quickly crumbled into dust. The walls themselves began to collapse moments later. The ceiling sagged in on itself before giving away completely, opening the view to the inky black void beyond. The stage finally collapsed in on itself, sending Laura plunging into the abyss below. Maria looked sadly down at her as she fell. A beautiful, serene smile crossed Laura's face as she gazed up at Maria. Maria smiled wanly back at her, knowing she was finally free. A second later, she was lifted upward along with the others, away from the theater, away from the abyss.

Ben looked down one last time as they were carried away from the theatre at the spot where Jody's ashes lay.

"Jody…" Ben whispered as the black charcoal that had once been her body rapidly turned into dust under the heat of the raging inferno.

"Thank you. Thank you for everything."

Maria followed his gaze, tears spilling down her face as the dust that now made up Jody's remains floated away into the darkness and out of sight.

"I love you Jody," Maria whispered as the theatre vanished. "I'll do the best I can to repair this broken world, I promise."

A loud wail erupted from somewhere in the darkness as the blackened remains of the theatre plunged into the abyss and out of sight. And then everything was gone.

CHAPTER 123

Maria opened her eyes. She was lying on the ground beside a frozen river, surrounded by a light dusting of snow. The sun shone brightly overhead. Judging by its position in the sky, it was around midday. Maria sighed and pushed herself into a sitting position. Her arms and back muscles, drenched with lactic acid, groaned in protest. She felt exhausted, but it was a good kind of tired, as if it were energy well spent. She smiled wanly. The river, now beginning to thaw so that the layer of ice broke apart into smaller chunks floating atop the water, sparkled magnificently under the bright winter sun. She wrapped her arms around her knees and stared out at the river as it thawed, savoring the feeling of the bright early afternoon sun on her face. For the first time in months, she felt truly at peace. It was finally over. She sighed, hanging her head. She only wished they could be here with her to see it.

"I'm sorry," she whispered. "I'm sorry I couldn't save you. Dad. Mom. Lilly." She felt a tear slide down her cheek and quickly wiped it away.

"I don't know where you are, but I hope wherever it is, you find peace there, as I have found mine. I may be able to move on, someday, but I'll never forget you. I will love you with all my heart until the day I move on from this place, and we can be together again." Another tear slid down her face. She didn't bother to wipe it away. "Or at least, I hope we can be together again." And then the dam that had been holding back the flood of her emotions burst, and she broke down, sobbing uncontrollably into her hands. Her tears seemed to go on forever, flooding the ground, melting the snow around her.

"C'mon, Maria, I'm gonna beat you to the river!"

Maria looked up.

"No way sis, I'm way faster than you!"

Two girls that couldn't have been older than nine or ten ran past her, their bare feet kicking up dirt as they ran, laughing, carefree. Their faces, flushed with color, shone brightly in the sunlight.

"Lilly…" Maria whispered.

"Last one there is a rotten egg!" Lilly shouted as the pair of them reached the river, both of them diving headfirst into the river. They both emerged a few seconds later, laughing.

"I beat you!" Maria laughed.

"No way!" Lilly shrieked, shoving her sister playfully.

"I got here first!"

They began splashing each other, laughing. Lilly tried to dunk her little sister, but Maria dodged her and grabbed her by the shoulders, dragging her underwater. They broke the surface, laughing joyously.

"You see them, don't you?"

Maria turned. Kaden was standing beside her, gazing pensively out at the sparkling blue water. Maria nodded. There was silence for a moment.

"Do you see your mother?" Maria asked finally.

Kaden was silent for a moment.

"Not here," he said calmly. "But I will, eventually, I'm sure."

"Where are they?" Maria asked.

Kaden remained silent.

"Do you know?" she tried again.

Kaden finally shook his head.

"Wherever they are, it's somewhere far beyond our reach," he said.

Maria sighed.

"Physically, at least. But we still have the memories."

Maria felt a tear slide down her cheek.

"It's all I have left of her," she choked out. "It's all I have left of any of them. The memories of playing in the river with my sister, of the campfires on those summer nights with my parents. We'd sing songs, we'd roast marshmallows, it was..." she choked back a sob. "It was the happiest I've ever felt."

Kaden nodded.

"When my mother died, I just..." he paused, choosing his next words carefully. "The only thing I could think about were the times we'd spent together when I was little, before I discovered my powers, before all of this started." He sighed heavily. "I just kept thinking about how I withdrew after I found out about my powers. Because I was scared. I didn't want her to find out. I was afraid she would hate me. I just keep thinking about all the nights she would cry to my dad about how she was losing me. It all feels so stupid now." He shook his head sadly. "I wasted so much time."

There was silence for a moment.

"You're right," Maria said resignedly. "They're beyond any of our reach. At least physically." She paused. "But you're wrong about one thing," she said, watching her younger self throw herself on Lilly's back, sending them both plunging beneath the surface. "They're not gone. Not completely."

The two little girls emerged, sputtering and laughing hysterically. She slid her hand into Kaden's.

"Don't give up hope," she said, smiling. But there was a deep sadness behind it that made Kaden want to cry. "My father left this world because he gave up hope." She looked out at the water, watching the two little girls splash each other, laughing joyfully. "We still have something to live for."

Kaden smiled.

"Promise me," he said. "Promise me you'll stay by me. I'll never give up hope. Not as long as I'm with you."

Maria smiled.

"Always."

They turned and walked back towards the cabin hand in hand, the shrieks of laughter gradually fading into the distance behind them.

EPILOGUE

"C'mon, dad, hurry up!" Laura shouted, laughing as she ran along the dirt path, her bare feet kicking up dirt and pine needles as she ran.

"Coming, honey! Wait for me!" Kaden called as he raced after her, sporting a pair of bright red swim trunks, a pair of bright blue beach towels flying behind him in his wake.

Maria, clad in a black silk bikini, hurried after them, laughing. The bright summer sun blazed overhead as the three of them charged towards the river.

"Last one in is a rotten egg!" Laura called as she burst out of the trees, her eyes set on the river's edge.

Maria smiled. For a split second, she saw her big sister Lilly racing towards the water's edge, laughing as she plunged into the slow-moving water. And then her six-year-old daughter, named after the woman Maria still missed dearly even years later, emerged, laughing and spitting up water, and the image was gone.

Kaden, laughing, jumped in after her headfirst. Maria watched from the bank as her husband picked up their daughter and spun her around as she kicked and screeched with laughter. She had come to think of Kaden as her husband over the last few years as he'd become a fully grown man. Not that he'd ever acted much like a little boy in the first place, but the physical maturation had certainly had its benefits. She'd lost her virginity to him several years ago, when they'd both been just teenagers. The act of making love had seemed foreign to her at first, but gradually they'd gotten used to each other, until it had become a nightly occurrence. This had gone on for a few months until Laura had been conceived. Laura had slept in their bed for the first year or so, until she was old enough that Maria was comfortable letting her sleep by herself. Maria had breastfed her, bathed her, helped her walk for the first time. She loved the little girl to death, and as Laura had started talking and walking on her own, the love had been reciprocated.

They'd been a family ever since. They'd chosen to stay in Jody's childhood home. A handful of times over the years, she and Kaden had discussed leaving, but had always reached the same conclusion. The house was a bit isolated, but they had plenty to eat, the setting was beautiful, and they were safe here. There was also something else, and although she'd never discussed it with Kaden, she was fairly sure he sensed it as well. Jody, or at least her spirit, was here, watching over them, keeping them safe. When Laura had been about a year old, just after she'd started talking, Maria had walked in on her laughing and grabbing at something Maria couldn't see. When Maria had asked her what it was, Laura had said:

"The lights, momma, don't you see them?"

She'd felt a strangely warm breeze brush past her a second later, as if there had been an invisible person in the room with them.

369

"All gone!" Laura had exclaimed happily.

When Kaden had gotten home that night, Maria hadn't said anything to him. She'd almost forgotten about it.

"Momma, c'mon!" Laura called happily as Kaden hoisted her onto his shoulders.

"Coming!" Maria called brightly. She waded slowly into cool blue water, shivering a little. In spite of the heat of the day, the water was still a bit chilly.

"Catch me mommy!" Laura laughed, springing off Kaden's shoulders.

Maria, caught slightly off guard, reached out and caught her daughter just before she went underwater.

"Be careful, honey," Kaden said, reaching out and picking up Laura.

Laura laughed and hugged her father.

"I love you, daddy," she giggled.

"Love you too, kid," Kaden said, holding her high above his head and spinning her around while she laughed joyously.

"Mind if we join you?" came a voice from the opposite bank.

All three of them looked up. A bikini clad teenage girl was standing at the water's edge, her long fluffy black hair tied back in a ponytail. She was smiling brightly at the three of them. Coming up the path a few feet behind her was a strongly built middle aged man clad in dark blue swim trunks, a tattoo of an anchor clearly visible on his left bicep. His short black hair was fading to gray in places.

"Hey," he said as he reached them, grinning broadly. "Bet you didn't think you'd see us again, did you?"

It took Maria a moment to realize who it was.

"Marianne!" she exclaimed happily. "Tyson!"

Kaden's face lit up as he recognized them.

"So good to see you!" he exclaimed, throwing his arms around Marianne.

"Yep, still alive and kicking!" Tyson joked, shaking Kaden's outstretched hand. "We were hoping we'd find our way back here one of these years," he said.

Marianne picked up Laura, who grinned back at her toothily.

"So, this is your daughter?" he asked, gesturing to Laura, who was laughing as Marianne spun her around high above her head.

"Yeah," Kaden said. "I see yours is all grown up."

Tyson laughed.

"Same goes for you, mate! I was still picturing the little boy we met in the forest all those years ago!"

Kaden laughed.

"Well glad to have you back," Kaden said, clapping Tyson on the back. "You two up for a swim?" Kaden asked.

Marianne, still grinning broadly, handed Laura back to her mother and socked Kaden playfully on the shoulder.

"What do you think we came here for?" she teased. "We're not here to see you, we just came to enjoy the water."

Kaden laughed and shoved her playfully.

"Reckon I still fight better than you," Kaden joked.

"You saved my life once, bud," Marianne giggled, playfully shoving him back. "But if you think you can beat me in a wrestling match, you're on!"

Kaden laughed and tackled her into the water. Tyson and Maria laughed as the two old playmates began to wrestle, Kaden finally surrendering with much laughter after Marianne managed to put him in a playful chokehold.

None of them noticed the pale figure standing a few feet away at the edge of the meadow, watching them, a bright, yet sad smile crossing her ghostly face. Her hair, which had been dark brown in life but was now as transparent as the rest of her, fluttered about her face in the light breeze. Her once soft chocolate brown eyes, in spite of their paleness, sparkled with warmth at the sight of them. They looked so happy together. In time, the rest of them would find their way here, and they would be together again, just as they had been all those years ago.

"Hey," came a nervous voice from behind her. She turned, coming face to face with a tall muscular, African American teenage boy clad in navy blue running shorts and a plain black t-shirt.

"Hey," she echoed, taken slightly aback at the realization that the boy could see her.

Dylan Teryon approached her with some trepidation, his head hung slightly.

"Look, I just wanted to say..." he began, his voice trembling.

"You don't have to be sorry," Jody said, smiling reassuringly at him.

"No, I do," Dylan insisted, standing next to her at the edge of the tree line, watching Kaden pick up a laughing Marianne by the waist and toss her back into the water.

"I did things back in those days that were...unforgivable..." The memory of the night when he'd almost set Jody's tent on fire flashed through his mind. "I hurt so many people, Jody," he went on. "I just don't know if..."

The rest of his words were lost as Jody wrapped her pale, spectral arms around his shoulders. Dylan began to cry. It was a feeling of love he had not experienced since his father had been alive.

"Shh..." Jody whispered. "You're okay, you're okay."

After a moment, they broke apart.

"What do you think they'd do if I went out there?" Dylan asked shakily, wiping his eyes with the sleeve of his t-shirt.

"I think they'd love to see you," Jody replied, smiling.

"Even after everything I did to them?" Dylan asked.

"Isolation," Jody said softly. "It makes us vulnerable. The people who are in the most pain are always cut off from the rest of the world. It's community that keeps us safe, friends that make us strong."

"I've been that way for a long time," Dylan replied sadly. "No matter where I've been, I've never felt like I fit in. Even at home, I just felt so angry all the time. I did a lot of bad things, even back then."

They stood in silence for a moment, the memory of slamming his fist through his mother's kitchen wall flashing through Dylan's mind.

"We're not a sum of our mistakes," Jody replied. "You can't let your trauma cut you off from the rest of the world, isolate you, tear you down, because then it wins."

"He wins," Dylan said softly, thinking of the magician.

Jody nodded solemnly.

"Our trauma doesn't define us," Dylan said, suddenly sounding more confident. "It's how we choose to respond to it, isn't it?"

Jody smiled.

"Finally, you're starting to get it."

Dylan, smiling wanly, took a few nervous steps towards the river. He paused, glancing back at Jody.

"So, what should I do?" he asked.

"What you do best," Jody said. "Overcome."

Dylan smiled broadly at her, and this time, there was no hint of sadness in it.

"Thank you," Dylan said. "For everything."

Jody smiled as Dylan turned and ran towards the river, doing a cannonball into the cool blue water, soaking his five stunned compatriots.

Jody watched as their shock at the sight of him quickly turned to laughter and hugs all around. She smiled as she watched Dylan pick up Laura and carry her around on his shoulders while the others stood around, laughing while Maria encouraged her beaming young daughter, any fear she might've had of the little boy who was no longer a little boy long gone. Jody closed her eyes, the warmth of the late afternoon sun, which was gradually retreating behind the trees, soothing her. She smiled wanly as she watched the six of them climb out of the river and start back towards the house where she'd grown up. Maybe, just maybe, there was hope for this world after all.

About the Author

Geoffrey Saemann is currently pursuing an undergraduate degree in Biochemistry at the University of Wisconsin Madison. He has been writing fiction stories since childhood and has submitted several to magazine and online contests. He wrote his first unpublished manuscript at the age of fourteen for an honors literature class. After walking away from writing during his late teen years, he has spent the last several years working on a number of unpublished short manuscripts, as well as his debut novel, *Firelight*. He moved to the Madison area in 2022.

THE TENTH STATION

THE TENTH SERIES

JOE LOOBY